Jacin Challenge

∞ ∞ ∞ ∞ ∞

M.K. Eidem

M.K. EIDEM

The Imperial Series

Cassandra's Challenge

Victoria's Challenge

Tornians

Grim

A Grim Holiday

Wray

Oryon

Ynyr

JACINDA'S CHALLENGE

Published by M.K. Eidem

Copyright © 2015 by Michelle K. Eidem

Cover Design by Judy Bullard

Edited by: www.A-Z_Media@outlook.com

This Book is licensed for your personal enjoyment only. The Book may not be re-sold or given away to other people. If you would like to share this novel with another person, please purchase an additional copy for each recipient. If you are reading this Book and did not purchase it or it was not purchased for your use only, then please buy an additional copy for each recipient.

No part of this book may be distributed in any format, in whole or in part without the express written consent of the author.

Thank you for respecting the author's hard work.

This is a work of fiction and is not a reflection or representation of any person living or dead. Any similarity is of pure coincidence.

∞ ∞ ∞ ∞ ∞

I'd like to thank my family for all their support during this exciting time of my life, especially my husband. I couldn't have done it without you. I'd also like to thank all my friends that have been there for me, answering questions and helping guide me, Judy, Reese, Sally, Julie, Fern, Beth, Susan and Narelle; Thanks, ladies!

∞ ∞ ∞ ∞ ∞

Prologue

"Brac, have my personal transport brought around," Lata told the head of her security detail.

"Queen Lata, there is a stoirme approaching."

"I don't care, Brac. I need to get out for a while. Inform the rest of the guards and have it brought around. I'm going to go see Barek and then I'll be down." Turning away, knowing Brac would follow her orders, Lata went to her son.

"I don't want to!" Lata heard her son's angry words before she sees him and smiles. Her son is so stubborn, so like his father.

"And just what is it that you don't want to do, young man?" she asks as she enters the room.

"Mama!" The angry, little-boy look immediately leaves Barek's face at his mother's words. Running across the room, he jumps into her arms knowing she will always be there for him, will always catch him.

"Hello, baby." Lata wraps her arms around her son's small body, kissing the top of his head before staring down lovingly at him. "So what is it you don't want to do?"

"I don't want to study, Mama! I want to play! I want to play with you!" He wiggles until his mother sets him down, takes her hand, and tries to pull her deeper into the room. "Come play with me, Mama!"

"Oh, Barek, I wish I could but I'm going out."

"Can I go with you, Mama? I always learn so much more with you." His violet eyes plead with her and he gives a smile so like his father's that it melts her heart. That smile had gotten him out of more scrapes with her than anything else. She just could never tell him no and the little scamp knew it.

Lata almost gave in. She loved spending time with her son. He always made the worst day bearable, but today she needed some alone time; time not to be the Queen, not to be a wife, not to be a mother, to just be her. Lata. A woman. She could not do that if Barek were with her.

"Your argument is very convincing, young man, and one day you will be an amazing Consul, but today you need to stay here with Nana."

"But, Mama, you always say you have more fun when I'm with you."

"And I do. I'll tell you what," she said quickly, her look stopping him from saying more. "You stay here and be a good boy for Nana and when I get back, we will go play in the gardens."

"But, Mama…"

"Enough, Barek!" Lata cringed at how sharp her words were. She really needed to get away. "I need to go." She pulls her hand from his and watches him cross his little arms across his chest, his eyes glaring at her. "You do as I say, young man, or I won't come back to see you today." Spinning around, she leaves the room.

∞ ∞ ∞ ∞ ∞

Lata was cursing herself as she drove through the strengthening stoirme. Why hadn't she listened to Brac? Why hadn't she stayed and played with Barek? Jotham was going to be so angry when he finds out she was out in this… and he had every right to be.

This was not an ordinary stoirme. This one had released its baisteach all at once, and now the roads were flooding making driving treacherous. If she hadn't been on the narrow road when it had started, she would have pulled over and allowed one of her guards, that were behind her, to drive. Instead, she forces herself to concentrate on her driving, to focus on making it home safely to her family. She finally relaxes as she rounds the final curve at the bottom of the hill.

A sudden rumbling sound catches her unaware and her eyes widen as she sees the hillside in front of her begin to move. Slamming on her brakes, she tries to stop her forward momentum but it is too late. The road is gone and the landslide sweeps her transport away.

"Jotham! Barek!" she screams, her last thoughts on her husband and son.

Chapter One

Jotham entered the royal tomb and froze, surprised to find Barek sitting on the bench Jotham had placed in front of Lata's final resting spot shortly after she met the ancestors. He was about to speak when Barek reached out to run a reverent finger over his mother's mouth in the portrait Jotham had carved into her tomb. He must have made a sound because Barek suddenly stiffened and looked his way.

"Father," he said pulling his hand away.

"Barek. I didn't realize you had returned to the Palace. I thought you would have stayed longer at the House of Knowledge."

"Victoria and Lucas were anxious to start their honeymoon. I can't blame them, not with the Guardian leaving so soon. So there was no reason to stay."

"Not even Amina?" Jotham watched his son's reaction carefully.

"Amina? What are you talking about?" Barek raised an eyebrow at him.

"You seemed interested."

"Amina is a child." His gaze returned to his mother.

"I was under the impression that she was the same age as Victoria."

"She is, but she hasn't had the same life experiences Tori has."

"No, but the first nine cycles of her life were spent on the Retribution. She has also been working with her father on the cyclotron propulsion system. I would say she is very mature for her age."

"What has you so interested in her, Father?"

"You were immediately at her side when Stannic appeared." Jotham again watched his son closely.

"She needed to be protected and I was the one closest to her."

"I see. My apologies, I must have misunderstood." Jotham looked to his wife's tomb. "Why are you here?" When Barek didn't immediately answer, Jotham gave him a sharp look. "Barek?"

"I found I couldn't remember her smile," Barek finally admitted quietly.

"What?" Jotham couldn't hide his shock.

"Tori had visuals of her family and I realized she looked like her mother. When the Chamberlains were rescued, even with Cyndy so sick, the resemblance was undeniable. Today at the Union, I realized that her brother, Brett, has Cyndy's smile too. That while he is her son, a part of her still lives on in him. It made me wonder about Mother's smile. If any of her lived on in me. This is the only place where I could come and see her."

"You know her royal portrait is in my private office."

"Yes, but as you said, it is your private office and I would never think to enter it without your knowledge. Here," Barek gestured to the tomb, "is the only other place besides the archives that has her image, and I couldn't remember…"

Jotham was at a loss for what to say to his son. When Lata died in a transport accident, Barek had only been five cycles and Jotham had been devastated. The pain he experienced every time he saw her image somewhere in the Palace had been unbearable. Therefore, he ordered them taken down, all except the one in his private office. That one he had covered. It took him nearly a cycle before he could finally uncover it. He had never given a thought to the fact that Barek might need to see her.

"I'm sorry, Barek. You should have said something. I never considered you would want a visual of her."

"You did what you needed to do." Standing, Barek turned to face him. "I knew how it upset you to hear her name, so I would just sneak out here to see her."

"You shouldn't have had to."

Barek just shrugged his shoulders. "It no longer matters, Father, and I have my answer."

"Which is?"

"I am my Father's son. I have nothing of my mother in me, which is what I deserve." Spinning on his heel, Barek left the tomb.

Jotham silently watched his son leave, too stunned by his words to try to stop him. What did he mean, *'which is what I deserve?'*

Moving, he sat down and looked to Lata. "What have I done, Lata?" he asked. "How have I failed not only you but our son?"

∞ ∞ ∞ ∞ ∞

Jotham let his mind wander back to when he first met Lata. It had been at the start of his fourth cycle at the Academy. He and Will Zafar had been joking around on their way to class. Will had pushed him as a dark-haired girl, chatting with another girl, stepped out of an open door. Lata's books went one way and Lata the other. Jotham had barely caught her before she hit the floor. She'd looked up at him with her incredible, brown eyes and he had been captivated.

He silently thanked the ancestors when he found out she was from the House of Protection, for he knew his father would never allow him to pursue her otherwise. The heir to the throne was not permitted to have a Union with anyone outside of his House and Jotham quickly realized that Lata was his life mate.

Jotham courted her for two cycles. It nearly killed him when he finished his last cycle at the Academy and went to serve his mandatory time in the Fleet. Royal family members were only required to serve one cycle in the Fleet. But he and Lata had kept in contact and she'd encouraged him to serve another cycle when he told her how much he enjoyed his duties. She still had another cycle in the Academy and then she could join him in the Fleet.

Lata had been excited to get into space, had been excited for it to be just 'them', away from all the prying eyes. Jotham had too, but it seemed the ancestors had other ideas. Jotham returned to Carina for Lata's graduation and as they prepared to go back to the Fleet, Jotham received word that his father and mother, King Kado and Queen Johanna, died in an accident.

Jotham and the entire planet had been in shock. With King Kado's sudden death, Jotham became the youngest person in Carinian history ever to assume a throne. At that moment, Jotham's world forever changed.

There was no way he could return to the Fleet and there was no way he was letting Lata go without him. Twenty days after his birthmark filled with color, Jotham took the throne and became the King of the House of Protection.

The next day, he made Lata his Queen.

Lata had been his rock through the entire ordeal. Never once had she faltered or complained. She had fully supported him as he assumed the responsibilities that so often took him away from her even as she struggled to understand her own responsibilities. They had both believed they would have cycles to learn about those responsibilities, but they'd been wrong.

They had both been so young at their Union and thought that as long as they were together they could handle anything. They had already decided that they wanted to wait a few cycles before they would start their family, giving each of them the time they needed to adjust to their new lives. Then Lata conceived.

It had been a joyous time in the House. It had also been a stressful time, for Lata insisted she continue her duties as Queen. However, she became so ill that the Royal Healer ordered her to remain in bed. Jotham tried to spend as much time with her as he could, but there was only so much time in the day.

Barek's birth had not been easy for Lata, and Jotham decided then and there that he would make sure he never forgot to take the Ollali juice again. Not until Lata was ready for a second child. She had died before that happened.

After Barek had been born, Lata became restless and returned to her Queen's duties. However, the enthusiasm she had for her duties was not the same as before she conceived. Classmates began returning from their tours with the Fleet telling Lata their tales of adventure. Lata felt it was the tour Jotham and Lata were supposed to take together. The *adventures* they were supposed to have together. Instead of her being able to experience them, she had become a mother and a Queen, all by the age of twenty.

Jotham had tried to be understanding. He knew that Lata's dream had been to travel the stars, a dream she'd willingly given up for him. Lata seemed to settle, seemed to return to her old self, but only after he finally allowed her to escape the Palace by driving her own transport. He hadn't liked it, but it seemed to give her the freedom she craved, and she returned to being the gentle, loving woman Jotham had fallen in love with.

"I shouldn't have allowed it, Lata," Jotham spoke quietly, raising tortured eyes to her portrait. "If I hadn't, you wouldn't have been driving that day. You wouldn't have lost control. You wouldn't have died and then Barek would know that while he doesn't have your smile, he has your laugh and your gentle ways. Not that he reveals either very often." Reaching out, he gently caressed her cheek. "What am I to do, Lata? I know what I saw today. Barek *is* interested in this girl, but can she handle being his Queen? I need your help, Lata. Our son needs your help."

A warm breeze brushed his cheek. It was his only answer and he lowered his head. After several moments he rose, kissing his fingers and placing them on her lips. "I will talk to you later, my love."

∞ ∞ ∞ ∞ ∞

Jotham entered his outer office to find Chesney, his personal aide, sitting at the desk he always seemed to be at. He rose as Jotham entered.

"Majesty, I've compiled for you the list of Assemblymen that will be attending the Annual Ball next week."

"List?" Jotham frowned at Chesney. "Chesney, I know who my Assemblymen are."

"Yes, Majesty, but if you remember there are several new ones with the recent elections. I've compiled a biography on each so you will be more familiar with them."

"Yes, of course. Thank you, Chesney." Taking the folder, Jotham entered his office and began to read.

Jotham frowned as he opened the last folder and looked at the visual. Why did this man look so familiar? Learning his name, his frown grew. Danton Michelakakis? Reading on, his eyes widened.

Was this possible?

Could one of Stephan Michelakakis' sons really be old enough to be an Assemblyman? Suddenly he realized he had just done the same thing Barek had with Amina because Danton had been born a cycle before Barek. He remembered how proud Stephan had been when he announced the birth of his first son, remembered how the man had shown everyone Danton's first visual, including Jotham.

Where had the time gone?

Leaning back in his chair, Jotham began to remember more about the Assemblyman that had died suddenly ten cycles earlier. Stephan had been an outspoken Assemblyman with strong beliefs and passionate delivery. He'd had definite ideas about what the House of Protection's role should be in the Coalition. Some Jotham had agreed with, others not so much, but all were well thought out and always presented with respect.

Jotham also remembered Stephan's wife… what was her name…? Looking back to the file in his hand he found it.

Jacinda…

Yes, that was it. She'd been a stunningly, beautiful woman. A great deal younger than Stephan, if Jotham remembered correctly. She'd also been from the House of Healing, her father being a powerful Assemblyman there. It had caused some debate within the Assembly, some felt that an Assemblyman's wife should be from the same House. It was an unrealistic expectation and Jotham had quickly weighed in, silencing Stephan's critics.

It had proven to be the right choice, for Stephan had gone on to be an Assemblyman whose opinion Jotham could rely on. His death, shortly before the destruction of Earth, had left big shoes to be filled and no one really had. Perhaps his son would.

Jacinda had seemed to retreat from the public eye after Stephan's death and now that Jotham thought about it, he couldn't remember seeing her anywhere since the sochraide. It was a shame because Jacinda Michelakakis' grace and beauty had always brightened any room she was in.

Michelakakis.... Jacinda Michelakakis... Amina Michelakakis... leaning forward Jotham pressed a button on his desk.

"Chesney, would you come in here, please? I have a job for you."

∞ ∞ ∞ ∞ ∞

Jacinda sat back on her heels, tipping her face up to the warmth of Carina's three suns and letting it soothe her. She was in her garden, tending to the last blossoms of the season feeling a sense of contentment that she hadn't felt in cycles. Her grandchildren had left several hours earlier and while she loved them, loved their exuberance and the energy they brought to her life, there were times she liked the quiet.

She knew her children worried about her, afraid she spent too much time alone, which was why they made sure to send their children to her house at least once a moon cycle. Sighing, she looked back to the house. It really was too big for just her and she should turn it over to Danton. As a newly elected Assemblyman, he would need a residence such as this in Pechora to entertain, but she found she couldn't let it go yet.

There were too many memories here. This was the house that Stephan had brought her to after their Union. This was the house where all her children were born. It was the garden where further up the path, her life mate had died picking her favorite flowers. Leaning down, Jacinda smelled one of the blossoms.

∞ ∞ ∞ ∞ ∞

This had never been the life Jacinda envisioned for herself all those cycles ago. She'd had such grand plans for her life and not one of them had included being involved in politics, especially not in the House of Protection politics.

She had grown up in a house that had been filled with politics and debates. She'd watched her mother stand beside her father. Watched her support him in every aspect of his life as an Assemblyman of the House of Healing. She knew it was the life they had both chosen and both loved. It just wasn't the life Jacinda wanted. Jacinda wanted to travel without worrying about appearances. She wanted to be just another citizen, not the daughter of a powerful Assemblyman. She'd known she didn't wish to be the wife of one.

One should be careful what they wished for… and what they wished against.

Jacinda returned home after her first tour of duty full of excitement and ready to start the next phase of her life. She found Stephan Michelakakis sitting at her parents' table and her heart had been lost.

Stephan had been amazingly handsome to her, and not just in the physical sense. Although he had been that. But he was a man who'd known who he was. *That* is what first attracted her to him. He'd known what he wanted out of life and was totally confident he could achieve it. He'd been so unlike the boys she'd been dealing with over the last two cycles. They thought they were men, yet they were still searching for their place in life. Stephan had listened to her, *really* listened to her. He would seriously consider what she was saying and not just to get her into his bed. The way it had made her feel was indescribable. He treated her like an equal, an adult. She'd found it so irresistible and sexy. They'd been true partners, friends, and life mates.

Their instant attraction to each other had caught both of them by surprise. Neither had been looking for a life mate and both knew there would be obstacles they would have to overcome. The first being Jacinda's parents, who had been shocked when they found out about the relationship. Jacinda's father, while older than Stephan, considered him a contemporary and not someone who should be interested in his daughter. It had taken some time, but eventually her father had come around, thanks to the prodding of her mother and once he saw how much they truly cared for each other.

The next obstacle they had faced had been the Assemblymen of the House of Protection who felt Stephan should not be allowed to serve if his wife were from another House. It had been an uncertain time until King Jotham had finally weighed in stating that an Assemblyman's wife did not need to be from the House of Protection for him to serve. While it had ended the debate, it hadn't changed the attitudes of some. Jacinda had just ignored the snide comments made to her by some of the other wives. Over time, as Stephan became more influential and Jacinda had more than proven she was up to the task of being an Assemblyman's wife, the comments ceased.

∞ ∞ ∞ ∞ ∞

"Madame Michelakakis?"

The voice of her housekeeper pulled Jacinda from her musings to find her standing only a few feet away.

"What is it, Myesha?"

"Madame, there is a messenger from the King at the door."

Jacinda frowned at Myesha's words. Why in the world would one of the King's messengers be coming here? Suddenly she realized the mistake. "He must be looking for Danton, Myesha. You can tell him his address."

"Yes, Madame, I thought that too, but Captain Deffand assured me his message is for you."

"Captain Deffand?" Jacinda didn't try to hide her surprise. Deffand was the head of King Jotham's security and had been for the last fifteen cycles. He wasn't a messenger. What in the world was going on?

Rising, Jacinda brushed the dirt from the knees of her pants then removed her gloves, dropping them into the basket of flowers she'd been cutting. Moving to Myesha, she handed her the basket. "Would you see to these for me please, Myesha, and I'll go see what is going on."

"Yes, ma'am."

Jacinda absently raised a hand to her hair making sure it was still pulled back as she'd arranged it that morning. She remembered Captain Deffand. He had always been present when the King addressed the Assembly. He was a tall, good-looking man who took his duty very seriously. He had never taken a wife, at least he hadn't when Stephan had been alive, but that could have changed in the last ten cycles.

Entering the entryway, Jacinda saw that time hadn't dimmed her image of the King's Captain. He was still handsome and although he had aged as they all had, it looked good on him. The look in his eyes told her he still took his duty very seriously.

"Captain Deffand, a pleasure to see you again." Jacinda held out her hand and after only the slightest of hesitation, he shook it.

"Madame Michelakakis, it is good to see you again too."

"Would you like to sit?" Jacinda gestured to the room behind her.

"Thank you, but no. King Jotham asked that I deliver this to you." Deffand held out the sealed envelope to her.

"King Jotham?" Jacinda was frowning again as she took the envelope, trying to figure out why the King would be sending her a message, let alone have his Captain deliver it.

"Yes, Madame. He also requested that I remain for your reply."

"Really," Jacinda raised an elegant eyebrow as she turned the envelope over. Seeing that the King's seal was still intact, she ran her finger underneath, breaking it. Pulling the single sheet out, she turned away from Deffand and read.

Why did Jotham wish to speak to her? About what? Why in person? Thinking how she could rearrange her plans for the next day, she looked to Deffand.

"Tell King Jotham I will be there at one tomorrow."

"I will let him know, Madame Michelakakis. A limisin will arrive here at 12:30 to transport you."

"No, Captain, I have some errands to run tomorrow. I will get myself to the Palace."

"But, Madame Michelakakis, the King…"

"I will make sure I am on time, Captain. I remember how pressed for time the King always is."

"Yes, Madame Michelakakis." Bowing, Deffand turned and left the residence.

Chapter Two

The next day, walking through the Public Wing of the House of Protection, Jacinda let the memories flow over her. It had been over ten cycles since she'd walked through this Wing. It was after the Annual Ball that welcomed in the new Assemblymen for the House of Protection. She and Stephan had attended as they always did and had enjoyed themselves immensely. They had chatted with longtime friends, nibbled on the delicious food and danced the night away. It had been an incredible evening. Less than a moon cycle later, she buried her life mate and she'd never entered the Palace again. Until today.

Stephan's office and that of every other Assemblyman's was in the Assembly Hall in Pechora. It was a large building in the center of the City that when a full Assembly was in session had room for the Assemblymen from all the other Houses.

The doors at the far end of the Public Wing blocked the first corridor that would lead to the King's Wing. When she approached, she stopped.

"Jacinda Michelakakis," she told one of the guards protecting the door. "I have an appointment with King Jotham."

Just as the guard raised his communicator to confirm her appointment, the door behind him opened and Captain Deffand stepped out."

"Madame Michelakakis," he nodded slightly to her.

"Captain Deffand," Jacinda returned his nod, smiling slightly. "As you can see I'm on time."

"I never thought you wouldn't be, Madame Michelakakis. If you'll follow me." He gestured for her to proceed him down the corridor. "The King is waiting for you in his private office."

Jacinda's eyebrow raised slightly at that, but she moved through the doorway. Why would Jotham want to speak to her in his private office?

They walked without speaking for several minutes as Jacinda reacquainted herself with her surroundings. She had traveled down this corridor before. If you turned left at its end, you would enter the Guest Wing used for off-planet dignitaries. She'd gone there once with Stephan when he had a meeting. Jacinda had accompanied him so she could entertain the man's wife. Turning right, you moved toward the Servant's Wing where all the staff lived if they chose to.

Guiding her to the right, Deffand led her passed the Servant's Wing to another set of guarded doors. These led to the Royal Wing and the King's Wing. The Royal Wing was to the right, and if she remembered correctly, it was where Queen Cassandra of the House of Knowledge had initially stayed when she arrived on Carina all those cycles ago. Before she'd been able to challenge Queen Yakira and claim her throne. What an amazing thing that had been. For a descendent of the lost Princess to actually return and reclaim her throne. Stephan would have loved to witness such a historic event. Unfortunately, he died two moon cycles before it occurred.

"Madame Michelakakis?" Deffand's question had her realizing she had stopped moving and was looking toward the Royal Wing. "Is everything alright?"

"Yes, Captain, forgive me, I was just thinking back to when Queen Cassandra arrived and stayed in that Wing." She nodded toward the Royal Wing. "Stephan would have loved to have witnessed the return of the true Queen."

"He was a good Assemblyman, Madame, and an even better man."

Jacinda looked up to the Captain and had to fight the tears that wanted to fill them at his sincere words. "He was, Captain, thank you for saying that."

"It is the truth, Madame. Assemblyman Michelakakis was well thought of and respected. His guidance in the Assembly has been sorely missed at times." He gestured to the corridor to his left and they slowly began to walk toward the King's Wing.

"Yes. Well, while I may not have my finger on the pulse of the Assembly anymore," she gave him a sideways smile. "I do still hear things and you've had your hands full lately."

"Yes, Madame," he replied noncommittally.

"So tell me, Captain, have you found your life mate yet?"

"I... my what?" Deffand's steps faltered.

"Your life mate. The last I knew you were single."

"I... yes, I was and still am."

"That's a shame, Captain."

"Shame, Madame?" Deffand raised his eyebrow at her, hearing the sincerity in her voice.

"Yes. No one should go through this life alone, Captain. Especially not a man like you. You have dedicated your life to the protection of our King and in doing so, have protected his people."

"That is why I remain single, Madame."

"I don't understand," she frowned at him.

"And neither do other women."

"No, Captain, what I don't understand is why you feel your life mate wouldn't understand your dedication to your King."

"I discovered early in my career, Madame, that women do not like to have a man leave unexpectedly with no explanation."

"That would be because they weren't your life mate."

"You are saying you never became… upset with your husband, when he was suddenly called away?" Deffand's tone was disbelieving.

"Sometimes," she admitted, "but being upset didn't mean I didn't understand. I knew who Stephan was before we had our Union and what it would mean. My father was also an Assemblyman, Captain. I grew up with him suddenly leaving, but Stephan and I also sat down and discussed it. If I couldn't have accepted that part of his life, then we wouldn't have had our Union."

"There are few woman that are that understanding, Madame," Deffand told her quietly.

"Oh, I don't know about that. I believe the right woman for you is out there somewhere, Captain. You just haven't met her yet. Perhaps I can help you with that." Jacinda gave him a smile before her gaze traveled to the portraits hanging along the walls. They were the portraits of the past Kings and Queens of the House of Protection. She knew the only time they were moved was when a new King took the throne and then they were moved down allowing the reigning monarchs the place of honor next to the doors of the King's Wing.

As they moved closer to the doors, Jacinda was saddened to see that only Jotham's portrait hung outside them. The space that had once held Lata's portrait remained empty, as it had been since her death.

Jacinda had never understood why Jotham had it removed. Maybe if he had taken another Queen, it would have been understandable, but he hadn't…. She wondered where the beautiful portrait had gone.

Deffand silently noted how Madame Michelakakis' eyes paused on the space where the Queen's portrait once hung. He hadn't even been in the Academy at the time of Lata's death, all those cycles ago. He remembered his shock the first day he'd been allowed to guard these doors and her portrait hadn't been there. Looking at the current guards, he nodded and they silently opened the doors.

Jacinda allowed Deffand to lead her into the King's Wing. There had been a time when Lata had been alive, that she would come visit the Queen here. They would walk through the gardens and talk, but that had been in the very early cycles when they both had been new to their roles and responsibilities.

∞ ∞ ∞ ∞ ∞

Jacinda and Stephan's Union had only been six moon cycles old when Jotham assumed the throne and made Lata his Queen. There had been dissent in the Assembly about her and Stephan's Union that Jotham's father, King Kado, had done nothing to stop. Jotham had immediately taken action informing all that an Assemblyman's spouse *could* come from another House, that only the heir to the throne must choose within it. It had been a relief to both her and Stephan.

While Jacinda had grown up in politics, she had never actually dealt with the inner workings of the Assembly wives. Each one of the wives was trying to position themselves in the best possible way with the Queen to help their husband. Queen Johanna had already chosen those she favored and those she just tolerated. She hadn't yet made up her mind about Jacinda before she had died.

When Lata became Queen, there had been a mad scramble among the wives with each trying to become a member of Lata's 'inner circle'. Most were hoping to be able to take advantage of Lata's youth and inexperience to forward their own agenda. Jacinda had been one of the few who had made no attempt. She had just silently watched as Lata carefully but calmly navigated the waves of comments and advice flowing around her. She had never appeared flustered or agitated. She would thank them, saying she would consider their advice and then make a kind comment about either the woman or her husband before moving on. She had acted like an actual Queen.

It was only when Jacinda found Lata in the garden one day, her shoulders slumped with her face in her hands, that Jacinda realized the toll it was taking on the young Queen. Lata and Jacinda's younger sister, Palma, had been best friends in the Academy and while Jacinda was several cycles ahead of them, she still remembered Lata coming to their house during breaks. Lata had always been a smiling, outgoing girl ready with a kind word and a gentle touch. Seeing her like that had hurt Jacinda's heart so she reached out to her.

At first, it had been stiff, as Lata thought Jacinda too wanted something from her. However, over time Lata realized Jacinda was just offering her friendship, no strings attached, and they had become friends. Much to the consternation of the older wives.

∞ ∞ ∞ ∞ ∞

"Madame Michelakakis?" Deffand's quiet question had her realizing her mind had drifted again as she walked passed the familiar rooms. But now she stood before the doors to the King's office, a place she had never been and it was time to put those memories away. Her smile told Deffand she was okay and he opened the door.

Inside sat, a man Jacinda knew was Chesney, the King's Personal Aide. He immediately rose as she entered.

"Madame Michelakakis," he greeted, "a pleasure to see you again."

"Mister Chesney, it's been a long time." Jacinda's voice was as warm as her smile. "How is your family?"

"Yes it has and they are well, thank you for asking. I will let King Jotham know you are here." Turning, he went to the doors that his desk seemed to be guarding.

"Madame Michelakakis," Deffand moved to face her, "it has been a pleasure to escort you today." He bowed slightly to her.

"The pleasure was all mine, Captain. It's been a long time since I've strolled down a corridor with a good-looking, young man." Jacinda laughed softly when Deffand began to flush and couldn't help but tease. "I will make sure to keep my eyes open for you."

∞ ∞ ∞ ∞ ∞

Jotham looked up from the report he was reading as the door to his private office opened and Chesney entered.

"King Jotham, Madame Michelakakis is here."

"Wonderful." Closing the folder, he rose and walked around his desk moving toward the door, surprising Chesney. In all Chesney's cycles in serving his King, never had Jotham gone out to greet someone, they came to him. "You've arranged for refreshments?" Jotham asked.

"Yes, Majesty."

"Good." Moving passed Chesney, Jotham entered the outer room to greet Jacinda. He paused when he heard her words, 'I will make sure to keep my eyes open for you,' and saw his Captain's cheeks darken slightly.

"Madame Michelakakis," Jotham spoke pulling her attention from his Captain to him.

Jotham's voice had Jacinda turning from Deffand to address the King and for a moment, she found herself speechless. Somehow, she had forgotten just how handsome Jotham Tibullus was. While Stephan had been her life mate and the only man she'd wanted to spend her life with, it didn't mean she still couldn't appreciate a good-looking male when she saw one. And Jotham had always been that.

Jotham was taller than Stephan by a good three inches. She'd forgotten that. She was able to look her husband in the eye when she wore two-inch heels and took care to make sure they were always shorter than that. It had become a habit. So now with Jotham, she had to tip her head back to look him in the eye. Jotham still had the thick, dark, unruly hair of his youth, although there was some gray starting if you looked close enough. Stephan's had already been fully gray at Jotham's age and Jotham's violet eyes, a testament to his being of royal blood, were nothing like Stephan's warm amber ones.

If the cut of Jotham's clothes was accurate, then time had not yet affected the King's physique either. He was still broad in the shoulders and trim at the waist and the tailoring of his shirt discreetly revealed the muscles of his chest and abs before it tucked into the waistband of his pants.

"King Jotham," she finally remembered to respond and bowed her head slightly to him.

"It's wonderful to see you again." Jotham gestured for her to proceed him into his office, which surprised him when he realized he truly was.

Jacinda Michelakakis was taller than he remembered. The top of her head just reaching his chin. Lata's hadn't reached his shoulder and her size had always made him feel that he needed to protect her. Jacinda gave off the aura of a strong, confident woman. One that could stand up for and by herself if need be.

She had shown that with how she'd handled the sudden death of her life mate.

Jotham remembered Stephan's sochraide well. The temple had been filled to capacity with representatives from every House, for Stephan Michelakakis had been well-liked and greatly respected outside of his own House. It had to have been a daunting task for Jacinda and her children that day, but they had all rallied around each other. Jacinda had gracefully accepted the condolences of each and every person there, even when you could see it was wearing on her. Her beautiful, golden skin had become pale and her usually bright and sparkling blue-green eyes had been dull and lifeless, filled with such sadness. He had been told she was the last to leave her life mate's grave… that her oldest son, Danton, had to convince her to leave.

Jotham had always meant to personally check up on her. It was the least he could have done for Stephan, but then Barek had been reported lost, Cassandra had arrived on Carina, and Dadrian's treasonous crimes had been revealed. Jotham was ashamed to admit he had forgotten all about Stephan's widow and family until yesterday.

Now he wondered how he could have, for Jacinda Michelakakis was an uncommonly beautiful woman. While he wasn't sure of her age, he knew she had been a good many cycles younger than Stephan at their Union. Jotham still believed that was the real reason why so many in the Assembly had protested their Union. It had nothing to do with what House Jacinda had come from, but that they envied her beauty and confidence and worried they would be found lacking. His father should have immediately put a stop to it, but he hadn't. Jotham had never understood why, but *he* ended the controversy when he became King. Moreover, while Stephan had thanked him, it had never stopped Stephan from expressing his opinion when he disagreed with Jotham. It had been something Jotham had greatly respected and missed. Now he felt like he had failed the man by not seeing to his family's welfare.

"Won't you sit?" Jotham asked gesturing to the couch along one side of the room.

Jacinda took in the room as she moved to the sofa. This was obviously where the King did the majority of his work. There were files piled on the large desk that faced the door as you entered. Behind the desk, a large window let in the light and scents from the King's Garden that lay outside. The wall opposite the couch, where she sat, contained shelves, filled with books and what appeared to be items given to the King by the other Houses.

"Your refreshments, Majesty," Chesney announced placing the tray down on the small table between the couch and the chair the King had moved to sit in.

"Thank you, Chesney, that will be all," Jotham dismissed him.

"Yes, Majesty. Madame." Giving each a small bow, Chesney left the room.

"Would you like me to pour, Majesty?" Jacinda looked at him, waiting for the King's reply before proceeding.

"Please," Jotham told her and watched as she gracefully poured two cups of the hot tea.

"Do you still take three sweeteners?" she asked, her hand poised above the sweetener.

"I... yes." Jotham frowned. How had she known? "How?"

"Did I know you liked your tea sweet?" Jacinda finished for him and smiled as she handed him the sweetened cup and saucer.

"Yes," he confirmed.

"Lata spoke of it once when we were having tea. She couldn't understand how you could take it so sweet." Jacinda shrugged her shoulders. "I guess I remembered it because Stephan liked his that way too."

"I see." Jotham took a sip of his perfectly sweetened tea then sat back even though he didn't fully understand. He had never realized Lata and Jacinda Michelakakis had been that close.

Jacinda picked up her own cup of unsweetened tea and sipped.

"You don't like your tea sweetened?"

"On occasion, but when I do, I like to use honey."

"I'll have Chesney bring some." Jotham moved to put his cup down when her words stopped him.

"No, Majesty, this is fine. As I said, I only occasionally sweeten it."

"If you are sure."

"I am." Jacinda continued to sip her tea, waiting for Jotham to tell her why she was here.

"I suppose you would like to know why I asked you here today."

"I am curious, yes."

"Well, I need to start out by apologizing for never having checked on you after Stephan's death."

Jacinda frowned and carefully set her cup down on the table. "Why would you check on me, Majesty?" she asked quietly looking up at him.

"Why?" Jotham gave her a slightly startled look at *her* question. "Well, because Stephan was an Assemblyman for my House for nearly forty cycles. You were his wife for thirty of those cycles. I should have made sure you were well and had what you needed."

"Thank you for the thought, Majesty, and I know that Stephan would have appreciated it, but I had what I needed. I had my children, grandchildren and the rest of my family to help me through that dark time. Thanks to them, I have recovered and am carrying on with my life as Stephan would have wanted me to. So now tell me, Majesty, what is it that *you* need from me?"

Jotham set his own cup down somewhat surprised at her bluntness then realized he shouldn't be. Stephan had been the same way, especially in private.

"I am hoping you can help me with a situation that has come to my attention."

"A situation?" Jacinda couldn't for the life of her think of anything she had the ability to help Jotham with.

"You are probably not aware of this yet, but I just recently returned from the House of Knowledge where I performed the Union of Lucas Zafar and Victoria Chamberlain."

"Really?" Jacinda didn't try to hide her surprise. She had heard nothing about this and she should have. A Royal wedding would have been the talk of the entire planet. "I would have thought the Queen would have wanted multiple balls for her niece to celebrate such a joyous event, especially after all they had survived together.

"I believe Cassandra did, but Tori and Lucas wanted it done before the Guardian's maiden voyage."

"Lucas Zafar is her first Captain, is he not? And she leaves in less than a moon cycle?"

"Yes."

"The Queen still could have arranged a more public Union."

"It is not what Lucas and Victoria wanted."

"The Queen just allowed them to dictate that to her?" Jacinda found that hard to believe. Everything she had ever heard and seen about Queen Cassandra was that of a woman who knew what she wanted and didn't stop until she achieved it. It's one of the reasons she and her niece had survived the destruction of their world.

"I don't think Cassandra really had a choice, not once Cyndy Chamberlain was done with her. If what Barek has told me is correct, then Madame Chamberlain has no qualms about letting the Queen know when she has overstepped her place."

"Really?" Jacinda couldn't believe it. The whole planet had heard about the incredible rescue of the Queen's family, the Chamberlains, from Earth nine cycles after it had been decimated by the Regulians. As of yet, the 'family' had made no public appearances and no visuals had been released. It made some believe it was just that, an incredible story, especially among the Queen's detractors of which there were still a few. "If Prince Barek is right, then I think I would very much like to meet this fearless Titan."

Jotham was captivated by the smile growing on Jacinda's face as she spoke. Her entire being seemed to light up especially her eyes. "She's more the size of a sprite than a Titan," Jotham told her.

"What?" Jacinda gave him a surprised look.

"She is even smaller than Tori. You have met Victoria, haven't you?"

"No, but I've seen visuals of her. She is quite small."

"Only by Carinian standards. Victoria is about average height for a female from Earth, or so I've been told, while her mother is quite a few inches shorter."

"Really? And she stood up to the Queen?" Jacinda's eyes sparkled.

"I don't believe Cyndy sees Cassandra as the 'Queen,' but as the younger sister of her husband."

Jacinda was silent for a moment, thinking before quietly saying, "I'm sure the Queen appreciates that, being seen as a 'person' instead of a 'title.'"

"I'm sure she does." Jotham paused then spoke his thoughts. "You sound as if you have some experience with that."

"With not being seen for who you really are?" Jacinda looked at Jotham wondering if he was really interested or just making polite conversation. She'd never really had a 'conversation' with him before. Yes, they had talked before but always about the current, polite, 'political' things and always in the presence of others. It had never veered toward the truly personal.

"Please, I am actually interested." Jotham saw her hesitation and was surprised to find he was. "I am just now realizing that while I have known you since you came to the House of Protection, I don't really *know* you."

"Actually you have known me since before that, Majesty. We were at the Academy together."

"Excuse me?" Jotham's shock was genuine.

"We were at the Academy together, Majesty," she repeated. "We actually attended several classes together even though I was a cycle ahead of you."

"We had classes together?" Jotham's shock grew. "Why don't I remember that?"

"I believe during those classes you and the High Admiral were more focused on the Hext sisters sitting in front of you than anything else."

"The Hext sisters?" Jotham couldn't stop the smile that broke out over his face or the rusty sounding laugh that escaped him. "Praise the ancestors, I haven't thought about those two in cycles."

"Yes, well they led both of you on a merry chase before you caught them."

"Caught them?" Jotham cleared his throat and forced his lips into a straight line before answering, but the sparkle remained in his eye. "I'm afraid I don't recall 'catching' them."

"Of course you don't," Jacinda's own lips twitched at the King's blatant lie. "No gentleman would remember such a thing."

"I still find it hard to believe I don't remember *you* from the Academy."

"I don't," Jacinda said without any censure. "You had every girl in the Academy trying to gain your attention. There was no reason for you to look at one who wasn't."

"And why weren't *you*?" The words escaped Jotham before he could stop them and cringed slightly at how that sounded, but Jacinda just laughed softly.

"Partly because I was from the House of Healing and knew nothing could come of it. I had no desire to become one of Prince Jotham's 'special friends,'" she said as she made air quotes. "But the main reason was that I had plans, Majesty, and those plans had absolutely nothing to do with politics. I grew up in it and I wanted to be known as *me*, not an Assemblyman's daughter. I had no desire to live the rest of my life in that fish bowl."

When Jotham's only response was to raise an eyebrow, she laughed again.

"No, it didn't turn out that way. The ancestors have the strangest sense of humor."

"Do you regret it?" Jotham asked.

"No. Stephan was worth every minute of it."

"I still find it hard to believe I never noticed you."

"As I said, Majesty, I was a cycle ahead of you. I'm sure you knew my sister though. She and Lata roomed together at the Academy."

"Your sister?" Jotham searched his mind trying to remember who Lata's roommate had been. "Palma? Palma Crocetti was your sister?"

"Is my sister and yes. She's Palma Metaxas now and lives in Kisurri. Lata used to come stay at our house during breaks."

"Yes, I remember that I just... I never made that connection before. I'm sorry."

"There's nothing to be sorry for, it really didn't involve you. Lata and I knew about it and it actually helped us both in those early cycles."

Jotham remembered those first cycles, remembered how Lata had struggled, remembered how she would cry in her bath where she thought he couldn't hear, remembered how he felt he had failed her. Jerking himself back from that painful memory, Jotham gave Jacinda a sharp look. How had the conversation strayed onto such a painful subject? This was so far away from what he had meant to talk to Jacinda about. It was time he got back to the topic at hand.

"Yes, well that has nothing to do with what I wished to speak to you about," Jotham told her coldly.

Jacinda stared at Jotham for a moment, hurt at his abrupt change then realized what he was doing. It was something he had always done if the conversation turned to Lata, not that it ever did anymore, but if it did, Jotham would always abruptly end the conversation. Jacinda had never understood it, but everyone grieved in his or her own way.

"Of course it's not," she replied coolly, "so maybe you should tell me why you summoned me here."

Jotham leaned back slightly surprised not only by her words but by the coolness of her tone and how remote her eyes had suddenly become when just moments before they had been sparkling. He knew he had caused it by his reaction and his words, but no one had ever 'voiced' their displeasure with him quite so eloquently or so politely in cycles.

"Summoned? You weren't *summoned*, Madame Michelakakis. I asked you here."

"When a King 'asks,' it is a summons, Majesty." Jacinda wasn't going to back down. Jotham was the one who had moved this from friendly to merely polite so that was where she would stay. "I am no longer the wife of an Assemblyman, so what possible 'situation' could I help you with?"

"Alright." Jotham rose and went to sit behind his desk, the place he should have been all along and gestured to the chair before it, indicating he wanted her to sit there. Opening the folder he had closed when he'd gone to greet her, he lifted the visual out then slid it across the desk to her.

Jacinda sat before picking it up. In the visual stood four people, all of whom she either knew or knew of. In the center was Lucas Zafar standing tall and proud in his Coalition dress uniform. The violet pants representing he was from the House of Protection were perfectly pressed. The left side of his white dress jacket displayed the medals he had earned and his newly acquired Captain's insignia was gleaming on its collar.

Standing next to Lucas was Victoria, her arms around her new husband's waist. She was literally glowing in the visual and it wasn't because of the incredible gown she was wearing although it was magnificent, one of Kia's creations Jacinda was sure. The violet sash around Victoria's waist was a surprise though. It stated that her loyalty was with her husband and *his* House, the House of Protection, not her aunt's House, the House of Knowledge.

On either side of the couple stood Prince Barek also wearing his dress uniform and Jacinda's great niece, Amina, in a solid violet gown that was a simpler version of Victoria's. Both were smiling at the happy couple. Jacinda found herself smiling. She had a visual very similar to this at home. It had been taken on her and Stephan's Union Day. It sat on her dresser, along with visuals of her children and grandchildren so she could see them every day and remember how very blessed she had been in her life. She hoped these young people were as equally blessed.

"It's a beautiful visual," she finally said, setting the visual down.

"It is. It's why I *asked* you here today," Jotham stated.

"I don't understand." Jacinda ignored his attempt to again act as if she hadn't been summoned.

"I believe my son has become interested in your niece, Amina."

"Great-niece," Jacinda corrected absently, her eyes returning to the visual, "and why would you say that?"

"Because I know my son and saw how he acted around her."

"He said something?" Picking the visual back up, she looked at it with a more critical eye giving particular attention to the expressions and body language of Amina and Barek. Nothing she saw there gave her the impression that they were looking anywhere other than at the happy couple."

"No."

"Then what makes you think he's interested?" Jacinda looked at Jotham.

"As I said. I know my son."

"So why are you telling *me* this?" Jacinda had a sneaking suspicion why but hoped she was wrong.

"I need to know more about this young woman before it goes any further." Jotham pointed to Amina in the visual. "While she is from the House of Protection, she does not reside here. Cassandra considers Amina a member of her family and would not be... pleased... to know that I was inquiring about her."

"I completely understand why," Jacinda told him feeling her anger begin to grow. "It's wrong."

"It is something that must be done if Barek is really interested in her and that is why I contacted you."

"Me?!!"

"Yes, Amina is a member of *your* family. *You* either have or can obtain the information I need to decide if this woman is worthy of my son."

Jacinda stared at him in shocked silence for several moments unable to believe what Jotham was asking of her. What gave him the right? Surging to her feet, she glared down at him.

"How dare you!"

"I *dare* because this woman might one day be the Queen of this House." He slowly began to rise. "I dare because I am the *King* and it is my duty to see that she is fit for the position! I dare because Barek is my *son*!"

"None of that gives you the right to decide the worth of someone! To decide if Amina and Barek are good for each other! That's for *them* to decide."

"The heir to the throne…"

"Must choose his Queen from his own House! Yes, I know! An archaic law that should have been dissolved cycles ago. I thought better of you, King Jotham." Jacinda let him hear the full disdain in her voice. "Especially since the High Admiral is not only a relative but a friend. *He* is from the House of Protection, but he is also the *King* of the House of Knowledge."

"That is only because Cassandra was already the Queen before their Union took place."

"So you are saying that if Barek were to fall in love with someone *not* from this House that he would have to wait until you *died* before he could make her is wife?"

"Don't be ridiculous. Barek would never put off his duty that way."

"Duty!" Jacinda spun away from him unable to believe what was coming out of Jotham's mouth. How could these words be coming from a man she and Stephan had so much respect for? A man they had supported and been honored to serve for so many cycles. She froze when her angry gaze suddenly found Lata's portrait, the one she'd wondered about for all these cycles, tucked away on a wall in the corner. Lata seemed to be staring at her, her eyes demanding something from her. But what?

"Was Lata just a duty, Majesty?" Jacinda spun back to him, her voice quiet but no less potent. "Is that why you've hidden her away? Why you never speak of her? She *loved* you! *You*! Not the Prince you were or the King you would become but Jotham Kado Tibullus!"

"How dare you!" Jotham's face flushed dark red at her accusation. "You know *nothing* about Lata and me! You have no right to question my decisions."

"I have every right! Not only because I am a citizen of this House but because Lata was my *friend*, and you have *erased* her. Not only from this House, but from its people! There are those that don't even know her name!" Jacinda was surprised at how angry she was about that. "She deserves better than that! Especially from the man she *loved*. The man she gave up all *her* dreams for! That you would act as your father did! With your own son! She would be ashamed of you!" Spinning on her heel, Jacinda stormed out of Jotham's office, uncaring about etiquette or protocol.

Chapter Three

"Thank you, Mother. I never expected this." Danton stared at the piece she'd just placed on the corner of his desk in his new office in the Assembly Hall. He had asked her for her assistance because he knew she would know the best way to organize his office, making sure it represented who he was and what he stood for. She had done that with his father's office and he knew that because his father had told him so.

Cycles ago when Danton had first told his father of his aspirations to follow him as an Assemblyman, Stephan had sat him down and told him the truth. That he wouldn't have been where he was, wouldn't have been able to accomplish what he had, if it hadn't been for Danton's mother. She was his sounding board. She gave him her honest opinion even if it differed significantly from his own. And she always stood at his side.

He had also confided in Danton that his mother hadn't wanted a life in politics. That she had always wanted a low-key life but because it was his dream, she'd willingly committed herself to the challenge and he hoped that the ancestors might one day bless Danton as he had been blessed.

All those reasons were why he had asked for his mother's assistance today for he had yet to find his life mate, but he hadn't expected this. This piece wasn't valuable monetarily, but it was irreplaceable to him because it had sat in that exact same spot on his father's desk for as long as Danton could remember. He remembered how his father would let him play with it. He remembered how the spherical balls, set up in a linear fashion would transfer their energy from one to the other until the last ball would swing out then come back to start the process all over again. When he'd gotten older, his father had confided in him that whenever he found himself struggling with an important decision he would start the balls moving. He said watching them helped calm him and cleared his thoughts, allowing him to focus. By the time they'd stop moving, he would know what the right decision was. To have it on his own desk now....

"It was always meant to be yours, Danton." Jacinda let her gaze travel over her first son. He was the image of her Stephan right down to his passion for serving his people in the best possible way. He still had much to learn and she wished Stephan were here to guide him, but she had faith in her first born. "You are following in your father's footsteps, not *because* of him, but because it was what *you* were meant to do. He would be so proud of you."

"I want to make him proud, Mother, but also you."

"Just be yourself, Danton. Follow your instincts and do what your heart tells you is right and I will always be proud of you. There are many that lose their way once they take this office. They become more concerned with their own wants and needs for success and power and forget about the people they are supposed to be serving."

"I will never do that, Mother."

"I know you think that now, Danton, but there will be many tests, many that will try to pressure you, to get you to think the way they do. Life isn't always black and white, Danton. What benefits one may often harm another and it will be up to you to decide whose needs are more important. It can be a daunting task, especially when others try to influence you and I don't just mean the other Assemblymen. The King will also try to influence you. Just remember that it is *your* decision to make and *you* are the one that must live with it."

"The King?" Danton didn't try to cover his shock. "Mother, you and father always supported King Jotham."

"We supported his reign, Danton, for King Jotham has always been a good and fair King, but we didn't just blindly support him." Jacinda thought about what he'd asked her several days earlier. "He is after all just a man and like all men he makes mistakes."

"I have never heard you speak like this, Mother."

"Perhaps because I never have, at least not to you. If your father were still alive, he would tell you this, but since he isn't it falls to me." Jacinda watched the deep frown that took over her son's face. "Do not worry so, Danton. You will find your way. You always have. Just know that there is no one within the House of Protection that you must bow down to, and I don't mean that you shouldn't be respectful. I just mean that you are all the same: Citizen, Assemblyman, or King. Your basic wants and needs are the same as anyone else's and no one person should take precedent over another's just because of their *position* within the House."

"Of course not, but still…"

"Danton," Jacinda walked up to her son gently framing his face with her hands. "Do you believe that the man or woman that prepares your food, that serves it to you, deserves less respect than you do now that you are an Assemblyman?"

"Of course not!"

"Do you believe that your rights are more important than theirs?"

"No."

"Why?"

"Because we are the same."

"Yes, you are. Just as King Jotham and every Assemblyman, you will meet are the same. They are no better and no worse than the rest of us. Yes," she saw him open his mouth and knew what he was about to say, "King Jotham deserves your respect because he carries a heavy burden, but he is still just a man."

∞ ∞ ∞ ∞ ∞

Jacinda was smiling as she left her son to finish settling into his office. It had been a good day. She hadn't been sure how she'd feel returning to this place. The last time she'd been here it had been to clean out Stephan's office. It had been a heart-wrenching day, filled with so many tears. Her children had wanted to help and in the end, she had let them carry out the boxes. However, the actual packing she had done alone. She'd needed to be alone with her memories and not have to worry how it was affecting her children.

There had been no tears today, at least not externally. She might have shed a few internally, but that was from seeing her first born sitting so straight and proud behind that desk, looking so much like his father. However, life went on and it was now Danton's turn to leave his mark.

Turning the corner, Jacinda cried out startled as she ran into someone and started to fall back. Strong hands gripped her upper arms preventing her fall.

∞ ∞ ∞ ∞ ∞

Barek moved quickly through the corridors of the Assembly Hall, hoping his swift pace would deter anyone from trying to stop him. He had a great many things to accomplish before he could return to the Bering and he wanted to get back there as soon as he could. He knew Gad was still holding out on them. His father showing up at Victoria's Union had proven that. What he wouldn't give to go a round with Rogue Stannic, but as

Stannic was an Assemblyman from the House of Knowledge, Cassandra was handling him. Barek would just have to satisfy himself with his son, and as Gad was part of the Coalition, Barek *would* handle him.

Deep in thought, Barek didn't look as he turned the corner and collided with someone. Instinctively, he reached out when he heard the soft, feminine cry.

"Are you alright?" he asked and looked down into wide, teal eyes that he felt he should know for some reason.

The deep voice had Jacinda looking up to find Prince Barek staring down at her, his eyes so like his father's full of concern. "I'm fine." Straightening, she took a small step back and Barek let his hands drop away. "I'm sorry, Prince Barek, I didn't mean to run into you."

"The fault is mine, Madame." Barek was still searching his mind trying to remember who she was. "I was in a hurry and not watching where I was going."

"Then perhaps we should agree that we are both at fault and leave it at that," Jacinda proposed smiling at him.

"Perhaps we should," Barek replied and found himself returning her smile. "Although I've never found fault with having a beautiful woman in my arms."

Jacinda's eyes widened for a moment, then she tipped her head back and the corridor filled with her beautiful laughter. "Oh, Prince Barek," she looked back at him. "You may look like your father, but you definitely have your mother's gift for giving a compliment."

"Well yes..." Barek began, meaning to move on, only to freeze when her words sank in. "My mother?"

"Yes, and I never knew anyone other than Lata, who could give such an inane compliment and appear completely sincere."

"And why would my compliment be inane? You are a beautiful woman."

"Who is older than your mother. But thank you, Prince Barek, you have truly made my day."

When she turned to leave, Barek's next words stopped her.

"You knew my mother?"

"Of course," Jacinda frowned up at him and saw something she didn't understand, hesitant curiosity.

"I'm sorry it's just..." Barek stared at her intently still trying to figure out who she was.

Jacinda finally realized part of what he was struggling with. "I'm sorry, Prince Barek, I should have introduced myself. I am Jacinda Michelakakis. Assemblyman Stephan Michelakakis was my husband."

"Of course!" Barek wanted to slap himself. How could he have forgotten? "My apologies, Madame Michelakakis, my mind was on other things."

"There is no apology necessary, Prince Barek. My Stephan has been gone nearly ten cycles now. There is no reason for you to remember me and please, call me Jacinda."

"Madame... Jacinda... I still should have remembered you because of your beauty alone."

"Definitely your mother's son." Jacinda felt herself blush only to be bumped by someone walking by.

"So you knew my mother through your husband?" Barek sent a dark look at the retreating back of the man who hadn't even stopped to apologize. He put an arm around Jacinda, guiding her out of the traffic flow and into a small alcove that overlooked the Hall's atrium.

"No, I was at the Academy when your mother was." Jacinda allowed herself to be led, finding she wanted to speak more with Barek about his mother. He seemed to need it. She might still be mad at Jotham for his earlier words, but she would not take that out on Barek. She owed Lata that. "She and my younger sister roomed together."

"Really? At the Academy? I never knew that."

"I was three cycles ahead of Lata, but I got to spend time with her when she would visit during their breaks. Although I could have done without some of the pranks she liked to pull," Jacinda smiled remembering.

"Pranks?" Barek's eyes widened in surprise.

"Yes, your mother loved to pull pranks. Didn't you know that?" She watched Barek slowly shake his head. "Oh, well, she especially liked to pull them when you weren't fully awake. I still find myself sometimes checking the salt shaker in the morning, just to make sure the top is on tight."

"She would loosen it?"

"Oh yes," Jacinda smiled at the memory. "Of course it was usually in retaliation for me short-sheeting her and my sister's bed, but still…"

"I've never heard this before."

"Yes, well we mothers have a certain reputation we must uphold, you know, and letting our children know we once did things we've told them not to…" Jacinda just shrugged her shoulders, but her smile never dimmed. "She also liked to take visuals when you weren't looking your best."

"She what?" Barek couldn't hide his shock.

"Oh nothing terrible," she quickly reassured him. "I remember one time I was trying out a new beauty treatment." She missed Barek's shocked look. "I was trying one of those Goryn-green mud packs," Jacinda shook her head remembering. "I had my hair wrapped in a black oil treatment and she snapped a visual. It cost me 100 credits to get it back from her."

"She blackmailed you?!!" Barek couldn't believe it.

"Of course she did. And all the while she had the sweetest smile on her face. Your mother knew how to handle herself, Prince Barek. Did you ever really doubt it?" She gave him a curious look. "She did graduate the top of her class at the Academy, you know. She might have looked sweet and innocent, but she was a strong, smart woman."

"There is just so much I don't know about her." The words seemed to escape out of his mouth on their own. "I always thought…"

"What?" Jacinda asked tipping her head to the side.

"That because of my father…"

"That it had all just been *given* to her?" Jacinda found she was suddenly angry at how little Barek actually knew about his mother. "Was it just given to *you*, Prince Barek? Are you just a figurehead or are you *actually* High Consul for the Coalition?"

Barek stiffened at the insult. "I have earned every position I have assumed, Madame Michelakakis," his voice as cold, as hard, as *royal* as she'd ever heard the King's.

"Yet you doubt that your mother had to… *before* she was Queen… *before* she was considered 'Royal'? When she was just someone Prince Jotham had taken an interest in?"

"I… I never considered…"

"That she might have struggled *more* than you had to, not because she was a Royal, but because she *wasn't* one? Your mother, at a very young age, handled all that pressure with no assistance from the Palace with a natural grace that I still envy. When she was suddenly thrust into the role of the Queen… I never once saw her be anything but kind and graceful, a real Queen." Jacinda's eyes turned sad as she remembered her friend. "Not only have I, but the House of Protection has greatly missed her gentle influence since her untimely death."

Barek was silent for several moments, finding his throat had tightened at Jacinda's heartfelt words. He had never given any thought to what it must have been like for his mother to be suddenly thrust into a role he'd been training his entire life for. And he still wasn't sure he was ready for. She had been so young.

"Just eighteen. Newly graduated from the Academy and ready to join the Coalition." As Jacinda spoke, Barek realized he'd said the last words aloud.

"I can't picture it. There is so much about her I don't know, don't remember." Barek couldn't believe he just said that to her, someone he really didn't know.

"What about her albums of visuals?"

"What albums?" he demanded.

"Lata had albums full of visuals of her trips with her family and of her time at the Academy. She always seemed to be taking visuals of your father and then there were the ones of you."

"Of me?"

"Of course. Oh, there were the 'official' visuals of you, but Lata had her own album of the ones she'd taken. She showed them to me once when she visited. There were ones of you in the bath. Of you sleeping in your crib. She even had one of you running around the King's garden, butt-naked." Jacinda laughed at his dumbstruck look.

"My mother visited you? In your home?" Barek coughed trying to cover his embarrassment and shock.

"Yes, with you. You don't remember?"

"I'm sorry, no."

"Well, you were very young. My first son, Danton, is only a cycle older than you so your mother and I would get together and swap stories. We were the only ones with new children and relied heavily on each other in the beginning."

"Why only in the beginning?"

Jacinda gave him a considering look. "I'm sure you are well aware of how Assemblymen try and," Jacinda hesitated over her next word, "position themselves around you and your father, hoping to forward their own agenda."

"Yes."

"Well the wives do the same with the Queen and when some became aware of how much time we were spending together it caused… tensions."

"My mother should have been allowed to spend her time with whoever she wished."

"And *you* know that is true only up to a point, especially with an Assemblyman's wife." Jacinda saw the understanding in his eyes. "So we began to curtail some of our meetings. Your mother began to reach out to some of her old Academy friends that were returning from their first tour in the Coalition and she began to find other ways to relieve the pressure."

"By driving," Barek spit out.

"Yes."

"Which is what ultimately killed her."

"It was an accident, Barek." Jacinda was unaware she had dropped his title. "Something no one could have foreseen or prevented." When Barek only tightened his lips, saying nothing she knew she needed to let the subject drop. "So you've never seen your mother's visuals?"

"No," he finally admitted.

"Would you like to?"

"What?"

"My sister, Palma, also has albums of visuals from that time. I'm sure she would be more than willing to share them with you. I know there are some visuals she took the day of your parents' Union. Palma assisted your mother on that day."

"I..."

"Palma lives in Kisurri now and I was planning on visiting her in a few days, so I could ask if you would like." Jacinda easily lied to Barek. She had no plans to visit her sister but plans change.

"Kisurri?"

"Yes," Jacinda followed her intuition, "hopefully while I'm there I'll be able to see the rest of my relatives. It's been too long since I've seen Javiera and Leander."

"Michelakakis? Leander and Javiera Michelakakis are related to you?"

"Why, yes. Leander is Stephan's brother's son. I haven't gotten to see them in awhile. Unfortunately, I missed Amina graduating from the Academy and I was hoping she would still be there." She saw Barek's eyes flare, then quickly go blank when she mentioned Amina. Maybe Jotham was on the right track about Barek's interest in Amina even if how he was going about it was all wrong.

"She is," Barek said revealing he was keeping tabs on Amina.

"Wonderful." Jacinda didn't ask how he knew, knowing it would raise his suspicion and looked at the watch on her wrist. "It will make the trip that much more enjoyable. I'm sorry, Prince Barek, but I have to go or I will be late for my next appointment."

"Of course, Madame... Jacinda. It's been a pleasure talking to you."

"Oh the pleasure has been all mine, Prince Barek, and as soon as I get those visuals I will have them delivered to you at the Palace."

"Thank you. I will be on planet until the Guardian departs."

Chapter Four

"This has been wonderful, Sis, having you here." Palma smiled at her older sister as they sat down at the street-side table in the heart of Kisurri soaking in the warmth of the midday suns, for a cup of coffee.

"It's been wonderful being here, Palma. I need to come visit more often."

"You do. You know you're always welcome." Reaching over Palma squeezed Jacinda's hand.

"I do." Putting her hand on top of Palma's she returned the squeeze. "Thank you, Palma, I know this was an unexpected trip."

"It was, but it's been fun going down memory lane. I know Lata would appreciate what you're doing for her son."

"I just can't understand it, Palma." Jacinda took a sip of her coffee enjoying the rich, full flavor for a moment before continuing. "I mean I always knew that publicly Jotham didn't like to talk about Lata, but I thought he at least talked about her to Barek. I can't imagine not talking about Stephan to our children. To have removed all the visuals of him from our home. I'll admit it hurt to look at them for a while, knowing he was gone." Jacinda's voice caught for a moment, "but now I find great comfort in looking at them and remembering."

"You are a strong woman, Jacinda. It's something I've always looked up to. I don't know if I ever told you that." Palma looked at her sister with eyes full of admiration. "I know I wasn't as supportive as I should have been when you married Stephan."

"Palma..."

"No, let me say this. I thought Stephan was too old for you, that he was making you sacrifice all those dreams you used to share with me. Suddenly you were like Mom."

Jacinda was probably the only person who fully understood what that meant. It wasn't that either of them hadn't loved their mother. She had been an amazing woman. Always polished, always polite, always ready to drop everything for her husband. Still she had taken care of her children, had loved them, but she had also demanded they act in a way that never reflected poorly on their father's position. While they'd both appreciated the lifestyle they'd been able to have thanks to that position, they both couldn't wait to escape the restrictions.

"It didn't take me long to realize it wasn't the same. Stephan wasn't just looking for someone that could help him advance his career."

"Our Union nearly ended his career."

"I know and that's when I realized he truly loved you."

"He did."

"Life is funny sometimes, isn't it? If you hadn't fallen in love with Stephan, you wouldn't have been in the House of Protection and been able to help Lata."

"I don't know that I did that much, Palma."

"You did more than you think. Lata told me about that day in the garden. How you found her crying. I know it's wrong of me, but I could just ring Queen Johanna's neck for how she treated Lata."

"Treated her? What are you talking about, Palma? Jotham made it perfectly clear that Lata was who he had chosen."

"Queen Johanna refused to believe it. She was sure Jotham would move on after his tour in the Coalition."

"Why?"

"Because while Lata may have been from the House of Protection, her family name carried no prestige. They were 'commoners' and as far as the Queen was concerned Lata would never be worthy of sitting beside Jotham."

"I always knew Johanna had some very… rigid… beliefs on who should be allowed within 'her' House, meaning me, but I never thought it extended to those from the House of Protection."

"Oh it did, and because of it Johanna made no effort at all to help Lata with the extra attention she was receiving. She gave her no training, no guidance."

"None at all?" Jacinda couldn't believe it.

"None. It really bothered Lata but she, like everyone else, thought it would be cycles before she would have to worry about it. When they were suddenly killed… Lata was petrified."

"It never showed."

"She told me once that your honest friendship meant a lot to her, that it got her through some difficult times, like when she'd visit your house with Barek."

"They were wonderful times. I was sorry they ended even though I understood why."

"I honestly believe that was a mistake. Lata shouldn't have caved to that pressure."

"Palma, you have to understand because Lata and I spent so much time together many believed she would influence Jotham to favor Stephan."

"So what? It's not as if Johanna didn't do the same thing with her 'favorites'."

"True, but Lata wasn't like that. She never played favorites."

"I know, but I believe if she had continued to visit you then she wouldn't have felt the need to escape the Palace by driving alone. I talked to her, Jacinda, the day before she died. Palma lowered her voice so no one would overhear. "Something was bothering her and I don't mean the usual things. I think it had more to do with seeing all our Academy friends going out, following their dreams, seeing the freedom they had to come and go as they pleased when she was always surrounded."

"She told you this?"

"No, it was more the sense I got from her. She told me that driving let her clear her head, let her be just Lata. Not the Queen. Not a wife. Not a mother."

"I wish I would have known she was struggling so. I mean, I was struggling too, but at least I had Mom to talk to."

"I know. I've always felt guilty that I didn't tell you about it, but if I had, Lata would never have confided in me."

"She was so young."

"Just twenty-four cycles when she met the ancestors. Can you imagine it, Jacinda? Our children are now older than she was when we lost her."

∞ ∞ ∞ ∞ ∞

"Jacinda?" The new voice had both women turning.

"Javiera," Jacinda smiled as she rose to hug the other woman. "I was going to call you later today."

"Of course you were," Javiera's voice held a teasing skepticism.

"I was!" Jacinda laughed at the woman she considered a niece. "Come. Sit down and join us. You remember my sister, Palma Metaxas."

"Of course. It's nice to see you again, Palma. How is your family?" As Javiera sat, Jacinda gestured to the server to bring another cup.

"They are well. Donau and his family are out with the Fleet while Tosha and her family are here in Kisurri. How about yours? Jacinda was just telling me that Amina was getting ready to go to Montreux. How exciting for you."

"It is."

"It sounds like you've had a lot of excitement lately. What with the Chamberlain's arriving, the Queen giving birth early and a Union. Do you have any visuals?" Jacinda asked looking to Javiera questioningly.

"It has been," Javiera stiffened slightly, "but I'm afraid I can't show you any visuals that the Queen hasn't officially released."

"Oh, Javiera, that's not what I meant." Jacinda reached over to cover her hand. "I would never ask that of you! I remember how irritating it was to have people approach me for information when Stephan was alive. What I meant was that I heard your family was at the Union and wondered if you had any visuals of *your* family. The last visual I have of your family, Dell is only three cycles."

"Oh, Jacinda," Javiera gave her a sheepish look. "I'm sorry, I should have known better. There have just been so many inquiries since Princess Sabah was born…" Javiera pulled out her personal comm and found the visuals before handing it to Jacinda.

"I understand and I should have been more specific." Jacinda took the comm from her and she and Palma leaned closer together as they swiped through them. "Oh my, what a beautiful visual, Javiera! They look so grown up." Jacinda's eyes traveled over the visual, taking in Leander and Javiera standing side-by-side in what she knew was the Queen's Garden, their children standing in front of them.

Dell was in front of his mother, looking young and uncomfortable as only a young boy could in his dress clothes. While Amina stood in front of her father, wearing the violet gown Jacinda had seen in Jotham's visual.

"That has to be one of Kia's creations," Palma said seeing the gown for the first time.

"It is. Victoria insisted she make Amina's too. Doesn't she look beautiful? And so grown up. Where did my baby go?" Javiera found her eyes welling up again at the thought.

"She grew up." Jacinda squeezed Javiera's hand understandingly. "They do that. They grow up, leave home and find their own way. Who knows where their path may lead them."

"I know. I'm so proud of her. I just thought I had prepared myself for this, but to see her standing there next to Victoria and knowing that one day that might be her…"

"We're never really ready," Palma told her. "I still look at Tosha and see my baby girl even though she's given me two grandbabies."

"Okay, now *that* I'm *not* ready for," Javiera told her laughing. "Neither of you look old enough to be grandmothers." She included Jacinda in her look, knowing Jacinda's second son, Ethan, had two young sons.

"Oh, I so need to come to Kisurri more," Jacinda shook her head laughing. "It is so good for my ego." The ringing of Jacinda's personal comm drew her attention and she reached into her bag to pull it out, smiling when she saw Danton's name appear on the screen.

"Hello, Danton."

"Mom! Where are you?" he demanded.

Jacinda frowned at her son's tone. "I'm in Kisurri, visiting Palma. Why? Has something happened?"

"No, but why didn't you let one of us know where you were going? What if something had happened and we needed to get hold of you?"

"Well it seems you *were* able to get hold of me just fine, so what did you need, Danton?" Her cool tone had Palma and Javiera looking at her curiously.

Silence reigned on the other end of the comm, as Danton sat back in his office chair feeling like a little boy who had just disappointed his mother. It had been cycles since he'd felt like that and found he didn't like it any more now than he did as a child.

"I'm sorry, Mom. I was just worried when I stopped by the house and it was locked up. Myesha wasn't there and not even Madame Nitzschke knew where you were."

"You went next door to the Nitzschke's?" Jacinda slapped a hand over her eyes and sighed heavily as she rested her elbow on the table. She would never hear the end of this, Madame Nitzschke's one goal in life was to know everything about everyone and then tell everyone else about it. By now, half of Pechora knew that Danton had 'lost' his mother and rumors would be flying. "Oh, Danton…"

"I didn't go to her door. She was walking by and I asked. I'm sorry. I know she's an irritating old lady, but I panicked."

"Why? Why would you panic? I am a grown woman, Danton. I've come and gone as I've pleased since before you were born."

"I know, but Mom…"

"But what?"

"We lost Dad so suddenly…. I just… I just couldn't take losing you like that."

"Oh Danton," Jacinda leaned back in her chair and felt her irritation fade away. "I've got a lot of life to live before I meet the ancestors. Now, why were you looking for me in the first place?"

Knowing he was forgiven, Danton quickly explained why he was looking for her.

"You do realize that it is only *three days* away, right?" Jacinda said exasperatedly.

"Of course."

"And that I have nothing to wear?"

"What do you mean? You have a closet full of gowns."

If Danton had been sitting next to her, his mother would have slugged him. "That are over *ten cycles old*!"

"So?" Danton was confused the way only a man could be when it came to clothing.

"You know, sometimes you are just like your father, and *no* that's not a compliment, Danton!"

"But…"

"I'm going to disconnect now, Danton. I will let you know when I am home." Jacinda jabbed the disconnect button wishing Danton could feel it where he was.

"Problem?"

Jacinda looked up to find both women giving her a concerned look. "Danton would apparently like me to attend the Annual Ball with him."

"And he just *now* asked you?" Javiera gave her an incredulous look.

"Apparently I have a 'closet full of gowns' that would do."

The two women looked at each other before they broke out laughing. "Oh, Jacinda, my nephew is such a *man*."

"Yes," Jacinda began to snicker with them, "he is."

"Well you know what this means, don't you?" Javiera said rising and received questioning looks from Palma and Jacinda. "We need to go see Kia."

∞ ∞ ∞ ∞ ∞

"He gave you *three days* notice!" Kia shrieked looking at the three women before her. "For King Jotham's Annual Assemblymen's Ball! Jacinda! Did you drop that boy on his head when he was a baby?" With her hands flying, Kia spun around and started screaming for her assistants.

Jacinda found herself wiping away the tears that were streaming down her cheeks at Kia's tirade. She'd forgotten how much she liked this woman. "No, Kia, I don't think I did," she told her following her deeper into her shop.

"Well, maybe you should have!" Kia spat over her shoulder. "Men! What do they think that 'poof' and amazing gowns just suddenly appear?!!"

"In his defense, Kia, Danton is a new Assemblyman and single. He has no idea how much time wives put into selecting their dress."

"Where did he think you were going to find a gown?"

"In my 'closet full' of gowns." Her words had Kia spinning around so quickly that Jacinda found herself taking a quick step back.

"Seriously?!!" Kia spat out. "He thought you'd just go into your closet and *pull out* something? You! You are Jacinda Michelakakis, the late Assemblyman Stephan Michelakakis' wife! *You* set the standard for elegance in the House of Protection! Every woman there tried to imitate you and never could! And he expects you to make your return wearing something ten cycles old? Oh, I could just wring that boy's neck!"

"I..." Jacinda looked at Kia in shock. "I... well thank you, Kia, but I'm not sure that's true."

"Don't argue with me, Jacinda Michelakakis. I'm a designer and I know what I saw and I know how many of those obnoxious women used to come to me demanding to know what you were going to be wearing so they could try to outdo you."

"They did?"

"Of course they did, especially that obnoxious Madame Pajari. She went as far once as to try and bribe one of my assistants to steal a design."

"Seriously? Adelaide Pajari did that?" Jacinda while surprised, could see Adelaide Pajari doing just that. Adelaide's husband, Elliott, had never been a very strong Assemblyman. He always wavered in his decisions, playing both sides. He would wait to see what the 'popular' vote was before he would cast his. He should have lost his position cycles ago, but still he kept being re-elected.

"Yes, so after that I banned her from my shop." Kia reached into a cabinet and pulled out a nondescript garment bag. "Now this just might work."

Gasping as one, all three women stared in astonishment at the gown revealed as Kia removed the protective covering. It was a long, trumpet mermaid-style gown in black. With a scooped neckline that was sheer, except for the violet beading around the edges that formed a thick 'necklace' before it moved down the bodice to create an intricate medallion snuggled between the bra cups.

"I designed this gown cycles ago, playing with what Cassandra had told me about Earth fashions. I've always loved it, but once we arrived here, there never seemed to be the appropriate occasion to present it to Cassandra."

"Why wouldn't there be?" Palma asked.

"Because it speaks too strongly of the House of Protection, so she could never wear it for a formal event, not now that she is the Queen," Kia told her.

"Kia, it's beautiful," Jacinda whispered, her eyes traveling over the gown taking in its detailed simplicity.

"Thank you and I think with just a few alterations it will fit you perfectly."

"Me?" Jacinda's eyes shot to Kia. "Kia, I love it. It's amazingly beautiful, but I couldn't possibly wear it. I'm too old for it."

"Oh please," Kia waved her hand dismissively. "I don't care how old you are. You don't look a day over forty cycles and when you were forty, you *so* would have worn this."

"I would have but…"

"But what?"

"I'm going with my *son*, Kia, not Stephan."

"So what? You are making your return, Jacinda, and I'm going to make sure you do it in style. Especially since that twit Adelaide will be there. What I wouldn't give to see her reaction when you walk in wearing this."

"I second that." Palma walked up to her sister, wrapping her arm around her waist.

"Palma…" Jacinda gave her sister a put-out look.

"At least try it on, Jacinda," Palma encouraged seeing the desire in her eyes. "You know you want to. If you don't like it, then we'll look for something else."

"I guess it couldn't hurt."

"Wonderful. Come. I'll help you into it. Zee! Thoma! Bring refreshments for the ladies and then my alteration box."

"Yes, Madame Juruas!" Both assistants who had silently entered the room immediately left to follow her orders.

∞ ∞ ∞ ∞ ∞

Jacinda slowly turned so she could see the back of the dress in the mirror. She hadn't realized when Kia had held it up that the beading of the scooped neckline hadn't just circled around the back. Oh no, that would have been too easy for one of Kia's creations. Instead, the 'necklace' had fallen halfway down her back with strings of beads radiating out from it. They attached to the sides of the dress making it conform to her body before it formed a jeweled belt at the small of her back.

"Here put these on."

Jacinda gripped Kia's shoulder as Kia lifted one of her feet to slide a strappy black four-inch heel that fit her perfectly.

"How did you know?"

"I still have your information on file, Jacinda." Kia looked up at her for a moment. "Did you really think I wouldn't? You were one of our first customers. You didn't have to come to us, Jacinda. Neither of us is directly related to you. There was no reason for you to give us your support."

"Of course there was. Yes, you were just starting out, Kia, and while you and Pazel were both young, your talent was undeniable. It's not like I didn't benefit from it."

"You gave us more than that." Slipping the other shoe on, Kia rose. "I know how you promoted us. How you encouraged others. Your standing in the House of Protection got so many women through the door."

"But it was your talent that kept them, Kia. You owe me nothing."

"We owe you everything." The vehemence in Kia's voice shocked Jacinda. "And now you will let me repay you. Come let's see what the others think." And Jacinda allowed herself to be led from the dressing room.

∞ ∞ ∞ ∞ ∞

"Oh, my ancestors!" Palma's cup and saucer rattled as she set it down on the small table in front of her. "Jacinda...."

"What?" Jacinda froze at her sister's words. "Do I look that bad?" She knew her sister would always tell her the unvarnished truth.

"NO!" Palma exclaimed her eyes running over her sister. "Jacinda, you look fabulous. Turn."

Jacinda took several steps as she turned, her golden-toned leg appearing through the high slit of the skirt while the single panel attached to the jeweled 'belt' at her lower back flowed gracefully behind her. She smiled as she heard Palma and Javiera's gasps when the daring back was revealed.

"Oh, Jacinda, you so have to get this gown," Javiera whispered.

"And the shoes. My ancestors, Jacinda, you have to get those shoes!"

"You don't think they make me too tall?" She stuck her leg out looking at the slender heel. "I don't want to overshadow Danton."

"You can never be too tall, Jacinda," Javiera told her absently her eyes still traveling over the gown.

"Yes, you can, especially when you're dancing."

"Seriously, Jacinda?" Palma gave her an exasperated look. "After all these cycles let it go."

"What are you talking about?" Javiera frowned at the two sisters. Even Kia looked at Palma questioningly.

"Henry Jezek and the Annual Holiday Ball for the House of Healing when we were still at the Academy. Henry's father was also an Assemblyman and they insisted that he and Jacinda dance together. I think they hoped it might start a romance."

"Right, like that was ever going to happen," Jacinda scoffed.

"Well not after that dance," Palma agreed.

"Why? What did this Henry Jezek do?"

"First, you have to understand Henry Jezek is short and Jacinda was wearing this fabulous pair of shoes that she had begged Mom for."

"I didn't *beg*, Palma."

"Oh, Mom, please?" Palma imitated in a high-pitched, girly voice that had Jacinda laughing. "Please… I promise I'll take care of them! They go perfectly with my gown. Please, Mama? I couldn't believe she caved." Palma shook her head smiling. "It was the 'Mama' that did it."

"Oh, like you didn't get your way too. You were 'Daddy's girl.' All you had to do was turn those big brown eyes of yours at him and he gave you everything you wanted."

"True," Palma smiled unrepentantly.

"Umm, excuse me," Javiera interrupted. "Henry Jezek?"

"Right, well with the shoes Jacinda wore, Henry's eye only came up to here." Palma put her hand level with her breasts.

"And he stared directly at them the entire valsa."

"Seriously?" Kia asked.

"Seriously and that wasn't the worst of it."

"What was?" Javiera asked.

"He kept licking his lips like he couldn't wait to taste them." Jacinda shivered in revulsion at the memory.

"Why the little foabhor! Why didn't you just walk away?"

"In the middle of the King's Annual Ball? In front of all the Assemblymen from the House of Healing? Mom and Dad would never have forgiven me. It was only one valsa."

"That you are still letting affect you. I know that's why you always wore low heels around Stephan."

"Stephan would never have done that." Jacinda couldn't believe her sister would even suggest such a thing. Stephan had been nothing like Henry.

"Of course not, but you still always made sure he was taller than you."

"Because he was."

"He wouldn't be with those heels," Palma gestured to the ones she was currently wearing.

"No." Jacinda suddenly found herself sad at the thought. Her Stephan would have loved this gown. "He wouldn't be."

"I'm sorry, Jacinda." Palma was instantly at her sister's side all teasing gone. "I didn't mean to upset you."

"You didn't." Jacinda squeezed her sister's hand. "It's just going to be so… odd being there without Stephan. Not helping him choose what to wear. Not standing beside him, reminding him of the wives' names he'd forgotten."

"But Danton will be at your side and that boy is going to need all the help you can give him. The only women he's ever interested in are the single ones."

"Isn't that the truth," Jacinda laughed, and that quickly her sadness evaporated. "I should send him a list of names to memorize just to torture him for giving me so little notice."

"It would serve him right," Palma agreed.

The rest of the afternoon passed pleasantly with the women chatting while Kia made slight alterations to the gown so it fit Jacinda perfectly.

"Kia, I can't thank you enough for doing this on such short notice. I know how in demand you are."

"It was nothing, Jacinda, especially not for you. Just make sure you instruct your son that the next woman he tries to pull this on may not be as understanding as his mother."

"Trust me, Kia, I will make sure he understands."

"Ladies, I have to go." Javiera looked to the message on her comm. "I've had a wonderful time this afternoon. Palma, we'll have to get together again soon."

"I'd like that, Javiera."

"Jacinda." Javiera walked over and hugged her. "Don't be a stranger. You know you are always welcome in our home."

"I know and know that you and yours are always welcome in mine. Montreux isn't that far from Pechora. Amina will always be welcome in my home if she needs to get away or just wants a home-cooked meal."

"Thank you, Jacinda. I will let her know. Maybe it will convince her to go."

"What do you mean? I thought she wanted to go. Is there a problem I can help with?"

"No. Not really. She's just working on something with her father. I can't talk about it, but she may put off Montreux until it's finished."

Jacinda looked at Javiera and realized whatever it was, she was upset she'd brought it up."

"Well, no worries. No one will hear anything from us. Will they?" Jacinda looked to Kia and Palma, who she both knew could keep a secret.

"Of course not," they immediately responded.

"You just let her know my offer is open-ended. Whenever she gets there, she is welcome in my home."

"Thank you, Jacinda. Now I have to go. Oh, I will send you that visual."

"Thank you, Javiera. Give Leander and Dell a kiss for me."

"I will."

Chapter Five

"Hello, gentleman." Jacinda smiled as she walked up to the two guards who were dressed in the colors of the House of Protection. They were protecting the door that led from the Public Wing to the more private wings of the Palace and she stopped several feet away. "I am Jacinda Michelakakis and I have something for Prince Barek."

The guards' hard stares traveled over her for a moment before moving to the package she carried. One lifted the comm attached to his wrist.

"We've received no notification to expect you," the larger of the two told her.

"You won't have. I didn't contact anyone to let them know I was coming."

"We can't let you pass, Madame Michelakakis."

"Of course not, I totally understand."

As Jacinda spoke, the door behind the guards opened and Captain Deffand followed by Prince Barek stepped out.

"Madame Michelakakis! How wonderful to see you again." The serious look on Barek's face turned into a blazing smile as he spoke.

"It's good to see you too, Prince Barek, and I thought you were going to call me Jacinda."

"Of course, I'm sorry, Jacinda," Barek blushed slightly to Deffand's amazement. "What brings you to the Palace today?"

"You do."

"Me?"

"Yes," Jacinda laughed at the confusion on Barek's face. "I returned from visiting my sister yesterday and have something for you."

As she offered the package she carried to Barek, the two guards immediately stepped between them knocking her back.

"What do you think you are doing?!!" Barek angrily shoved his way through the guards to find Jacinda standing several feet away, her face pale. The package she had been carrying lay on the floor. "Jacinda, are you alright?"

"I…" Swallowing hard, she took a deep breath trying to calm her racing heart. "Yes. Of course, I am. I don't know what I was thinking."

Barek spun around to confront the two guards, but before he could, Deffand spoke. "They were doing their job, Prince Barek."

"Since when is shoving a woman their *job*, Captain?" Barek's rage was easily heard.

"Prince Barek," Jacinda's soft but firm voice interrupted him and pulled his furious gaze from the Captain to her. "Captain Deffand is correct. The fault is mine. It goes against every protocol for me to directly hand you a package that hasn't been inspected by your security first."

"That gives them no right…"

"It gives them every right," Jacinda again interrupted. "They do not know me and were protecting their future King, as they should."

Leaning down, she picked up the package of visuals she'd gotten from Palma, along with one she'd 'accidently' slipped in and extended it to Deffand.

"Captain."

"Thank you, Madame Michelakakis." Deffand took the package.

"Are those the visuals?" Barek's question was directed at Jacinda, but his eyes were locked on the package now in Deffand's hands.

"Yes, and I have to thank you." She saw the confusion on his face. "Palma and I had a wonderful time going down memory lane. We laughed until our stomachs hurt. We tried to attach comments to each one for you, about who's in the visual, when and where it was taken. I took the liberty of making hard copies of them, but they are also on the memory foil that's inside. If you have any questions just contact me and I will do the best I can."

"I... I can never thank you enough for this, Jacinda." Barek's voice was tight as he spoke. "You have no idea what it means to me."

"Your mother was my friend, Prince Barek. She would have done the same for one of mine if the situation were reversed." She gave him a warm smile. "Now I will get out of your way for you seem to be on your way somewhere. I will see you tomorrow night."

"Tomorrow night?" Barek's question halted Jacinda as she started to turn away.

"Yes, at the Assemblyman's Ball."

"You will be there?"

"Yes. My first son, Danton, is now an Assemblyman and asked me to accompany him."

"Then I will save a dance for you," Barek smiled at her.

"I look forward to it, Prince Barek." With a nod, Jacinda turned and left.

∞ ∞ ∞ ∞ ∞

Deffand watched the gentle sway of Jacinda Michelakakis' hips as she walked away. She was truly a beautiful woman inside and out and he wondered if he would ever find a woman half as beautiful and kind. He pulled his thoughts away from what he wanted, to what was in his hands.

"These are visuals of the Queen?" His gaze traveled to Barek to see he too was watching Jacinda leave.

"Yes." Barek extended his hand. "You and I both know Jacinda Michelakakis would never cause harm to the House of Protection."

"I know that, Sire, but there are still protocols that must be followed."

"Those are private visuals, Deffand. Of my mother before she became Queen. Jacinda's sister was kind enough to share them with me. I won't allow someone else to view them, especially before I do."

Deffand could see that Barek was adamant about this and sighed heavily. Barek didn't demand much. He had always seemed to understand the need for security, unlike his late brother, Dadrian, who had always pushed everything. For Barek to be this insistent meant these visuals were extremely important to him. Still he couldn't just hand them over to him.

"I will personally walk this package through security. It can be scanned and tested without being opened. No one will view what is yours, Sire. That is the best I can do."

Deffand watched Barek struggle and knew Barek wanted to argue further even while he knew he was right. Finally, Barek nodded jerkily.

"Do it, but I want that package waiting for me in my personal quarters by the time I return."

"It will be done, Sire."

∞ ∞ ∞ ∞ ∞

"Yoo-hoo… Jacinda…"

The high-pitched, scratchy voice had Jacinda cringing slightly. She should have known her luck couldn't hold out forever. That she'd managed to get into her house the night before and then out again this morning without Madame Nitzschke catching her had been a miracle, but now it was time to face the music. Turning, she forced a smile on her face.

"Hello, Madame Nitzschke. How are you this beautiful day?" Jacinda watched as her neighbor came teetering up the sidewalk. Jacinda tried not to shudder at the outfit her meddlesome neighbor was wearing. It was one of her 'signature' outfits, that had never been in style, even though Madame Nitzschke seemed to think it had. A knee-length, multicolored skirt with vertical stripes over leggings that if you looked at them too long gave you vertigo. Her shirt, while black and white had horizontal stripes with dots splattered in-between them. Her outfit was completed by a wide-brimmed, straw hat with a garden of artificial flowers banded around it and short-heeled, ankle-high, red boots on her feet.

Madame Nitzschke had been a fixture in their neighborhood since before she and Stephan had purchased their home. She was the only child of an Assemblyman that had met the ancestors before Stephan had become one. It was rumored that her life mate had been killed while serving in the Coalition, in a surprise attack by the Regulians along the border. Because of it, she had never had a Union. Instead, she'd made it her life's work to know everything about everyone in the neighborhood.

"It could be nicer. It's too cloudy." She put a hand on the top of her hat, keeping it in place as she squinted up at the half-dozen, fluffy, white clouds floating across the sky. "Looks like we might have a stoirme."

"Really?" Jacinda glanced up not seeing a single stoirme cloud.

"Yes. I'm glad to see you are okay, Jacinda."

"Why wouldn't I be?"

"Well, because you just *disappeared* there for several days."

"I didn't *disappear*, Madame Nitzschke. I went to visit my sister in Kisurri."

"Really?" Madame Nitzschke's tone let Jacinda know she didn't believe her. "Without telling *anyone*?"

Jacinda had to bite her tongue to stop from telling the old biddy to mind her own business. In her heart, she knew Madame Nitzschke was actually concerned and that her nosiness came from being lonely.

"I did tell someone. I told Myesha."

"But not your son."

"No, Madame Nitzschke, I did not call my son to tell him where I was. I am a grown woman and don't have to account for my comings and goings to *anyone*."

"He came pounding on *my* door in a panic."

"Danton did no such thing!" While Jacinda was willing to humor Madame Nitzschke to a point, she wouldn't let her outright lie. "You were walking by as Danton was leaving. He told me so when he called me on my comm."

"Well he was in a panic and I can understand why with the men you 'entertain' in your home, especially that last one. My goodness, he barely looked older than Danton. You should be ashamed of yourself, Jacinda."

"Excuse me!"

"You heard me, young lady. You were the wife of a well-respected Assemblyman. You owe it to him and those who supported him to make sure your actions are above reproach."

Jacinda felt her face flush and her blood begin to boil. That this self-righteous old… That she felt she had the right to judge her. "Madame Nitzschke, I understand and sympathize with the fact that you have no family of your own, that you have nothing better to do with your time than interfere in other people's lives. But it does not give you the right to judge me, or whom I see. I thank you for your concern, now if you will excuse me, I was on my way in." Spinning around, Jacinda walked away before she said something she would regret.

Jacinda barely stopped herself from slamming her front door. How dare that condescending, old biddy think she had the right to tell her who she could 'entertain' in her own house. Not that she ever did. It had taken nearly five cycles after Stephan died before she had even considered dating again, let alone 'entertaining' a man. Not that there hadn't been offers.

It seemed there were many men who thought that as a widow she would welcome their subtle, and not so subtle advances. She hadn't, not until Oran Halloran. Oran had been an old family friend from the House of Healing. A few cycles older than her, they became reacquainted when he traveled to Pechora for a business meeting. Oran was also a widower and his business brought him to the city every few weeks. Slowly they had begun to see each other, both tentative about starting a new relationship. It hadn't lasted long. After just one night of intimacy, six moon cycles into the relationship, and it had ended. It had felt terribly awkward to Jacinda and while they occasionally still had dinner together, neither of them had wanted to pursue the relationship further.

Her second attempt had lasted longer. With a man Jacinda thought she could spend the rest of her life with. Paul had been a quiet, unassuming man and after Stephan, Jacinda thought that was what she wanted. She'd been wrong. She found herself bored and unchallenged. Paul had been a nice enough man, but he wasn't someone she wanted to spend the remainder of her life with.

After she'd ended it with Paul, she'd sat down on the bench Stephan had placed in 'her garden' as he liked to call it, and really thought about what she wanted for the rest of her life. It had been an enlightening experience for her, because it was only then that she had fully realized how many of her wants and needs had become a reflection of Stephan's. It hadn't been something he demanded or something she'd done consciously, but still it had happened.

They'd been a cohesive unit doing what was necessary to forward what they both wanted, but when she'd thought back about it, Stephan's needs had always been the ones that took the forefront. With their children grown, Jacinda had wanted them to start traveling more. She wanted to enjoy her husband without the constraints brought on by him being an Assemblyman.

Stephan had promised that he would start taking more time off and that they would travel, but something had always come up. A vote he just couldn't miss. A committee he just had to chair. A ball they just had to go to. And in the end, it had been that 'just' that had caught up with them.

Jacinda had loved her life with Stephan. If she could, she would change nothing about it except for the way it ended. But now… it wasn't the way she wanted to spend the rest of her life. She wasn't going to be a replacement as she would have been for Oran and she wasn't going to settle, as she would have with Paul. She was going to live what remained of her life exactly the way she wanted.

Frowning, her thoughts returned to Madame Nitzschke's final words. Who was the 'younger' man she'd been talking about? Searching her mind, she began to laugh. Praise the ancestors, the old biddy was referring to Deffand, the Captain of the King's Guard. Still laughing, Jacinda moved away from the door.

∞ ∞ ∞ ∞ ∞

Barek entered his private rooms in the King's Wing and immediately saw the package sitting in the center of his desk. Dropping the files from his latest interview with Gad Stannic on a corner, he rounded the desk, never taking his gaze from the package. Sitting in his chair, he continued to stare at the package for several minutes before slowly reaching out to pull it toward him.

Turning the envelope over, he saw that its seal was still intact. Deffand had kept his word, not that Barek had ever truly doubted it. Deffand had always been a man of honor. Reaching into his desk, he pulled out a thin blade. Slowly sliding it under the seal, he broke it then set it aside as he carefully tipped the package's contents onto his desk.

The memory foil Jacinda had spoken of was the first thing to skitter across the desk followed by a facedown stack of visuals, many more than Barek had expected. Picking up the foil first, he held it between his thumb and forefinger trying to imagine what wonders it held before carefully putting it in a drawer of his desk for safekeeping. Gathering the visuals into one pile, he turned them over and a girl he had never seen before looked out at him.

She appeared to be about fourteen cycles in the visual and she was making funny faces for whoever was taking the visual. Her head was tipped to the side with her tongue sticking out and even though both her brown eyes were looking at the tip of her nose, you could see the sparkle of laughter in them.

As he studied the visual closer, he realized he recognized where she was, in a dorm room at the Academy. Even without the caption below, there was no mistaking that drab, gray, wall color or the smallness of the room. *Introducing myself to my new roommate* it read. Carefully, he set the visual to the side and picked up the next.

First day of classes. This one read and it showed two young girls, this time they were standing tall and proud in their academy uniforms. It was easy to tell who was who for the taller girl on the right greatly resembled Jacinda while the shorter one could only be his mother. Barek's eyes greedily traveled over her, taking in the darkness of the hair that hung down, just touching her shoulders. Barek ran a hand through his own hair. It was thick, full and wavy, a little longer than regulation, but he knew if he could touch his mother's in the visual it would feel the same.

A small smile touched the corners of his mouth as he found something he and his mother had in common. His smile grew as he continued through the visuals. Each one had some humorous comment about why it was being taken and Barek felt like he was getting to know his mother as a person for the first time, watching her grow older. His hand stilled over the next visual and he felt his heart beat harder.

His father's face took up half of the visual, the top of his head cut off. His mother's took up the other half, the top of her head cut off too as if one of them was taking it. But it was his father's expression that captured Barek's attention this time, for he had never seen it on his face before. It was happy, carefree joy, the kind of feeling Barek wasn't sure he had ever experienced before. His father's eyes sparkled in the visual and no one seeing him would doubt, that at that moment, he thought his world was perfect.

Barek noted how the visuals began to change after that, rarely was there one of his mother that didn't include his father, but she seemed happy. Especially in the one of her gazing up at Jotham, even Barek could see the love shining in her eyes. She had truly loved his father.

The last visual had him frowning. It didn't belong. His eyes traveled over the half dozen rows of visuals laid out before him on the desk's surface before returning to the one in his hand of the Michelakakis family. It had been recently taken at Victoria's Union and he remembered how beautiful Amina had looked that day.

Amina... he let his eyes travel over her smiling face. She was so young... too young.

"Barek?"

His father's voice had Barek quickly slipping the visual into a drawer before he answered. "In my office."

Jotham entered Barek's office and froze. What he'd come to talk to his son about disappeared from his mind as he saw the visuals lined up across the top of Barek's desk. Slowly he moved forward, his gaze greedily taking in his late wife's face.

"Where did you get these?" he whispered.

"From Jacinda Michelakakis, she got them from her sister."

"Palma," Jotham supplied the name.

"Yes."

"She and Lata were roommates for all six cycles they were at the Academy."

"So Jacinda told me."

"Jacinda?" Jotham lifted his gaze from the visuals to frown at his first son. When had his son become familiar enough with Jacinda Michelakakis to use her first name?

"Yes. I literally ran into her in the Assembly Hall. We talked for a time and she offered to obtain these for me."

"Why?"

"What do you mean, why?" Barek frowned at his father's question.

"Why would she offer to do this for you? What did she want in return?"

"Nothing. Jacinda said that she and my mother had been friends, even before she was an Assemblyman's wife and Mother was the Queen. She told me that Mother loved to take visuals and that she would have shown me these herself had she lived, that it was the least she could do for her friend."

Jotham said nothing, just reached down and turned the visual of his and Lata's faces around so it was upright to him. He could remember when this was taken. They'd been alone in Lata's room, something they were never supposed to be, but William had helped him sneak in that night and then out again before the dawn. He hadn't realized Lata had given Palma the visual.

"You snuck into the girl's dorm?"

Barek's shocked question made Jotham realize he had spoken out loud and Jotham felt his face start to flush.

"Yes," he admitted. "I was in my last cycle at the Academy. Graduation was just weeks away and I would be leaving to serve in the Coalition. Palma was gone for a few days and your mother and I didn't want to be separated."

"You and she..."

"That is none of your business, Barek," Jotham told him gruffly before relenting, "but no. Your mother was only sixteen cycles at the time. She was too young and I would never have pressured her like that. We had plans..." he trailed off.

"What were they?"

Jotham smiled at his son, but there was no happiness in it. "We were going to travel the universe together. Your mother couldn't wait to get into space, it was her life-long dream to see other worlds, to see Carina growing smaller as we left and then grow larger when we returned."

"Why didn't she ever get to?"

"You know why, my parents died."

"But that didn't mean she had to give up her dream."

"You think I would let your mother go into space without me? Do you realize what could have happened to her out there without me?"

"Yes. I believe I do, but that is not what I meant. Why didn't you let her experience those things when she was the Queen? You could have taken her into space. Let her experience her dream."

"When there was no heir?" Jotham's gaze hardened as he looked at his son. "The House of Protection had already been thrown into turmoil because my father had yet to give me any actual responsibility and your mother...."

"What about her?" Barek demanded

"Barek... you have to understand... or maybe not because I never did. My mother, Queen Johanna, never reached out to Lata. She never tried to ease the transition for her. My mother... she never believed Lata was my life mate. She wanted me to choose one from a strong bloodline. Lata's family... they were... are good, strong people but they were too... common for my mother. It's not something she ever verbalized, but you better than anyone understand that what we *don't* say is sometimes more important than what we do."

Barek was silent for several moments thinking about everything his father had just told him. He wondered if his father realized this was the most personal conversation they had ever had about their family. "Why not later? After I'd been born?"

"At first because Lata needed to fully recover. Then she refused to leave you, and then…" Jotham truly looked at his son, at the man he had become and knew he had to tell him the truth. "Then there were rumblings of a challenge… because of Lata's heritage."

"Who would *dare*?" Barek demanded, enraged at the thought.

"It matters not. We silenced them."

"By mother again giving up her dream."

"For the moment, yes. I promised Lata that we would go off planet, that I would do everything within my power to see that she achieved her dreams…."

"And then she died."

"Yes."

The word was torn from Jotham and Barek couldn't doubt his anguish. Barek slowly began to gather up the visuals from his desk, looking at each one with new eyes.

Jotham watched his son gather the fragments of his mother's short life and Jacinda's words suddenly resonated within him, and he realized she was right. He had significantly harmed not only his Queen with how he handled his loss, but also his son.

"There are albums of visuals, you know."

"What do you mean?" Barek's hands stilled over the last visual on his desk.

"Madame Michelakakis was right. Lata did love to take visuals. It was what she wanted to be for the Coalition, a visual historian, not unlike what Kyle Zafar does. Since it wasn't 'suitable' for a Queen to take visuals as she met the people, she instead took them of you."

"Of me?"

"Yes. I don't think there was a day that passed that she didn't take a visual of you."

"I've never seen them."

"My fault." Jotham looked his son in the eye as he admitted his failing. "I didn't react well to your mother's loss, Barek. Every visual I saw of her... or that I knew she took..."

"I understand."

"No. You don't. And I hope you never do. To know, I failed her in so many ways."

Barek saw the pain that filled his father's eyes and didn't know what to say or how to ease it.

"I always thought I would have the time to make it up to her." Slowly he handed the visual he still held out to Barek. "To show her that I understood what she had given up... for me... but I didn't."

"Would you have done it differently? If you could?" Barek took the visual from his father's hand. "Would you have changed anything?"

"Only the ending," Jotham whispered. "I will find the albums for you. Your mother would want you to have them." Turning Jotham left the room.

Chapter Six

For the third time in less than two weeks, Jacinda found herself in the Public Wing of the Palace. This time on the arm of her son as he led her to the Ball Room and she could feel the muscles in his arm tensing with each step they took.

"Relax, Danton. You will do fine." Her words traveled only as far as his ears as she squeezed his arm reassuringly. "They are just men, like you."

"I know." Danton looked to his mother. "Did I tell you how beautiful you look?"

Jacinda chuckled, her eyes twinkling as they looked up at him. "You are just trying to make up for that 'you have a closetful of gowns' comment."

Danton had the grace to blush. "Well, yes, that was an entirely inappropriate comment for me to make and I'm sorry." He let his gaze travel over what she was wearing and knew it hadn't come from her closet. "You do look beautiful, Mother."

"Thank you, Danton." Jacinda knew he was sincere and silently thanked Stephan for giving her such a wonderful son. She knew Danton was going to do a fantastic job as an Assemblyman; his nervousness was proof of that. If he were already comfortable with his new responsibilities, *then* she would be worried.

Together they paused at the entrance of the Ball Room each taking in the room before them. For Danton, it was his first time seeing the Ball Room decorated for an Assemblymen only event. He'd only been here for 'family' and 'public' events and it had never looked like this.

For Jacinda, it was like entering an old, familiar room. She'd spent so much time in this room in the past and it appeared not much had changed. The same tables were still set up, tall ones for those who wished to stand and lower ones with chairs for those that preferred to sit and talk. The food area was still being set up along the same wall, serving only the finest the House of Protection had to offer. Waiters wandered through those gathered offering them crystal flutes filled with the finest House wines.

Banners of violet floated down from ceiling to floor between the doors that opened to allow the perfumed air from the garden to flow into the room. The crystal chandeliers were polished so they sparkled. Right now, they blazed brightly lighting the entire room but Jacinda knew that as the night progressed they would be dimmed and would send out shards of color, illuminating those that chose to dance.

"I..." Danton trailed off.

"It's amazing, isn't it?" Jacinda smiled at her son. "And now you are a part of it, Danton. Come, let's get a drink." She and Danton had no more than picked up their flutes when a familiar voiced called out.

"Jacinda? Jacinda Michelakakis. Is that you?"

Turning around, a smile broke out across Jacinda's face as Evadne Terwilliger moved toward her. Evadne was the wife of Assemblyman Evander Terwilliger, the longest sitting Assemblyman in the House of Protection. Evander was a powerful man and Evadne was considered the reigning 'Queen' of the wives. They had also been good friends with her and Stephan.

"Evadne." Jacinda hugged her old friend. "How are you?"

"I am fine. But you... let me look at you." Evadne stepped back, holding Jacinda's hands out so she could run a critical eye over her old friend. "Praise the ancestors, Jacinda! How do you keep getting more beautiful the older you get? If you weren't my friend, I think I would hate you."

Jacinda tipped her head back and laughed. "I need to see you more often, Evadne. You are good for my ego."

"You have no ego, Jacinda, it's one of the things I love most about you."

"Of course I do and it's the dress that is so beautiful, not me."

"It is a stunner. Turn," Evadne ordered.

Jacinda knew better than to argue when Evadne got that look in her eye so she made a slow turn revealing the starburst back.

"This has to be one of Kia's creations."

"It is." Jacinda finished turning to face Evadne. "I was lucky enough to be in Kisurri when Danton invited me to join him tonight." Jacinda turned to Danton, who had been standing quietly behind her and put her hand on her son's arm bringing him forward. "You remember my first son, Danton, don't you, Evadne?"

"Why yes, of course." Evadne's gaze ran over Danton. "You look just like your father, Danton." She leaned in and whispered loudly. "If it hadn't been for my Evander and Jacinda here, I would have made a play for that man."

Danton stiffened slightly not sure how to respond until his mother started to laugh.

"Evadne Terwilliger, you stop that right now," Jacinda admonished her friend, knowing this was how Evadne vetted many a new Assemblyman. "Danton might take you seriously and then where would you be?"

"With two gorgeous men?" Evadne wiggled her eyebrows up and down at Jacinda.

"You, Evadne, are incorrigible and I will not have you corrupting my son."

"But what if I want to be corrupted, Mother?" Danton smoothly leaned over and kissed the back of Evadne's hand. As he rose, he watched Madame Terwilliger blush.

"Definitely your father's son," Evadne was slightly breathless as she spoke. "He did that exact same thing at *his* first Assembly Ball."

"Evadne, are you trying to replace me with a younger model?" Evander Terwilliger walked up behind his wife and put a possessive hand on her lower back.

"You know I would never leave you, Evander, but if I were…" She smiled up at her husband before her eyes returned to Danton.

"Danton Michelakakis, Assemblyman Terwilliger," Danton introduced himself as he held his hand out to the senior Assemblyman.

"Evander, Danton, there is no need for titles between us as we are equals."

"No, we are not," Danton instantly denied. "Assembly… Evander, but I hope one day we will be."

Evander silently assessed Danton for several moments before nodding his approval at his response. "I have no doubt of it, Danton, that is unless you entice my wife away. I always had to keep a close eye on her when your father was single."

"Oh, Evander!" Evadne playfully slapped her husband's arm. "You are going to give Danton here a terrible opinion of me."

"I could never have a terrible opinion of a woman as beautiful as you, Madame Terwilliger."

Evander watched his wife of over fifty cycles blush at the heartfelt compliment and knew having a Michelakakis back in the Assembly was going to be interesting. "Definitely your father's son." His gaze turned to Jacinda. "Jacinda, it's wonderful to see you again and don't you look amazing."

"Thank you, Evander." Leaning over Jacinda kissed her old friend's cheek. "It's wonderful to be back even if it's only for a night."

"I wish it were more than that. You and Stephan always found a way to liven up this event."

"I don't believe we did it alone." Jacinda's eyes were sparkling as she spoke. "As I remember, you and Evadne were the ones responsible for Assemblyman Cote and his wife's incredible dance."

Evander burst out laughing, drawing the attention of those nearby before he straightened and his face became expressionless. "I have no idea what you could possibly be referring to, Madame Michelakakis. As I remember it, I was talking to King Jotham when that occurred."

"Of course you were, Evander." Jacinda didn't try to keep the laughter from her voice.

"Jacinda? What are *you* doing here?"

Danton watched all humor leave his mother's eyes, her face becoming an expressionless mask at the nasally question. Looking to the Terwilligers, he saw it was the same. Turning, he watched a thin, bird-like woman walk up to them, her eyebrows drawn so tightly together that they nearly touched.

"Hello, Adelaide." Jacinda turned to face the one Assemblyman's wife that she had never been able to stand.

"What are you doing here, Jacinda?" Adelaide asked again stopping several steps away, making no attempt to keep her voice down. "You are no longer the wife of an Assemblyman."

"No, I'm not." Jacinda readily agreed.

"My dear, is there a problem here?" Assemblyman Pajari walked up to his wife. Where his wife was thin and angular with sharp features, Elliott was soft and round, but his eyes were just as beady as his wife's as they traveled over Jacinda.

"Yes. I was just trying to discover how an 'outsider' could have been allowed into this esteemed gathering."

"Now, my dear, I'm sure there is a reasonable explanation as to how Madame Michelakakis was able to gain entrance."

"My mother is here because she was gracious enough to accompany me, Assemblyman Pajari." Danton angrily eyed the other man, not liking his tone nor how his eyes seemed fixed on his mother's chest.

"Your mother?" Elliott frowned, looking from Jacinda to Danton, his confusion easily seen.

"Yes, Elliott," Evander spoke, his tone neutral. "It seems you forgot to read up on the new Assemblymen. Again. Danton here is Stephan and Jacinda's first son. He will be taking Turner's seat in the Assembly."

"I must have missed that." Elliott gave Danton an assessing look but made no move to welcome him into the Assembly.

"That makes no difference," Adelaide piped in, all but sneering. "This is a Ball for the Assemblymen and their *wives*, not their *mothers*."

"An Assemblyman has always been allowed to bring whoever he wished to this Ball, Adelaide," Evadne reminded her in a hard voice.

"Of course he is, but for some reason this new Assemblyman doesn't understand that means someone 'significant' in his life."

"My mother *is* 'significant' in my life, Madame Pajari," Danton ground out.

"Yes, yes of course, but you are obviously too young to understand my meaning. It is for an Assemblyman's potential wife, not his *mother*. Your mother should have explained that to you, but I suppose she was so desperate to be seen as 'important' again that she didn't care how it reflected on you."

"Potential *wife*?" Jacinda finally spoke and while her words were polite they carried the cloying sweet hint of sarcasm. "Was that what Bebe Bouchard was? A potential wife?" She turned her gaze to Elliott and watched the flush that started to climb his neck.

"Bebe Bouchard?" Adelaide choked out, her face paling.

"Yes, Bebe Bouchard," Jacinda said loud enough to draw the attention of those near her.

"I have no idea who you are talking about," Adelaide denied.

"You don't? How strange. I'm sure Elliott introduced her as your niece," Jacinda frowned as if confused. "But wait, I must have misunderstood, it has been over twenty cycles because you are an only child. Aren't you, Adelaide?"

"Yes," Adelaide forced out through tight lips. "So you see…"

"So she must have been *your* niece, Elliott. Is that right?" Jacinda's gaze pierced the Assemblyman's refusing to allow him to look away.

"Um… no, I too am an only child," he finally admitted, his wife sending him an angry look.

"Really? Then who was she? Why was she with you?"

"As I said, you are mistaken, Jacinda."

"Oh no, Adelaide, I am not," Jacinda cut her off. "I remember her quite distinctly. We were all surprised when Elliott arrived with her on his arm instead of you. He was positively bubbly which was confusing after he told us you were in Atrato, recovering from some illness. We were all very concerned. Weren't we, Evadne?" Jacinda looked to her friend and saw her fighting a smile.

"Yes," Evadne nodded her agreement. "I do recall that."

Jacinda knew she had just put Adelaide Pajari in her pompous place and was going to let it end there, but the little twit just wouldn't let it go.

"Neither of you know what you are talking about! I can only hope that your son has a better memory than you do and knows his place in the Assembly. Otherwise, he won't remain there long."

"Really, Adelaide, you want to go there?" Jacinda's eyes went cold and her voice hard as she glared at the other woman. If this b'osh wanted to attack her son, then the gloves were coming off. "Because *I* distinctly remember a great deal more about that particular ball. I remember how Bebe danced with your husband. How she was pressed so tightly up against him that others stopped and stared." She watched as Adelaide turned bright red before she spun around and stomped off. Elliott quickly followed looking like he wanted to crawl into a hole.

Silence reigned for several moments before Evadne broke out laughing and wrapped her arms around Jacinda. "Oh, Jacinda, I have indeed missed you. The look on Adelaide's face... priceless."

"I've wanted to put that self-important little b'osh in her place for cycles but now..." Jacinda looked to Danton. "I'm sorry, Danton."

"Don't be, Mother. It sounds like that was a long time coming."

"It was, but you have to work with Elliott and I've just made that more difficult for you."

"Don't worry about it, Jacinda," Evander reassured her. "I'm sure you son will be able to handle him."

∞ ∞ ∞ ∞ ∞

Jotham and Barek silently followed their guard as they entered the Public Wing of the House of Protection. Tonight was the annual Assemblymen's Ball, an event that Jotham knew he had to attend but one he no longer enjoyed. Every cycle he had to choose a wife from one of the Assemblymen to dance with and then for weeks after, he would have to deal with the rumors that he was favoring that Assemblyman.

"Father."

"Yes?" Jotham looked to his son. It had been cycles since Barek had been on planet for this event, normally he was out with the Fleet.

"Would you mind if I took the first dance for the night?" Barek looked at his father as Jotham approached the closed door to the ballroom.

"You wish to address the Assemblymen?"

"No, I'll leave that to you. I just thought I could help deflect the rumors of favoritism you always have to deal with after the Ball."

"You know of that?" Jotham hadn't realized his son had.

"Of course, I may not always be here, but that doesn't mean I don't know what is happening here."

"No. Of course not." Jotham looked at his son with new eyes. "I would appreciate you taking the first dance." Jotham began to smile. "It will be interesting to see the Assemblymen's reaction. Do you have someone in mind?"

"Yes," was all Barek was able to say as Deffand opened the doors and their arrival was announced.

∞ ∞ ∞ ∞ ∞

Everyone in the room turned as the music that had been softly playing changed. The doors to the ballroom, that had been closed when the last Assemblyman had arrived, now opened to reveal not only King Jotham but also Prince Barek, both looking amazingly handsome.

Barek wore his official Coalition uniform, pants of deep violet with a black stripe running down the outside of each leg and a pristine white jacket, displaying his rank and medals for all to see.

Jotham was not wearing his full 'royal' attire, which consisted of his crown and robe. Jacinda knew he wore this during the opening of the Assembly. But he still wore a subtler and more comfortable version of it. His jacket was solid, House of Protection violet, the royal crest of an arrow emblazoned across his chest in black that matched his pants. The combination gave him an aura of power and strength that he seemed to carry easily.

Jacinda hadn't been sure how she would feel at seeing Jotham again after their last meeting. She was still angry about what he had asked her to do, but in hindsight it had been what prompted her to offer to get the visuals for Barek. Seeing him now, she found herself struggling to maintain that anger.

∞ ∞ ∞ ∞ ∞

Jotham moved through the crowd stopping to say a word to an Assemblyman and his wife here and there on his way to the steps that would lead him to the seats slightly raised where the King and Queen always sat. He accepted the fluted goblet of wine from a servant before he ascended to where he would address his Assemblymen.

"Greetings and welcome to the Assembly Ball," Jotham began.

"Greetings," the room responded to him.

"Tonight I am honored to welcome back those of you who have served me and our people so well and faithfully in the past." He raised his glass slightly. "And to welcome those new to our Assembly, who I am sure will do the same. Assemblyman Dobos and Madame Dobos," Jotham found the new Assemblyman in the room and raised his glass to him. "Welcome."

"Welcome," the room repeated.

"Assemblyman Gully and Madame Gully," Jotham acknowledged the second new Assemblyman. "Welcome."

"Welcome," the room again repeated.

"Assemblyman Danton Michelakakis," Jotham stressed the first name slightly and paused for a moment when he realized who was standing next to Danton. "Welcome." This time when Jotham raised his glass he drank.

"Welcome!" The room seemed to be more enthusiastic this time and it warmed Jacinda's heart as she too drank to the new Assemblymen.

Typically, Jotham would now be required to officially start the Ball by choosing a woman to dance with. Instead, and to the shock of many, he turned and walked up the steps to take his seat.

Barek, handing his glass to a passing waiter, smiled and nodded to those he passed, but did not stop moving until he reached Danton and Jacinda Michelakakis.

"Danton," Barek extended his hand. "It's been a long time."

Danton shook Barek's hand, his face revealing none of his surprise or confusion at being singled out. "It has, Prince Barek."

"With your permission, I would like to steal your mother away for the opening dance." Barek extended his hand to Jacinda.

"I would be honored, Prince Barek." Jacinda placed her hand in his and as Barek led her to the center of the dance floor, the music started.

∞ ∞ ∞ ∞ ∞

Jotham leaned back in his chair, his eyes focused on Jacinda as his son confidently maneuvered her around the dance floor. She looked beautiful, easily the most beautiful woman in the room despite her age, or maybe because of it. She smiled and laughed as she danced, comfortable and confident with who she was and her place in the world. So many women when they danced with either himself or Barek would giggle and flirt and it wasn't only the young ones. Some of the older, more experienced women would try to use the time to advance their husband's agenda. Jotham knew Jacinda was doing neither with Barek, she was simply enjoying his company. Would it be the same if she were dancing with him?

∞ ∞ ∞ ∞ ∞

Jacinda smiled up at Barek as he led her around the room for the first valsa of the night. "So to what do I owe this honor, Prince Barek?"

Barek smiled down at her, liking how she wasn't afraid to ask the question. "I wanted to speak to you privately and knew this would be the best way to do it."

"Privately?" Jacinda raised a beautifully arched eyebrow at him. "You consider this *private*?" she asked knowing every eye in the room was following them.

"Yes." Barek grinned at her. "Everyone might be *watching*, but no one can *hear* what we are saying."

Jacinda found herself laughing at his logic. "That is true. So what did you need to speak 'privately' to me about?"

"I wanted to thank you for the visuals."

"They cleared security?"

"Of course, there was never any doubt they would but…"

"There are protocols. I am not insulted, Prince Barek," Jacinda reassured him. "Actually I find it a relief that your security is so vigilant."

"Why?"

"Because you are the future King, but more importantly, you are the son of one of my friends. Lata would want me to watch out for you."

"Do you really believe that?"

Jacinda wondered if Barek realized how much he revealed with that simple question.

"Yes, I do. Your mother loved you, Barek, very much. Her eyes would light up every time she talked about you. I swear if she could have she would have spent every moment of her day with you."

"I thank you for that."

"You don't need to thank someone for speaking the truth."

"Of course I do."

Jacinda waited a moment before continuing. "So tell me. Why are you starting the Ball instead of your father?"

"Besides wanting to dance with a beautiful woman?" Barek gave her an incredible smile.

"I'm sure that line works with the younger women, Prince Barek, but it won't distract me from my query."

"Of course it won't. You, Madame Michelakakis, are unlike any other woman." His lips quirked slightly. "I suppose the answer is since I was here I thought I could deflect some of the rumors my father has always had to deal with after selecting his dance partner."

"Ah, of course, about him favoring one Assemblyman over another."

"Yes, but as I said before, the main reason is to thank you for the visuals. I looked at them last night and…"

"And?"

"And it allowed me to see my mother in a different light. And my father."

"To see them as more than the figureheads you've always known them to be."

"Yes. To see that she stood in some of the same places I have… it's something I had never considered before."

"I'm glad you enjoyed them."

"I did, as did my father."

"King Jotham saw them?" Jacinda wasn't sure why she was surprised, but she was.

"Yes, he came in while I was looking at them. He's promised to find her visual albums because of it, so I need to thank you for that too."

"I'm glad. Lata would want you to have them. Family was everything to her."

"Speaking of family… there was a visual included in the packet that I believe was placed there by mistake."

"I'm sorry?" Jacinda frowned up at him.

"There was a visual of the Michelakakis family… Leander Michelakakis' family," he clarified.

"So that's where it disappeared to," Jacinda feigned innocently. "I am so sorry, Prince Barek. Javiera sent me the visual via my comm, and it must have gotten mixed up with yours."

"I will make sure it is returned to you."

"Oh, that's not necessary. When I couldn't find it, I just had another one printed. It's already framed and on my wall."

The music ended before Barek could respond and he led her back to Danton. "Thank you for the dance, Madame Michelakakis." And giving her a slight bow turned to join his father.

∞ ∞ ∞ ∞ ∞

"My, my, my. Aren't you just full of surprises tonight, Jacinda." Evadne ran an assessing eye over her friend after Prince Barek walked away.

"Why, Evadne, whatever do you mean?" Jacinda asked, her eyes sparkling as she turned to her son and held out her hand. "Danton. Shall we?"

"I would love to, Mother." Taking her hand, Danton led her to the dance floor.

∞ ∞ ∞ ∞ ∞

The rest of the evening passed quickly for Jacinda. She danced, she caught up with old friends, and she was able to introduce her son to some of the most influential men on Carina. Over all, except for its start, it had been a perfect night.

She watched as Jotham made his way around the room, making a point to talk to every Assemblyman and their wife. It surprised her how long it had taken him to make his rounds, for normally he left long before the last dance whose first notes had just started to play.

She was just about to ask her son to join her for the last dance when she suddenly found Jotham standing before her.

"King Jotham," she bowed slightly.

"Madame Michelakakis. Would you do me the honor?" Jotham held out his hand, palm up.

Jacinda paused for only a moment before she placed her hand in his. "The honor is mine, Majesty."

Eyes followed the couple as the King led Jacinda to the floor. They watched with interest as his hand went to her waist, his fingers just brushing the bare skin of her lower back as her hand settled delicately on one of his broad shoulders. After a moment, with their other hands clasped, they began to move as one to the music.

Jacinda silently but confidently allowed Jotham to lead her around the dance floor, ignoring the looks they were receiving. She wasn't sure why Jotham had singled her out like this. It was common knowledge that he rarely danced more than the first dance at any Ball, and never the last, not since Lata died.

"I would like to thank you," Jotham's words were spoken quietly so no one dancing close to them could hear.

"For what, Majesty?" Jacinda found she had to look up to meet his eyes, even in her heels.

"For what you did for my son. The visuals…" Jotham paused seeming to gather his thoughts but Jacinda spoke first.

"I didn't do it for you. I did it for Barek… and for Lata." She watched Jotham's eyes darken with pain.

"Yes, well thank you anyway."

They danced silently for several moments.

"How did you know?" The quietly spoken, tortured words had Jacinda's eyes shooting up to Jotham.

"Know?"

"That he needed to see them? Barek has always kept his feelings about his mother close, even from me. He never once asked if there were any visuals."

"Perhaps that is because you've made it abundantly clear that *you* don't wish to see any visuals. Barek has always been sensitive, like his mother. He would never intentionally want to cause you pain."

"Yet he said something to you."

Jacinda saw the flash of pain in Jotham's eyes before it quickly disappeared and she realized it hurt Jotham, that he felt he had failed his son. "He didn't actually say anything, Majesty. We were talking and he made a comment that so reminded me of Lata that I mentioned it. It seemed to surprise him, that something of Lata lived on in him."

"He mentioned something like that to me after Victoria's Union."

"Yes, well that would make sense."

"Why?"

"Why?" Jacinda frowned up at him. "Because Unions are about families, they are about love and new beginnings. They inherently make us think about where we come from, who we come from. I've never attended a Union where I haven't thought of my parents. For Victoria's to have Barek thinking about his mother is only natural, especially when Victoria's mother miraculously returned from the dead."

"I never gave it a thought."

"No, but Lata was your wife, Majesty, and the relationship between a husband and wife is very different than that between a mother and child."

"That is true." Hearing the music begin to change Jotham suddenly realized how quickly this time had passed and how he didn't want it to end. His next words were out of his mouth before he could stop them. "Have lunch with me tomorrow."

"I… what?" Jacinda couldn't hide her surprise.

"I have enjoyed talking to you, Jacinda. Which is surprising considering how our last one ended. I would like to continue this conversation and since we both need to eat..."

"I... alright." Jacinda couldn't believe she was agreeing to this. "At noon?"

"Will one work for you? I should be able to clear my schedule by then."

"Alright. One it is."

The dance ended and Jotham took a step back. A quieter tune began to fill in the background conversations. Turning to lead Jacinda across the floor to Danton he suddenly stopped and looked at her. "What was it that Barek said that reminded you of Lata?"

Jacinda found herself blushing. "You know we literally ran into each other, don't you?"

"Yes."

"Well, after we decided we were both at fault for not looking where we were going he informed me he'd never found fault with having a beautiful woman in his arms. That's when I informed him that he was definitely his mother's son because only Lata could give such an inane compliment and make you believe she was completely sincere."

Jotham stared at her silently for several moments then tipped his head back and laughed, a deep laugh that few rarely heard from their King.

"You are right, Madame Michelakakis, my Lata truly did know how to deliver a compliment." Turning he led her across the floor. When they were just steps away from Danton, he leaned down to whisper in her ear. "But, in this case, my son was stating the truth. You truly are a beautiful woman, Jacinda."

∞ ∞ ∞ ∞ ∞

Adelaide Pajari stood beside her husband, silently fuming, her eyes never leaving the couple now alone on the dance floor. Jacinda Michelakakis! How Adelaide despised the woman.

She didn't belong here. Never had. Not as the mother of an Assemblyman and especially not when she'd been the wife of one. This is the House of Protection and *her* parents were both from the House of Healing.

Adelaide believed Jotham's greatest mistake, well besides having a Union with that little nobody, was to endorse Stephan and Jacinda's Union. He should have done neither, for Jotham was a direct male descendant of King Shesha and his Union should have been to someone whose royal background was just as strong, like her. It was what his mother had wanted. She, Adelaide Pajari, could trace her own ancestry back to King Shesha's daughter.

Adelaide's father and his father and his father had all been Assemblymen for the House of Protection. Her mother had been a member of Queen Johanna's inner circle and it had been agreed that Jotham would wed her. Instead, the King and Queen had suddenly died and Jotham had married *Lata* and she'd been forced to accept Elliott Pajari as her husband to maintain her family's position after her father lost his seat in the Assembly.

Now Jotham openly danced with a woman from a weaker House. A woman who had nothing to offer him, who couldn't influence a vote in his favor. Even his son had danced with the woman. Well, she wouldn't allow her family to lose out again. Adelaide had arranged for her daughter, Shosha, to be assigned to the Guardian. Once it left, Shosha would gain the affections of Prince Barek, thanks to her ancestry and her mother's maneuvering. If not, there was always the option Rani had taken to conceive Dadrian. Of course, Jotham had refused to wed Rani but Adelaide would make sure that didn't happen to her daughter.

Chapter Seven

Jacinda checked her hair one last time in the mirror then stuck her tongue out at herself, before heading out the front door. Why was she fussing like this? Why was she nervous? She'd met with Jotham before. What made this time so different?

'Because you are both single this time,' that little voice in her head answered.

'Ridiculous!' Jacinda thought to herself. She and Jotham had both been single at the Academy and she hadn't felt like this around him. Sure, he had been handsome and charming back then too. Girls would stop and watch as he and Will Zafar would walk by, but he represented everything she was trying to get away from. Politics. Being in the public eye.

So why was she having lunch with him? It would only stir up rumors if others found out. Well, it was too late to back out now and really what's the worst that could happen?

Driving through the imposing gate of the House of Protection, Jacinda was just getting out of her transport when she found Captain Deffand approaching her.

"Captain," she greeted.

"Madame Michelakakis," Deffand smiled at her as he held out his hand. "If you don't mind, I thought I would drive your transport and take you to an entrance that is closer to the King's Wing. It will save you a long walk."

Jacinda was silent for a moment, realizing what he wasn't saying. He was going to drive to the private, secure entrance where King Jotham's transports were kept. Where people could come and go in total privacy. Reaching out, she gave her transport fob to Deffand.

"Of course, Captain." Moving around to the passenger side of her transport, she found Deffand there first, opening the door for her to slide in. "Thank you, Captain."

"Madame Michelakakis."

It was a short, silent drive, and Deffand expertly handled the transport, slowing down only so the guards lining the outside of the Palace could verify who was driving and that the transport posed no threat.

"You and your men do a good job protecting the King."

"Thank you, Madame Michelakakis. It is our only priority."

When the vehicle pulled up to the entrance, Chesney was there to greet her. "Madame Michelakakis, welcome." Mister Chesney approached her smiling.

"Mister Chesney, I'm pleased to see you again."

"You too, Madame Michelakakis. If you would follow me, King Jotham is currently on a call but wished for me to reassure you that he would not be long and for me to escort you to the King's Garden."

"Of course," Jacinda nodded her head not at all surprised that Jotham had been detained. There were many times when Stephan would arrive late for a meal because something had occurred and he had only been an Assemblyman. As King, she imagined it was a hundred times worse.

Following Chesney, Jacinda realized she really was a great deal closer to the King's Wing than she'd thought. Especially with the corridor that Chesney was leading her down. She had expected to enter the hallway that connected the Royal Wing to the King's Wing. Instead, she was entering what appeared to be the King's sitting room.

"This way to the garden," Chesney gestured with the sweep of his arm for her to proceed him through the open doors on the other side of the room.

Stepping out, Jacinda found herself in the most beautiful garden she had ever seen. Whereas her garden was nearing the end of its last full bloom for the season, this one was nowhere close. "It's beautiful."

"It is and there is always something blooming."

"I can see that." Jacinda looked expectantly down the path. "Am I allowed to explore the garden while I wait for the King?"

"Of course, Madame Michelakakis. If you follow this path, it will lead you to where you will be having your lunch today."

"We're eating in the garden?" Jacinda's smile was brilliant at the thought.

"Yes, Ma'am, as it is such a beautiful day King Jotham thought you would enjoy it."

"He thought right. Thank you, Mister Chesney." Turning, she started down the path.

∞ ∞ ∞ ∞ ∞

"As I've said before, Assemblyman Pajari, I am not going to support anything less than a full funding for our joint venture with the House of Knowledge. We are the House of Protection and this new system falls under the authority of this House."

"But, Majesty, the House of Knowledge is more than able to absorb the full cost of the program. They are the wealthiest of all the Houses and we could use those funds for more important things."

"There is nothing more important than the protection of our people, Pajari, and it matters not that the House of Knowledge can fully fund it. The House of Protection will do its part. Now, this discussion is finished. Good day."

Jotham disconnected the call and rubbed the back of his neck, trying to relieve the tense muscles. Dealing with Elliott Pajari always irritated him. He couldn't stand the Assemblyman and if it were in his power he would have his seat taken from him, but there were very specific grounds in which an Assemblyman could be removed and irritating the King wasn't one of them unfortunately.

"Majesty."

Chesney's voice had him looking up to find the man had entered his office while he'd been lost in thought.

"Madame Michelakakis has arrived. She is currently touring the gardens."

"Thank you, Chesney." Turning in his chair, he gazed out the window that overlooked the garden and watched as Jacinda moved along the path pausing every now and then to smell a flower. Rising, he walked around his desk. "Give us twenty minutes then have the meal brought out and make sure we are not disturbed."

"Yes, Majesty."

∞ ∞ ∞ ∞ ∞

Jacinda couldn't believe the beauty of this garden. She remembered its sorry state the first time Lata had shown it to her. Queen Johanna had no affinity for gardens, feeling it was beneath her to waste her valuable time on it. She left it to her gardeners to care for, demanding only that they produce the blooms she desired for inside the Palace.

Lata, on the other hand, had enjoyed being in the garden, had often helped Jacinda's own mother in her garden when she would visit. She'd told Jacinda she found it peaceful here because she knew no one could bother her.

Now the garden was a showplace, written of, spoken about, and envied by all who loved gardening. Once a cycle, Jotham opened the garden to students from Montreux who were in their last cycle of studying floriculture.

Jacinda thought Lata would have liked that, to know that what she had imagined and created continued to influence generations of young minds. Walking along the path, Jacinda's breath caught at what suddenly appeared before her. She was in the center of the garden, it was a well-manicured area walled in by flowers with a beautiful table set up, but that wasn't what captured her attention. Her eyes started to fill as she approached. There, in the center, grew an amazing rose bush.

"It's called the Tausendjahriger Rosenstock." Jotham walked up quietly behind her.

"Yes, I know." Jacinda tipped her head slightly to the side to acknowledge Jotham's arrival, but her gaze never left the bush. For not only was it beautiful, but it was massive. Apparently, the soil of the House of Protection agreed with it.

"You know of it?"

"Yes," Jacinda carefully reached out capturing a blooming rose between two fingers then leaned down to take its amazing scent deep into her lungs. It reminded her of her mother. "I'm so glad it thrives here."

"What do you mean *here*?" Jotham frowned at her. "You've seen this plant before? The Royal Gardener has never been able to discover where it came from. He could find no record of a plant that bloomed such a deep violet."

"Yes, I've seen it." She turned to look at Jotham. "Lata didn't tell you?"

"No."

"It was a gift to Lata from my mother after the birth of Prince Barek."

"I don't understand."

"The original plant, the 'mother' if you will, has been in my family for hundreds of generations. Every woman receives a cutting from the 'mother' when she has a child. It is only when the caretaker of the 'mother' dies, does it pass on to the oldest daughter and the cycle repeats.

"So how did Lata end up with it?"

"Well if you mean 'it' as in this is the 'mother,' then you'd be wrong. This is what has grown from the cutting *my* mother gave Lata. The 'mother' now resides in my garden. As for why Lata received a cutting, that's because my mother considered her a third daughter."

"Lata never told me." Jotham looked at the plant with new eyes.

"I'm surprised. She and I talked extensively about her plans for this garden and I know she contacted my mother with her questions. She wanted to imitate my mother's garden. She always loved to walk in it when she came to visit."

"I don't remember her being there that often."

"I believe it was mostly during her last two cycles at the Academy when you were serving in the Fleet. It allowed her to escape the constant scrutiny she found herself under."

"She never said a word."

"Yes, well Lata was like that, wasn't she? She was always willing to help another, but rarely asking for any herself."

"Majesty."

Turning, Jotham found Chesney had entered the inner garden followed by servants carrying their lunch.

"Are you ready for lunch, Majesty?"

Jotham turned to Jacinda. "Madame Michelakakis?"

"Yes, of course." Jacinda allowed Jotham to lead her to the table then sat down in the chair he held out for her. "It smells wonderful." She smiled at the servants as they placed several covered plates before them.

"I hope you think so, I wasn't sure what you might like so I had my chef prepare several dishes. So if you don't like one, don't feel obligated to eat it."

"That's very kind of you, but rest assured I've never been a fussy eater. I'm sure I will like whatever has been prepared."

"I hope so, my Chef seemed to think you would enjoy a mustard dressing."

One of the servants removed the dome from the smaller plate, revealing a beautiful salad made up of delicate greens and thinly sliced vegetables.

"I do, very much. How nice of Chef Safford to remember that." Jacinda looked at his plate. "You seem to prefer the beryl cheese dressing."

"Yes, it's always been a weakness of mine." Jotham smiled at her then nodded to the servant to reveal the main course of perfectly cooked Zebu with a side of well-seasoned pratai bruite.

"This looks wonderful."

"Good," Jotham smiled then looked at the servants. "I will let you know when we are ready for dessert."

"Of course, Majesty." After a series of bows, the servants left them alone.

Jotham lifted his forc, knowing Jacinda would not begin to eat until he did. It was one of those protocols he found pointless when not eating at an official event. Taking a bite of his salad, he enjoyed the sharp, creamy flavor of the dressing. They ate in silence for several minutes each enjoying their meal.

Jotham found he liked that about Jacinda, that she didn't feel the need to make mindless small talk during the meal. How many meals had he had to endure where the woman... or man sitting beside him felt they needed to speak the entire time? How did they expect him to enjoy his meal if they kept asking him questions?

He also liked how Jacinda made no attempt to curb her enjoyment of the meal. Already there wasn't a single leaf of salad left on her plate and she was making a good dent in her Zebu. He'd seen so many women just push their food around their plate, in his presence, making it look as if they'd eaten when they hadn't taken a bite. Did they really think they fooled him? That he would frown on them actually eating?

"Is something wrong?"

Jotham found himself flushing when Jacinda's gaze captured his and he realized he'd been staring.

"Do I have something stuck between my teeth?"

"No," Jotham quickly denied. "Of course not, I was just..."

"Staring."

"I, yes, I guess I was. I'm sorry. I was just enjoying how much you were enjoying your food."

"What's not to enjoy? Chef Safford is a genius with food."

"He is, but I've found that most women when eating with me rarely eat much."

"Really?" Jacinda's eyes widened with shock. "Then they are truly missing out on a rare treat. I remember how I would hardly eat when there was an Assembly event at the Palace just so I was able to sample everything Safford offered."

Jotham tipped his head back and laughed enjoying Jacinda's honesty. "You know I never realized just how much we had in common. There are times I do the same thing, especially when Safford is making his Fudge Torta."

"Oh don't even mention that!"

"You don't like his Fudge Torta?" Jotham frowned.

"No, I don't. I *love* it!"

"Good."

Jacinda wasn't sure when Jotham had signaled for the servants that they were ready for dessert. The servants arrived quickly clearing the now empty dishes and placing a covered one before each of them. With a flourish, they removed the cover and Jacinda gasped as her gaze flew to Jotham.

"Fudge Torta," she whispered.

"When Chef Safford discovered who I was having lunch with, he insisted that this was what we would be having for dessert."

"Bless him." Without waiting for Jotham, Jacinda took a bite of her slice. "Oh, this is so good."

"It is," Jotham agreed taking his own bite.

"You know," Jacinda leaned over slightly as if she were about to tell Jotham a royal secret. "There's something I have to confess to you."

"And what would that be?" Jotham asked enjoying the teasing light in her eyes.

"Stephan once tried to bribe Safford."

"He what?" Jotham leaned back in shock. What was she talking about? Never in his life would he believe Stephan Michelakakis would bribe anyone.

"He tried to bribe Safford into giving up his Fudge Torta recipe."

"His recipe?" Jotham just stared at her.

"Yes, you see my fortieth birthday was coming up and Stephan wanted to surprise me with it."

"Stephan knew how to bake?" Now Jotham was truly shocked.

"Oh, ancestors no!" Jacinda waved a hand laughing. "The only time Stephan ever entered the kitchen was when he was raiding it for a midnight snack. No, he was going to have our housekeeper, Myesha, make it. Or he would have, but Safford refused to give up his 'secret' recipe."

"Really," Jotham replied. "I find that hard to believe, especially for you. I was told Safford insisted on making the entire meal today personally." He watched Jacinda begin to blush with pleasure.

"He did? What a wonderful man he is."

"Yet he still didn't give Stephan his recipe," Jotham reminded her wondering why her warm words for his Chef bothered him.

"No, he didn't. Instead, he made the Torta himself and had it delivered to our home," Jacinda smiled softly remembering. "You should have seen the kids' reactions. Stephan and I had plans to go out that night. By the time we got back the kids were pretty much in a fudge coma."

"Ate that much, did they?"

"Oh yeah, more than half of it gone by the time we got home."

"Safford sent you a large one?"

"Yes, thank goodness, or I never would have gotten a second piece."

Later, after they'd both completely finished their Torta, Jotham and Jacinda decided a walk was in order.

Jotham watched, his hands clasped loosely behind him, as Jacinda leaned over to smell a flower.

"What are you thinking so hard about?" Jacinda turned to look at him and could see she had surprised him.

"You." The word was out before he could stop it.

"Me? What about me?"

"You are someone I thought I knew, yet every time we speak I learn something new, about you, about Lata, about my home."

He looked over her shoulder at the rose bush. "Our lives have always been intertwined and I didn't even realize it."

"I think 'intertwined' is a bit strong."

"Do you? I wonder. Tell me again why I don't remember you from the Academy?"

"Because you only had eyes for Lata." Jacinda smiled and began to walk again.

"I had been at the Academy for two cycles before I met Lata. You were in the class ahead of me. Why did we never meet?"

"Do you want the truth?"

"Please."

"I avoided you."

"You avoided me! Why? What did I do?"

"Nothing!" Jacinda quickly reassured him. "You didn't do anything. It was because of *who* you were. What you represented."

"What did I represent?"

"Everything I was trying to get away from. Politics. Being in the public eye. Having your every move scrutinized."

"I don't understand."

Jacinda sighed heavily. She really didn't want to get into this. "You know who my parents were, don't you?"

"Your father was a powerful Assemblyman for the House of Healing. Some would go as far to say that in his time, he was more powerful than King Adon."

Jacinda just shrugged her shoulders. It wasn't anything she hadn't heard growing up. "Perhaps, but he learned a great deal from *his* father, who had also been an Assemblyman, along with my mother's father. They served together."

"That I didn't know."

"Yes, well, I'm sure you can understand the event their Union became. King Adon himself attended."

Jotham nodded his understanding. For a King to attend the Union of an Assemblyman was rare because it gave the appearance of favoritism. To attend one of an Assemblyman's child... It would have reflected extremely well on both families.

"It wasn't long after their Union that Dad himself became an Assemblyman and Mom conceived me. From the time I could walk and talk I was in the public eye. I was schooled on what I could do and what I couldn't. It's the reason I decided to go to the Academy instead of a private school."

"I don't understand."

"The influence of the House of Healing isn't as strong at the Academy as others are, say the House of Protection, especially for an Assemblyman's *daughter*. At the Academy, I could discover who I was without worrying about how it reflected on my parents. To be seen with you, even when everyone knew nothing would ever come from it, well that would have erased all I was trying to achieve."

"And why could nothing have come from it?"

"Because I was from the House of Healing. We both know that the heir to the throne, in any House, must wed someone from within that House."

"I see." Jotham walked silently for a few minutes thinking. "But that never stopped you from befriending Lata."

"Of course not. That archaic law only applies to future rulers, the 'commoners' as your mother liked to refer to us, have been intermingling for generations."

"My mother actually called you a 'commoner'?" Jotham couldn't believe it.

"Yes. She did not approve of one of her Assemblyman having a Union with someone *not* from the House of Protection."

"I've never understood why she felt that way. Or my father for that matter."

"Yes, well I know this is going to sound terrible and I don't mean to make light of what you went through, but had you not become King, Stephan would have been forced to resign his seat in the Assembly."

"I think you are overstating that possibility."

"I'm not." Jacinda turned hard eyes to Jotham. "I read the 'official' letter Stephan received from King Kado, informing him that he had to choose between serving the House of Protection or having a 'common' wife."

"I..." Jotham couldn't believe what he was hearing but he in no way doubted Jacinda's words. He could see his father doing such a thing and it would explain the shock in the eyes of so many when he'd declared that an Assemblyman could serve in his Assembly even if his wife was from a different House. "I'm sorry, Jacinda. I never knew he'd done that."

"It's not your fault, Majesty, and after all these cycles I shouldn't let it still bother me so."

"Please, Jacinda, I feel we have known each other too long to use titles. Call me Jotham."

"I... alright... Jotham." Jacinda found herself stuttering slightly.

"So tell me about your other children. Ethan and Stephanie, isn't it?"

"Yes, you have a good memory or should I be thanking Chesney for reminding you?" Jacinda was charmed when Jotham's face flushed then felt ashamed of herself. "I'm sorry, I shouldn't have said that. There's no possible way for you to remember the name of every child of every Assemblyman. Especially one who has been gone ten cycles now."

"Some are easier to remember than others, but that's not always a good thing."

"You couldn't possibly be referring to Shosha Pajari and the tantrum she threw at the Assemblymen's picnic, would you?"

"As a matter of fact I was. You remember that too?" Jotham's eyes began to twinkle.

"Of course, it was days before my hearing came back. Who would have thought not getting a second piece of cake could be so traumatic to a ten-cycle?"

"Yes, well apparently her mother promised it to her if she was good."

"Ahh, the old bribery trick. So of course when she didn't receive her reward, she did the one thing Adelaide didn't want her to."

"Yes."

"Ethan and his family live in Comorin. He now runs his father-in-law's business and Kasmira restores artwork. They have two sons; Eliron and Roland." Jacinda answered Jotham's original question. "They're eleven and eight now."

"I find it hard to believe you are a grandmother." Jotham ran an assessing eye over her knowing neither of his grandmothers ever looked like her.

"Thank you," Jacinda blushed slightly at the compliment. "They are a joy. Stephanie is out with the Fleet. I'm hoping she'll be home next month."

"She's been out a while?"

"Yes. Nearly two cycles, every time she was scheduled to come home something always interfered."

"What does she do?"

"She works in security, that's all she'll ever tell me." Jacinda saw the understanding in Jotham's eyes. "So I don't ask many questions going with the no news is good news philosophy."

"Sometimes that's the best we can do when it comes to our children."

"Yes."

Jotham saw that Jacinda wanted to say something but was hesitating. "Say what you wish, Jacinda."

Jacinda tipped her head to the side slightly then nodded. "I just wanted to say how sorry I am over you losing Dadrian. I know I sent a note at the time but… it doesn't seem adequate. I don't know what I would do if I lost one of mine. To know that their future is gone. That everything they were destined to do and accomplish was taken away by something as minor as a loose runner on the stairs. And for you to have witnessed it… I am truly sorry, Jotham."

Jotham's entire body tensed at Jacinda's words.

∞ ∞ ∞ ∞ ∞

Dadrian.

His second son, Dadrian.

His son that didn't come from Lata.

Jotham turned away from Jacinda, his chest heaving as he tried to stop those thoughts of betrayal. Not only his but Dadrian's. Which one was worse? Jotham's for allowing him to be conceived? Not that he remembered much of it, and in doing so betraying his Queen, his life mate, Lata. Or Dadrian's for conspiring with the Regulians in an attempt to murder his brother?

Jotham had always known Dadrian had problems, and he blamed himself for them. Because every time Jotham looked at Dadrian all he saw was his own weakness. Somehow Dadrian had always known that and Jotham believed that's what drove him to give the Fleet's location to the Regulians, so they could assassinate Barek and force Jotham to declare him the future King of the House of Protection.

So many had died because of Dadrian's treason. Fourteen hundred and twenty-one brave men and women of the Coalition to be exact including the entire crew of the Talon. For a time, Jotham had believed Barek was among the dead. The Fleet had been in chaos, no one knew how the Regulians were able to conduct speed attacks on the Fleet. Or how they knew where they were.

William Zafar, Jotham's life-long friend, confidant, and blood relative had been the Admiral of the Fleet at the time. He had saved Cassandra and Victoria from Earth when the Regulians had destroyed it, and in doing so changed history. Cassandra was a direct descendant from the lost Princess of the House of Knowledge, its one true heir, and someone didn't want her to assume her throne. It was why the Regulians had destroyed Earth and Cassandra was bound and determined to discover who it was.

In doing so, she discovered Dadrian's transmissions to Barek, while he'd been out with the Fleet, and then been able to link them to the transmissions sent to the Regulians with the Fleet's location. She'd discovered two traitors; one from the House of Knowledge and one from the House of Protection.

The day Dadrian died was the day Jotham's friend and confidante, and the woman he loved told Jotham and Barek what they had discovered. Jotham had been in denial, not wanting to believe it was possible. But when Dadrian came charging in, Jotham had seen the truth as Dadrian saw the brother, he thought dead, standing there instead.

Dadrian had run from the room. He had run from facing what he'd done and in doing so he tripped on the runner at the top of the stairwell in the Royal Wing and fallen to his death.

The next days passed in a blur for Jotham. The House of Protection and the entire planet went into mourning. Yet Jotham couldn't mourn. Not for Dadrian. He just went through the motions trying to decide what to do. He needed to report Dadrian's betrayal to the Grand Assembly, the one that was convening to witness Cassandra's Challenge of Queen Yakira, the appointed Queen for the House of Knowledge.

Jotham had gone to tell William and Cassandra that, and to apologize to them for what his son had done, especially to Cassandra. He knew Dadrian's betrayal had cost him more than his throne, it had cost him his friendship with William. They both surprised him that day. First, Cassandra by destroying the evidence she had against Dadrian, and then William by assuring him Dadrian's actions in no way affected their friendship.

Together they convinced him that the harm that would be caused by him reporting this to the Assembly outweighed any good that could come from it. Dadrian was dead. There would be no further attacks on the Fleet because of him. The one that would truly suffer if it were revealed was Barek, and then Dadrian would win and that wasn't justice.

∞ ∞ ∞ ∞ ∞

"I am sorry, Jotham."

Jacinda's voice and the gentle touch on his arm brought him back to the present.

"I didn't know Dadrian well, but I know you must have loved him a great deal and still miss him. Barek too. To lose a sibling like that…" Jacinda was shocked when Jotham ripped his arm from her grip then rounded on her. The rage pouring off him had her taking a startled step back.

"You know nothing about it, Madame Michelakakis!" Jotham's body vibrated with the anger that he was trying to control. "And I would like you to keep your pathetic words of solace to yourself!"

"I..."

"Majesty," Chesney appeared from nowhere, his eyes wide at what he had just witnessed. "I'm sorry to interrupt, Sire, but the High Admiral is on the comm. He says it's urgent."

Jotham found he couldn't speak, shame choking him as his mind replayed the words he'd just said to Jacinda. How could he have said something like that to her? She was just trying to help. She had no clue what Dadrian had done. He was the one to start the discussion of children. It was only natural for the conversation to turn to Dadrian.

Jacinda stepped away from him in fear... no woman had ever had to do that with him before... maybe Dadrian had gotten that from him.

Meaning to apologize, Jotham found Jacinda had turned her back on him and was moving toward Chesney.

"Would you mind showing me back to my transport, Mister Chesney? I'm afraid I've gotten myself totally turned around in the garden and I have an appointment I can't be late for."

Chesney looked to Jotham and at his stiff nod spoke, "Of course, Madame Michelakakis."

"Thank you. That way the King won't be delayed in seeing to his duties." Jacinda turned to Jotham, her face perfectly neutral. "Please thank Safford for a wonderful meal, Majesty. Goodbye."

Chapter Eight

"What can I do for you, High Admiral?" Jotham asked sitting down at his desk.

"King Jotham, I'm calling to inform you of some information that has been discovered, concerning the House of Protection, after our latest 'interview' with Gad Stannic.

"Gad Stannic? I thought he and his father, former Assemblyman Rogue Stannic, were a Coalition and House of Knowledge problem."

"They were and are, but now it seems that Rogue Stannic was also communicating on a regular basis with someone from the House of Protection."

"For what purpose?"

"That's not entirely clear at the moment, but it seems to have something to do with Prince Barek."

"Is he in danger?" Jotham demanded.

"I don't believe so. The communications seem to be geared more toward who will be his future Queen."

"I see." Jotham was silent for a moment wondering if someone else had noticed Barek's interest in Amina. "Why would Stannic be interested in this?"

"That is what is still unclear, but I wanted to inform you before Barek did."

"Barek knows of this?"

"He was interviewing Gad when it was hinted at. Going through Rogue's confiscated files, we found some evidence of the correspondence but haven't yet determined who in the House of Protection it is going to. They bounce from planet to planet. It's going to take some time to sort out."

"Even for Cassandra?"

William was silent for a moment. "I haven't informed her of it yet. I'm on the Bering and she's caring for Sabah."

"Sabah! What's wrong with Sabah?" Jotham shouted into the comm. Cassandra's daughter and future Queen was only several moon cycles old. If something had happened to her...

"Nothing's 'wrong' with her, she just has a little sniffle. Do you really think I'd be on the Bering if something was wrong with my daughter?"

"No. Of course, you wouldn't. I'm sorry. It seems to be my day to overreact."

Silence greeted Jotham's statement.

"Jotham, we are on a fully secure line."

"I never doubted it."

"And you are not only my King but my friend. Tell *me* what's wrong?"

Jotham found himself chuckling at William referring to him as his King, for in reality William was now the King of the House of Knowledge.

"Is that so, *King* William?" Jotham's chuckles grew when he heard William's groan. He hated when someone used that title.

"Stop trying to change the subject, Jotham. Talk to me."

"What do you know about Jacinda Michelakakis?"

"Jacinda Michelakakis?" Whatever William had thought was bothering Jotham, it hadn't been a woman. "Well, let me think. She's Leander Michelakakis' aunt through her Union with his father's brother, Stephan. Stephan was a powerful and effective Assemblyman for the House of Protection until his untimely death. What ten cycles ago now?"

"Yes."

"But you know all that, so what are you really asking?"

"Do you remember her from before that? From the Academy?"

"Sure, she was a cycle ahead of us."

"You seriously remember that?"

"Of course. She was seriously stunning."

"She still is," Jotham informed him.

William leaned back in his chair on the other end of the comm, stunned. Jotham was showing an interest in a woman? After all these cycles?

"So I've been told."

"Who told you that?" Jotham demanded before he could stop himself.

"I was with Cassandra when Javiera told her how she had run into Jacinda and her sister, Palma, the other day when she'd been out of the Palace. Apparently, Jacinda's oldest son is following in his father's footsteps."

"Danton, yes. He's the image of his father."

"Well, apparently he still has a lot to learn about women."

"What do you mean?"

"It's what Javiera couldn't wait to share with Cassandra. Apparently, while she was having coffee with Jacinda and Palma, Danton called asking his mother to attend the Assemblyman's Ball with him."

"When was this?" Jotham searched his mind. It had only been a week ago that he first met with Jacinda. Since then, she'd met with Barek, traveled to and from Kisurri, attended the Ball, and had lunch with him.

"Four days ago now," William informed him.

"What!" Jotham couldn't believe it. Even *he* knew that a woman could spend months trying to find the right gown. To give your own mother only a three day notice... was Danton insane?

"The Ball was last night, wasn't it?"

"Yes. Jacinda looked... amazing."

"Did she now?" Yes, Jotham was clearly interested in this woman, William thought.

"What else did Javiera say?"

"That they went straight to Kia who just happened to have the most amazing dress, Javiera's words, that was not only in violet but fit Jacinda perfectly."

"It did. I can't believe it."

"I can't believe she let her son live after the comment he made."

"What comment?"

"Apparently, when Jacinda scolded him for not giving her more time to find a dress he informed her he hadn't thought it would be a problem since she had a closet full."

"She let the boy live?"

"Those were my exact words and Cassandra informed me a mother's love for her child truly knows no bounds, but that if I tried that with her, I should fear for my life."

"You are much too wise to say something like that, Will. Think it, yes. Say it, never."

"Too true. So you chose Jacinda for the opening dance?" William was not going to be distracted. Jotham was upset about something.

"No. Barek did."

"Barek? Barek opened the Ball?" William couldn't believe it. Never before had Jotham allowed Barek to assume what was essentially the King's duty.

"Yes. He thought it would help deflect the traditional rumors that always surface of me favoring one Assemblyman over another. He also had a personal agenda."

"Personal agenda? Jotham, what are you talking about?"

"Barek wanted to thank Jacinda for obtaining some visuals of Lata from when she was at the Academy. She got them from her sister, Palma."

"Why would he need to get them from Palma? Lata was always taking visuals." William didn't miss that Jotham actually 'said' Lata's name. It was the first time in cycles he'd heard it cross his lips.

"Yes, well, they've been in storage for cycles. I never gave it a thought that Barek would want to see them. When he and Jacinda literally ran into each other in the Assembly Hall, they spoke for a while. Somehow, out of what was said, Jacinda realized Barek had never seen any visuals of his mother that weren't 'official' ones and even then only the one in my private office."

"Jotham…" William didn't know what to say. He'd never realized Jotham had taken it that far, especially not with Barek.

"I know." Jotham leaned back in his chair closing his eyes. "I just shut down after Lata was killed. I'm not sure I ever really realized how much until just recently." Opening his eyes, he straightened. "So anyway, Jacinda got him the visuals, which just goes to show what a truly good woman she is, especially after how our previous meeting ended."

"Previous meeting?" William looked up as his assistant on the Bering silently entered and tapped his wrist, indicating that he was going to be late for another meeting. William shook his head and gave him a silent signal they'd developed over the cycles that told him everything else could wait. He and Jotham were talking in a way that they hadn't since those few cycles they served in the Fleet together. Since before Jotham became King, and he was working his way up through the ranks. Nothing short of the Regulians attacking was going to take priority over this.

"I asked Jacinda to come to the Palace last week. I had a situation I thought she could help me with."

"Did she?" William was intrigued at how evasive Jotham was being.

"No. Instead, she got angry, royally pissed off to be honest. She stood right up to me, Will, and told me I was wrong. I can't remember the last time someone did that to me or treated me as if I were just a normal man... unless it was Cassandra... or Cyndy Chamberlain."

"Cyndy is a little spitfire," William agreed. "Especially now that she's regaining her health. I hope she continues to be."

"Is there a problem?" Jotham heard the concern in William's voice.

"Not yet, and not one she's allowing her family to see, but it's growing."

"Can I help?"

"I'll let you know. Now back to Jacinda. What did you say to her, Jotham? You didn't... proposition her."

"Ancestors no!" Jotham shot out of his chair. "It was the first time I'd seen the woman in over ten cycles!"

"Then what was it?"

"Nothing I want to talk about."

William let it go, knowing eventually when he was ready, Jotham would tell him.

"Have I dishonored my life mate again, Will? With my actions?"

William could barely hear the question let alone answer it. "What?"

"Have I again dishonored my life mate?"

"Jotham! You have never dishonored Lata!"

"Haven't I? What about Rani? What about Dadrian?"

"Jotham..." William struggled for words. "As your friend, I can honestly say I never understood how Rani happened, but I wasn't there. As for Dadrian, he was a grown man. He made his own choices."

"He was so young, Will."

"He was older than you were when you took the throne, Jotham." William's anger was easily heard. "He was given every opportunity in life and he exploited every one. You know this! You can't hold yourself responsible for what he did!"

"If it were Kayden? Or Lucas? Would you not feel you were somehow responsible because of how you raised or didn't raise them?"

"I don't know how I would feel, Jotham, and I hope I never have to find out, but in the end they are their own men."

"What if you can see yourself in them? What if you find yourself wondering if he could have learned it from you?"

"Jotham! What the fuck are you talking about?!!" William raged. "You, of all people, are *nothing* like Dadrian! What happened to make you think you could be?"

"I was having lunch with Jacinda before you called."

The pause on the other end of the comm was deafening as William tried to follow the conversation. "O...kay."

"Last night, at the Ball, I couldn't take my eyes off her. It was as if every light in the room was focused on her, revealing what a beautiful creature she really was. She drew people to her, Will, with her warmth and honesty."

"Alright..."

"I asked her for the last dance."

"You..." William found himself speechless. While a King or Queen always opened an event by either dancing with their spouse or someone else, the last dance was always reserved for only the spouse. Since Lata's death, Jotham had never danced it.

"I know. But I was making my way around the room, speaking to the Assemblymen and I hadn't yet talked to Danton. To be honest, I don't think I ever did."

"So you invited her to lunch."

"Yes. The words just escaped my mouth. When we danced, we talked, truly talked. She had no agenda. She wasn't trying to draw my attention. She just had it. And as the music started to fade, I found I didn't want it to end, that I didn't want to let her go. So I asked her to come to lunch."

"Just her?"

"Yes. We ate in the garden."

"*Your* garden?"

"Yes."

"I take it, it didn't go well?"

"It went perfectly. The weather was perfect. Safford remembered her love of Fudge Torta."

"Everyone loves his Fudge Torta," William muttered remembering everything he'd tried to get that temperamental chef to give the recipe to Hutu. In the end, it had been Cassandra telling him that she 'craved' it during her pregnancies that had finally swayed the man. "So what happened?"

"I frightened her, Will."

"What?" William's disbelief could be heard through the comm.

"We had finished our lunch and were walking through the garden. We were talking and laughing, learning more about each other." Jotham paused remembering how he'd been feeling at that moment. It had been as if, for the first time since Lata's death, that he felt like he could just breathe around a woman. That she wasn't *trying* to attract his attention, that she wasn't trying to become his Queen. "The conversation naturally turned to our children. I'm even the one that started it. Jacinda began to try and express how sorry she was for Dadrian's death. That she felt the card she sent was inadequate for a loved child. That it must have been terrible for Barek to lose a sibling... I lost my temper."

"Jotham, you never lose your temper."

"I did, Will. I was so enraged that this wonderful woman would waste her sympathies on Dadrian after what he had done."

"She didn't know."

"I know that!" Jotham nearly shouted. "But it didn't stop me from reacting. I lashed out at her, Will. I lashed out so violently that she felt the need to move away from me. I had just convinced her to call me Jotham and then I did that."

William understood what Jotham wasn't saying. Few were allowed the honor of using just his first name. It was reserved only for those that truly mattered to him. Everyone else he kept at a distance by demanding they use his title. For him to request it of Jacinda meant his feelings were even more engaged than William had first thought.

"She told me goodbye, Will."

Jotham's softly spoken words brought him back to the conversation. "What?"

"When she left, she asked me to thank Safford for a wonderful meal, called me Majesty, then said, 'Goodbye.'"

William's mind was in turmoil as he tried to process everything his friend had just said. He knew Jotham, and as much as it pained him to say it when it came to women, Jotham was inexperienced.

Yes, he was a King.

Yes, he was used to dealing with women.

Just not in his personal life.

From the time Jotham had been a sixteen-cycle, Lata had been it for him. He'd never even looked at another woman, which was why he didn't remember Jacinda from the Academy. He'd never strayed from Lata, not even with the many women his mother had thrown his way when they'd been out in the Fleet. William would watch Jotham go back to quarters every night to either talk to or leave a message for Lata, depending on the time back on Carina.

It's why what happened with Rani had been so shocking.

"You need to contact her, Jotham. You need to explain."

"Explain? Explain what?" Jotham demanded. "That the son she thinks I should be grieving for was actually a traitor?"

"No, but you could explain that you didn't mean to frighten her, that the memories just overwhelmed you. From everything you've said about her, Jacinda Michelakakis is a very caring woman. She will understand."

"Then what? What's the point? It's not like we're going to develop a relationship."

"Why not?"

"Why not?" Jotham couldn't believe what William had just said. "Will, I barely know the woman."

"Yet you have strong feelings for her. Jotham, it took you less than a day to know that Lata was the woman for you. Why would you think this would be any different?"

"Because I've had my life mate."

"Yes, and so has Jacinda from what I've heard, but that doesn't mean you can't fall in love again. You both have your families, Jotham. You both have pasts, but that doesn't mean you can't still have a future… together."

"Lata…"

"Would want you to be happy. Just as I want Cassandra to be if something should ever happen to me. There are no guarantees in this life, Jotham, especially not ours. It's what makes me cherish every moment I have with my wife."

"Cassandra would let you have it if she heard you talking like this, Will."

"She already has."

"You talked about this?" Jotham couldn't believe it. "With her?"

"Yes, and she hated the conversation. She refused to listen until I forced her into a chair and made her. I'm a good deal older than her, Jotham, it's not a secret. The chances are good I will meet the ancestors before her and I know how she will react. She'll do what she did during the Challenge. She'll make sure everyone else is taken care of, our family, our friends, and our people, and she'll forget to take care of herself. That's my job, whether I'm alive or not, even if that means another man has to do it. I would do anything to make sure she's happy."

"Just like you were willing to give her up so she could be Queen."

"If that would have assured her happiness then yes. I'm just glad it never came to that."

"Lata and I never discussed it."

"Why would you? You were both so young. It's only as we get older that we begin to realize that another's happiness could matter more than our own."

"I would give anything to speak to her one last time, to have the chance to settle all that was left unsaid."

"Then do it."

"What?"

"Do you really think she isn't listening, Jotham? That Lata hasn't been watching over you all these cycles?"

"What are you saying?"

"I'm saying that I've come to believe that the ancestors play a bigger part in our lives than we've ever given them credit for. I believe they watch and are willing to give us guidance if we are only willing to ask and listen." William paused for a moment. "I used to have dreams of Kayden."

"He's your son, William. It's only natural."

"No. Not my Kayden but the Kayden that disappeared with the Princess from the House of Knowledge. We had several conversations, ones I didn't always agree with, but in the end he told me something I couldn't argue with."

"What?"

"That I couldn't 'protect' what was mine if I wasn't 'with' what was mine. You can't either, not if you let Jacinda go."

Chapter Nine

Jacinda didn't relax her grip on the steering wheel of her transport as she drove home. She didn't let herself think about what had just happened back at the Palace. If she did, she knew she would have to pull over.

There just ahead was her driveway. Pulling in, she slowly relaxed each finger then shut off the transport and leaned back in her seat. Finally, she allowed her thoughts free reign.

Jotham was a complicated man with many facets. She'd always known that. He had to be to deal with everything it took to be King. Yet in all the cycles she'd known him, she'd never *once* heard of him lashing out like that.

It had been a beautiful day, the gardens had been lush, and their lunch together had been wonderful. She couldn't remember the last time she'd been so at ease with a man. She and Jotham had so much in common, had shared so many of the same life experiences that the conversation had just flowed. It had felt as if they were becoming more than just associates but truly becoming friends.

At least until the talk had turned to Dadrian.

Dadrian.

Yes, there had been rumors that *Dadrian* could get violent, but *never* about Jotham.

Could it have been kept hidden?

"No!" The sound of her own voice had Jacinda jerking slightly in the seat. No, there was no way that was possible. She'd known Jotham nearly her entire life. She had seen him in too many tense situations and he'd *never* become violent.

She should have realized he wouldn't want to talk about the loss of his son. He still rarely talked about Lata and it had been nearly thirty-five cycles since *she'd* met the ancestors. It had barely been ten cycles since Dadrian had.

She had overstepped her boundaries talking about Dadrian. She could see that now, but in that moment, she'd felt so close to Jotham. He hadn't been a King to her then. Jotham had been a friend. A man. A man, she was surprised to discover she was beginning to have strong feelings for.

He had been on her mind since that meeting when she had stormed out of his office. If she were honest with herself, she would admit that it was why she let Kia talk her into that dress.

Okay, it hadn't taken much talking, but still.

She'd wanted to look amazing last night, not just for Danton but for herself, and maybe just a little to see Jotham's reaction.

When they danced last night, she still had to look up at him even in those heels, it had just seemed so right and a feeling she hadn't felt in cycles returned. It had grown during their lunch today as they discovered more about each other. Walking through the garden with him had seemed so natural, as if they'd been doing it for cycles.

Then it had all gone wrong and she still didn't fully understand why.

Exiting her transport, she moved up her walk. Entering her home still fuming, she barely stopped herself from slamming the door. Still, for him to treat her that way, to speak to her that way. King or not, no man did!

"No one!" Jacinda muttered.

"No one what?"

Jacinda's eyes quickly scanned her living room looking for the source of the voice.

"Stephanie!" Jacinda was immediately across the room wrapping her arms around her daughter. "I thought you weren't going to be on planet until after the next moon cycle!"

"Yes, well plans change." Stephanie hugged her mother back before she ran a critical eye over her, taking in the angry slash of color across her cheeks. "Who's got you so upset?" Whoever it was, Stephanie would make sure he never did it again. Her mother was a very special, precious woman and no one was allowed to anger her, not when Stephanie was around.

"What? Oh no one," Jacinda waved a dismissive hand. "It's not important. What's important is that you're home." Jacinda wrapped her arms around her again. "Oh, I've missed you."

"I've missed you too, Mom."

As one, they moved to sit. Jacinda looked at her daughter and while part of her heart broke that she was no longer her little girl, another part swelled with pride at the strong, independent woman she had become.

"So when did you get in? How long can you stay? Do your brothers know your back?"

Stephanie found herself laughing as her mother fired questions at her. It was good to be home.

"I landed just a few hours ago. I'm going to be on planet for several moon cycles and no I haven't contacted Danton or Ethan yet."

"Several moon cycles?" Jacinda didn't try to hide her shock. Ever since Stephanie had joined the Coalition, she'd never been on planet longer than three weeks and that had been when her father died.

"What's wrong? Are you alright?" Jacinda ran a more critical eye over her daughter taking in the stress around her eyes and the nearly faded bruise on her cheek. "What happened?"

"Nothing happened, Mom." Stephanie knew the instant her mom noticed the bruise for her eyes narrowed. "It happened during a training exercise. Honestly, I'm fine."

"Then why are you here for so long?" Jacinda demanded.

"Gee, Mom, it sounds like you don't want me here," Stephanie teased, knowing it would distract her mother.

"Oh stop that! You know that's not true!"

"I know, Mom," she quickly reassured her. "And actually I'm only going to be in Pechora for a week, then I'm off to Kisurri."

"Kisurri?"

"Yes. I've been accepted into a new advanced training program being taught by Peter Chamberlain. He'll be teaching it in the training facility within the House of Knowledge."

"Training program?" Jacinda frowned. She hadn't heard anything about it.

"Yes, on Earth, Peter Chamberlain was the leader of a Shock Troop."

"They had Shock Troops on Earth?"

"I believe they called them Special Forces, but it is essentially the same thing. He taught some moves to his sister and daughter. They're now taught to every cadet at the Academy. To learn directly from him though… it's a great honor."

"One I'm sure you've earned. You've always worked hard, Stephanie, and while I'll admit your choice of career has always worried me," Jacinda held up her hand to silence the mouth she saw open. "I'm your mother. It's my job to worry. That said, I also know you wouldn't have advanced so far, so quickly if you didn't excel in your chosen field. So I'm not at all surprised that you were accepted into this new program."

"Thanks, Mom."

"You're welcome. Now tell me everything you've been doing."

∞ ∞ ∞ ∞ ∞

"Majesty."

Jotham looked up from the report he'd been staring at blindly for the last thirty minutes. "Yes, Chesney?"

"Did you need me for anything else tonight?"

"Tonight?" Spinning around in his chair, Jotham looked out the window to find the garden bathed in moonlight. When had it gotten so late?

"I'm sorry, Chesney. I didn't realize it was so late." He turned back to face Chesney. "Go home, I'm sure Helen is wondering where you are."

"She's used to it, Majesty. If you need me to stay longer, she would understand."

"No. We've done enough for the day and thank you for clearing my schedule earlier, Chesney. I know it wasn't easy."

"I was happy to do it, Majesty." And Chesney really was. As far as he was concerned, the King worked too hard. He might cancel a meeting, but it was always because something more important needed his attention. It was never for a personal reason and never because of a woman. A wonderful woman, as far as Chesney was concerned. "If you'll forgive me for saying it, but you should do it more often. I'm just sorry I had to interrupt and that Madame Michelakakis had to leave."

"Yes… Well… it was for the best."

"I'm sorry, I don't understand, Sire."

"You had to have overheard what was being said as you walked up, Chesney."

"Yes, Sire." Chesney looked at his feet. "I'm sorry I didn't mean to eavesdrop."

"I know that, Chesney. You have always been loyal and discrete. I don't know what I would do without you after all these cycles."

"Thank you, Majesty." Chesney beamed at him.

"Go home to your wife, Chesney. I will see you tomorrow."

"Yes, Sire." Chesney turned to leave then paused. "She's a wonderful woman, Sire."

"She would have to be to put up with you for all these cycles, now wouldn't she?" Jotham smiled as he teased his assistant.

"Yes, Majesty, my Helen is, but I wasn't referring to her. I was referring to Madame Michelakakis." Chesney watched his King's smile immediately disappear.

"I'm aware of that, Chesney." Jotham hoped that would end the conversation. It was one of the things Jotham most appreciated about Chesney. He rarely said unnecessary things. Apparently he felt this was necessary.

"I will never forget the day she came to the aid of my youngest," Chesney continued.

"What?" Jotham gave him a confused look.

"It must be more than twenty cycles now. Helen was out shopping in the market with all three children and Tara wandered away from her. Helen was frantic and was just about to call me when Madame Michelakakis came walking up to her with Tara in her arms. It seems Madame Michelakakis found Tara crying behind some crates and was able to coax her out. I hadn't even realized she knew I had a wife, let alone children." Chesney remembered how shocked he had been when his wife had told him how Jacinda had stayed and talked to her. How she had made sure that Helen was okay too. Assuring her that the same thing had happened to her with her youngest, Stephanie, and that it didn't make her a terrible mother. "So many Assemblyman's wives tend to ignore the families of the House staff."

"What are you talking about?" Jotham had never heard this before, had never noticed it happening. "Why have you never said anything?"

"It never occurred to me, Sire. The only reason I mention it now is so you know that Madame Michelakakis isn't like that. She is a wonderful, caring woman. She still inquires on my family."

"I see. Well, thank you, Chesney."

"She will understand and forgive the… sharpness of your words," Chesney pressed further.

"Thank you, Chesney. Goodnight." This time he made sure Chesney couldn't mistake he was finished discussing this.

"Yes, Sire. Goodnight to you too."

∞ ∞ ∞ ∞ ∞

"Are you ready for a coffee?" Jacinda switched the bags in her hands as she looked at Stephanie. They had been shopping all morning and made a good attempt at clearing out the shops of Pechora.

"I'm always ready for coffee," Stephanie declared, silently wondering where her mother got her energy. They had been out all morning and her mother showed no sign of slowing down. Stephanie got less of a work out during a training session.

"Pittaluga's? It's just down the street and they still have that Torte you love."

"How do you remember stuff like that, Mom?"

"Oh, I guess there are just certain things a mother never forgets. Like how you'd always beg to go there for your birthday."

"True, but it's been cycles since I've been home for my birthday."

"I know, but I still come here on that day and have a piece for you."

"Seriously?" Stephanie stopped in the middle of the sidewalk and turned shocked eyes to her mother. She never knew her mother did that.

"It always made me feel like I had a little piece of you with me, even though you were so far away."

Before Stephanie could say anything, she was bumped into from behind.

"Pardon me," the deep voice said as strong hands gripped her elbows.

"Captain Deffand?" Jacinda's tone was welcoming.

"Madame Michelakakis?" Deffand's eyes ran from her to the woman who was quickly pulling away from his grasp. She was beautiful and he knew he had never seen her before.

"How wonderful to see you again. Stephanie, this is Captain Deffand, Captain of the King's Guard. Captain Deffand, my daughter, Stephanie."

"Captain," Stephanie gave him a cool nod, silently cursing.

"Miss Michelakakis," Deffand nodded to her slightly.

"It's Lieutenant actually."

"Excuse me?" Deffand's eyes widened in surprise.

"It's Lieutenant Michelakakis, sir. I serve in the Coalition. Security."

"Security? Which ship are you serving on?"

Stephanie stiffened as Deffand ran a disbelieving eye over her.

"I just finished my tour on the Retribution. I'm now investigating other options for my skills."

"I see."

Jacinda raised a brow, her gaze going from Deffand to her daughter. "Captain, we were just about to go to Pittaluga's for coffee. Would you care to join us?"

"Thank you, Madame Michelakakis, but I'm afraid I can't. Maybe next time?" He bowed and turned to go.

"I'll hold you to that, Captain. And Captain," Jacinda waited until he looked at her. "Please call me Jacinda."

Stephanie watched as the King's Captain blushed. "Of course. I apologize… Jacinda, but only if you call me Nicholas." Deffand gave her a boyish half smile.

"I would be honored, Nicholas, and I will hold you to that coffee."

"Lieutenant Michelakakis," Deffand bowed again then left.

Jacinda let her gaze run over her daughter as Pittaluga himself sat them at her favorite table. It was in a sunny but private corner of the restaurant which still allowed her to people watch.

"It is wonderful to have you with us again, Madame Michelakakis. You also, Miss Stephanie. Will you be wanting a piece of my Dobos Torte?"

Stephanie found herself laughing at how Mister Pittaluga addressed her and was unwilling to correct the man who had been serving her Dobos Torte since her fifth birthday.

"I will be, Mister Pittaluga. It's been too long."

"I agree, Miss Stephanie. Would you like me to place your bags behind the counter so they're not in your way, Madame Michelakakis?"

"Thank you, Mister Pittaluga." Jacinda smiled at the man as she handed him her bags. "That would be wonderful."

"Anything for you, Madame Michelakakis. I will be right back with your coffee."

Jacinda settled herself into her chair and looked at her daughter. "So? Are you going to tell me?"

"Tell you what, Mother?"

Jacinda smiled slightly at her words, knowing her daughter's defense mechanism that had her call her 'Mother' instead of Mom.

"Why you were so cool to Captain Deffand?" She watched Stephanie look away, another tell.

"I don't know what you mean, Mother."

"Don't you 'mother' me, Stephanie Anne. I know you. I remember every word of what you told me your 'dream' man was."

"MOM!" Stephanie quickly lowered her voice when she realized the attention they were drawing. "I was only a ten-cycle when I told you that!" she hissed.

"Well has it changed?"

"No, but I have."

"What do you mean?"

"I mean that I've grown up and come to realize I can't always have what I want. Not if it interferes withwhat I really want."

"What?" Jacinda frowned at her daughter.

"Mom... you don't understand." Stephanie leaned back and forced herself to smile at Mister Pittaluga as he brought their coffee and inhaled deeply. "Thank you, Mister Pittaluga, this smells wonderful. No one makes coffee like you."

"You are most welcome, Miss Stephanie. Your Dobos Torte will be out shortly. When I informed Luis who it was for, he stated he would make sure it was perfect."

Jacinda took a sip of her amazing coffee and waited until Pittaluga was out of hearing range before she turned her gaze back to her daughter. "Tell me what I don't understand, Stephanie."

Stephanie sat back in her chair and assessed her mother. She knew that look, had received it too many times in her life to not know that in this her mother would not let her fib her way out.

"Captain Deffand is the head of the King's guard," she began.

"Yes, I know that."

"Did you know that he was the youngest ever to assume that position?"

"No. No, I didn't."

"Also in the entire history of the House of Protection, a woman has never been allowed to guard the King."

"What?" Jacinda looked at her daughter in shock.

"Never has a woman been allowed to be a member of the Royal Guard. King or Queen's, even though over a third of the Coalition's Security forces are women."

"I… I didn't know that either."

"Well I want to change that and I can't if I'm anything but professional with the Captain of the King's Guard."

"Stephanie…" Jacinda put her hand over Stephanie's.

"I can't be like you, Mom! I can't give up all my dreams, let myself become the one thing I never wanted to be, all because of a man."

Jacinda jerked her hand away at her daughter's criticism of her life. She forced a smile on her lips as Pittaluga approached with two pieces of the cake Stephanie so loved.

"Thank you, Mister Pittaluga."

"You are most welcome, Madame Michelakakis. Enjoy."

"Mom, I didn't mean that the way it sounded." Stephanie waited until Pittaluga was out of earshot before speaking.

Jacinda took a small tasteless bite of her Torte, giving her mind time to process what her daughter had just accused her of. Did she truly think she had 'given up her dreams' to be with her father? That she had become the one thing she never wanted to be? She was right… to a point… but only to a point. It was true she had never wanted a life in politics, had wanted a life out of the public eye. If given a choice, she would never have chosen it, but it was Stephan's dream to serve and it was no hardship, no sacrifice to help him achieve his dream. She silently and vocally thanked her mother for preparing her for the world where she seemed to know she was destined to live.

"I think you did." Jacinda turned hard eyes to her daughter. "I believe you owe me an explanation. Just what makes you think I 'gave up all my dreams' to be with your father?"

"Mom. Aunt Palma and I would talk when I'd go to visit. She told me how all you ever wanted was to serve in the Coalition, to never be involved in politics again."

"And because of that, you believe I resented my life with your father?"

"I wouldn't say resent, but it couldn't have been what you really wanted!"

"No. It wasn't." Jacinda agreed, her eyes pinning Stephanie. "It was more! More than I could ever imagine! Your father and I were a team. We worked together, raised a family, and in the end he gave me a dream I didn't even know I wanted. How dare you think you have the right to judge my life!"

"Mom! That's not what I'm doing."

"Sounds like it to me."

"I'm just saying I want to fulfill my dreams, not support someone else's."

"Then what?" Jacinda demanded. "When you achieve this goal of yours to be the first woman in the King's Guard, what then?"

"What?"

"There's more to life than work, Stephanie. It's something your father never truly understood because he loved what he did. In that, you and your father are alike."

"What do you mean?"

Jacinda eyed her daughter. She was a full-grown woman, no longer her daddy's little girl who thought the suns rose and set in him, that he was perfect.

"You're right to a point, that I would have preferred to not be involved in politics. If I hadn't loved your father, I wouldn't have been, but I don't regret it. My only regret is that I allowed your father to serve so long."

"What are you talking about?"

"There is so much about your father's and my life that you don't know, Stephanie. You've always viewed us through the eyes of a child or as your parents. You just assumed we were here to serve you and your brothers. Its only now, that *you* are older that you realize we were more than that. You see me as a woman who gave up her dreams for a man, but what you don't understand is… he *was* my dream. Was it a perfect dream? No, but that's what made it special and ours. Your father fully understood what he was asking of me when he asked me to be his wife. It's why he promised me he would not serve past his sixty-fifth cycle if he were still serving then."

"But…" Stephanie looked at her in shock, knowing her father was still serving at seventy.

"It's the only promise he didn't keep to me." Jacinda gave her a sad smile, "and it was my fault. I should have pressed harder. I knew he was tiring easier, but he was so happy to serve, to be involved in shaping the world his children and grandchildren would live in. Maybe if I had…"

"Mom," Stephanie reached out and gripped her hand. "It wasn't your fault."

"No, but I should have taken better care of him. Should have made him see that it was time to slow down."

"Dad never slowed down."

"No. He didn't. He always insisted that life was for living."

"He did say that. It was some of his last words to me before I left on the tour before he died. He said, *Stephanie, life is a wonderful thing. Live it. Don't be afraid to risk yourself, to risk others judging you. Take the path it sometimes makes no sense to take and when you do, you will find you are where you were always meant to be. That's living, Stephie, not just existing.*"

Jacinda let her tears run unashamedly down her cheeks as she listened to her life mate's last words to the only other woman to have captured his heart. His daughter.

"Good words." Jacinda gave her a watery smile. "I hope you follow them, Stephanie, because he gave you the secret to how he lived his life, even when it was hard. And he had an amazing one."

"He did, thanks to you and your support."

"He gave as much to me. Maybe you don't see it that way, but the truth is, he was the one who allowed me to travel that path I was sure I didn't want to take and by doing so I got him, my children, and an amazing life. I got to become the person I was always supposed to be. Not the one I thought I was."

"I'm sorry, Mom. I should have realized…"

"It's fine, Stephie." Jacinda used Stephan's pet name for her letting her know she was forgiven. "I said the same things to my mother, only I was much younger than you when I said them and was much more adamant I was right."

"You did?"

"Yes, before I left for the Academy. She wanted me to stay and go to a school within the House of Healing where I would be accessible to those she considered 'worthy' of her daughter."

"Really? Did she have someone in mind?" Stephanie found herself asking.

"Unfortunately, yes," Jacinda grimaced remembering.

"Who?" Stephanie's eyes sparkled with curiosity after her mother's reaction.

"It was ridiculous. I mean he was a child and a whiny one at that. How she could imagine, I might one day be interested in him…"

"*Who* mother!"

"Prince Yusuf," Jacinda whispered.

"Prince Yusuf!" Stephanie nearly shouted drawing the attention of nearby tables.

"Stephanie!" Jacinda hissed. "Lower your voice."

"Sorry, Mom." She immediately lowered her voice. "But *Prince* Yusuf? Who is now *King* Yusuf?"

"Yes." Jacinda rested her forehead in her hand at the memory. "What could my mother have possibly been thinking? He's nine cycles younger than me!"

"Dad was twenty cycles older than you," Stephanie reminded her.

"Yes, but that was different." Jacinda bit out.

"Really?" Stephanie smiled at her mother's reaction. It was a rare thing for her to see her flustered. "How?"

"Your father and I were both *adults* when we met. Yusuf was *five* when my mother started her plotting. I couldn't believe it. He wasn't even out of school when I met Stephan. How would you like me trying to get you interested in Athol Allerd when you were fourteen."

"Ewww, Mother! Athol Allerd! He was the neighborhood terror!" She leaned across the table and whispered. "He was always picking his nose!"

"So you understand."

"Are you saying…." Stephanie's eyes widened.

"I would never *say* such a thing, Stephanie Anne! Yusuf is the King of the House of Healing and deserves my respect."

"Oh, Mother," Stephanie eyed her mother with new respect. "You are soooo bad."

"Thank you, my dear," Jacinda smiled benignly at her daughter. "Now let's enjoy this amazing Torte then finish buying out Pechora."

Chapter Ten

"Majesty! Majesty!"

Jotham absently waved at those that were calling out his name as he entered the Assembly Hall for the first session of the new Assembly. Assembly Guards were holding back the yelling crowds. While he wore his crown, he had foregone the Royal robe. It was something he now only wore for the most formal of occasions that included meeting the Kings and Queens of the other Houses.

Moving through the Hall, he paused before the closed doors that separated him from the Assembly that waited for him to officially open the new cycle. This was the fortieth time he had done this and he wondered when it had become routine for him.

He could still remember how anxious he had been that first time he addressed this Assembly after his father's death. He'd been twenty, just returning from his second tour with the Fleet, and newly wed. He stood before that Assembly and saw the doubt in so many eyes. Doubt that he would be able to step into the role he had suddenly been thrust. Doubt that he could take command of this Assembly and live up to those that came before him.

He, himself, had doubted it. Lata hadn't. She had proudly walked beside him as they entered that Assembly. He remembered how it had filled him with such pride to see her sitting there, so regally. She let no one intimidate her. She was his Queen and she had only been eighteen cycles.

He still remembered the first time he had to address the Assembly after her death. He couldn't look to where she should have been. If he had, he never would have made it through that speech.

"Majesty?"

Deffand's question pulled Jotham from his memories. "Open the doors, Captain."

"Yes, Majesty." Deffand nodded to the guards at the doors.

As they opened them, the Assembly's Sergeant at Arms announced his arrival.

"All rise for the King of the House of Protection," he shouted and everyone rose.

Jotham slowly walked down the aisle, nodding to an Assemblyman here and there, as he approached the podium. Why did he feel no excitement, no anticipation for the coming cycle? Turning, he looked to the empty Royal area and felt his heart lurch. Lata should be there. She should be sitting there, smiling up at him as she always had and for just a moment he swore she was. Her smile was as bright and her eyes as full of love as they had always been, then she slowly faded away. Yet she left behind a joy and sense that he was exactly where he was supposed to be that he hadn't felt in cycles.

The sound of the Assembly moving restlessly as he stood silently at the podium finally broke through to him and he forced his gaze away from Lata's empty seat.

"Today marks my fortieth address to this esteemed Assembly and I am honored to be able to deliver it to you. Forty cycles... where has the time gone?" Jotham let his gaze travel over the Assemblymen gathered on the floor before moving to the people in the balconies.

"It seems like only yesterday that I addressed you for the first time. Many of you weren't even born then, yet here you sit, where others once sat. Where others once stood."

"They were dedicated men and women who wanted to make their House and their world a better place for their children. Some were Assemblymen. Some served in the Coalition. Some were those who performed the necessary, yet unglamorous day-to-day tasks that it takes for our society to function properly."

"Those of you before me have the daunting task of living up to the standards they set and they set them high. As Assemblymen, you must always remember that you serve the *people* of this great House. You must make sure that the laws you enact, that the decisions you make are always in *their* best interest, even when they may not be in your own."

"You owe it to those who made it possible for you to be where you are today. Assemblymen like Pedahel Watson, Roxbert Botterill, and Stephan Michelakakis. They all dedicated their lives to the advancement of their people."

"You owe it to those that are to come, your children and your children's children to do this. But most of all you owe it to those that are here now. Look around you," he ordered and waited until they did. "See the people you serve. See their hopes and dreams and know that what you do in this room directly affects those dreams."

"Yet even with all of that responsibility and power, *you* are not more important than those that serve in the Coalition. They willingly protect us all, risking their very lives to do so."

"And *you* are not more important than those that serve quietly in the background. The ones that do the necessary day-to-day activities that make our society work. They and the families that support them are as important as any Assemblyman or member of the Coalition."

"Queen Lata came from such a strong and proud people." He heard the gasp that echoed through the hall at the mention of Lata. "Many considered them commoners, but I say to you there is no such thing, not in this House. I look at you, my people, and I don't see one 'common' person anywhere. Each of you is extraordinary in your own way and you do extraordinary things every day. Never think that it goes unnoticed by your King."

Applause thundered through the hall, the majority coming from the balconies where people were shouting their approval and Jotham acknowledged them with a small nod.

"In a few weeks, the Guardian, the new flagship for the House of Protection, will be leaving to join the Fleet to protect us from our enemies. And while it's Captain, Lucas Zafar, is from the House of Protection, there are members from every House serving on her. It is a true representation of the best of Carina." Jotham thought about what William had told him before and decided to see what he could stir up.

"We are a great people. We have a great future. The only thing that can stop us is us." He heard the confused whispers. "A people cannot have a great future if they don't learn from the mistakes of their past. Ten cycles ago one of ours was responsible for the death of billions."

He heard the rumbles of disagreement begin to filter through the hall. He knew what they were thinking, Audric had been from the House of Knowledge, not the House of Protection.

"It matters *not* which House Audric claimed! He was Carinian! One of us and that makes *all* of us responsible for his actions!" Jotham's claim echoed in the hall. "Actions caused by greed and the belief of his self-importance. We must remain vigilant so that it never happens again. So that when we become history," Jotham touched his chest, "future generations can look back at this time and celebrate our accomplishments, not be disgusted by our short comings. The choice rests with you."

Jotham stepped away from the podium and applause slowly began to build. By the time he reached the doors to exit, the entire Assembly was on its feet showing their support for their King.

∞ ∞ ∞ ∞ ∞

"Well, that was an... interesting speech." Stephanie took a sip of her wine as she switched off the comm she'd turned on so she and her mother could watch the King's speech. "I can't believe he mentioned Dad after all these cycles."

"Your father and Jotham always had a great respect for each other," Jacinda said absently thinking about what *had* been said. Especially the last part and wondered what was going on. She'd heard too many of these speeches to not realize he was sending a message, but to who?

"I guess I just never realized it before."

"Why, does it *worry* you?" Jacinda gave her daughter a sharp look, knowing her tones.

"It's just... I told you what I want to do."

"To become the first woman accepted into the King's Guard."

"Yes. Getting accepted into Captain Chamberlain's elite training program is the first step. When I graduate from it, there will then be no excuse for them to refuse my application. No one else will have the specialized training I will."

"And that's what you truly want?" Jacinda closely watched her daughter's reaction and found herself surprised at the emotion she heard in her voice.

"More than anything. I can't explain it, Mom, but I *need* to be there. My heart and soul tell me I do. I don't know why, but if I'm not..."

"If you're not?"

"Then I can't follow that harder path that will take me to where I'm meant to be." Stephanie turned tear-filled eyes to her mother, pleading for her understanding.

Jacinda felt her own throat tighten at the absolute belief she heard in her daughter's voice. How long had it been since she'd been that sure of the path she needed to be on? How long had it been since she had to truly work and sacrifice for something? Cycles for sure. Since she'd lost Stephan, nothing had truly challenged her enough to make her move outside her comfort zone. Not until... Jotham. Her gaze flew to the now dark comm. That couldn't be right... could it?

"Mom?"

"I'm sorry, honey. What?" Jacinda forced her gaze away from the dark screen.

"Are you alright?"

"Of course I am." Jacinda waved a dismissive hand. "If you believe that you are meant to be a member of the King's Guard then you will be. I've never known you to fail at something once you've set your mind to it. And I will be there, in the front row, proudly watching as you make history when they pin that insignia on your chest."

"Thanks, Mom." Stephanie rose to hug her mother. "You don't know what your support means to me."

"I will always support you." Jacinda hugged her back. "You're my daughter."

∞ ∞ ∞ ∞ ∞

Jotham sat back in the limisin, watching the lights of Pechora pass as they drove back to the Palace. Across from him, Deffand sat silently watching him.

"What's on your mind, Nicholas?" Jotham looked to his Captain, using his first name to let him know he could speak freely.

"I found your speech... interesting."

"Did you?"

"Yes. Is there a threat that I am unaware of?"

Jotham ran an assessing eye over his Captain. He shouldn't have been surprised that Nicholas had caught what he wasn't saying. He had been Jotham's Captain for fifteen cycles and before that served as a member of his Guard. He, more than most, knew how Jotham spoke when he was silently trying to make a point.

"No 'threat' but the High Admiral discovered that Rogue Stannic has been regularly communicating with someone from the House of Protection, concerning Barek."

"I'll increase his security immediately."

"No. Barek is aware of the situation and will handle it." Jotham saw Nicholas frown. "The communications seem to be of a more personal nature as in trying to influence who he might choose as his Queen."

"I wasn't aware Prince Barek was currently involved with anyone."

"He's not. As I said, he is aware of the communications and will take precautions."

"Still I would feel better assigning more guards."

"I will discuss it with him, but you know that his answer will be no."

"Yes, Majesty."

"He won't be on planet much longer, Nicholas, and you know Barek refuses to get involved with anyone while he's on tour."

"I believe the High Admiral was the same way... until he met Queen Cassandra."

Jotham found himself laughing, "Yes, well that is true but I highly doubt Barek will find himself in the same situation."

"If you say so, Majesty."

"What did you think about the rest of the speech?"

"It wasn't what you had planned on saying."

"Was it that obvious?"

"No, but I was there when you and Chesney discussed the points you wanted to cover."

"Of course, I'd forgotten."

"It was a rousing speech, Sire. Maybe not as much to a few of the Assemblymen, but to those that aren't, it validated that what they did mattered."

"Which Assemblymen?" Jotham demanded.

"Pajari for one, although if not for Madame Pajari jabbing him awake I don't think he would have heard a word."

"I can't understand how that man can continue to be re-elected."

"It has more to do with his wife than him. There are those that feel that having someone of 'Royal' blood as their Assemblyman will get their voices 'heard' more easily."

"They are wrong."

"I know this, just as I know you voiced your support of Danton Michelakakis."

"I did no such thing."

"You mentioned his father as one of the most important Assemblymen of your reign. It elevated his position within the Assembly even though he is newly elected."

"That was not my intention."

"But it is what was surmised by many Assemblymen, especially after what occurred at the Ball."

"What 'occurred' at the Ball?" Jotham asked frowning.

"Prince Barek opened the Ball by dancing with Jacinda."

"He did that to prevent the rumors that always occur when I dance with one of the wives."

"Of course, and it might have, had *you* not chosen her for the final dance. A dance you haven't danced since the death of Queen Lata. *That* didn't go unnoticed."

"She is the widow of an important Assemblyman. It would have been rude of me to not dance with her."

"Agreed, but it was the *final* dance. You, Majesty, are single. She is single. It started people wondering."

"Let them wonder."

"Yes, Majesty."

Jotham frowned at Deffand. Over the cycles, he'd learned when Deffand wasn't saying something. "What's really bothering you, Nicholas?"

"Not 'bothering,' Majesty, rather wondering."

"Wondering what?"

"If maybe there isn't more to your relationship with Jacinda than you are letting on."

"With *Jacinda*? You feel you are well acquainted enough with her to use her first name?" Jotham found he didn't like that.

"She insisted the last time we spoke."

"I see." But he didn't. "She and I don't have a 'relationship.'"

"May I ask why not? She is an amazing woman."

"Excuse me?" Jotham wasn't used to anyone questioning him, especially not about his personal life. "You overstep, Captain!"

"Pardons, Majesty." Deffand snapped his jaw shut and saw they were entering the Palace grounds. "Will you be wanting to return directly to your Wing, Majesty, or should I notify the guards that you will be in your gardens?"

Jotham looked at his Captain, took in his stiff posture, and knew he had overreacted, again. Deffand would willingly sacrifice his life for his. He wasn't trying to further his own agenda with his question.

It seemed his Assemblymen weren't the only ones that needed reminding that they were no more important than anyone else.

"I believe I would like to walk in the garden. Would you join me, Nicholas?"

"If you wish, Majesty."

∞ ∞ ∞ ∞ ∞

Jotham let the fragrance of the night blooming flowers fill his senses as he wandered along the discreetly lit path of the garden. "Jacinda Michelakakis is an amazing woman." When Deffand didn't reply he looked to him and found him several steps behind him, his eyes scanning the area. "Let the guards on the walls do their job, Nicholas. You are off-duty."

"I am never off-duty, Sire."

"You are as of right now. I asked you to join me so we could talk. Not so you could guard me."

"If that is what you wish, Majesty."

"It is. Now Jacinda Michelakakis."

"I agree, she is a truly amazing woman. One I don't think I've ever met the likes of."

"She intrigues you." Jotham found he couldn't contain his surprise.

"Yes, she's led an amazing life and yet she doesn't seem to see it that way. I'm not sure I would be the Captain of your Guard if it wasn't for her."

"Why would you say that?"

"It was one of my first days as a member of your Guard. There was a dinner, in your Wing, for a select number of Assemblymen and their wives to meet some dignitary, I don't remember who."

"Yet you remember Jacinda."

"Yes. I was dreadfully ill that night, but I refused to tell Captain Rutherford. It was my first 'real' assignment and I wasn't about to call in sick. I stood at that wall, guarding the door as course after course was brought in and tried not to vomit. I was just about to excuse myself when Jacinda rose from her seat and asked if I would escort her to the restroom."

"I don't remember that." Jotham thought back, but there had been so many dinners.

"Yes, well as soon as the door closed she grabbed my arm, dragged me into the room with her, shoved a glass of water into my hand and ordered me to drink. She then went on to berate me about men who were too stubborn to admit when they were sick and just how was I supposed to protect the King when I could barely stand." Nicholas smiled at the memory. "No woman had ever dressed me down so well, except for maybe my mother."

"She does have a talent for letting a man know when they've done something she perceives as incredibly stupid."

"She does. Anyway, she refused to return to the table until she was sure I would make it through the rest of the night. We both know Rutherford would have dismissed me if I had left my post for any other reason than to watch over a guest."

"Jacinda would have known that too."

"Yes."

"And she never approached you about it?" Jotham already knew the answer. "Never asked for any special favors in return?"

"Never."

"I've had my life mate, Nicholas."

"As has Jacinda, that doesn't mean you can't have another."

"Spoken like one who's never had a life mate." Jotham's laugh held no humor.

"No, I haven't, and it's doubtful I'll ever find one. I never had the honor of meeting Queen Lata, Majesty, but I can't believe your life mate would want you to spend your life alone... Not when there is someone you obviously care about."

∞ ∞ ∞ ∞ ∞

It was later that night as Jotham lay in his bed, alone, that he truly thought about what Deffand had said. It just wasn't possible.

"Why?" The sweetest voice he ever heard asked.

Jackknifing up, Jotham found he wasn't in his bed. He wasn't even in the Palace. He was back at the Academy, in Lata's room, leaning against the wall along her bed, holding her in his arms as he'd done so often when they'd stolen time together.

"Why what?" he asked and closed his eyes as his arms tightened around her, enjoying the feeling of her sinking into them.

"Why isn't a relationship possible between you and Jacinda?"

"What?" Jotham's eyes flew open and he looked down at her, but it wasn't Lata's sixteen-cycle eyes he was looking into, it was the eyes of his wife, his Queen, the ones that knew him so well.

"Why is a relationship with Jacinda impossible?" Lata's warm hand pressed against his pounding heart as she pushed slightly away. "I'm with the ancestors, Jotham, but you're not."

"That doesn't matter!" His tone was angry but still he held her.

"It does." Lata's soft voice cut through his angry one. "It's been so long, Jotham. You've suffered so much. Did you think I couldn't feel it? That just because I was gone that a part of me wasn't still connected to you?"

"Then how can you possibly want..."

"You to be happy again? To find love again?"

"Stop!"

"I won't stop, my love, because I love you!" Lata framed his face with her hands. "You were my first and only love, Jotham. We had such plans. So many dreams."

"I'm sorry I couldn't give them to you." He felt the crushing weight of it descend again.

"Jotham, you did! Don't you see? Was it the way we planned? No, but that doesn't mean you still didn't give them to me." She tipped her head to the side. "Do you remember our first anniversary?"

"I remember you wanted to go away to Messene. We didn't go."

"You had a meeting, so instead you brought Messene to me. You had the Chef get all his ingredients from Messene. You ordered him to make only 'authentic' Messene dishes."

"They were awful," Jotham half-smiled as he remembered the disaster that meal had been.

"Because you never asked him if he *could* make authentic Messene dishes. He had no clue," Lata laughed.

"I wanted it to be so special for you."

"It was. I was with you."

"I was always with you."

"Not like that you weren't. You cleared the *whole* day. It wasn't enough time to *travel* to Messene, but it was better. You gave me your *time*. *No one* interrupted us for the entire day! We laughed, we talked, we loved. We created Barek that day. It was a happy time."

"It was."

"You can be happy again, my love. Can love again. You can if you let yourself."

"It would never be the same."

"Of course not, but that doesn't make it wrong. It doesn't mean you can't. Love is a precious gift. Don't let it pass you by."

Chapter Eleven

"I'll get it, Mom!" Stephanie called out as she walked up to answer the knocking on the door. Opening it, she was momentarily stunned to find Captain Deffand standing there.

"Lieutenant Michelakakis."

"Captain Deffand."

"May I come in?" he asked raising an eyebrow slightly.

"Oh. Yes. Of course."

"Stephie, who's here?"

Deffand pulled his eyes from Stephanie to see Jacinda walking toward him. "Madame Michelakakis." He noted her look and corrected himself. "Jacinda."

"Much better, Nicholas. So to what do we owe this unexpected pleasure?"

Deffand reached inside his jacket to the concealed inner pocket and withdrew the sealed envelope the King had asked him to deliver, and handed it to Jacinda.

Stephanie looked on confused. Why was the Captain of the King's Guard delivering a message to her mother and why did her mother seem so hesitant to take it?

Jacinda slowly reached out and took the envelope from Nicholas. Without even opening it, she knew it was from Jotham. He was the only one the Captain of his Guard would deliver a message for. What could he possible want to say to her?

Breaking the seal on the envelope, she walked across the room toward the open doors that led to the garden to give herself some privacy. She pulled out the folded piece of paper and read the words written in Jotham's own hand.

Madame Michelakakis,

I feel the need to apologize for the way I spoke to you the other day.

I know your words were heartfelt and I didn't mean for my response to alarm you.

I would like the chance to repair any damage my actions may have caused and invite you to dine with me tomorrow night.

I await your response.

King Jotham

Jacinda reread the note, feeling the weight of the paper between her fingers and taking in the House of Protection arrow imbedded in it. Jotham's initials were along the shaft, telling her it was from his personal stock. She'd seen enough 'correspondence' to know it was always on a lightweight paper with just the arrow.

How was she supposed to respond to this? She understood why Jotham felt the need to apologize. It had been so out of character for him to react that way, to allow his emotions to be revealed like that. She'd witnessed Jotham's anger before and seen him put someone in their place, both during dinners she and Stephan had attended. But he'd always done it politely, so coolly that some missed the rebuke altogether. And he *never* raised his voice and he *never* revealed his emotions.

It was something she'd always admired... and wondered about. Had he really become that controlled? That cold? Where had the young man Lata had said was so warm and romantic gone?

She had gotten a glimpse of him during their lunch, but the words in this note came from the cool, controlled man she'd known for cycles. It was the other man that intrigued her, he was the one she wanted to get to know better.

He had asked her to call him Jotham, but he'd signed this note 'King' Jotham. Again sending mixed signals. Did he want to have dinner with Madame Michelakakis, the widow of an Assemblyman and the mother of a new one, to make sure he hadn't offended her? Or did he want to have it with Jacinda, a woman because he was interested?

Jacinda couldn't decide which one she wanted it to be. Was she really interested in trying to start a personal relationship with Jotham? He was an attractive man. They had a long history together even if Jotham was only starting to realize it. They had a lot in common: both had lost their life mates, both had grown up in politics, and they both knew it could never go anywhere.

Jacinda looked through the doors to her mother's rose bush. The one she'd transplanted here after her mother's death. She'd been so worried the 'mother' wouldn't thrive here. After all, it had always grown in House of Healing soil. She could still remember her amazement when it bloomed that first time. The root her mother had given her had bloomed violet, just as Lata's had. She remembered calling her mother distraught about it.

Her mother had laughed and said it was the way of the plant. It would bloom the color of the House where it was planted. Yet the 'mother' hadn't changed to violet. Instead it bloomed the deep golden color of the House of Healing. It was only after Stephan's death that it had begun to change, blooming the gold *and* the violet of the House of Protection.

Jacinda hadn't understood why and she wished that *her* mother had been alive to ask. Had she known it would happen? If she had, why hadn't she said anything?

Yet none of that really mattered. She was just trying to distract herself from doing what she knew needed to be done. Turning back, she found both Nicholas and Stephanie watching her.

"Stephanie, while I go respond to this," she waved the note in her hand, "would you please keep Nicholas entertained? There's some wine." She gestured to the bottle she'd opened right before he had arrived. "I won't be long." With a forced smile, she left the room.

∞ ∞ ∞ ∞ ∞

"So are you going to 'entertain' me, Lieutenant?" Deffand couldn't believe he was flirting with Jacinda's daughter. She was a member of the Coalition. Her brother was an Assemblyman. And on top of all that, she was nearly ten cycles younger than him.

Stephanie looked at Deffand in shock. Sure, she'd been approached by men before, powerful men. Her mother was an amazingly beautiful woman and she'd been compared to her all her life. For her mother, it had been an asset, but for Stephanie it had been a hindrance. Too many men saw only her looks and refused to believe there was anything else to her. She had fought that attitude since the Academy, and to find it again in the Captain of the King's Guard, hurt more than she thought possible.

"I am not 'entertainment,' Captain," she spit out.

"Of course not! I'm sorry, Lieutenant, I never meant to imply..." He took a deep breath and forced himself to continue. "You are obviously a beautiful woman, but that doesn't excuse my words. You are a member of the Coalition. A highly decorated one. For me to imply any less insults me more than you."

"You investigated me?"

"I... yes. You are the child of Stephan and Jacinda Michelakakis. Your brother is now an Assemblyman. It is part of my responsibility to know about anyone who has access to someone who has access to the King."

"*That's* why you had me investigated?"

"In part."

"And the other part?"

Nicholas found himself struggling to maintain eye contact with Stephanie. "That was entirely personal," he finally admitted.

Stephanie found her breath catching. If this was any man other than the Captain of the King's Guard she would be all over him. She had thought of nothing other than him over the last few days, but to reach her goals, she had to resist him.

"Then you know why I'm on planet."

"You have been accepted into the first class ever taught by Captain Chamberlain. That speaks for itself in your abilities. I've met Peter Chamberlain, he is an amazing man, with great skills. Anyone trained by him will be a great asset to wherever they choose to serve."

"I hope you still feel that way when I apply for the King's Guard."

"What!" Nicholas found himself taking a step back as her words struck him. "You... you wish to be a member of the *King's Guard*?!!"

"Yes." Stephanie stood proud as she stared him down.

"But..."

"But what?"

"You are...."

"I am what? A woman? Are you saying that as a woman I am unable to protect my King?"

"Stephanie! That's enough!" Jacinda's voice cut through the tension growing between the two.

∞ ∞ ∞ ∞ ∞

Jacinda walked into her bedroom, Stephan and hers bedroom, and walked to the desk that used to be his. Sitting down, she opened the desk and pulled out a sheet of her own stationery, and penned her response to King Jotham.

After a moment's hesitation and a great deal of regret, she sealed her response and returned to her living room only to be shocked at what she heard.

"Stephanie! That's enough!"

∞ ∞ ∞ ∞ ∞

"Madame Michelakakis, the fault here is mine," Deffand spoke first.

"Excuse me?"

"My... words to your daughter were inappropriate. I apologize, Lieutenant." Deffand bowed stiffly to Stephanie. "If you have finished your response then I shall deliver it to King Jotham."

"Yes." Jacinda handed it to him and found she was as reluctant to let go of her response as she had been to receive his request. "It was wonderful to see you again, Nicholas. Please, don't be a stranger. No matter what else occurs in our lives, you are always welcome in this house."

"Thank you, Jacinda. I may take you up on that."

"I hope you do, Nicholas. The older I grow, the more I cherish those I call friends. Be well."

"You also. Lieutenant." Bowing once again, he turned and left.

∞ ∞ ∞ ∞ ∞

"Mother, what's going on?"

"What do you mean, Stephanie?"

"Why was the King's Captain coming here?" She gestured to the door Deffand had exited through. "What message was he delivering to you? Who was it from?"

"Stephanie, you are a smart, intelligent woman, I shouldn't have to explain the obvious to you."

"Mother!" Stephanie ran a hand through her hair. "Are you telling me that message was from King Jotham?"

"As I said, smart and intelligent." Jacinda walked over and took a sip out of her glass of wine.

"But why would he be sending you a private message? You're not involved with the Assembly anymore."

"No, I'm not."

"So why then the private message? Why have it delivered by his own Captain? If it were any other woman but you, I would think..."

"Would think what?"

"Well, that there was some type of... personal relationship between the two."

"You don't think that Jotham would want that with me?" Jacinda raised an eyebrow at her daughter.

"Mom, are you telling me..."

"I'm telling you nothing. I'm just wondering why you would think it impossible for Jotham and I to become involved?"

"I... a... well... You're my mother."

"I am aware of that."

"He is the King."

"I'm aware of that too. He is also just a man, Stephanie. A man with a lot of responsibility. We've known each other since the Academy. We have a lot of history together. A lot in common."

"Yeah, but still..."

"Still what?"

"I... I guess I just never thought of you with anyone else but Dad. I mean I know he's been gone ten cycles now, but still."

"I will always love your father, Stephanie. He was my life mate, but that doesn't mean I want to remain alone for the rest of my life. Stephan wouldn't want that."

"I know but... Jotham?"

"Relax, Jotham and I are not involved that way." She saw the tension leave her daughter's body.

"Then why all the secrecy."

"Because, just look how you reacted to a simple note of apology. Others would think just what you did if they found out."

"Apology? Why did the King feel he needed to apologize to you?"

"It was just a misunderstanding that's now been resolved. Let it go, Stephanie."

∞ ∞ ∞ ∞ ∞

Jotham sat in the garden and silently looked at the envelope Deffand had brought him. It had taken him two days to write it. Two days, where he thought about what Will had said and what Chesney and Nicholas had said. But mostly about the dream he had with Lata.

Had he really talked to Lata as Will said he had with Kayden? Or was it just his mind telling him what he wanted to hear? In the end, he decided the least he needed to do was apologize for his actions, and Jacinda's response would dictate his next action. Opening the envelope, he pulled out the single piece of paper and read.

Majesty,
While I thank you for your apology, it is unnecessary.
I am the one who is sorry for overstepping the bounds of propriety and causing you discomfort.
No amends are necessary and you can rest assured the incident is forgotten.
May the ancestors watch over you.
Madame Michelakakis

Jotham reread the cool, impersonal words and felt a pain unlike any he had felt in cycles, maybe ever. She was refusing him, that came through loud and clear in her response.

She wasn't going to have dinner with him. Or do anything else with him for that matter.

Rising, he found himself walking to the center of the garden to Lata's rose bush. It was such a beautiful thing, he knew Lata would love to see it like this. To know that it still flourished.

A gift.

Like love.

A gift from Jacinda's mother.

Jacinda had known her mother loved Lata as if she were one of her own. Had known about the gift and it hadn't upset her.

A child that *wasn't* hers and yet Jotham had found it hard to love a son that *was* his. A son that didn't come from his Lata and somehow Dadrian had known that. Was that why he had acted the way he had?

What did that say about Jotham as a man? That he withheld his full love, his full acceptance from his own child?

Jacinda had made the right decision not to get involved with him.

Obviously, he was a man who didn't know how to love.

Turning, he walked away from the bush not noticing that the bush drooped slightly.

∞ ∞ ∞ ∞ ∞

It was several weeks later while eating first meal that Jacinda found herself once again watching Jotham on her comm. Stephanie had left for Kisurri. Danton was busy with the Assembly and Ethan and his children had visited earlier in the week. Life had returned to its normal routine. So why was she so unsettled?

Looking at Jotham's face broadcast from the space station, Bering, the christening ceremony had been going on for nearly an hour and she thought he looked tired as he moved to the podium. He stood before a massive window that gave a magnificent view of the Guardian, ready to depart on its maiden voyage.

"For thousands of cycles our people have gone into space. We have created vessels to carry us and as in ancient times we named them, for they nurture and care for those on board when they are so far from home. Today we christen the Guardian. May the ancestors watch over those she carries and return them safely to us."

Everyone watched as a bottle of the best champagne the House of Protection produced was shot out of a launch tube to shatter against the Guardian's hull. Slowly, she began to back out of the space station, to the applause and toasts of those invited to the ceremony.

Leaning forward, Jacinda turned off the comm and sent a silent prayer up to the ancestors to watch over those brave souls on the Guardian. That they returned safe and whole and if they could especially watch out over Prince Barek, she would be eternally grateful for she didn't think Jotham could survive the loss of another son.

∞ ∞ ∞ ∞ ∞

"You look tired, my old friend." William leaned back in the chair in his office on the Bering.

"I'm fine. How are you doing? Your first son just left on the flagship of the House of Protection."

"Lucas will be fine. Neither of us would have allowed him to assume such an important position if we didn't believe it."

"True. Still he's out there without you."

"So is Barek. They've both been there before. They'll be fine, especially with Victoria with them."

"Yes she'll keep them in line," Jotham agreed smiling.

"And what she can't handle, Amina will."

"Amina? Amina is on the Guardian?"

"Yes." William frowned at Jotham's reaction. "Her program for detecting the Regulians new stealth ship is nearly finished. It just needs real-time testing. She wanted to be on board to handle any corrections that might need to be made."

"Why wasn't I informed?" Jotham demanded. "Was Barek?"

"Why would you be? Why would he? It's a Coalition matter." When Jotham opened his mouth only to snap it shut, William raised an eyebrow. "What aren't you telling me, Jotham?"

"Nothing I'm sure of."

"Bullshit, you're sure enough to question a personnel change that shouldn't concern you at all."

"Amina is a member of the House of Protection. One of my people. I'm always concerned about them."

"She is also a member of the House of Knowledge. Cassandra thinks of her as a niece. Do you really think I'd put someone my wife loves in harm's way?"

"No..."

"But... I hear the 'but,' Jotham. What's going on? Why would Barek be interested?" *'Why would Barek be interested?'* William thought to himself, then it hit him. "Barek is *interested?*" He half rose from his seat. "In *Amina*!"

"I believe so," Jotham finally admitted. "Sit, Will. Barek hasn't admitted as much, but... I know my son. I saw how he looked at her during Victoria's Union. How he instantly moved to protect her when Stannic stormed in."

"Do you have a problem with that?" Will could see it on Jotham's face.

"No. Yes. Damn it, Will, she is so young!" There he'd finally said it. It wasn't that he thought Amina wasn't 'worthy' of Barek. It wasn't that he had a problem that she currently resided in the House of Knowledge. It was her *age*.

"She's the same age Lata was," William reminded him quietly.

"I know and that worked out so well, didn't it."

"Jotham...." Will gave his friend a sympathetic look. "Lata didn't die because of her *age*. She died because she got caught in a landslide."

"She shouldn't have been there!" Jotham surged to his feet. "She should have been in the Palace where she was safe."

"Life is a risk, Jotham." He watched his friend begin to pace. "You have to live it or what's the point?"

"And you would feel this way if it was Cassandra?"

"Jotham, I watched her stop breathing on the Retribution. Valerian attacked her during the Challenge. You didn't see what she went through to deliver Sabah. Do you really think I haven't felt what you've felt? I've just been lucky enough to not lose her."

"You have been," Jotham agreed with him.

"What's really going on, Jotham? I don't feel like this is about Amina and Barek. I think it's about you and Jacinda."

"There is no me and Jacinda."

"Why not?" When Jotham didn't answer, William frowned. "Jotham, why isn't there a you and Jacinda?"

"Because that's what she wanted. I screwed up. In the garden. I sent her a note apologizing. Her response was very cool, letting me know she wasn't interested in pursuing a relationship."

"You sent her a note?!!" William didn't try to hide his disbelief.

"Yes." Jotham gave him a confused look. "What else was I supposed to do?"

"How did you sign the note?"

"'*King Jotham*,' of course."

"Seriously?" William gave him an exasperated look. "Is that how you signed notes to Lata?"

"Of course not! I wasn't King when we met."

"Don't be obtuse, Jotham. You know exactly what I mean."

Jotham began pacing again. "I signed them '*Jotham*,'" he finally admitted.

"Why?"

"Why? Because it was Lata. It was personal. She never saw me as my position."

"Jacinda does?"

"No," Jotham finally admitted.

"Then why send her a Royal apology instead of a personal one?" William leaned back in his chair steepling his fingers under his chin. "You addressed her as Madame Michelakakis too, didn't you?"

"Yes."

"And you really expected her to respond warmly?"

"I..."

"You were protecting yourself, Jotham." William rose to move to the front of his desk and leaned back against it, crossing his arms over his chest.

"I was?"

"Of course. No man likes to be rejected, especially from a woman like Jacinda. I can still remember how it felt when she rejected me."

"What?" Jotham stopped pacing to stare at his life-long friend in shock. "When? She's only been widowed for ten cycles. You've been married to Cassandra all that time!"

William raised an eyebrow at how passionate Jotham had suddenly become, he was even clenching his fists. Oh yes, his old friend was definitely interested in Jacinda Michelakakis.

"Relax!" William ordered trying not to laugh. "It was back when we were in the Academy."

"The Academy?" Jotham frowned, his fingers relaxing. "You said you remembered her. You never said you dated her."

"Because I didn't. Did you not hear me say she rejected me?"

"She did? When? I don't remember you even pursuing her."

"Yes. It was right before she graduated and you don't remember because I didn't 'pursue' her. I happened to sit next to her in the cafeteria."

"*Happened* to sit next to?" It was Jotham's turn to be disbelieving.

"Okay, I followed her in and made sure to sit next to her," William laughed. "She was beautiful, even though she went to great lengths to downplay it."

"I never noticed."

"That's because she wasn't Lata and she avoided you... and me."

"Why?"

"That's what I wanted to know too, after all I was a good-looking man. She was a good-looking woman. It should have been simple."

"You honestly didn't put it to her that way." Jotham found himself smiling at the thought. Even *he* knew you couldn't approach a woman like that.

"Of course not." William was affronted that Jotham would even suggest such a thing. "I was a smooth guy back then, remember?"

They both laughed as they remembered Will's past as the playboy of the Academy.

"Yes, the girls all loved you."

"They did. All but Jacinda."

"You saw her as a challenge."

"Yes, after all I was seventeen and knew it all."

"We sure thought we did, didn't we?"

"Yes. Jacinda set me straight, politely of course." William frowned as he thought back over that conversation. "You know I think that was the first truly serious conversation I ever had with a woman. I know after it, I thought about my future differently."

"What are you talking about, Will?"

"Jacinda... after all my best lines had no effect on her, I finally just flat out asked her why and do you know what she said?"

"No."

"She said that while I was a handsome, smart, intelligent man she had no desire to one day be the wife of the High Admiral."

"She said that?"

"Yes, amazing isn't it? That she seemed to see my future so clearly. Until that moment, I had never given the future that much thought. I just wanted to get out into the Fleet. The thought that I might one day have this position," he looked around his office. "I never believed I had that potential, Jacinda did. After that conversation, I buckled down with my studies and took our training a lot more seriously."

Jotham was silent for several moments thinking back over that time. Will *had* suddenly changed during their fifth cycle. He'd always been near the top of the class, but suddenly he was acing everything. He became the guy to beat and he still had records on the walls of the Academy.

"She saw you for what you really were, not what you were trying to project."

"Just as she sees you for who you really are. A man first, and then a King, unless you make her view you differently."

"Which is what happened with how I addressed that note."

"Yes." Will eyed his friend trying to decide what to say then decided to just say it. "I've known you all my life, Jotham. We've seen each other through some good times and some bad ones."

"We have."

"One of the things I've admired most about you is steadfastness. Once you decide on something or someone, that's it. You're solid. That doesn't mean you're inflexible and can't change when necessary, but not about what's important. You knew Lata was your Queen from the moment you saw her and you never changed your mind. You stood beside me when I arrived on Carina with Cassandra when we both knew you had doubts. You did that because of your faith in me."

"I seem to recall not being as supportive as I could have been."

"Totally understandable. You are my friend, more than my friend, and you were looking out for me. Let me look out for you now."

"In what way?"

"By telling you to pursue Jacinda."

"She isn't interested, Will." Jotham found he had to look away from his oldest friend.

"She isn't interested in the *King*," William stressed. "She's interested in *you*. In *Jotham*. I've never known you to back down from something just because it was challenging, Jotham. Don't start now."

"What if it ends badly?"

"Would you have given up one day with Lata just because it ended badly?"

"No."

"Then don't do it with Jacinda. She's a mature woman who knows who she is and what she wants. She's not going to play games with you, Jotham. She's going to tell you what she really thinks. Can you handle that?"

"You say that as if no one has ever told me no before. As if everyone bows before me."

"Of course you are right, my King," Will smirked as he stood at attention and gave Jotham a full Royal bow.

Jotham reached out and shoved Will. "You're an idiot. How does Cassandra put up with you?"

"She loves me." Will laughed before turning serious. "Take the chance, Jotham, at least then you'll know for sure."

Chapter Twelve

"Jacinda?"

Jacinda turned when Myesha called out her name. "Myesha, what are you still doing here? I thought you'd left to visit your grandchildren for a few days."

"I was just on my way out when the comm rang."

"It did?" Rising, Jacinda brushed the dirt from her knees. "I didn't hear it."

"Yes, well... I told him I would find you."

"Him?"

"Yes... King Jotham."

"King Jotham is on the comm?"

"Yes." Myesha gave her a speculative look.

Slowly, Jacinda removed her gloves and moved to the house. "Alright. Thank you, Myesha, have a good time with your grandkids."

"I'll see you in a few days." Myesha had worked for Jacinda and Stephan most of her life. She and Jacinda were friends, but she knew there were times when Jacinda wasn't able to confide in her and this was one of those times.

"Alright," Jacinda spoke absently as she moved into the house. She wanted to berate herself when she stopped at the mirror to make sure she looked presentable. Taking a deep breath, she moved to sit down in front of the comm.

"King Jotham," she greeted, forcing a pleasant expression on her face, "to what do I owe this unexpected call?"

"Hello, Jacinda." Jotham let his gaze travel over her face taking in the warm, dewy glow of her skin, telling him she had just come in from outside. He also took in the cool look in her eyes, telling him she was still upset with him. "How are you?"

"I'm fine. You?" She forced herself to ask and realized he looked even more tired than he had earlier.

"I'm fine. I've just returned from the Bering."

"Yes, I saw the christening."

An uncomfortable silence followed her words. "Jacinda...." He closed his eyes and rubbed his temples. "I'm sorry, for the way I acted in the garden and for the note I sent."

"You're sorry for your apology?" Jacinda found herself teasing him, wanting to ease some of the pressure he was obviously under.

"No!" His gaze captured hers through the comm. "I'm just sorry for how I delivered it."

"You didn't. Nicholas did." Jacinda felt her breath catch as she was suddenly pinned by Jotham's amazing, violet eyes. She had forgotten just how beautiful those eyes were.

"Are you teasing me, Jacinda Michelakakis?"

"Obviously not very well if you have to ask."

"You'll forgive me then?" A hopeful look passed over his face.

"There's nothing to forgive. I overstepped."

"You didn't. You were only showing your concern, as a true friend would. My relationship with Dadrian... it's complicated and I would prefer not to discuss it right now. Can we just let that go for now, Jacinda?"

Jacinda let her gaze travel over Jotham's face. She heard the sincerity in his voice and saw it on his face. She had never lost a child. Who was she to judge how someone handled it? "We can do that," she told him quietly.

"Thank you." Jotham felt a weight lift and decided to push while she seemed agreeable. "Have dinner with me tonight."

"King Jotham..."

"Jotham," he interrupted. "Please, Jacinda. Call me Jotham." He watched her look away, watched her take a deep breath, and knew their future hinged on her next words.

"Alright." She met his gaze head on. "Jotham."

"Good, now have dinner with me tonight."

"Jotham, I don't think that's a good idea."

"Why?"

"Why? Because you are the King."

"So?"

"So?" Jacinda asked growing flustered.

Jotham found he liked the flush that was beginning to grow on her cheeks. He found he liked stirring Jacinda Michelakakis up. He wondered how far he could take it.

"Yes. So. I've been King nearly my entire life. It's not like I did anything to deserve or earn the position, it just is."

"You may not have done anything to *deserve* it, Jotham, but over the last forty cycles you've certainly *earned* it. The House of Protection has flourished under your reign. The true test of any monarch is if when he leaves his House it is better off than when it was placed into his care. You've certainly done that with the House of Protection."

Jotham found it hard to speak after her heartfelt words. Was this what he'd been missing since Lata had died. The absolute support of someone that knew he wasn't perfect. That knew he was just a man.

"Thank you, Jacinda. You don't know what that means to me, especially coming from you." He paused for a moment. "Have dinner with me tonight."

"Jotham..."

"Do you already have plans?"

"No, but..."

"Then have dinner with me. Save me from having to eat a miserable dinner alone."

"Oh please, Safford has never made a miserable dinner in his life."

"True, but I would still be eating it alone."

Jacinda's mouth dropped open as Jotham pouted at her over the comm. It was adorable. It was unexpected. It was irresistible.

"Did that look work with Lata?" she found herself asking then could have kicked herself when his expression froze. Damn it, she'd done it again. She knew Jotham didn't talk about Lata the way she did Stephan. Why did she keep forgetting that?

Jotham forced himself to breath, to not respond the way he had for the last thirty cycles. Jacinda wasn't trying to be hurtful. She was a caring, loving woman and she spoke of those she loved and cared about even if they were now with the ancestors.

"Most of the time," he admitted giving her a slightly uncomfortable look. "It got me out of a great many misunderstandings when we were first seeing one another."

"I can see why." Jacinda only paused for a moment before responding. She knew what it had taken for him to tell her that. "It works very well."

"So that means you will be having dinner with me tonight?" Jotham jumped all over her words.

"Jotham, there's no way you can just clear your schedule on such short notice."

"I can. I am the King." He smiled as his words caused her to laugh.

"Yes, you are, but my guess is that some of those people have been waiting a very long time to meet with you. You can't just cancel."

Jotham found his smile fading. "True, but I still want to have dinner with you."

"How about a late meal? After your scheduled meetings? What time do you think you will be done?" She saw him look down and knew he was looking at his schedule and saw him frown.

"My last meeting starts at nine."

"Seriously? You let Chesney schedule you until nine at night?"

Jotham heard the outrage in her voice, yet wasn't sure who it was directed at. "Being King doesn't have set hours," he began.

"Of course it doesn't. It's a twenty-four/seven job, but that's for emergencies and events. It doesn't mean your *daily* appointments need to run that late! Chesney needs to realize you have a life! That you need time..."

"Jacinda!" Jotham's words cut off her growing tirade.

"What!"

"Chesney scheduled it that way because I asked him to." Silence greeted his statement.

"Why would you do that?" she asked confusion clearly seen on her face.

"Because it keeps me busy," he admitted.

"Jotham..."

"Have dinner with me."

"You have a meeting."

"Have desert with me then. I'll have Safford make Fudge Torta."

"Oh, you don't play fair."

"I'll play anyway I need to if it means I'll get to see you tonight." Jotham saw the shock on her face. "I *need* to see you tonight, Jacinda."

"Alright." Jacinda found she couldn't refuse him, not when he spoke so honestly. "But not for dinner and not for Torta. It's not fair of you to ask Safford to make it on such short notice."

"He wouldn't mind."

"I would. Your Chef does an amazing job, Jotham. He's in early every day making sure your meals and the meals for anyone you have a meeting with are properly prepared. To expect him to suddenly extend his day for me..."

"As I said, for you, he wouldn't mind. I don't know how you've charmed so many of my House, but you have."

"I think you are overstating that."

"I don't. I'll have the limisin pick you up at 9:30."

"I'll drive myself."

"But..."

"Jotham, I'll drive myself," she said firmly.

"Fine." Jotham finally agreed, but he wasn't happy about it. "Drive up to the secure area. I'll have Deffand meet you and bring you to my private chambers."

"Alright, I'll see you then."

"Until then." Jotham nodded then ended the comm.

∞ ∞ ∞ ∞ ∞

Jacinda leaned back in her chair and couldn't believe what she'd just agreed to. Did she really want to do this? To start something that couldn't go anywhere? Yet she was drawn to Jotham in a way she hadn't been to any other man, and that included Stephan. She and Stephan, because of their age difference, sometimes struggled to find common ground. She'd found it invigorating in the early cycles, she'd learned so much when she thought she knew it all. It had sometimes been a trial, but she wouldn't change a minute of it.

Yet it wasn't that way with Jotham. They had the same reference points, knew the same people, and were at the Academy together. It was something she'd never had with Stephan and she found she liked it.

Looking at the clock, she realized she had time for a short nap before she needed to leave. Rising, she went to lie down.

∞ ∞ ∞ ∞ ∞

"Do you realize how beautiful you are?"

Jacinda opened her eyes to find she was staring up into her life mate's warm brown ones. "It will fade with age."

"Yours won't because it's not just on the outside. Your beauty runs through your entire being. You are gold, Jacinda. House of Healing gold."

"I'm glad you think so." Reaching up she cupped the cheek she so loved.

"I don't think it. I know it." Leaning down Stephan gently kissed her lips. "I realized it the first moment I saw you, sitting there across your parent's table, your eyes so suspicious."

"I was so sure it was a set-up, at least until my dad said you were from the House of Protection."

"I'll never forget the moment you realized it. You raised that eyebrow at me like you do." He gently caressed said eyebrow. "And it was like a challenge, one I was more than willing to accept."

"I didn't realize I was doing it."

"You always do it, my love. You always conveyed so much with this eyebrow. Amusement. Shock. Understanding.

Questions. Anger. I so relied on this eyebrow," he gently touched it, "during our life together, especially when dealing with other wives. Somehow, you always seemed to guide me without having to say a word."

"You give me too much credit, Stephan. You were the one with the silver tongue. All you ever had to do was open your mouth and women fell all over you, me included. Every woman in the House of Protection hated me, not because I was from the House of Healing, but because I'd captured your heart."

"You did that, my love, and you still have it, even though I am gone."

"Stephan..."

"Shhh, my love." Stephan pulled her close. "Don't cry, you know how I hate it when you do that."

"I just miss you so much, Stephan. So much."

"I know. You've been alone for too long. You were never meant to be alone."

"What are you saying?" Jacinda looked up at him not sure if she was hopeful or frightened. "Will I be joining you soon?"

"No! Jacinda, no," he instantly denied.

"Why not? Don't you want me with you?"

"Of course I do! And that day will come and then it will be forever, but you still have so much life to live. There is still so much you need to do."

"What are you talking about?" She gave a slight yank on the hair he liked to let grow just to feel her fingers in it. "I've lived my life. I've had my life mate. I've had my children. What else is there left for me to do?"

"To do? To live. To love. To make a difference in the lives of those to come."

"How am I supposed to do that?"

"By being who you are. By becoming who you were always meant to be. You've already started down the path, my love. There will be difficulties and trials. That's life, but I know you will weather them because when you love, it is always strong and pure."

∞ ∞ ∞ ∞ ∞

Jacinda awoke and felt a sense of contentment she hadn't felt in cycles. Those first few cycles after Stephan's passing she'd hated going to bed. It was so empty and when she'd wake, for just a moment, she always expected to find Stephan there.

Jacinda had always been able to feel Stephan's presence when she really needed it. Had always known he was watching over her. Still it had been hard. Her mother had taught her to believe in the ancestors, to believe that they watched over those they loved. Many Carinians didn't. They thought it was nonsense. Maybe when she had been younger she had been one of those people, but not since her mother's passing.

Jacinda still remembered how she heard her voice that day, telling her she needed to check on Stephanie. Stephanie had somehow managed to climb out of the day crib she had put her in while she'd dealt with a service man. When she rushed in to check on her, she'd found her prying off the safety cover for one of the power sources in the room. Had she succeeded, she could have been killed. From that day on, she never doubted that the ancestors watched over them.

It had never been like this.

To feel Stephan's touch. To really hear his voice. But what was he really trying to tell her?

∞ ∞ ∞ ∞ ∞

Jotham tried not to rush his meeting with Pajari. The Assemblyman drove him crazy. He had never known Elliott to have an original thought, to make a stand, yet he always seemed to end up on the most popular side of any issue and get re-elected.

"I understand your point, Assemblyman Pajari, but until all the facts are in I refuse to pass judgment on what might just be an honest mistake."

"Honest mistake! Majesty, that's just not possible! Have you not heard what is being said by the House of Growth?"

"Rumors, Elliott, and I will place no substance in them. Now, if that's all. It's been a long day and I'm ready to retire for the night." Jotham reached for the button that would signal Chesney.

"Of course, Majesty. I will discuss this with you again later."

"Do that." Jotham looked to the door as Chesney entered. "Please see Assemblyman Pajari out, Chesney."

"Of course, Majesty. Assemblyman Pajari." Chesney gestured for him to proceed to the outer office then turned back to Jotham. "Majesty, I had a variety of refreshments delivered to your chambers. Will you be needing me any longer tonight?"

"No, Chesney, thank you. Have a good night."

"You also, Majesty."

∞ ∞ ∞ ∞ ∞

Pajari quickly moved away from where he'd been eavesdropping near Jotham's office door, pretending to look at a painting as Chesney entered the outer office closing the connecting doors.

"If you'd follow me, Assemblyman Pajari, I'll escort you to the Public Wing so you can get to your transport." Chesney turned off the light on his desk and moved to the door.

"Thank you, Mister... Chesney."

Chesney heard the slightest of pauses and knew Pajari had to search for his name. Even though Chesney had been Jotham's assistant for over twenty cycles and Pajari had been an Assemblyman for all of them.

"No thanks necessary, Assemblyman Pajari." He waited for the Assemblyman to proceed him then closed the door.

"King Jotham is meeting with someone else tonight?" Pajari waited until they were outside the King's Wing before asking.

"Pardon me?" Chesney looked to the Assemblyman.

"He seemed distracted during our meeting. As if something else was on his mind."

"I'm sure you're mistaken, Assemblyman Pajari. The King takes every meeting he has seriously, especially one with an Assemblyman."

"Is that who he's meeting with now?"

"I wouldn't know, Assemblyman."

"But you schedule all his meetings!"

"Yes, I do."

"So you would know."

"I am not at liberty to discuss the King's itinerary with you, Assemblyman Pajari. Ahh, here we are." Chesney opened the door that separated the Public Wing from the hallway that led to the inner Wings and nodded to the guards. "Have a nice evening, Assemblyman Pajari."

With a huff, Pajari walked through and Chesney rolled his eyes as he shut the door. This wasn't the first time Pajari had tried to pump him for information on the King. Nearly every Assemblyman did to a point but they were at least subtle. Pajari was always obvious, sometimes painfully so. Some things never changed.

Thinking about how Pajari would react if he discovered just *who* Jotham was meeting with Chesney smiled. He couldn't wait to get back to work tomorrow to see how the night went. Whistling, he walked to the secure area where his transport was parked.

∞ ∞ ∞ ∞ ∞

Jotham found himself eagerly striding toward his private chambers, something he hadn't done in cycles. Jacinda should be arriving soon and he wanted to make sure everything was perfect. Entering, he came to an abrupt halt finding Jacinda already there, studying the label on the bottle of wine.

"You're early," he said letting the door close behind him and stepping deeper into the room.

"I am." Jacinda put the bottle back on the table and smiled at him. "I hope you don't mind."

"No. Never. I was just hoping to be here to greet you."

"I asked Nicholas not to say anything. He said you were in a meeting and I know how those can go. I didn't want you to feel like you needed to rush."

"It was with Pajari," Jotham found himself sharing something he never shared.

"Oh." Jacinda grimaced slightly. "You have my sympathies. I don't know how you put up with that man."

"He isn't that bad." When Jacinda raised an eyebrow, he laughed. "Okay, yes he is, but over the cycles I've learned to zone him out."

"You would have to."

"Would you like something to drink? Chesney said he sent up a variety, but I only see the wine."

"That's because I sent the rest back and yes, I'd love a glass. I always looked forward to having your House wine when there was a dinner at the Palace."

"You did?" Jotham expertly opened the bottle.

"Yes, it's very good."

"It is, but I was referring to you sending the other beverages back."

"Oh, well, for some reason they sent up caffeinated coffee and energized tea. If you were to drink that this late at night, you would never get to sleep. I told... I'm afraid I didn't catch his name, to replace both with decaffeinated."

"That would be Morven. I... thank you. I never gave that a thought."

"Chesney should have. It's one thing to drink it when you're up early and have a busy day, but after a certain time you need to switch so you can shut down and get the rest you need."

He poured a generous amount of wine into a crystal glass. "In his defense, Chesney knows I usually work late into the night."

Jacinda took the glass he extended before turning to sit on the couch. "That's no excuse."

Jotham liked her sitting there, so comfortable and at ease on his couch. She tucked a leg under her and rested one arm along its low back. Did she know how beautiful she looked sitting there? But it was more than her looks, it was her concern for him. She sat there as if she were always meant to be there. Maybe she was.

"So are you going to instruct him in how to properly handle his duties?" Jotham asked as he poured himself a glass of wine.

"Of course not," she immediately replied. "I would never presume like that."

Jotham gave her a sharp look, but her amazing blue-green eyes sparkled and her lips hinted at a smile as they touched the rim of her glass to take a sip of wine.

Moving to the couch, he imitated her pose laying his hand over hers. "What if I want you to presume?"

"Jotham...."

"Do you know how long it's been since someone has done what you just did for me?" While he looked her in the eye, his fingers ran over the top of her hand, gently caressing the soft skin.

"What did I do?" Jacinda was surprised to find herself slightly breathless.

"You took care of me. You saw something you felt could adversely affect me and corrected it. You didn't ask. You just did it."

"I believe your staff does that too."

"Not like this. They know I like my coffee strong and sweet. When I ask for it, that's what I get, day or night. I am the King after all."

"You're also a man."

"I honestly think you are the only one that sees me that way."

Jacinda's eyes searched his face and saw he was serious. "As a woman, I find that hard to believe, but I do understand how you might. Stephan was always being approached by people, no matter where we were and no matter if it was appropriate. He was their Assemblyman and they felt that gave them the right to interrupt, to intrude, and to ask things they'd never ask someone else. Your position is much more powerful, more important. It's... more comforting for some to see you as a figurehead rather than a man. Men make mistakes, have bad days. Figureheads don't, they're just there to serve us."

"It seems that way sometimes."

"But you are a man, Jotham." She turned her hand over to squeeze his hand. "A powerful, important man, yes, but still you have the right to just be a man too. You have the right to have a life beyond your position."

"I'm not sure I know how to any longer."

"Well, let's start with this. Tell me about your day."

"What?" Jotham frowned at her.

"Tell me about your day. It's a normal conversation to have at the end of the day and you've obviously had a long one."

"Are you subtly trying to tell me I look tired?" He enjoyed the darkening of her cheeks as he teased her.

"Maybe a little." She instinctively reached out with the hand holding her wine, only to stop just shy of touching him.

"Please. Do." The words were out before he could stop them and he was rewarded by the light brush of a finger against his temple.

"I watched the ceremony on the Bering today. You didn't speak until ten, even though the ceremony started an hour before. That means you were there, at the latest, by eight. Which means you were on your way to the Bering by six."

"Half past six," Jotham corrected. "I've recently acquired a new ship designed by the House of Knowledge. It's shortened my travel time immensely."

"I'm glad, but you've still been going all day, without a break from what I can tell, and now you're sitting here with me."

"It's the best thing that's happened to me today. The only thing I've had to look forward to since our lunch together if you want to know the truth."

"I always want the truth." A knock on the door stopped her from saying more.

"Enter," Jotham ordered and tightened his hand around hers when she tried to pull away.

Jacinda watched as the man she'd ordered about earlier, wheeled in a new cart.

"Morven, this is Jacinda Michelakakis. Jacinda, Morven Blac."

"It's nice to meet you, Madame," he nodded to her slightly.

"You also, Morven. I apologize for not introducing myself before. It was very rude of me."

"Think nothing of it, Madame." He looked to Jotham. "Would there be anything else, Majesty?"

"No, Morven. Thank you and thank you for seeing to Jacinda's request so quickly."

"I..." Morven's eyes went from the clasped hands on the couch to Jacinda, then back to Jotham. "It was no problem, Majesty. Goodnight."

"Goodnight, Morven."

Jacinda finished her wine, then leaned forward to set the glass on the table. "I should be going."

"What? Why?"

"It's getting late and you need to rest." She went to rise.

"Please. Stay a little longer. Tell me about your day."

"Jotham..."

"Please?" Leaning over, he refilled her glass and handed it back to her and waited.

"You are incorrigible sometimes, Jotham Tibullus." Jacinda took a sip of her wine. "Let's see, what did I do today?" She tapped a finger from her freed hand against her lip. "I started out by having coffee in the garden and catching up on some correspondence until the Christening Ceremony started. After that, I ran a few errands then spent the rest of the afternoon weeding the garden."

"You don't have someone to take care of that?"

"I have a gardener. He comes in every couple weeks to do the majority of the work, but I like to putter in it too." She smiled at him. "After that I got a call to have drinks and here I am."

"And I'm glad you're here." Jotham captured her hand again, this time lacing their fingers together.

She tipped her head to the side slightly. "Why am I here, Jotham?" Her eyes sharpened. "Tell me it has nothing to do with Amina and Barek because I'm not going to help you with that."

Jotham looked at her and found himself chuckling. "No, it doesn't. You know, Will was right about you. You don't play games. You say what you think."

"Will? You talked to William Zafar about me? Why would you do that?" Jacinda jerked her hand from his, hurt by the thought that he would do that.

"Jacinda," Jotham quickly set his glass down as she did and grabbed her arm to stop her from rising. "It's not what you think. Well, it might be because I don't know what you are thinking. All I know is that I needed to talk to someone about what I was feeling, about *you*. Will is the only person I could do that with."

Jacinda stopped trying to pull away and looked at him. "I don't understand."

"Will is my oldest friend. I've known him all my life. We've been through life and death together."

"I know all *that*. What I don't understand is why you felt you needed to talk to him about *me*."

"Because I screwed up. With you. More than once." He shook his head disgusted with himself. "And I don't understand why!" Now it was Jotham who tried to rise and Jacinda who stopped him.

"Talk to me, Jotham."

Jotham looked down at the hand on his arm. It was so soft, he'd felt how soft and so delicate looking. But it was also strong.

But it wasn't her actual strength that was holding him. It was the strength of her feelings... for him... that held him.

"I don't know what to say. You..." He closed his eyes and covered her hand with his.

"I?"

"I look at you, talk to you and the rest of the world goes away. All its demands. All its pressures. Maybe for only a minute but for that minute I can breathe, I can relax, for the first time in cycles." He reached up to cup one of her cheeks. "Then I say or do something stupid and you're gone. It all comes crashing back down on me, worse than before."

"Jotham..." Jacinda felt her eyes start to fill.

"Will saw it. Saw me struggling. He's probably the only one who would. So he cornered me, demanding to know what was wrong. I found it all pouring out of me. I didn't do it to hurt you."

Jacinda looked up at him silently for several moments, then nuzzled her cheek against his hand. "Alright."

Jotham's eyes widened slightly. "That's it? Alright?"

"Do you want it not to be?"

"No! But still..." he took a deep breath. "You are too understanding, Jacinda."

"Oh I don't know about that, just ask my children, but I understand your needing someone to talk to in confidence."

"Thank you."

"Oh don't thank me yet, you still haven't told me what he said."

"What he said?"

"Yes. The High Admiral hardly knows me. It's been cycles since I last spoke to him and that was when he was still an

Admiral and Stephan was alive. At a Royal dinner, if I remember correctly. In honor of some new mining treaty. We were seated next to one another."

"Well, he remembers you, from the Academy actually."

"Really?"

"Yes. It seems you made quite an impression on him."

"How could I have possibly done that?"

"Well," reaching out he picked up their glasses, handed her one, then settled back on the couch. Once she did the same, he laced his fingers back through hers and continued. "It seems that my best friend had a crush on you back in the Academy."

"What!" Jacinda nearly choked on the amazing wine she'd just taken a sip of.

"Yes, and he couldn't understand why you weren't just as enamored with him as he was with you." Jotham knew he was embellishing the story slightly, but liked how Jacinda blushed the way he told it.

"I... I never knew."

"You don't remember your 'date' with him?"

"Date? I never 'dated' Will Zafar!"

"He claims it changed his life. That it made him the man he is today."

Jacinda opened her mouth, then snapped it shut taking in the teasing glimmer in his violet eyes. Praise the ancestors, he was irresistible. "Jotham Tibullus, you are lying to me."

"I am not. Maybe stretching the truth slightly, but I couldn't resist." He gave her his most disarming smile, one he hadn't used in cycles. "You are just so cute when you are all riled up."

"Cute? Are you seriously calling me *cute*? I haven't been called that since I was a child."

"That's because everyone else only sees how seriously beautiful you are. They overlook the 'cuteness.'"

Jacinda found she didn't know how to respond to that. To Jotham actual seeing her as more than just a pretty face. So few did.

"Tell me more about this 'life-changing' date I supposedly had with William Zafar."

"Well... it wasn't really a *date*. He was trying to get you to go on one with him."

Jacinda frowned as she searched her memory but couldn't remember anything. Yes, she'd had classes with Will, as he went by back then. She remembered how he always seemed to breeze through the classes, barely applying himself while she would study every night and admitted she struggled with the physical training required. She had never been a weak woman but then again she never wanted to be one that was ever mistaken for a man either. Jacinda liked being a woman. The only time she remembered ever talking to Will one-on-one was...

"Are you talking about the cafeteria?"

"That would be it."

"How in the name of the ancestors could those, what had they been fifteen minutes, have changed his life?" She turned a sharp eye on him. "You made that up just to get a reaction out of me."

"Well, while I'll admit I like teasing you, and that I have embellished the story slightly, Will's exact words were, 'that it was the first truly serious conversation he ever had with a woman and that after it he thought about his future differently.'"

Jacinda's eyes searched his. "You're serious."

"Absolutely."

"What could I have possibly said...."

"You told him you had no desire to be the wife of the High Admiral."

"I did?" Jacinda frowned. "I don't remember that. I remember that I always thought he never fully applied himself. He had so much potential but seemed more interested in girls. But then again he was a seventeen-cycle boy."

"Yes, but you made him think, made him see himself differently. And I for one have to thank you. Can you imagine what our world would have been like if Will had been a different man?"

"No. He is the hero of the Battle of Fayal. He brought the lost Princess home and discovered that Prince Audric was a traitor. Thanks to that, I still have my daughter."

"What are you talking about?" Jotham stiffened.

"Ten cycles ago, when the Regulians were making those speed attacks against the Fleet. Do you remember them?"

"Yes," Jotham said through tense lips.

" My daughter, my youngest, Stephanie, was assigned to the Talon."

"I..." Jotham didn't know what to say.

"The Retribution was returning to Carina with Cassandra. No one but Will knew she was the lost Princess, the true Queen. He let everyone believe he had been taken in by a much younger woman."

"Yes," Jotham remembered, he'd thought so too.

"But he still made sure she was protected. He pulled extra security from other ships to guarantee it. He pulled Stephanie from the Talon. If he hadn't..."

"She would have died with the rest of the Talon's crew when the ship experienced rapid decompression."

"Yes. It took days before she was able to contact me and tell me she was alive."

"I'm sorry, Jacinda."

"It wasn't your fault." Reaching up she touched his cheek. "It's something that's always in the back of every parent's mind when their child is serving in the Fleet. The thought that they might not come home. I'm just thankful she's on planet right now. Not that I'm going to get to see her much."

"Why not? If she's on leave, isn't she here?"

"She's not on leave. Well, she was." She raised an eyebrow at him. "Didn't Nicholas tell you we bumped into him several weeks ago?"

"No. He never said a word."

"Oh well, we did. Anyway, Stephie was only here for a week. Now she's in Kisurri training with Captain Chamberlain."

"She was accepted into Peter's first class?" Jotham couldn't hide his shock. "The elimination process was *brutal*."

"So she told me. It's why she was so thrilled to be accepted." Jacinda looked down at her wrist unit amazed at how much time had passed. "I should go."

"No, please stay, you haven't even had dessert yet."

"Jotham, I'm fine and it's late. I'm sure you have a full day scheduled tomorrow. You need to rest."

"Not yet." Rising he extended his hand. "There's something I've been wanting to do since the Ball. Will you indulge me?"

Jacinda looked up at him and suddenly realized Jotham rarely 'indulged' himself, let alone asked for someone else to. She found she couldn't deny him and was intrigued by what he was about to ask of her and reached out to take his hand. "Alright."

Jotham pulled her to her feet then led her to the center of the room before he released her hand to move to the wall comm. After pressing several buttons, he turned to face her. Slowly he walked back to her and watched her eyes widen as the music started.

"Ever since the Ball, I've wanted to dance with you again. I've wanted to hold you the way I really wanted to."

She was surprised when Jotham pulled her flush against his body instead of holding her at the appropriate distance. "Jotham?"

"Do you mind?" He looked down at her, enjoying the curve of her neck when she tipped her head back to look up at him. She enjoyed how her steps instinctively matched his, how his hand nearly spanned her lower back when he brought her even closer. It was amazing how her breasts felt pressed against his chest.

"No," she moved her hand from its traditional place on his shoulder further up so her fingers could brush the skin along his neck. "I don't mind at all."

They danced silently for several moments, Jotham curling the hand clasped in his to his chest.

"This is how we should always dance," he whispered against her temple. He felt her smile against his chest and wondered what she was thinking. He should have realized she would tell him.

"Can you imagine the look on Adelaide Pajari's face if we did?"

Jotham smiled at the thought. "It can't get anymore... pinched than it already is."

"Oh yes, it can. You've only ever seen her 'the King is near' face."

"She has another one?" he asked rubbing his cheek against the hair she'd left down, enjoying its silky feel and hint of roses.

"Oh yes. It looks like she's biting down on a sour citron."

"Seriously?" He leaned back slightly to stare down at her. "I would like to see that."

"Oh, no you wouldn't." She tipped her head back to smile up at him. "It's not a pretty sight."

"You are though. Here in my arms." Jotham's feet stilled and his hands shifted so they framed her face as his eyes stared intensely down into hers. "I'm going to kiss you, Jacinda. If you don't want me to, say so now."

Jacinda felt her heart begin to pound with an anticipation she hadn't felt in cycles. It was as if she were a girl again and about to experience her first kiss.

Jotham's lips barely brushed over hers, testing her willingness. When the hand on the back of his neck tightened, encouraging him, he brushed them again increasing the pressure.

"Jotham, stop teasing me," she demanded against his lips, her nails sinking into his scalp.

So Jotham pressed his lips firmly against hers and Jacinda felt her world tilt.

Jotham kissed her like a starving man, capturing her lips in a kiss so deep and hard she felt it all the way down to the toes she was standing on to try to get closer to him.

When was the last time she'd been kissed like this? With such passion? With such obvious need? It wrapped around her and tilted her world off its axis. Groaning, she wrapped her arms around his neck and held on.

Jotham couldn't believe how amazing Jacinda felt as he ran a hand down her back, pressing her closer against him. How perfectly her body molded against his. Her lips were so soft. She was so responsive. When had any first kiss ever felt so... natural?

It hadn't with Lata. Their first kiss had been a fumbling of noses and lips and she'd been so young, so innocent. He could still remember the first time they'd truly been together. It had been the night of their Union and it had been both their first times. He knew no one would believe Lata had been his first, not even Will, but she had been. He had always known there could be serious repercussions if he ever acted foolishly. Then, at sixteen he'd met Lata.

Jacinda pulled her mouth from Jotham's to look at him. The passion she felt coming from him suddenly seemed.... subdued and she didn't know why. "Jotham?"

Jotham saw the question in her eyes and wanted to kick himself. How had he allowed himself to be distracted by the past? He rested his forehead on hers. "I'm sorry."

"For what?" She saw the conflict in his eyes. "Talk to me, Jotham. Tell me the truth. That's the only way this even has a chance of working."

Leaning back he told her bluntly. "I was thinking of Lata." He watched her pale.

Jacinda jerked her arms from around his neck. She couldn't believe how that hurt or how much guilt she felt because she hadn't given Stephan one thought during that kiss.

"I see." When she moved to leave his embrace he refused to let her.

"I'm sorry."

"There's no reason to be sorry for being honest, Jotham." Reaching up she touched his cheek.

"There is if it hurts you."

"No." Slowly she took a step back and this time he let her. "Pretending would hurt more. You loved Lata. I know that. I loved Stephan. It's not something either of us can or should deny." Turning, she reached down and picked up their glasses, handing him his.

"No." Jotham took his glass from her and watched her sit down on the couch. "Where does that leave *us*?"

"I honestly don't know." Jacinda took a bracing sip before looking up at him still standing there, looking so confused. "Maybe nowhere."

"I refuse to accept that. I think about you all the time, Jacinda. I walked in the garden the other night and wished you were with me."

"Me or Lata?"

"*You!*" Jotham set his glass down and ran a frustrated hand through his hair. "I know I'm no good at this. I have so little experience."

"No good at what?"

"Relationships. With a woman. Lata was the only one I ever really had one with and that was so long ago..."

Jacinda slumped back into the couch trying to figure out what Jotham was telling her. "Are you saying that..." she snapped her jaw shut, she knew she had to be wrong.

"Ask Jacinda, no pretending."

"Alright, are you saying that Lata was your *first*?" She hoped she wouldn't have to get more explicit than that.

"Yes, just as I was hers."

"I... I never once considered that." Jacinda raised an eyebrow as she thought. "But the more I think of it, the more it makes sense. Lata was two cycles younger than you. Only eighteen at your Union."

"Yes. I never would have pressured her like that."

"You never... strayed, when you were away from her?"

"No. Would you have strayed from Stephan after you had met him?"

"No. Never." There was no doubt in her voice.

"So you understand."

"I do." Jacinda gave him an understanding look. "I remember how hard it was to reach out that first time after Stephan's death. I was lonely and alone, it had been four cycles and he was an old family friend. It didn't work out."

"There was another?"

"Hmmm... several cycles later. He was everything I once thought I wanted."

"Which was?"

"Quiet. Unassuming. Undemanding. Not in the public eye. I found myself quickly bored out of my mind." Jacinda found herself smiling sadly as she remembered Paul. "He was a good man."

"Just not for you."

"No. You?"

Jotham knew she was asking him to share and wondered how much he could. "I honestly can't tell you how Rani happened. I barely remember it. I just knew she wasn't someone I wanted to remain with, but then she discovered she had conceived and..."

"You were as shocked as the rest of us," she finished for him.

"Yes."

"The others?"

"Others?"

Jacinda gave him a small smile. "You've always done an excellent job at keeping your private life... well private, Jotham. Except for Rani, there's never been any talk about your other women."

"Is that what you think?"

"I... well... yes."

"The reason there's been no talk, Jacinda, is because there's been no one since Rani. I couldn't believe I'd done that. It felt like I had betrayed Lata and after that I couldn't allow any other woman close."

"What?!!" Jacinda shot straight up off the couch. "Jotham, that's been over thirty cycles ago!"

"I know that."

"So I'm only the..."

"Second woman I've seriously kissed? Yes."

"You don't count Rani?"

"I don't remember ever kissing her."

"I see."

"Do you? Because I don't. I'm attracted to you, Jacinda. Very attracted, but I feel like I'm sixteen again and have no clue what I'm doing."

"Thank the ancestors it's not just me."

"You feel that way too?"

"Yes," Jacinda found herself laughing. "I haven't been kissed like that... well, I'm not sure I ever have, but I'm like you, Jotham, just trying to find my way. I never once thought that might include you."

A firm knock on the door interrupted him from saying more.

"Enter," Jotham ordered, not happy at the interruption.

"Majesty," Deffand stepped in bowing slightly. "Sorry for the interruption, but the High Admiral in on the comm. He says it's important."

Jotham knew it would have to be for Will to call him at this time of night. "Alright. Jacinda." He turned to her, his eyes full of regret.

"It's okay. I need to be going anyway."

"I..." He wanted to ask her to stay, but he had no idea what Will needed, or how long it would take. "I'm sorry."

"Don't be. It's late and these things happen."

"Unfortunately they do. Deffand, you will see Jacinda to her transport." He gave his Captain a hard look.

"Of course, Majesty."

"Jacinda." He turned, pulling her close.

"It's alright, Jotham." She let her hands rest on his chest, gently moving them in a soothing motion. "I understand."

"Thank you." Ignoring Deffand, he leaned down capturing her lips in a hard kiss. "I'll contact you tomorrow."

"Okay," she whispered slightly breathless then reached up to caress his cheek. "Remember, no caffeinated drinks this late at night then you'll be able to get a good night's sleep."

"Thank you." Jotham found himself kissing the tip of her nose before he forced himself to step away and leave the room.

∞ ∞ ∞ ∞ ∞

"Thank you for the escort, Nicholas." Jacinda entered the code that opened the door to her transport.

"It was my pleasure, Jacinda, truly." Nicholas paused then found himself asking. "How is your daughter? Did she get to Kisurri okay?"

"Don't you know?" Jacinda found herself having to fight to hide her smile.

"How would I know?" Nicholas frowned at her.

"Well, you *are* the Captain of King Jotham's Guard."

"Yes, but I would never abuse that power for a personal situation."

"And is my daughter a 'personal situation'?"

"I..." Nicholas felt his skin darkening.

Jacinda took pity on the man. "She made it there just fine, Nicholas. I don't expect to hear from her again for several weeks, but I will let you know when I do."

"I... thank you, Jacinda. You will drive carefully?"

"I always do, Nicholas. You make sure you get some sleep too. You can't do your job if you're exhausted." With one last smile, she slipped into her transport.

∞ ∞ ∞ ∞ ∞

Jacinda found herself smiling as she drove through the quiet streets of Pechora. She'd never had a night like this one before. Stephan had been experienced, something he'd been proud of and Jacinda had never had anything to complain about. She'd enjoyed everything he'd shown her, everything she'd experienced with him.

Yet with Jotham it was different. Neither of them was sure of themselves. Both had doubts, fears left by the lives they'd lived. But they still seemed to be finding their way to each other.

She couldn't wait to see what tomorrow would bring.

A sudden flash was her only warning, causing her to look to her right just as her transport was suddenly struck on the passenger's side, sliding the entire vehicle across the road until it slammed into a luminaire pole.

∞ ∞ ∞ ∞ ∞

"Madame! Madame! Are you alright?"

Jacinda shook her head and tried to focus on the face that was in front of her. What was going on?

"Madame! Madame, can you tell me your name?"

"Jacinda... Jacinda Michelakakis," she told him and wondered why her voice sounded so strange. Forcing her mind to function she took in the situation around her. She was still sitting in her transport, but instead of it being the beautiful vehicle Stephan had insisted she had to have, it was now half its normal size and its windshield was shattered.

"What happened?" she asked lifting a hand to her suddenly aching head.

"You were involved in an accident, Madame Michelakakis."

"An accident? Was anyone hurt?"

"Just you, ma'am."

"Me? I'm not hurt." But she grimaced as she moved to show him.

"Please, ma'am, be still."

"I'm fine, young man. A little shaken up but otherwise fine. If you'd just help me out of my transport."

"Yes, ma'am." Reluctantly he helped her out.

Jacinda took in the scene around her and felt her heart drop. There was another transport, its front-end crushed in, just a few feet away from hers. A young man no more than eighteen cycles sitting on the curb his head in his hands.

"I thought you said no one else was hurt!" She turned hard eyes to the man helping her.

"He isn't hurt, ma'am, not a scratch on him. He's just upset that he wrecked his father's transport." He gave the boy a disgusted look.

"You're sure he's not hurt?"

"Yes, ma'am. Ma'am, is there someone I can call to come get you?

"My transport's not drivable?"

"No, ma'am, and honestly I wouldn't let you drive even if it was. You've got a pretty good bump on your head. I'd like to have you transported to a medical unit, just to have you checked out."

"No, I'm fine. If you would call my son for me, I'd appreciate it. His name is Danton. Assemblyman Danton Michelakakis and his comm contact is..."

Chapter Thirteen

"Anything I need to be aware of?" Deffand demanded from his second-in-command Lieutenant Kort Green. After seeing Jacinda to her transport last night, he had finally ended his shift for the day and done as she had recommended and gotten some sleep. Now, ten hours later, he was back at the Palace ready to protect his King.

"Nothing pressing. King Jotham has meetings in his office all day so he won't be leaving the Palace." He flipped a page. "The guards along the south perimeter reported that a group of kids attempted to gain access to the outer wall overnight."

"What?!!"

"They were apprehended twenty feet from the wall. They carried no weapons and were petrified when confronted. It seems the boys were trying to impress the girls, who were with them, which made them brave enough to sneak up and touch the wall."

"Stupid kids," Deffand muttered. "They could have been killed."

"Yes, and that was strongly explained to them and their parents when they arrived to retrieve them. We won't be having any problems from them again."

"Good."

Green turned another page. "There will be groups of children from Pechora touring the Public Wing today for Heritage Day."

"Is it that time of cycle again?" Deffand groaned.

"I'm afraid so."

"Double the guards on all doors and put a set on the *inside* of the corridor leading from the Public Wing. It never fails, somehow one of those little brats finds a way in."

"Already done," Green grinned at him. "They are inventive, aren't they?"

"That's one word for them. Anything else?"

"No." He was just about to close the report when one more thing caught his eye. "Oh, Pechora transit reported that they responded to an accident early this morning involving the family member of an Assemblyman."

"Injuries?"

"Just bumps and bruises. She was lucky. All her transport safety devices deployed. Her transport, on the other hand, is a total loss."

"It was that serious an accident?"

"The other transport was going twice the limit and struck her directly on the passenger side as she was going through an intersection."

"She was taken to the hospital?"

"No, she refused and insisted they call her son to pick her up."

"Her son..." Deffand started to get a sick feeling in his stomach and grabbed the report from Green rapidly reading until he found what he hoped he wouldn't. "Jacinda Michelakakis."

"Yes," Green frowned at him. "She's the mother..."

"Of Danton Michelakakis. Why wasn't I immediately made aware of this?!!" Deffand demanded his eyes piercing Green's.

"I... it was late, sir. She wasn't seriously injured. There was no reason to contact you."

"Do you know who this *is*?"

"She's the mother of an Assemblyman."

"She is also the widow of Assemblyman Stephan Michelakakis and..." Deffand cut off the rest of the sentence and headed for the door as he snapped out orders. "Get the men ready. *All* of them! Notify Scheer to prepare the King's transport."

∞ ∞ ∞ ∞ ∞

Chesney sighed silently as he reviewed his King's schedule. It was full again. The first moon cycle at the start of a new Assembly was like this. Everyone wanting to make sure the King heard about what *they* thought needed accomplished.

Looking across the room, he watched Assemblyman Fiala reading through the stack of papers he'd brought with him as he sat, waiting for his appointment with the King. It was Chesney's job to try and keep the King on schedule, to make sure meetings didn't go longer than their allotted time. He could already tell he was going to have a hard time doing that today.

His eyes shifted to the door when it opened, then widened when Deffand came with a barely contained intensity that, without a word told Chesney something was wrong. Very wrong, and that the King's entire schedule was ruined.

"Who is with King Jotham?"

"Assemblyman Terwilliger."

If anyone other than Deffand had moved to interrupt one of the King's meetings, Chesney would have been on his feet blocking him, but after all the cycles they'd worked together he knew Deffand would never interrupt if it weren't urgent.

Turning back to his desk, he began to pull out what he would need to change the King's schedule.

∞ ∞ ∞ ∞ ∞

"You're looking well, Majesty." Terwilliger leaned back and let his gaze travel over Jotham and realized his words were true.

Jotham did look well. He looked well-rested and... happy? When was the last time he'd seen his King happy.

"Thank you, Evander. I am feeling well and you?"

"Very well, Majesty. Excited about the new cycle."

"As am I."

"I'm also excited to be working with Danton Michelakakis."

"I have high hopes for him."

"I agree. I've watched him grow over the cycles and he is truly his father's son. He will be a great asset to this House."

"You will help guide him?"

"Of course, Majesty. We've already had lunch together. He has some very... unique ideas. I don't agree with all of them, but..."

"You didn't expect to."

"No," Terwilliger smiled at Jotham. "I didn't always agree with his father, but I always respected Stephan."

"Good, now..."

Jotham frowned when the door to his office was suddenly thrust open. Chesney knew he was with Terwilliger and didn't want to be interrupted. But it wasn't Chesney who entered. It was Deffand.

"Majesty, I need to speak to you. Privately." His gaze shot to Assemblyman Terwilliger, who instantly got the silent message and stood.

"I'll just step out, Majesty." With a slight bow, he did just that shutting the door behind him. Turning, he saw Chesney moving efficiently but with an urgency that made him think his meeting with Jotham was over.

∞ ∞ ∞ ∞ ∞

"What's happened, Deffand," Jotham demanded bracing himself to hear that the Regulians had attacked again.

"I just received a report that last night, while returning home, Jacinda was involved in a transport accident." Deffand watched as all color left Jotham's face.

"Jacinda..." The word barely made it past his suddenly numb lips.

"The report states that she was not seriously injured," Deffand hurriedly informed him. "Only bumped and bruised. She refused to go to the hospital and Danton drove her home."

"She's alive?"

"Yes, Majesty!"

Jotham turned to his comm, refusing to let his fingers tremble as he punched in the code that would connect him to Jacinda, cursing at the time it took for someone to answer.

"Hello?"

The voice he'd been praying to hear came across the comm, but the screen remained dark.

"Unblock the feed, Jacinda!" he demanded.

"Jotham?"

"Who else would it be! Un. Block. The. Feed."

"Jotham, now's not really the best time."

"*Damn it, Jacinda!*" He slammed his fist down on his desk. "I know about the accident! Let me see you before I go out of my mind!"

As the blank screen dissolved, Jotham's breath caught. Before him, the most beautiful woman he'd ever seen sat, her hair loose, a lump the size of an Alder egg on her forehead and an eye starting to turn black.

"Jacinda..."

"I know. I look hideous, that's why I didn't want you to see me."

"Do you think I fucking care how you *look*? Why haven't you seen a doctor? Why aren't you in the hospital? Why did I have to find out about it from *Deffand*?"

With each sentence, Jotham's rage grew louder until it echoed off the walls.

"Jotham..."

"I'll be there shortly, Jacinda."

"What? Wait! No! Jotham, I'm fine! There's no reason for you to come here."

"No reason," Jotham's hard gaze traveled over her face on the screen as he spit out his next words. "For an intelligent woman, there are times when you are just plain *stupid*, Jacinda!" And with that he disconnected the call.

"Deffand, have my limisin readied," Jotham ordered as he rounded his desk heading for the door.

"It already is, Majesty, as are extra guards."

Entering the outer office Jotham ignored the Assemblymen, his gaze zeroing in on Chesney.

"Clear my day, Chesney."

"Already working on it, Majesty." But Jotham didn't hear him, he was already gone.

∞ ∞ ∞ ∞ ∞

Jacinda let her head fall to the back of her chair when Jotham disconnected. She'd never seen him so irate. Or so... scared, for that's what she'd seen in his eyes, hiding behind the anger. Fear. For her.

How could she have been so stupid not to realize the accident would be reported to the Palace? Not because of the budding relationship between her and Jotham because no one knew about that. But because anything involving an

Assemblyman or a member of his family was always reported to the Palace. She hadn't thought about it since Stephan was dead, but Danton was now an Assemblyman and as his mother it would be reported.

Maybe the accident had rattled her brain more than she'd thought. Now Jotham had found out second-hand and, of course, it had to have brought back memories of Lata. Of the transport accident, she'd been killed in.

She should have called Chesney so he could let Jotham know what had happened, but it had taken her hours to convince Danton she was okay even after Dr. Portman left, and by then he'd already contacted Ethan and Stephanie so she'd had to reassure them too.

Carina's first sun was just starting to rise when she'd finally been able to climb into her bed and collapse. She was only half way through her first cup of coffee when Jotham had called.

She had recognized his code immediately and blocked the live feed hoping to get away with the old ploy of saying she'd yet to fix her face. True but still.... She should have known better, this was Jotham she was talking about, and he knew her better than that.

Her stalling had only made it worse for him when that was what she'd been trying to avoid. Well, there was nothing she could do about it now. Rising she went to the kitchen, refilled her cup and poured a second before returning to the living room to wait.

∞ ∞ ∞ ∞ ∞

Jotham's finger's strummed impatiently on the seat of the limisin as it drove through Pechora. What could she have possibly been thinking, trying to keep this from him! Did she think he wouldn't find out? That he wouldn't care? She could have been killed, and he would have had to find out the same way he had with Lata.

No, he wasn't going there. He wasn't going to lose someone else he loved that way!

His fingers stilled.

Loved?

Where had that word come from?

It wasn't possible. Yes, he cared a great deal about Jacinda but love.... It was for the young. For those who hadn't found their life mates and failed them. He couldn't love Jacinda.

"Majesty."

Deffand's voice broke through Jotham's thoughts.

"We are here, Sire."

Jotham looked out his window to see that indeed, they had arrived at Jacinda's house. He could tell it was her house, although he had never been here before. It was stylish and naturally elegant just like its owner.

"I have guards stationed throughout the neighborhood and around the house. Just notify me when you are ready to leave." With that, Deffand stepped out putting his body between his King and the open area on the other side of the door.

Jotham stepped out of the limisin and strode up the walkway that led to the door that was opening as he approached.

∞ ∞ ∞ ∞ ∞

Jacinda rose as she heard the sound of multiple transports pulling into her drive. She knew one would be Jotham's limisin while the rest would be the large special transports that carried his security. Oh, Madame Nitzschke was going to have a field day with this.

Opening the door, she felt her breath catch at the imposing figure Jotham made striding so confidently and so angrily up her walk. Stepping back, she allowed him to enter before closing the door and shutting the rest of the world out.

"I've got coffee in the..." she trailed off as she turned to find him standing mere inches from her.

"Why didn't you call me?" The whispered words were made even more poignant by the trembling hand that carefully reached out to gently touch the bump on her forehead.

"I'm sorry," and she truly was. "I just wasn't thinking. They wanted me to go to the hospital, but I refused."

"Which was stupid!" While his voice was harsh, his touch remained gentle.

"It wasn't. I knew I was fine."

"You just said you weren't thinking straight!"

"About *calling* you, not how I *was*. I couldn't drive my transport home so I called Danton."

"You should have called *me*!"

"Don't be ridiculous!" She gave him a disbelieving look as she took a step back. "I couldn't have called *you* to come pick me up."

Jotham grabbed both of her arms, pulling her to her toes demanding, "Why the fuck not?"

Her gasp of pain had him paling and instantly he eased his grip, although he didn't let her go. "You're hurt worse than you said. Come on, you're going to see a doctor."

"No! Jotham, I'm fine! And I have seen a doctor."

"What? The report said you refused to go to the hospital."

"I did, but that doesn't mean I didn't call my personal doctor." She saw the relief in his eyes. "I just didn't want to be poked and prodded by a bunch of strangers. Dr. Portman has been my doctor for over twenty cycles and before him, his father was. I knew he would give me an honest assessment and he did. I have an alder egg-sized bump on my head but thanks to said head's hardness, it did no permanent damage. It's just going to leave a lovely, multicolored-bruise that will also affect my eye. I also have an assortment of bruises, mostly from my seat restraint, that will be sore for several days. Otherwise, I'm fine."

"Is that what he really said?" Jotham would be contacting him.

"Yes. Do you really think Danton would have left me alone if he hadn't?"

"That depends on whether you told him that or Dr. Portman did."

Jacinda laughed then grimaced when it caused her head to ache. "My son would never have fallen for that, Jotham. He had to hear it directly from Portman."

"So he wouldn't take your word for it."

"No more than you will. Would you like Portman's code or will you just have Chesney find it for you?"

Jotham had the grace to look guilty but still said, "I'll take the code."

"Men."

Jacinda waved her hands up in mock disgust, but Jotham noticed they didn't go as high nor were they as animated as they normally were. Jotham again asked the question she didn't answer.

Leading her to the couch, he carefully positioned her so she was facing him, making sure it caused her no pain. Then he framed her face in his hands, kissing first the bump on her forehead, then the darkening bruise around her eye before asking, "Why couldn't you call me, Jacinda?"

Looking at him she felt all his concern, all his fear, and also all his confusion. He really didn't understand. "Oh, Jotham," she let the uninjured side of her forehead rest against his while her hands rubbed his chest, trying to sooth him. "You are the King. I couldn't just call you even if I wanted to."

"Why not?" His voice broke on the last word.

"Because... I don't have your code."

She felt him jerk back as if shot by a stunner. "What? What do you mean? I've called you."

"Yes, but you don't really believe that just because you call someone that they would be able to call you back, do you?" She raised an eyebrow at him. "Your code is always blocked, Jotham. If it wasn't, you'd have thousands of calls a day."

"I..."

"You'd forgotten that, hadn't you?"

"I... yes, I guess I had. I'll make sure that is corrected. I want you to be able to call me, Jacinda. Whenever you want, whenever you need. I never want to experience what I did this morning again. It was too much like..." he couldn't finish.

But she knew he was referring to Lata's death. "I'm sorry." Leaning forward, she kissed him gently. "So sorry." She kissed him again trying to convey all her regret for what he had gone through, trying to make him understand that she would never willingly put him through that.

Chapter Fourteen

Jotham closed his eyes and sank into the kiss.
He thought he had lost this.
Again.
Another transport accident.
Another woman he loved.
But she wasn't lost. She was in his arms. Kissing him and he was never going to let her out of them again. It seems Will had been right. When he decided on a woman that was it. His heart had decided on Jacinda and he wasn't going to waste one more precious moment of their time together.

∞ ∞ ∞ ∞ ∞

Jacinda felt the shift. Suddenly, a kiss she started went from her trying to comfort Jotham to him swamping her with a need so powerful it stole her breath. Her hands fisted into his shirt as her world began to tilt.
Suddenly, she realized the world wasn't tilting; *she was*.
Jotham had lifted her off the couch and into his arms.
"Where's your bedroom?" he demanded against her lips.
"Down the hall and to the left." She found herself instantly answering him.
Jotham wasted no time carrying her down the hall. He'd wasted enough of it because of his pride and insecurity. He was done with that. He wasn't just going after what he wanted. He was going to get it.
Moving to the foot of the bed, he shifted his grip letting her slide down his body as he deepened the kiss, slipping his tongue between her lips. Truly tasting her for the first time and she tasted better than Fudge Torta.

Carefully, remembering her bruises, he ran his hands up her back keeping her flush against him. He enjoyed the silky feel of whatever she was wearing. He vaguely remembered it being long, black and clingy when she had opened the front door. He had other concerns then.

Now he just wanted it off so he could touch her skin.

As his hands reached her neck, he pulled back slightly breaking the kiss to look down at her. Jacinda's face was tilted up to his, her lips moist from his kiss, her blue-green eyes full of desire and even bruised, she was the most beautiful thing he had ever seen.

Slowly, watching her the whole time, his fingers slid down the soft skin on either side of her neck to slip under the silky material, slowly moving it aside, exposing the beautiful skin of her shoulders before it fell away. What it had been concealing was breathtaking.

Lace straps graced her shoulders moving down to a modest bodice of more lace that perfectly conformed to her large, full breasts before the silky material returned flowing to the floor.

"Beautiful." Leaning down slightly, he kissed the soft skin where her neck and shoulder met and felt her tremble slightly. "Shh," he whispered against her skin. "It's alright, Jacinda."

"I know," she said and tipped her head to the side, giving his lips easier access to the area they wanted.

Kissing his way down along her shoulder, his fingers slid the straps out of the way then pulled them down her arms taking the bodice with it.

And it was his turn to tremble because of the bruising he revealed.

"Jacinda..."

Carefully, so carefully, he kissed the offensive bruise that slashed its way across her body. It started at her shoulder, traveling between her breasts on down to disappear around her waist. He knew it came from the transport restraint that had kept her safe.

"It's fine, Jotham."

"It's not," the anger in his voice at odds with the softness of his lips, "but at least you are safe."

He continued to kiss his way along the mark, leaving the dark path only when he reached the inside curve of a breast. Using his nose, he nuzzled the abundant globe, drawing in the unique scent that was Jacinda. Sweetness, warmth, and just the hint of roses. He would never smell a rose again and not think of her.

He continued to circle the golden flesh, kissing, licking and nipping his away around it until he finally reached its high, taut summit. He paused for only a moment, his hot breath bathing the dark, turgid peak before he consumed it.

"Jotham!"

As she called out his name, he felt her fingers sink into his hair, pulling him closer and he drew harder on her, wanting to hear it again.

His hands tightened on her hips, rubbing his throbbing shaft still painfully encased in his pants against her now naked abdomen. He nudged her to take a step back and lowered her onto the bed. Following her down, he braced himself on his elbows and turned his attention to her other breast, making sure it didn't feel neglected.

∞ ∞ ∞ ∞ ∞

Jacinda dug her fingers deeper into Jotham's thick, dark hair keeping his mouth exactly where she needed it to receive the most pleasure. She wasn't a young girl that didn't know what she was doing, who didn't know what was needed to give and receive pleasure. Yet with Jotham, everything was new, exciting and slightly frightening.

She knew she wasn't a young woman. She was a mother, a widow, and a grandmother. Yet when he looked at her, all that faded away and she was just Jacinda, a woman who desired a man.

When Jotham had kissed her the night before it had curled her toes, but the kiss he gave her today.... it curled around her soul and reawakened parts of her she'd forgotten existed.

When he'd carried her, so easily, she'd felt like a young girl again, in the arms of her hero. She'd worried when he started to remove her nightgown. She was battered and bruised, but instead of being repelled, his eyes had filled with the concern of a man more concerned about her than himself. Every bruise, every hurt he kissed felt like a balm that did more to ease her pain than the pills Dr. Portman had given her.

Now, even as she felt his need pressing against her, he laid over her making sure not to press too heavily, concerned he could harm her. He was a true gentleman.

And she wanted all of him.

"Jotham... you're teasing me again."

The look she received, when Jotham stopped teasing her other nipple, made her breath catch.

"You think I am teasing you?" His amazing violet eyes were nearly black, his voice nearly a growl.

"Yes!"

"Well we can't have that now, can we?"

∞ ∞ ∞ ∞ ∞

JACINDA'S CHALLENGE

Jacinda's words burned through Jotham's system. Driving him on. He thought, for a moment, that he would need to be gentle with Jacinda. It was their first time together and she had been injured, but he had underestimated her.

Jacinda was a mature woman.

She didn't play around.

She told him exactly what she wanted and it was the same as he did.

He was going to give them what they both wanted.

With regret, he abandoned her breasts but that regret quickly turned to an amazing new discovery as he moved further down her body. He kissed a faded scar that he would ask her about later, and the red marks he knew were left from having her children.

Each spot he kissed drew him closer to her instead of away, as it might have in his younger, stupider cycles. Now he saw them as symbols of a life well-lived and he wanted to be a part of it.

Jotham was a King. Before that, he had been a Prince. Yet even then, he had never kneeled. Before anyone. It wasn't done. As he gazed at her dark chestnut curls, trimmed so beautifully, he found himself sliding between her legs and sinking into them, knowing it was the only way to honestly worship at the most feminine altar.

∞ ∞ ∞ ∞ ∞

Jacinda's eyes widened when Jotham went to his knees between her legs. Yes, Stephan had gone down on her, but for Jotham to do it? He was the King. Kings never kneeled, not even for their wives. It was an urban legend that while a King might satisfy a woman this way, he always laid across the bed, his knees never touching the floor.

"Jotham..." she rose up to her elbows, looking down at him.

"Shh," he said, his thumbs gently separating her damp curls. He knew they were that way because of him. It made him want to see how damp he could get her with just his kisses. He decided to find out.

Finally revealing her woman's nub, he leaned forward to taste the budding fruit.

"Jotham!"

His eyes shot up and felt his heart stutter. Jacinda was on her elbows, her head falling back, her long, lush hair streaming behind her. The breasts he so enjoyed moments earlier were thrust up forming full and proud peaks as she lost herself in what he was doing to her.

He had never seen anything so beautiful.

Never felt so powerful. He wanted more.

Closing his mouth around her, he tugged harder on her nub, his tongue licking causing her to groan.

"More please, Jotham."

And he gave her more, attacking her nub as if he as a starving man and she was the only thing that would sustain him.

∞ ∞ ∞ ∞ ∞

Jacinda couldn't believe what Jotham was doing to her.

What he was making her feel.

Never in her life had she felt this... need, coming from a man. All centered on her.

It was powerful.

It was humbling.

She didn't want it to end but already she could feel her orgasm building.

It had started when he kissed her, then the marks left from her accident. When he turned his attention to her breasts, every tug of his mouth had felt directly connected to her womb.

Now he was driving her higher with that same mouth and she was so close. She just needed a little more.

As if Jotham knew exactly what she needed, he slid a finger along her wet folds before slipping the thick digit slowly into her. Moving as deep as he could before retreating to add another, filling her, stretching her.

When his fingers twisted, finding that *exact* spot she needed she cried out, her heels digging into his shoulders as the orgasm exploded through her.

∞ ∞ ∞ ∞ ∞

Jotham could feel how close she was.

Could feel it in the tensing of her muscles, in her breathless cries and the tremors that were growing stronger. It wouldn't take much to send her over and he knew what it was.

Sliding a finger along her lush, full, lower lips, he coated it in her juices then slowly pressed against her opening with a finger demanding entry and she granted it. He pressed as far as he could into her tight softness then withdrew adding another finger stretching her as he knew she'd need to be to accept him.

Twisting his wrist, he crooked his fingers rubbing that spot he knew would send her over the edge and was rewarded by her cry of release.

∞ ∞ ∞ ∞ ∞

Jacinda's eyes tried to focus when Jotham rose from between her legs. She heard the unmistakable rustling of clothing being removed and then he was moving her to where he wanted her on the bed and slipped back between her legs.

The pressure as the head of Jotham's shaft demanded entrance finally had her eyes clearing and her breath caught at what she saw on Jotham's face.

"Jotham..."

"I need you, Jacinda." His voice was rough and so full of such restrained passion that her heart, that was just starting to return to its normal beat, sped up again.

"Then take me. I'm here."

She was shocked at what her words unleashed. With her permission, Jotham surged forward filling her completely with one stroke. His balls slapping against her with the strength of the move as he caged her beneath him.

"I'm not going to last long," he warned, capturing her lips as he pulled nearly completely out then quickly surged back into her.

"It doesn't matter," she gasped when he finally released her lips, lifting her hips to meet him thrust for thrust.

"It does." Jotham continued to thrust into her and felt that tingle he hadn't felt for cycles start down his spine. He felt his balls draw up and knew he was moments away from heaven. He refused to go without her and reached down between their bodies, caressing her nub in a way he somehow knew would drive her crazy.

"Jotham..."

"You will come for me again, Jacinda." He rubbed faster as he continued to pound into her.

"Jotham!" Jacinda couldn't believe that she was about to come again, it hadn't happened since she'd been such a much younger woman.

"Come!" he ordered. "I command it!" And she did.

∞ ∞ ∞ ∞ ∞

Jacinda was boneless. She could tell by the way her body melted around Jotham when he pulled her with him as he rolled onto his back after shouting out his release. There wasn't a part of him she couldn't feel. Not his chest pressing so firmly against her. Not his arms wrapped so securely around her. Not his lips pressed against her temple. With an arm around his waist, Jacinda let her mind absorb everything that had happened, and as she did she began to chuckle. A chuckle that turned into a full-blown laugh.

∞ ∞ ∞ ∞ ∞

Jotham rolled onto his back pulling Jacinda with him, having just experienced one of the most explosive releases of his life. It had felt so amazing that he found he didn't want it to end, not so much the release, but the feeling of being so connected with another living being.

He was sure Jacinda felt the same way, especially with how her leg settled so intimately between his, the way her arm wrapped around his waist as her head rested on his chest. That was until she started to laugh. He frowned when she looked up at him, her eyes full of mirth.

"I command you?" she chuckled. "Seriously?"

Before he could comment, she buried her face back into his chest.

"Praise the ancestors, Jotham, only *you* could have said something like that."

Jotham felt his color rise as he thought of how arrogant that must have sounded, but then again she had obeyed him...

"It seems to me that you liked it."

Jacinda's laughter trailed off. Resting her chin on his chest, she looked back to him.

"I did like it," she admitted, blushing. "I liked it a lot. I can think of only one thing you did that I didn't like."

"I did something you didn't like?" Jotham was instantly frowning.

"Mm-hmm." Pressing a hand against his stomach, she sat up unconcerned about her nudity.

"What did I do?" Jotham asked trying not to let her touch distract him from this all important answer. He wanted to please Jacinda, always.

"You stripped so quickly that I didn't get to enjoy the show."

"I... What?"

"I wanted to watch you strip." Her hand caressed the well-defined muscles of his chest. "You have no idea how many women have fantasized about seeing you naked."

"What?!!"

Jacinda smiled at the shocked look on Jotham's face.

"They talk about this chest." Leaning down she scattered kisses across it, paying special attention to each flat dark nipple until they pebbled with pleasure. "They wonder if it can be as magnificent as it looks in your jackets or if it is just the tailoring."

She'd never doubted it was him.

"They talk about this trim waist of yours." She eased her way down his body, kissing each individual muscle with her touch, as they became even more pronounced.

"We have all seen that incredible visual of you at the Academy. The one of you coming out of the pool, grinning, in those tiny trunks that revealed more than they covered. Including these abs."

Hearing Jotham groan, she looked up at him through her lashes.

"I hate that visual," he told her. "I tried to have it destroyed."

"Generations of women on Carina would have revolted." She knew they would have, for that visual was legendary. "I know for a fact that it still hangs, framed, in the girl's dorm at the Academy."

"Tell me you're joking."

Jacinda chuckled at the horrified look on Jotham's face but continued to kiss her way down his body.

"I'm afraid not, and every woman on Carina wants to know if you still have all eight of those incredibly tight abs."

Jotham arched up, groaning as her fingers just grazed the head of his rapidly recovering shaft.

"As you can tell, I don't," he groaned.

"No, you don't." Jacinda gave him a sassy little grin. "Just six. I am sooo disappointed." Sliding further down his body, slipping between his legs, her mouth replaced her fingers.

"Jacinda!"

She ignored him as she took his large, bulbous head deep into her mouth. She'd seldom done this for Stephan. Not because she didn't enjoy it, but because as their marriage went on, Stephan didn't. She'd never understood it, but she'd respected his wishes.

Jotham didn't seem to feel the same way. If the way his fingers were sinking into her hair, guiding her movements was any indication. Fisting the base of his shaft so he wouldn't choke her, she took as much of him in as she could. While her other hand cupped his heavy balls, gently rolling them.

Her tongue glided along the bulging vein on the underside of his shaft, feeling its rapid pulse before swirling around its head, capturing the pulse of essence he gave her. Moaning at his sweet taste, her cheeks hollowed as she sucked harder, wanting more.

"Ancestors! Don't stop, Jacinda!" Jotham pleaded, his breathing ragged, his fingers tightening in her hair as his hips pumped faster and deeper into the hot moist heat of her mouth. She felt his balls tighten in her hand and knew he was close. Going back down, she took him deep into her throat, swallowed, and Jotham exploded.

∞ ∞ ∞ ∞ ∞

Jotham collapsed onto his back, trying to regain control of his breathing and his mind after what Jacinda had just done to him. He would have never expected... never thought.... Praise the ancestors! How could a day have gone from terrible to incredible in such a short time?

His only thought after being told about her transport accident was to get to her side. To make sure she really was alive. When he'd been en route to Lata's accident, they only told him that it was serious. No one told him she had no chance of surviving it.

Today, Deffand had said Jacinda's accident was serious too, but that Jacinda was okay. He hadn't believed it, not until he *really* saw her. Held her. Kissed her. She'd changed his world. In more ways than one.

Feeling her move, he raised his head to look down at her and felt his world shift again. Her amazing teal eyes where luminous, her cheeks flushed. His fingers were still intertwined in her chestnut curls. Carefully shifting his grip, he encouraged her to move up his body until he could capture her lips in a tender kiss.

"You are an amazing woman, Jacinda," he murmured against her lips.

"Hmmm," she curled up into his arms, kissing him back. She was about to say more when her stomach spoke instead.

Jotham's eyes filled with mirth. "Hungry?"

Jacinda blushed slightly, "A little." Pressing a hand against his stomach she sat up, then heard his stomach rumble. "I'd say you are too. Come on, let's go see what's in the kitchen."

Chapter Fifteen

Jotham watched as Jacinda moved efficiently around her kitchen. Making coffee, getting plates and cups from the cupboards, selecting ingredients out of the cool unit. When was the last time he'd actually sat in a kitchen and watched someone prepare a meal?

Had he ever?

Searching his memory, he realized it had been back when he was a boy. He had been at the Zafar cabin and Will's mom had made them all first meal.

Since then his meals had always been brought to him.

He found he liked watching it be prepared, especially when it was by Jacinda who he knew was naked under that thin, silky robe she wore.

"What's put that look on your face?" Jacinda asked as she set a plate of fruit and pastries in front of him before turning to retrieve the pot of coffee. Sitting down, she poured them both a cup then slid the sweetener toward him.

"What look?" he asked innocently, taking a sip of the coffee he'd sweetened.

Jacinda just raised an eyebrow at him and he chuckled.

"Alright. I was just thinking how I liked watching you make me a meal, especially when I know what's under this robe or should I say isn't." He reached out to run a hand over the golden skin of a leg that had been exposed when she crossed them as she sat.

Her lips twitched and she raised her own cup to take a sip. "You, Jotham Tibullus, are incorrigible. Eat," she ordered.

Jotham did, but he kept his hand on her knee the entire time and the meal passed in a comfortable silence.

"How are you feeling?" His hand tightened on her knee, turning her swivel seat so she faced him. He saw her grimace a few times while eating.

"I'm fine."

"Jacinda." He gripped her chin, searching her eyes and saw the pain she was trying to hide from him. "Did Portman give you anything for pain?"

"Yes, he gave me some pills."

"Where are they?"

"On the nightstand, next to my bed."

"Stay here, I'll get them for you."

"Alright," she put a hand on his chest, her fingers caressing the skin left bare by his unbuttoned shirt. "Thank you."

Leaning down he gave her a gentle kiss. "Anytime. Now stay put."

The pills were easy to find and Jotham was quickly returning to her when he heard her moving around in the kitchen. He should have known she wouldn't listen to him. As he got closer, he realized she was actually talking to someone.

"I'm fine, Danton. Really. There's no need for you to come over."

Entering the kitchen, he found her facing him, talking on the comm.

"Mom, you were in a serious accident last night." Danton's voice filled the room.

"I know that, Danton, I was there."

"What were you doing out at that time of night?" he demanded.

"Excuse me?" The coolness of her tone along with Jacinda's raising that expressive eyebrow of hers at the screen should have warned Danton that he was treading on thin ice.

It did Jotham.

"There is no reason for a woman your age to be out that late." Danton continued, seemingly unaware he had just insulted his mother.

"A woman *my age*?"

Jotham literally cringed at Danton's words. Did the boy have a death wish? No man said something like that to a woman, mother or not.

"Mom, you know what I mean."

"No, Danton Lee Michelakakis, I do not. Why don't you just explain to me why a woman *my age* shouldn't be out at that time of night?"

"It wasn't night, Mother. It was *past midnight!*"

"And your point?" Movement in the doorway had Jacinda looking up to see Jotham silently standing there.

"Where could you have possibly been at that time?"

Jacinda took a deep breath and forced herself to calm as she turned her attention back to her son.

"Danton, I am a grown woman and I don't need to explain to *you* where I go and who I see. No matter what time it is."

"Are you saying you were... *with someone?!!*" The last two words were whispered in disbelieving horror.

"I am not saying that. What I am saying is that if I were, it would be none of *my son's* business. Now I thank you for coming and getting me last night, Danton, and I thank you for your concern today, but I'm fine and I'm ending this conversation before one of us says something truly hurtful. I'll talk to you later this week. I love you, Danton." And with that she disconnected.

Jotham walked over to the sink and filled a glass of water before he moved to stand in front of her. "Are you okay?"

"Yes." Reaching up she squeezed his hand holding her pill bottle. "I'm sorry you had to hear that."

"I'm not. You could have just told him you were coming from the Palace." He set the glass of water down and after reading the instruction on the bottle shook out a pill and handed it to her. "Take that."

"Thanks." She tossed the pill into her mouth then drank it down. "I couldn't have."

"Why not?"

"Because there is no reason for me to be there that late."

"I'm not a reason?"

Though he tried to hide it, she heard the hurt in his voice.

"Jotham..." Rising she stepped into his slack arms, framed his face with her hands and looked him straight in the eyes. "Of course you are, but you can't possibly want it to become common knowledge that I'm visiting you late at night."

"I can't?"

Jacinda frowned up at him.

Turning his head, he kissed the inside of her palm, "Can we go sit in the other room?" he asked.

Nodding, Jacinda turned and led him into the living room.

∞ ∞ ∞ ∞ ∞

Jotham rubbed his hands on his thighs as he sat next to her on the couch, surprised to discover how nervous he was. Giving himself a moment to calm he let his gaze travel around the room he barely noticed earlier and his eyes widened.

Sitting on the low table in front of them were framed visuals, in all different shapes and sizes of the Michelakakis family. One was of just the kids, young and obviously on a vacation somewhere, sitting in the sand, smiling up at whoever was taking their image.

Another was of Danton, sitting on Stephan's shoulders, laughing as he pulled his father's ears.

There was Stephan and Jacinda, the Academy building directly behind them, standing next to their daughter who was in her graduation uniform.

As he continued to look around, he found more and more visuals documenting Jacinda's life with not only her children but with Stephan. Some were formal and he could tell they had been taken at an Assembly event. When he looked above the mantle, there for all to see was a portrait of Stephan looking down at them.

"Jotham?"

Jacinda's voice brought his eyes back to her. "Stephan was a very lucky man."

Jacinda's eyes followed to where Jotham's had been and frowned. "I don't understand."

"You still have his portrait hanging there. You still have visuals of him out."

"Why wouldn't I?"

"I couldn't. After Lata. It hurt too much to see her face and know she was gone."

Jacinda was silent for several moments trying to organize her thoughts. "Every person grieves differently, Jotham. I would be lying if I said there weren't times when I look at that portrait and cry. Or that when I look at this visual," she picked one up that had all three of her children piled on Stephan's back as he crawled on all fours around the room, giving them a ride, "that I don't rage he isn't still with me." Carefully she put the visual back. "But I could never pack them away. Stephan might be gone, but he will always be part of my life."

"That is why he's a very lucky man. You remember him."

"You remember Lata, Jotham. In your own way. You have her portrait hanging in your private office."

"Which you don't approve of," he reminded her.

Jacinda felt shame fill her as she remembered her words to Jotham. "I'm sorry, Jotham." She leaned over to squeeze his hand. "I should never have said that. It isn't my place."

"Then whose place is it? If not someone who was her friend?" Jotham surged to his feet and found himself pacing. "I loved Lata. I still love her."

"I know that." Jacinda's concerned gaze followed him.

"But...." He looked at her, saw her concern, and finally admitted something he never had before. "She was growing unhappy with our life together."

"What? She told you that?" Jacinda couldn't hide her shock.

"Not in so many words, but I knew Lata. The constant pressure was getting to her and I wasn't helping."

"I'm sure you were doing what you could, Jotham. You were under a lot of pressure too."

"Yes, but not like Lata. At least I had some experience and training at what would be expected. Lata didn't. When she conceived..."

"When she conceived?"

"She was angry, so hurt."

"I don't understand."

"We talked about it, about waiting at least four cycles before we had children. She wanted to be more comfortable with her duties before she conceived. I agreed, then I got caught up with my duties and forgot to take the Ollali juice." Jotham tipped his head back looking up at the ceiling. "If only I hadn't forgotten."

"Then you wouldn't have Barek, Jotham." Rising she went to his side and waited until he looked at her. "Lata loved Barek. She wouldn't have changed anything if it meant losing him."

"You can't know that."

"I can. Lata and I used to talk, a lot. I told you that. She and Barek used to come here, in those early cycles. We would sit and talk the way new mothers do and watch our sons grow. She made a comment once, I thought I understood what she was talking about, but now I see I didn't, not then, but I do now."

"What did she say?"

"That while it hadn't been how she had wanted it, she wouldn't have changed anything that happened. Not if it meant she didn't have Barek. It seemed a little strange to me, but I thought she was referring to being restricted to bed for so long."

"She said that?"

"Yes."

"Why did you say 'early cycles'? She stopped coming here?"

"Not long after Barek's first birthday." Jacinda went over to a multi-tier table on the far side of the room and picked up a visual tucked in the back on the bottom shelf before walking back to hand it to him. "We used the self-timer to take this. It was the last time she visited."

Jotham looked at the visual and felt his eyes fill. Staring out at him was his Lata, sitting on the floor next to Jacinda, each of them were holding their sons and they were all smiling, even the boys.

"Why did she stop coming?" he asked quietly.

"There were grumblings about favoritism from some of the other wives."

"So? She was the Queen. What they thought didn't matter. She could do as she pleased."

"We're talking about Lata here, Jotham." Reaching out she touched her friend's image. "She was a truly nice and loving person. She was still learning to navigate the self-centered and hurtful world that politics can sometimes be."

"It is why she wanted to go driving so often. She needed to get away from it."

"I wish I would have known it had gotten so bad, but after I had Ethan and Stephanie, she seemed to pull even further away from me."

"That was probably my fault," he said sadly, handing her back the visual.

"I don't understand," frowning she looked up at him.

"After Barek was born I made sure to never forget the Ollali juice again. I didn't want to force another pregnancy on her, but as time went on, I began to push for her to have another child. I didn't want Barek to grow up alone and lonely like I did."

"And?"

"And she refused to even consider it."

"I... I'm sorry, Jotham." Turning she went to put the visual back.

"We argued about it the night before she died. Maybe if we hadn't..."

"You can't think like that, Jotham. Not only is it wrong but Lata wouldn't want you to. She had an accident. A senseless accident. If she hadn't, you *would* have had more children together and a long, happy life."

"But that accident did happen." Walking over to her he wrapped his arms around her, pulling her close, letting her warmth sooth him. "Lata's and our chance at that long and happy life disappeared. I'm not going to lose that chance again."

"Jotham..." She rested her hands and forehead on his chest.

"I want you in my life, Jacinda." With a gentle finger under her chin, he tipped her face up. "In my bed. I planned on moving slower than this, planned on letting both of us get used to the idea first, but you had an *accident* last night and I'm not going to chance losing another woman."

"I'm fine. Really."

"That doesn't matter! What matters is that you could have been killed and no one would have known to notify *me*! That is unacceptable. I should have been the one you called. I should have been the one to come get you. I want everyone to know that."

"You want to make an official announcement?" Her fingers dug into his skin, her mind churning at what that would mean not only to her but to her children.

"No, not official, because it's no one's business but ours, but I don't want to hide it either. I want us to spend time together. Openly."

Jacinda found herself relaxing at his words. She wasn't sure how this was going to work, wasn't sure it would, but she knew she wanted the chance too. "How open?" She found herself teasing as she slid her hands up and over his shoulders taking his shirt with them.

"As open as you want." Leaning down, he captured her lips as his hands loosened the ties holding her robe together.

∞ ∞ ∞ ∞ ∞

Jacinda leaned back against the door Jotham had just walked out of and she wrapped her arms around her waist. What an amazing, unexpected, exhilarating day it had turned out to be. Never in her wildest dreams could she have imagined what happened here today.

It wasn't just the sex that had surprised her, although that had been incredible. Jotham's stamina had amazed her. He was an intense lover but not a selfish one. She couldn't remember the last time she'd come so many times.

But it was more than that, it was the quiet moments, the looks he gave her, the words. She wouldn't have recognized that in her younger cycles, but she did now. Love was more than the physical act, more than those three little words, although they mattered too. It was the little day-to-day things that were the true signs of love, and Jotham had given her all those things today. Well, all but those three words, but then she hadn't given them to him either.

The ringing of her comm had her pushing away from the door to answer it.

"You will rest." Jotham's voice filled the room before his face could even fill the screen.

Jacinda gave him an exasperated look. "I told you I would."

"Then why aren't you?" he demanded.

"Umm, because you left less than two minutes ago?"

"Oh." Jotham had the grace to look contrite.

"I am and will be fine, Jotham. Stop worrying about me."

"Not going to happen. Especially when I'm not with you."

"Jotham..."

"Get used to it, Jacinda. Now I'm sending you my personal code. It will go directly to my wrist comm. Call me if you need to. For anything."

Jacinda saw his eyes turn hard.

"I mean it, Jacinda. You. Will. Call. Me. I can't go through what I did this morning again."

"I will, Jotham." Jacinda's eyes softened as she looked at him. "I promise. I'm home. I'm safe and I'm not going anywhere. I'm going to make some calls. Reschedule some appointments and then rest. At least until you call me again."

"I will unless you've changed your mind about coming to the Palace." He looked hopeful.

"No, I haven't, so I'll talk to you later." Smiling, she disconnected the call.

∞ ∞ ∞ ∞ ∞

Jotham sat back, looking to Deffand, who sat silently across from him. "You understand what this means. Correct?"

"Yes, Majesty. I will start the selection process to increase the number of Royal Guards, as soon as we return to the Palace. I will also make sure all guards know she has full access to the Palace."

"Good."

"I received some information earlier that you are going to want to know about the accident."

Jotham's eyes sharpened on Deffand. "Tell me."

"Because Jacinda is the mother of an Assemblyman, Pechora transit automatically did a closer investigation of Jacinda's transport, making sure nothing had been tampered with. They found something very interesting."

"Her transport was tampered with?!!" Jotham sat straight up in his chair.

"No. No tampering, but Jacinda's transport was no ordinary transport."

"What are you talking about Deffand!"

"It seems Stephan Michelakakis took his wife's safety very seriously. He special-ordered her transport. Its frame was reinforced. Its windows were impact resistant as were its sides. It should have easily withstood the speed of that impact."

"Why didn't it?" Jotham demanded.

"That's what Pechora transit wanted to know once they discovered the modifications to Jacinda's transport. After talking to the manufacturer, they realized that the boy had to be going at least four times the legal limit to cause that amount of damage and it was not the first time he's caused an accident."

Jotham paled at the thought and thanked Stephan for seeing to Jacinda's safety even when he was with the ancestors. "How does he still have a license? How was the boy able to walk away unscathed?"

"I don't know, Majesty. He should have been killed instantly at that speed. The ancestors must have been watching over him."

"And Jacinda."

"Yes."

Silence reigned as the limisin traveled through the gates of the Palace.

"I want the boy charged, Deffand."

"The process has already been started, Majesty. Majesty," Deffand hesitated.

"What's your question, Deffand?"

"Do you want him charged as an assassination attempt?"

Jotham eyed Deffand, seriously thinking about it. He wanted to. He wanted that boy to pay for the harm he'd caused Jacinda, but he also knew Jacinda would never see it that way.

"No. Let it run as an Assemblyman's mother, that will be harsh enough."

"As you wish, Majesty."

"And Deffand."

"Majesty?"

"Make sure he never drives again."

"Yes, Majesty."

∞ ∞ ∞ ∞ ∞

Jotham was surprised when he entered the outer office and found Chesney sitting at his desk.

"What are you still doing here, Chesney?"

"I was notified that you were returning and knew you would want to be informed of the changes to your schedule."

"Yes, well come into my office, Chesney and we'll discuss how my schedule is going to be changing."

∞ ∞ ∞ ∞ ∞

Chesney looked at the schedule in his hand in disbelief. When they had entered Jotham's office, the King walked behind his desk, sat down and picked up a pen and had begun making alterations to the schedule it had taken him all day to arrange. After several minutes, he handed it back to him.

"You... you are no longer going to be taking meetings after six?" Chesney looked at Jotham and knew the shock in his voice was easily heard.

"Unless they are official dinners or events then no. Also, I will eventually be cutting back on my early morning ones also."

"I... I will immediately start reorganizing your schedule, Majesty."

"Tomorrow is early enough, Chesney. I'll keep what you have in the morning."

"Yes, Majesty."

"Also, Chesney, Jacinda Michelakakis is going to be spending a great deal more time here in the Palace. Anytime she arrives, calls or sends a message I am to be notified immediately."

"I... Yes, Majesty!" Chesney couldn't keep a smile from breaking out across his face.

The King and Jacinda Michelakakis.

They would be the perfect couple.

Jotham watched the smile break across Chesney's normally stoic face and remembered Chesney telling him of his affection for Jacinda.

"Do you have something to say, Chesney?"

"I... Just that I'm very happy for you, Majesty, and I will see to it. Madame Michelakakis is a wonderful woman."

"She is." Jotham sat back in his chair forming his fingers in a temple and putting them against his chin. Chesney was someone he trusted. Never in all the cycles that Chesney had served him had he ever given Jotham cause to doubt his loyalty or discretion. He would need to rely on him even more now. "When Jacinda was returning home last night she was involved in a transport accident."

"What!" Chesney shot straight up in his chair. "Is she alright?" he demanded forgetting for a moment who he was talking to, making Jotham smile.

"She is bumped, bruised and a little sore but otherwise fine. It's where I've been today."

"Completely understandable, Majesty. Is there anything I can do? Helen would be more than willing to go over and stay with her if you like."

"Thank you, Chesney, and thank your wife, but Jacinda has assured me she is fine. I will be calling her tonight to verify that."

"Good." Chesney nodded his approval. "Do you need me to prepare any official announcement?"

"No, there will be no announcement."

"Yes, Majesty." Chesney rose then paused.

"What is it, Chesney?"

"Majesty, while I know Madame Michelakakis is a wonderful, warm, caring woman there will be many that will not approve of this relationship. Some in your own Assembly."

"What are you talking about, Chesney?"

"She is not from the House of Protection, only the widow of someone who was."

"She has been a member of this House for nearly forty cycles. She is the widow of one of our most important Assemblymen!"

"Yes, Majesty, but for the purists that still doesn't make her from the House of Protection, especially with her heritage."

"You mean because her father and grandfathers were Assemblymen in the House of Healing?"

"Yes."

"I understand what you are saying, Chesney, but I don't need their 'approval' and neither does Jacinda."

"Of course not, Majesty. I just wanted you to be aware."

"Thank you, Chesney. Is there anything else you feel I need to be made aware of?"

"No, Majesty." Bowing Chesney left the room.

Chapter Sixteen

"Did you rest?"

Jacinda smiled at Jotham's question. She had taken her portable comm to bed with her, something she hadn't done in cycles because she knew Jotham was going to be calling.

"Hello to you too and yes I did."

Jotham had the grace to look abashed for a moment then she saw him reach out as if he were touching the bruise on her face.

"It's gotten darker."

"It's going to, Jotham, at least for a while. You can't tell me you've never had a black eye."

"I have, but that doesn't mean *you* should. Can't Portman do something?"

"He's done what he can, you know this since you talked to... or should I say tried to intimidate him into telling you my personal, private, medical information."

"He called you?"

"Of course he called me. Otherwise, he never would have given you any information. King or not, some things, not even you have the right to know."

"You mean like the scar you have on your side?"

"My scar? You asked Portman about my *scar*!"

Jacinda sat straight up in bed revealing she was wearing another beautiful nightgown this time in a bronze color that accentuated her skin tone.

"No." His eyes ran appreciatively over her. "I'm asking you."

"Why would you possibly want to know about that?" Jacinda laid back down settling the covers under her breasts.

"Because it is a part of you."

"Jotham..." Jacinda's eyes softened.

"You fascinate me, Jacinda." The intensity in his eyes held hers. "Don't you know that? Not because of your beauty, but because of your faults. They are what make you who you are and I want to know you."

How was she supposed to stay irritated with him when he said something like that?

"It's not a very interesting story," she finally said.

"Tell me anyway."

Jacinda watched Jotham settle back and realized he was laying in his bed too, talking on his personal comm, just like she was. It made her feel closer to him.

"We were on vacation in the Lake Baku Region, visiting Stephan's brother, Leander's father, when I suddenly got sick."

"Sick!" Jotham shot straight up in bed. "What do you mean sick?"

"I had some trouble carrying Stephanie," Jacinda shrugged. "My gallbladder was damaged. It had been manageable, but for some reason that weekend it flared up so badly that it had to be removed."

"You're okay now?"

"Jotham, I'm fine. It was over twenty cycles ago. I told you it wasn't an interesting story." She frowned as she remembered. "Stephan and I had already decided not to have more children, but that took the matter out of our hands."

"That doesn't matter. The only thing that does is that you are okay."

"I am."

"Tell me more about your life, Jacinda. Tell me about your time with the Fleet."

Jacinda's smile returned as she settled deeper into her bed. "Well, let's see, there was that party at the Rodham space station..."

∞ ∞ ∞ ∞ ∞

Jotham lay back in his bed smiling as Jacinda went on and on about her time in the Fleet when she worked in communications. He could tell by her tone that she'd loved every moment of it. It made him wonder if Lata would have felt the same way had she'd gotten to go.

"What's put that look on your face?"

Jacinda's soft question brought his thoughts back to the present. "I'm sorry, my mind wandered." He watched her smile sleepily.

"To where?" When Jotham didn't immediately answer she had her answer. "To Lata."

"Yes." Jotham watched her closely, surprised to see she wasn't upset.

"She was a part of your life, Jotham. A major part. It's not going to upset me to hear you talk about her, to hear that you still think about her. I do that with Stephan all the time."

"That's different."

"Why? Because I had him longer than you had Lata? I thank the ancestors I did, but even if I didn't, he'd still be a part of me. An important part. Just like Lata is to you."

Jotham could see the honesty in her eyes. He could see that his thinking about Lata, talking about Lata, didn't upset her at all. So he did. "I was just wondering if Lata would have enjoyed her time in the Coalition as much as you did. If she'd had the chance."

"She might have, but she wanted you more, Jotham." Jacinda's tone held no doubt. "She didn't have to wed you right then, Jotham. She could have put off the Union until after she served. She chose not to."

"I've never been sure of that."

"Jotham." Jacinda hoped she was saying the right thing. "I can't tell you with any certainty that there weren't moments Lata didn't doubt her decision. There were times when I doubted deciding to wed Stephan."

"You did?"

"Of course. I loved Stephan, never doubt that, but there were times in the early cycles when I wondered if love was enough. If what we had could withstand all the outside pressures and demands. *I* was changing my life. Not him. Just as Lata changed hers for you. But I'll never believe she regretted it any more than I did."

∞ ∞ ∞ ∞ ∞

Jotham found himself smiling when he woke the next morning. When was the last time that had happened? He and Jacinda had talked late into the night. He wasn't sure who had finally disconnected the transmission. Maybe it had self-terminated when they'd both drifted off to sleep.

All he knew was the only way it could have been better was if he'd been able to sleep with her in his arms, been able to wake with her in them.

Rising, he quickly dressed, wanting to get through his duties for the day so he could go see Jacinda.

∞ ∞ ∞ ∞ ∞

"Good morning, Chesney," he greeted as he entered his outer office.

"Good morning, Majesty." Chesney smiled in response to the King's good mood. "Your coffee is waiting for you on your desk along with the files you will need for your comm meeting with Birgin Casar."

"Thank you. Anything else I need to be made aware of?"

"Hagar called a few minutes ago. The High Admiral would like you to call him when you have a moment. No emergency. He will be at the Palace for the day."

Jotham looked at his wrist unit. He had time. "I'll contact him now. Let me know when Casar is on the line."

"Yes, Majesty."

∞ ∞ ∞ ∞ ∞

"What did you need, Will?" Jotham asked when the call connected, taking a sip of his coffee.

"I said it wasn't urgent, Jotham," William responded.

"I know, but I have back-to-back meetings all morning. Now is the best chance I'll have to talk to you."

"Oh, well, okay."

Jotham frowned, Will seemed nervous... uncomfortable. What in the name of the ancestors was going on?

"What's wrong, Will?"

"Nothing. Nothing's *wrong*. It's just.... Cassandra said *I* was the one to do this and... damn it I can't believe I'm finding this so hard."

Jotham watched Will run a frustrated hand through his hair. "What?" Jotham demanded "Will, just spit it out!"

"I... we... Cassandra and I..."

"Will!"

"We would like to ask you to be Sabah's second father," he said in a rush.

Jotham fell back in his chair, stunned.

"You would like *me*..." Jotham's voice trailed off. Never before had he been asked to be a second father. It was an honor reserved for only the most trusted of friends. A promise to help guide and raise that child if its parents couldn't. While Will was Barek's second father, Jotham had never been asked to be one for *any* of Will's five sons.

"We would. *I* would. It's something Cassandra and I have argued about every time we've had a child."

"Cassandra didn't feel I was the appropriate choice. I can understand that, Will. Especially after Dadrian."

"*No*, Jotham! That has nothing to do with it. For the record, *Cassandra* always thought you should be, after all, you are my best and life-long friend. Who better to entrust the raising of our children to?"

"*You* preferred I not..."

The words could barely be heard as they passed Jotham's lips, but William did.

"I never thought it would be appropriate and didn't want to put you in the position where you'd have to refuse me."

"Why would I refuse, Will? I don't understand?"

"Jotham, it's one thing for *me* to be second father to Barek. He's the future King. But for *you* to be one to *mine*... the impression it would give others of favoritism... "

"Would be intense."

"Yes. We both know Lucas had to overcome a great deal because I am his father. With you as his second father..."

"No one would believe he ever achieved anything on his own."

"No, and while I know Lucas or any of my boys for that matter, could care less what others think about them, it still would have been difficult to handle."

"Yes." Jotham nodded. "I can see that."

"Even with Kayden, Jacob and Willie, I still refused to ask you. They are the Royal sons of the House of Knowledge, but they also carry the House of Protection Arrow on their forearms. They will always have to straddle two Houses and if *you* were to be their second father, then *they* are your second sons, meaning they could be placed in line to take the throne."

"That's ridiculous, Will," Jotham raised his hand dismissively. "Barek will take the throne."

"Yes, but what if something were to happen to him. Jotham... think about it... You would be forced to choose a new heir. Who would it be?"

Jotham frowned, giving Will's question serious thought. Who *would* he choose? He thought over all those who had the bloodline to assume the throne. Out of all of them, the only one he would ever have chosen was Will. But Will was now the King of the House of Knowledge and the High Admiral, there is no way *he* could take the throne. So, he *would* have looked to one of Will's sons, especially if he were their second father.

Will was also right on that point that by law, his agreeing to be a second father meant that he was accepting that child as if he/she were his own. And for Jotham to accept, by law, put that child in line to inherit the throne. He had never considered that before.

"The purists in both Houses would go ballistic," Will said after a few minutes.

"You're right," Jotham agreed. "I never considered that before. I just always assumed..."

"That I didn't think you worthy of it? That's bullshit, Jotham, and you know it!" bracing his hands on his desk, Will leaned closer to the comm, his eyes full of rage. "I didn't have to make you my sons' second father to know you would automatically watch over them if I were gone. The same way you know whether I'm Barek's second father or not, I will always watch over him."

"I... you're right, Will. I'm sorry."

"You should be. Of all the pea-brained, idiotic... if I were there, I'd punch you in the face, Jotham."

As Will blustered on, Jotham smiled. Will rarely lost his temper like this and he enjoyed seeing it. He also knew Will meant every word he was saying. Will was one of the few people who actually could hit Jotham without any consequences.

"So why are you asking me to be second father to Sabah?"

"Because you are my *closest* friend! She is my *daughter*! There is no one else I would trust her with other than you."

Jotham felt his throat tighten. "Cassandra feels the same way?"

"Yes."

"But her brother...."

"We've made Peter the second father to all the boys, but Sabah... Sabah's different, Jotham. She's going to be the Queen one day. A strong, beautiful, and powerful Queen. Peter has no understanding of what all that entails. You do. You are the only one that could ever guide her, without bias. So will you?"

"I would be honored, Will."

Jotham watched all the tension leave Will's face and was shocked to realize Will had actually been worried he would refuse.

"Good. We are planning on having a small, intimate ceremony next week to make it official."

"You were that sure of me?"

"Cassandra was. So you can make it on such short notice? Maybe spend a few days? We could catch up, maybe do a little sparring with Peter."

"I'll clear it." Jotham paused. "I hear he's quite good."

"Peter's exceptional. Anyone who passes his classes is going to be an Elite of the security forces."

"I'll keep that in mind." Jotham paused for a moment. "Will, I'd like to bring someone with me if that's okay."

"Jacinda?" Will's eyes sharpened on Jotham.

"Yes."

"By all means, Jotham." A smile broke across his face. "Cassandra is dying to meet her."

"Why?" Jotham frowned at his friend's smile. "What have you been telling your wife, William?" he demanded suspiciously.

"Only that our friend has fallen in love. I have to warn you though, Cassandra is skeptical."

"That I love Jacinda?"

"No, that Jacinda isn't using you. For some reason, my wife has gone all protective over you."

Jotham laughed at the putout expression on Will's face. "Poor Will. I always told you I was the better looking of us."

"You're pretty, but I'm handsome." It was a life-long argument.

"Maybe Cassandra likes pretty better," Jotham teased.

"You stay away from my wife, Tibullus!"

Laughing, Jotham disconnected the call.

Now he just had to convince Jacinda to go.

∞ ∞ ∞ ∞ ∞

"You want me to what?" Jacinda pulled back against the arms that were wrapped around her to look up at Jotham in shock.

It had been three days since they had physically gotten to see each other. First, Ethan and his family had come to check on her, and then Jotham had an official dinner he'd had to attend.

Today, to Jacinda's surprise, her new transport was delivered, weeks earlier than expected. She knew Jotham had something to do with it, but before she could bring it up, he had asked her to accompany him to the House of Knowledge.

"Come with me," he said again.

"Jotham, you're going to a private event between you and the King and Queen of the House of Knowledge. They aren't going to want a stranger there."

"I want you there, and you're not a stranger. You know Will and you know Javiera."

"Jotham..."

"Please, Jacinda." His eyes pleaded with hers. "I have to go and I want you with me. I want to spend time with you. I want you to meet my friends. I want them to know you're in my life."

"I thought we were going to take this slow, nothing official."

"This isn't 'official.' This is you and me, going to visit people we both know. Together."

Jacinda gazed at him silently for a moment, taking in the depth of desire he had for this blazing from his violet eyes. "Oh alright, but I need to know how formal this is going to be so I can pack accordingly."

"It's not going to be anything 'formal,' Jacinda." When she just raised that expressive eyebrow at him, he laughed. "Honestly, there are no official events planned. The second father ceremony is going to be held in Cassandra's private garden."

Jacinda knew Jotham thought he was telling her the truth, but if there was one thing she had learned from her mother growing up, it was that when dealing with a Royal, you needed to be prepared for anything. Plans could change with only a moment's notice and you needed to be able to adapt.

It was advice she'd taken to heart when she wed Stephan. As irritating as she found it, there *were* times when appearances mattered. To be able to stand confidently beside her man, and know that no fault could be found with *him* because of *her,* was important to her.

Jacinda knew it stemmed from those early moon cycles when Queen Johanna had singled her out for her sharp critiques. The worst had been when she happened to wear a pair of earrings her parents had given her when she turned sixteen. She had forgotten about the House of Healing symbol at their base. Jotham's mother had immediately zeroed in on them. She made sure every other wife witnessed the humiliating dressing down she delivered.

Stephan had been enraged when he heard about it. That, on top of King Kado's letter, had him reconsidering if he could continue to serve a King and Queen that were so narrow-minded.

Johanna and Kado both died before Stephan had to make that decision, and one of Jotham's first decrees had been to validate her and Stephan's Union, making it known he supported them. She doubted any of them had truly understood how that one act would change all their lives.

"Jacinda?"

Jotham's question, along with his arms tightening around her, had Jacinda's mind returning to the present.

"When do we leave and how long will we be there?"

Jotham smiled, "Three days and we'll be there for at least that long."

"Jotham Tibullus!" she playfully slapped his chest shaking her head.

"What?" he asked confused.

"If I have to explain it, you wouldn't understand." She knew he had a staff that was used to packing for such things, that all he had to do was tell them he was going. She, on the other hand, would be rushing for the next three days to prepare and pack for the trip. But that was for later, right now she was in Jotham's arms and she wanted to enjoy it. Stretching up, she kissed him lightly.

"So tell me, Your Royal Highness," she asked teasingly. "What do you know about my new transport arriving two weeks early?"

"I don't know what you are talking about." Jotham's instantly blank expression was a dead giveaway.

"Really?" She raised an eyebrow slightly. "I talked to Mister Taggs two days ago and he informed me that the earliest he could get me a new transport was two weeks."

"And?"

"And low and behold, he calls me this morning to tell me it's arrived early."

"Well that's good, right?" Jotham tried to kiss her, but gentle fingers on his lips stopped him.

"What did you do, Jotham?" She wasn't going to let this go.

"Why do you think I did anything?" He kissed her fingers instead.

"Because the only way that transport could have been built and delivered so quickly would be because of your influence."

"You refused to use one of my limisins, and I refused to allow you to not have adequate transportation."

"So you're saying it's my fault?" her twitching lips softened her words.

"No, not your *fault*, but you made things more difficult. All you had to do was allow me to assign you a driver."

"And why would I do that, Jotham Tibullus?" She meant her question to be teasing, but Jotham didn't react that way.

"Because you could have been killed!" Jotham's hands suddenly shifted to her upper arms, lifting her so they were eye to eye. "If you had been in a limisin you would have been safe!"

"Jotham!" Her eyes widened in shock at the true rage in his voice, her hands resting on his shoulders. "He still would have hit me," she said trying to calm him.

"But you would have been in the back and wouldn't have taken the full brunt of the attack."

"It wasn't an attack! It was an accident."

"Do you really think that matters if you're dead?!!" Jotham shouted.

"Jotham." She framed his face with her hands, her eyes searching his. She'd never seen him this upset before. "It's alright. I'm here and I'm safe."

"I'm not losing you." His mouth captured hers, his tongue plunging inside, staking his claim. Jacinda was his, his to hold, his to protect, his to love. And he wouldn't lose her. He knew he was being irrational, but he couldn't stop himself because he would never survive losing someone else he loved.

Feeling Jacinda's arms wrap around his neck, he bent down and swept her off her feet quickly carrying her to his bedchamber.

He wanted her.

Needed her.

In *his* bed.

The only woman to be there since Lata.

Laying her down in the center of the bed, he pulled back, breaking off the kiss. He looked down at her and what he saw stole his breath.

She had casually pulled her hair back in combs when she arrived. They had fallen away during his embrace and now her long chestnut hair fanned out around her framing her in its silken beauty.

Reaching down, he slowly pulled the loose blouse out of the tailored pants it was tucked in to, revealing that 'uninteresting' scar she had told him about. Leaning down, he reverently kissed it, thanking the ancestors that she had survived, knowing she had downplayed its severity.

"Jotham..." She sank her fingers into his thick, lush hair trying to pull his mouth back to hers.

Jotham knew what she wanted, but there were other areas his mouth wanted to explore before returning to that wondrous place. Places he didn't feel he had given enough attention to before.

Such as the indentation at her side where her waist was. No, it wasn't the narrow waist of a younger woman, one fresh out of the Academy, taut and firm. It was the waist of a mature woman that had successfully carried three children. A little softer. A little wider. With the feathery marks left from those experiences. It aroused him. Kissing it, he moved higher. Where he discovered a smattering of freckles, he had missed before. They seemed strategically placed, beckoning him to follow where they led. So he did, but only after making sure he suitably appreciated each one.

In return, they led him to the valley between the peaks he loved to worship at and revealed what they wanted him to see. There between her breasts, previously covered by bruising, lay three small, faint, connected spiral suns.

The first on the inner, underside curve of her left breast.

The second cradled between them.

While the third rested along the upper curve of her right breast.

It was the royal symbol for the House of Healing!

Yet not.

What were they doing on Jacinda?

"Jacinda..." He lifted his mouth away from the first symbol to stare up at her.

"Hmmm?" she asked looking up at him with desire-filled eyes.

"What are these doing on you?"

"What?"

"These marks. They are the Royal symbols for the House of Healing."

"No, they're not. They're similar, but not the same. Only the men of the House of Healing carry that symbol and it's always on their hand."

"Yet here it is on you." He watched the flush that ran up her body. "Jacinda..."

"I didn't think we were 'talking' right now." She tried to distract him by pulling her blouse over her head.

"We'll get to that. Now tell me how this mark came to be on your body." He smiled gently at her putout look. It was adorable. Jacinda was too used to no one challenging her. He wanted to spend the rest of his life putting that look there.

"It really is nothing. Just family legend whispered in the depths of the night."

Jotham rolled to his side, propping his head on one hand as the other rested on her stomach, giving his fingers access to all three marks.

"Tell me anyway."

Jacinda huffed but knew that look that said Jotham wouldn't be swayed.

"Family legend, on my mother's side, tells of how cycles ago... so many cycles that no one really knows, a woman in my family fell in love with a Royal from the House of Healing. The

King didn't approve and the prince wed someone else, but not before my ancestor conceived."

"And the Prince never claimed his child?" Jotham couldn't believe it.

"He was never informed, especially since the child was female and no threat to the throne."

"Yet she carried the royal mark."

"She did, in the same spot I do, but her daughter didn't nor her granddaughter, but her great granddaughter did."

"It only appears every third generation?"

"Yes, but only down the direct female line."

"Like Cassandra in the House of Knowledge."

Jacinda frowned slightly, "In a way I guess you're right, but it's not the same."

"Why not?"

"Because only a King can rule the House of Healing. A King with the full mark." She gently touched Jotham's mark on his right forearm. The Arrow, representing that he was the King of the House of Protection, proudly blazing full of color.

Jotham thought about her words, thought about how William's sons with Cassandra, while House of Knowledge, still bore his House's symbol. Now a female from the House of Healing carried its royal mark. Something never before heard of. "Perhaps things are changing."

"Some things can change. Some things can't." She moved his hand so it cupped her breast, arching up slightly into it.

Jotham's fingers instinctively tightened over the full globe. "You are trying to distract me."

"Is it working?"

"Yes." Leaning down he captured her nipple, sucking it deep into his mouth, his tongue lapping at it.

"Damn." She ran frustrated nails down his back, wanting to touch skin, not fabric. "Why aren't you naked? I want you naked!"

With a pop, he released her breast and gave her a look that had her channel flooding with desire.

"Do you now?"

"Yes. Please, Jotham. Don't tease me. I need to feel you inside me."

All the teasing left Jotham's face, replaced by a need that took her breath away. "Then you'll have me." Pushing up to his knees, he ripped his shirt off before his hands made short work of both their pants. Settling between legs that welcomed him, he paused at her entrance.

"You are *mine*!" he proclaimed and thrust deep making sure he claimed every part of her.

"Yes!" Arching off the bed, she accepted his claim and made one of her one. "And you are *mine*!"

"*Yours*!" he acknowledged.

∞ ∞ ∞ ∞ ∞

Jacinda wrapped her arms around Jotham's neck, pulling his mouth down to hers as she met him thrust for thrust. Her body tightening around him. His words had triggered something deep inside her, something she never expected to feel again.

Love.

She. Loved. Jotham.

Her heart stuttered slightly at the enormity of it.

Ripping his mouth from hers, Jotham glared down, his violet eyes glowing. He felt something shift. "Don't you hold back on me, Jacinda. I want everything!" With that, he increased his thrusts knowing from the way she trembled that she was close.

"Give it to me, Jacinda!" Jotham ordered. "Come for me!"

"Jotham!" His words sent her over the edge, and as her orgasm exploded through her, Jotham thrust one final time and followed her.

∞ ∞ ∞ ∞ ∞

Jacinda tried to catch her breath, as she lay draped across Jotham's heaving chest. He only remembered, at the last moment, to not crush her by rolling onto his back taking her with him.

Her mind was still trying to absorb what her heart knew was true. She loved Jotham Tibullus. The King of the House of Protection. How was this ever going to work?

"What's going on in that mind of yours?" Jotham's deep voice had her propping an elbow on his chest, resting her head on her hand to look down at him. He lay on his back, eyes closed, a relaxed, satisfied expression on his face.

"What makes you think my mind can think at all?"

"Because I can hear it." He opened those amazing eyes to look up at her. "Also you are starting to tense up."

"Oh," she said, giving him a sheepish look. Should she tell him? She was too old to play games, but still, she needed some time to process this. It wasn't something she could just blurt out.

"Jacinda?" Jotham's satisfied expression began to turn into a frown. "What's wrong?" he demanded again.

"Nothing, just thinking."

"About?"

"Lots of things. You have to know that it doesn't matter that you can turn me into mush, I'm still not going to agree to ride around in a limisin."

"Why not?"

"Because life is meant to be lived."

"Damn it! You were in an accident, Jacinda!"

When he tried to rise, she refused to let him. "Yes. Which could have happened anywhere. In any type of transport. I could fall down a flight of stairs." She felt him stiffen as she mentioned how Dadrian died. "Or I could die picking flowers in the garden." Which was how Stephan died. "I'm not going to live my life in fear, Jotham."

"I'm not asking you to."

"You are to a point. I promise I'm not going to take unnecessary risks. I have too much to live for. I drive what amounts to the safest transport on the planet. I don't drive fast. I don't drive in bad weather. I take every precaution."

"That doesn't always matter."

"No, it doesn't." Reaching out she cupped his cheek. "That's life, Jotham. I'm going to live mine, fully. Let me. Enjoy it with me."

Chapter Seventeen

"Jacinda Michelakakis! I will speak to you!"

Jacinda briefly closed her eyes hearing the high-pitched, scratchy voice of Madame Nitzschke. She had just closed her front door and was heading down her sidewalk to her transport. She had Deffand leave it parked out front when he had driven her home the night before.

She and Jotham had just been finishing up a late meal when Chesney notified him that something had occurred that needed his attention. Jotham had wanted her to stay, but it was late and she knew it would be better if she wasn't seen driving away from the Palace in the early morning hours.

Jotham hadn't liked it, her accident still weighed heavily on his mind and he demanded that if she refused to take a limisin, then she would allow Deffand to drive her. Jacinda remembered opening her mouth to argue, but then realized it was a small thing to allow. So she had agreed, knowing it gave Jotham a sense of comfort.

Deffand had driven her transport, with Jacinda sitting beside him, not in the back, as he would have liked. They were followed by another transport so he could return to the Palace. She had him park in her driveway, and after he walked her to the door, he left.

Now Madame Nitzschke was tottering down her walk as Jacinda was on her way out to shop for the trip to Kisurri, and apparently it was too much to ask that she not run into the neighborhood gossip.

"Hello, Madame Nitzschke. How are you today?"

"I would be much better if you would stop having all these *male* visitors!"

"Excuse me?" Jacinda bristled at the condemnation in the old woman's tone.

"You heard me! It's an embarrassment to the entire neighborhood what you are doing! That man is half your age! He comes and goes, day and night! Assemblyman Stephan would be rolling over in his grave if he knew how you were disrespecting him!"

Jacinda felt her rage growing as each word passed the old biddy's lips. She knew Madame Nitzschke kept an eye on everyone in the neighborhood. For cycles, she'd found it comforting, knowing her children couldn't get away with anything. Now she found it intrusive. The interfering but caring woman Madame Nitzschke had once been was now a judgmental one, and Jacinda would not tolerate it. Later she might laugh over the thought that Madame Nitzschke thought she was involved with Deffand, but right now it infuriated her.

"Madame Nitzschke," Jacinda bit out. "While I have always respected your position in the community, I will not tolerate you thinking you have the right to judge me or my life. Who comes and goes from my house and when they come or go, are none of your business! Now if you will excuse me, I was on my way out."

Turning from her, Jacinda walked to her transport and left the woman glaring at her.

∞ ∞ ∞ ∞ ∞

"Mother?"

Hearing her name called out, Jacinda looked to her left and smiled seeing her son striding toward her. "Danton."

"How are you?" Kissing her cheek, he reached for the bags she carried. "Here let me take those for you."

"I'm good. I was just going to head to Pittaluga's for coffee. Can you join me?"

Danton twisted his wrist to check the time. "Yes. I have an hour before my next meeting."

"Wonderful." Slipping her arm through her son's, she let him lead her down the street.

"Madame Michelakakis!" Mister Pittaluga rushed forward to greet her. "You are here! You are well! I was so concerned when I heard of your accident!"

"Hello, Mister Pittaluga. Thank you for your concern, but I am fine. "How are you today?"

"I am wonderful now that you are here and you've brought Assemblyman Michelakakis. Wonderful! Would you like your usual table?"

"Please." Jacinda was startled for only a moment hearing Pittaluga address Danton as Assemblyman Michelakakis. For a moment, it was as if Stephan were at her side.

Danton was frowning when he sat down at the table Pittaluga had led them to.

"Can I take those for you, Assemblyman Michelakakis?" Pittaluga gestured to the bags he carried.

"Thank you." He handed them to him.

Pittaluga nodded, "I will be right back with your coffee."

"What's got you frowning all of a sudden?" Jacinda asked once Pittaluga walked away.

"He was flirting with you," Danton's frown deepened.

"What? Who? You mean Mister Pittaluga?" Jacinda asked, surprised.

"Yes."

"And you have a problem with that?"

"I... well yes. You're my mother."

"Danton, we've been over this before. While I may be your mother, I was and still am a woman first."

"I know that, but still..."

Jacinda suddenly realized that Danton was truly struggling with this and sat back in her chair gathering her thoughts. She understood that Stephan's sudden death had shaken all her children, but it had hit Danton the hardest, because he so idolized his father. She remembered all those late night talks the two of them would have, sitting in Stephan's office discussing hundreds of different things. She knew he wished his father were here to guide him now that he was an Assemblyman.

Since Stephan's death, Danton had taken his roll of first son very seriously. He made sure he checked on her, by calling her or stopping in. And while she appreciated it, he needed to understand she was still going to live her life. A life she hoped included Jotham.

Before she could speak, Pittaluga arrived with their coffee and a plate of sweets.

"Here you are."

"Oh, Mister Pittaluga, you spoil me." Jacinda looked at the plate with all her favorite bites and several of Danton's too.

"Impossible, Madame. Is there anything else I can get for you?"

"Yes. I'm going to need several pounds of your wonderful coffee blend for my sister before I go."

"I will see to it." Smiling Pittaluga bowed slightly then left them.

"Danton. I love you. You are my first male, but you are not my keeper. Not even your father was that."

"Mother..."

"Let me finish." Danton immediately snapped his mouth shut, even at his age that certain 'mother's tone' still worked.

"Your father was my life mate and I miss him immensely, but he would no more want me to stop living my life than I would want him to if the situation were reversed."

"But..."

"But nothing." She knew she had to start broaching this subject with Danton even if it made him uncomfortable. "What that means is that I'm going to live and enjoy my life, and if that involves seeing other men, then I am and you're just going to have to deal with it."

"Mother!"

"You see women don't you, Danton?"

"Of course, but that's different."

"Why?"

"Because it just is! The thought of you..." Danton's face began to turn red.

"Of me?" Jacinda knew exactly what he was thinking, but was going to make him say it.

"Mom, you can't possibly be thinking of seriously becoming involved with someone other than Dad!"

"Why not?"

"Because Dad was your life mate."

"Yes, and no one could ever replace him, but that doesn't mean I can't fall in love again, that I can't share my life with someone else."

"I just never considered it." Danton took a deep sip from the cup in front of him. "It's going to take some getting used to." He set his cup down and gave her a hard look. "I also want to approve anyone you might be thinking of seeing."

Jacinda looked at him in shock, then began to chuckle. "You want to 'approve' my dates?"

"Yes. You don't know the kind of men that are out there, Mom. You've been protected all your life.

She raised an eyebrow at him. "I know exactly what kind of men are 'out' there. I have been on 'dates' since your father died, Danton."

"What?" Danton's eyes widened in shocked. "How? Who? When? Why didn't you tell me?"

"Because it was none of your business, it was mine. All you need to know is that *I* know what is right for *me*." She slid the plate of treats toward him "Now have one of Pittaluga's pastries."

Still slightly shocked, Danton reached out, chose his favorite pastry and bit into it.

∞ ∞ ∞ ∞ ∞

"Thank you, Mister Pittaluga. You will add this to my account?"

"Of course, Madame Michelakakis," Pittaluga held out the bags to her. "There are two individual bags of coffee in your bags."

"I'll take those." Danton took the bags. "Thank you, Mister Pittaluga."

"Always a pleasure, Assemblyman Michelakakis." Bowing slightly, he turned to greet another customer.

"Do you need a lift home?" Danton looked at his wrist unit and knew he would be pushing it, but he didn't want his mother to have to use a jitney.

"No, my transport is just around the corner. I have a little more shopping to do, so I'll just drop off the bags in it." She paused to pull her ringing comm out of her shoulder bag. Seeing Jotham's code she silenced it, not wanting to speak to him on the street and in front of Danton.

"You have your new transport already?" Danton frowned watching her silence her comm.

"Yes, apparently Mister Taggs was able to obtain one sooner than he expected." She started walking again.

"Then my call to him did some good," Danton nodded satisfied.

"You called him?" Jacinda bit her lip, knowing it was Jotham's call that made the difference.

"Yes, I know you told me to let you handle it, but I hated the thought of you without a way to get around."

"Thank you, Danton." She stopped next to her transport unlocking and opening the back door so he could set her packages inside."

"So you're sending coffee to Aunt Palma now?"

"No, I'm actually going to Kisurri later this week."

"You are?"

"Yes." She looked down as her comm rang again with Jotham's code and frowned, why was he calling again?

"Why?"

"Hmmm," Danton's question brought her back to the present. Silencing the call, she looked to Danton. "Oh, because I was invited. I'll be gone about a week. I was going to call and tell you tonight so you wouldn't think I'd 'disappeared' again."

"Disappeared?" It was Danton's turn to frown.

"Yes, that's what Madame Nitzschke is telling everyone."

"I'm sorry, Mother. I was just worried. Myesha was gone and she was there."

"Yes, well, Myesha is going to be there off and on while I'm gone, but feel free to check in on her if you want," she teased.

"You think I won't?"

"I know you will, Danton. Myesha is a part of the family. I just don't want you to be concerned if she isn't there. I'll ask her to either call you or leave a note if she goes to visit her children."

"I'd appreciate that because you're right, she is part of the family." Danton looked at his wrist unit. "I have to go, Mom, or I'll be late for my meeting."

"Go." Jacinda kissed his cheek. "I'll talk to you when I get back."

Jacinda watched Danton walk away, proud of the man he'd become then slipped into her transport to return Jotham's call.

∞ ∞ ∞ ∞ ∞

"Where have you been?" Jotham demanded answering her call on the second ring.

Jacinda was surprised by the abruptness of his words. "I was out shopping and didn't want to talk to you on the street. What's wrong?"

"There's been a development and I need to leave for Kisurri tonight."

"Oh." She tried not to be disappointed. She hadn't realized how much she had been looking forward to spending time with Jotham.

"I know it's rushing you, but can you be ready to leave by nine?"

"You still want me to go with you?"

"Of course! I could handle some things over the comm if you need more time, but we'd still need to leave by the rising of the first sun."

"You'd do that?" Jacinda sat there unable to hide the disbelieving look on her face. "Delay an important trip? For me?"

"I would, but I can only delay for so long." He looked away to take something handed to him by Chesney, she assumed, and she noticed the fatigue around his eyes.

"Did you get *any* sleep last night?" she asked quietly.

"No." He wrote on what was given to him, then handed it back.

"I'll be at the Palace as soon as I can. No later than eight." She knew she would have to rush, but anything she forgot she could purchase in Kisurri.

"Really?" Jotham's eyes shot back to her in disbelief.

"On one condition."

"What's that?"

"You try and get some rest between now and then."

"I can only promise to try."

"Don't make me come over there and force you."

"You're going to put me to bed?" Jotham found he was grinning at the thought, and knew he wouldn't be getting any rest if she did.

"Get that look off your face, Jotham Tibullus." Jacinda fought her own grin. "That was supposed to be a threat."

"It wasn't a very good one."

"I can see that." She watched something else get handed to him. "You're obviously busy and I have a lot I need to accomplish if I'm going to be there on time, so I'm going to disconnect and get to it."

"Do you need me to send someone over to assist you? I'm sure Chesney can..."

"I'm sure Chesney has more than enough to do assisting you. I'll be fine." She quickly reassured him. "I'll see you when I get there. Try to get some rest."

With that, she quickly disconnected.

JACINDA'S CHALLENGE

∞ ∞ ∞ ∞ ∞

"Jacinda Michelakakis, what is going on?" Myesha unzipped yet another piece of luggage for her to pack.

"What are you talking about, Myesha?" She pulled out yet another outfit that, while formal, wasn't too formal to pack. "I told you I was going to Kisurri, I'm just going a few days earlier than planned."

"Yet you are packing the way you used to when Stephan was alive, and you knew what you wore reflected not only on him but on the House of Protection."

Jacinda paused, looking at her friend uncertainly. "I am?"

"Yes. Why are you really going to Kisurri?"

Jacinda slowly walked over to the bed. She carefully folded and put the outfit in the luggage before sitting down on the bed. "I'm not going by myself, Myesha," she quietly confided.

"I could tell that. What I can't figure out is why all the secrecy." Myesha sat next to her long-time friend. "We used to talk about everything."

"I know, but this is... unexpected and complicated..."

"Jacinda, you are starting to scare me." Myesha took her hand and squeezed it. "You were the wife of one of the most influential Assemblymen in the history of the House of Protection. You set the standard for grace, style, and what an Assemblyman's wife should be. Now you're acting as if you have to somehow step it up for this man. Why? There can't possibly be a man on the planet whose life you believe could demand more of you than what your life with Stephan did."

"There is," Jacinda whispered.

"Impossible. For that to be true, it would have to be King..." Myesha's voice trailed off, her eyes widening as she realized what she was saying. What Jacinda wasn't denying.

"Jacinda..."

"As I said, it was unexpected and is complicated."

"Jotham..." Myesha could only whisper.

"Yes. You can't tell anyone, Myesha."

"The children don't know?"

"No, very few know."

"You were coming from the Palace when you had your accident."

"Yes."

"You are going to Kisurri with Jotham."

"Yes."

"Praise the ancestors, Jacinda." Myesha surged to her feet, running a shaky hand threw her hair. "He's the *King*!"

"I know that."

"He asked you to accompany him?" Her pacing slowed as she gave her a considering look. "To the House of Knowledge?"

"Yes."

"He is not trying to hide it, not if he's taking you *there*. The High Admiral is one of his oldest friends."

"I know. I knew them both in the Academy."

"You did?"

"Yes."

"King Jotham has fallen in love again!" A smile broke out across Myesha's face. "Jotham is in love."

"He hasn't said that, Myesha."

Myesha only paused for a moment. "That doesn't matter. He will. He danced with you, the last dance at the Assemblymen's Ball. You're spending time with him at the Palace. He is taking you with him to Kisurri, to the House of Knowledge."

"We are trying to keep it unofficial."

"Right, because it will so remain unofficial once you're seen in Kisurri with him."

Jacinda grimaced. "Hopefully that won't happen. We're going for Princess Sabah's christening. There are no public events planned."

"Good luck with that."

"Which is why I'm having so much trouble packing."

"Well, this isn't going." Myesha reached in and pulled out the outfit Jacinda had just folded and put in the luggage. "There are too many visuals of you in this. Why didn't you go shopping?"

"I was," Jacinda defended herself, but smiled as her friend moved around her room in a determined fashion. "But then Jotham called and we need to leave sooner."

She watched Myesha go deep into her closet, returning with several hanging bags. Bags that contained clothing she'd purchased for the upcoming Assembly cycle with Stephan. The one he never got the chance to serve at.

"These will be perfect."

"I had forgotten about those."

"I know." She paused to look at her. "Will you be okay wearing them... with Jotham?"

"I..." Jacinda seriously thought about it. Those outfits had been bought when Stephan had been alive, but he never saw her in them and they would be perfect. "Yes, I'll be okay with it."

"Good. Now for your shoes...."

∞ ∞ ∞ ∞ ∞

"Majesty, Madame Michelakakis has just entered the Palace grounds." Chesney stepped into Jotham's office informing him.

"She is? Already?" He looked at the time and saw she was several hours early.

"Have Deffand meet her."

"He is already on the way, Majesty. He ordered the guards to notify him as soon as she passed the gate."

"Good, have her things put on my shuttle."

"Of course, Majesty. I'll also have yours loaded. Would you like her escorted directly to the shuttle or to your private quarters?"

Jotham looked around his desk and started to gather up his papers. There was nothing here he couldn't do on the shuttle. If they left now while it would be late when they arrived, they would still be able to get a good night's sleep and it had been too long since he'd seen Jacinda.

"Have Deffand escort her to the shuttle and inform the pilot that we'll be leaving as soon as everyone is on board."

"Yes, Majesty."

Chapter Eighteen

Jacinda silently watched as Jotham answered yet another comm, signed another document, and gave Chesney another order. It had been that way for two hours, Jotham sitting at his desk on the shuttle furiously working.

When Jotham arrived on the shuttle, he had immediately zeroed in on her, wrapping her up in his arms and soundly kissing her. While the shuttle had taken off, he sat next to her, telling her of the explosion on Nuga, an important mining planet for the Coalition. At first it was believed to be the Regulians, but now they believed members of the House of Knowledge and the House of Protection were involved, which was why they were heading to Kisurri early.

Jacinda had silently absorbed it all, not wanting to believe it was possible but knew from experience that evil could exist where you least expected it. So, when Jotham had risen after takeoff and moved to the desk, she had said nothing, knowing how important this work was. But now after watching the fatigue grow on his face and in his tone, after listening to some of the comms he was receiving that had nothing to do with the matter at hand, she was beginning to grow angry.

She was seeing too many similarities between Jotham and Stephan.

They were both dedicated workaholics who didn't know when it was time to quit.

She lost Stephan because she hadn't made him slow down, hadn't made sure he had gotten enough rest. If she had done those things, maybe she wouldn't have found him dead in the garden from a massive heart attack, maybe she wouldn't have lost him dozens of cycles before she should have.

She and Jotham were just beginning this journey together. They were both a little tentative, both a little unsure, but if there was one thing Jacinda was sure of, it was she wanted to create a life with Jotham. A real, true, happy life. One that involved them really *being* together, not her just sitting here watching him work himself to death. She had been down this path before with Stephan, and she wasn't going to make the same mistakes again.

She was going to start as she meant to finish. Something she used to tell her children. It was time she did the same. Rising, she walked around to where Jotham was sitting and took the pen from his hand.

"Jacinda, what are you doing?" Jotham frowned up at her.

"You need to rest, Jotham. This can wait."

"I need to get this done."

"The world isn't going to end if you don't sign off this minute on a report about a proposed new hospital. Not one of the last five comms has been about Nuga. It's time for you to rest."

Chesney entered the room carrying another stack of papers.

"Are any of those related to Nuga?" Jacinda demanded, shocking both Jotham and Chesney.

"Ahh," Chesney looked at the paper then back to Jacinda. "No."

"Then they can wait as can any comms not related to Nuga. Jotham needs to get some sleep before we arrive in Kisurri. The first sun will be rising only a few hours after we arrive and I'm sure the High Admiral will be up."

"I..." Chesney's gaze flew to Jotham, obviously not sure what he should do.

"Jacinda, I need to get this done."

"Not tonight." She glared at him for a moment then turned her attention to Chesney. "That will be all, Mister Chesney, and please make sure everyone else knows they are not to disturb the King."

"I...yes... Madame," Chesney stuttered, quietly shutting the door as he quickly left.

"What do you think you are doing, Jacinda?" Jotham watched as she gathered up all the scattered papers on the desk, unconcerned she was mixing them up and shoved them into a drawer before slamming it shut.

"I'm doing what Chesney should be doing. What you should be smart enough to do and what I should have done with Stephan. I'm saying *enough,* and I'm meaning it. You're exhausted. What you're working on can wait, so it's going to. Now come, you're going to lay down and rest."

∞ ∞ ∞ ∞ ∞

Jotham allowed her to pull him up and lead him back to the bedroom of the shuttle. It was a room he rarely used, preferring to work while en route, but right now he had to admit the bed looked good, especially if Jacinda were lying down next to him.

He hadn't realized how much time had passed since the shuttle had taken off. He only meant to clear a few things up, but it seemed he had become immersed in his duties, as he always did.

Jacinda was right. He was tired. He should have realized it and stopped, but even with fatigue making him sluggish, he hadn't missed her reference to Stephan and the guilt she seemed to carry.

Once in the room, he kicked off his shoes and let himself groan as he rolled onto the bed. Yes, he should have realized he needed this. Rolling onto his back, he opened his arms.

"Rest with me."

Having kicked off her own shoes in the outer room, Jacinda climbed onto the bed and settled into his arms with a contented sigh.

With Jacinda in his arms, Jotham closed his eyes and felt the chaos of his world drift away. How had she known he needed this?

He needed to ask her.

He needed to ask her why she felt guilty about Stephan's death.

And he would.

In just a minute.

∞ ∞ ∞ ∞ ∞

Jacinda knew the moment Jotham feel asleep. It didn't take long, a testament to just how exhausted he really was.

Why had she let him push so hard?

Why hadn't she said something sooner?

Was she destined to make the same mistakes again?

∞ ∞ ∞ ∞ ∞

"You made no mistakes, my love."

"Stephan?" Searching for his voice she found she was in her garden, the three suns high overhead.

"Here, my love."

She found him kneeling in front of the 'mother' rose bush, clipping roses. It was exactly where he had been when he died.

"Get up!" She immediately reached to make him.

"Jacinda, it was no more this bush's fault that I died than it was yours."

"It was. If I had been firmer... paid more attention... gotten to you sooner."

"It would have made no difference. It was my time to join the ancestors. I had done all I was supposed to and it was time to move on."

"No! We were supposed to have many more cycles together. You were supposed to be here to see your son become an Assemblyman, to witness your daughter's Union! You were supposed to grow old with me! Carinians now easily live a hundreds cycles. I wanted to share them with you."

"Oh, my love. I did witness Danton become an Assemblyman. From here. A part of me will always live on in him, thanks to you, just as a part of me lives on in Ethan and Stephanie. That's what makes you my life mate. My life continues because of you. You allowed me to have the life I was meant to have. Without you, none of it would have been possible."

"Oh, Stephan."

"Now it is time for you to do the same for Jotham."

"What?"

"Did you ever wonder about this plant," he gestured to the rose bush. "Why its blooms changed?"

"Mother told me it would bloom the House color of the soil it was planted in."

"Yet it remained Healing Gold until after I met the ancestors."

"Yes."

"Your mother wasn't entirely correct in her assumption. She didn't know the whole story behind it."

"And you do?"

"I do now. You see, my love, the prince that loved your ancestor, the one that gave you this mark." Stephan's finger gently traced the three spiral suns that adorned her chest.

Looking down Jacinda suddenly realized she was wearing Stephan's favorite nightgown, the one he'd had specially made to reveal those marks.

"His name was Dallan, and he truly loved Pascua. As proof of that love, he gave her the Tausendjahriger Rosenstock, the ancient symbol of love."

"If he truly loved her he would have stayed with her."

"Oh, but it wasn't that simple. For you see, he also loved the woman that would become his Queen."

"What! That's impossible."

"Is it? Do you not, my love, also love Jotham?"

"But... but that's different! It never would have occurred if you were still alive!"

"Are you so sure about that, my love?" Stephan looked at her with no censure in his eyes. "I know you would never have betrayed me, never would have broken your vows to me, but *feelings* are about neither of those things. They just are, and Prince Dallan, unfortunately, had them for two women at the same time. One he had known for cycles and had grown to love. The other one he instantly fell in love with as soon as he met her. One he made his Queen and the other gave him his daughter. Both women knew about the other, but once Dallan said his vows to Rohanna he totally committed himself to her and never saw Pascua again. Instead, he sent the bush."

"I don't understand."

"It's not the soil that causes the blooms color, Jacinda, not in the 'mother,' it is the love between its caretaker and the man she loves."

"But I was its caretaker before you died and it only produced golden blooms."

"That's because you are a royal and although you loved me, someone from the House of Protection, *I* wasn't royal."

"But..."

"Jotham *is* royal and that's why the 'mother' now blooms two colors. You love Jotham, a royal from the House of Protection. The plant understands that and acknowledges that love."

"But I didn't love him when it changed!"

"It doesn't matter, the plant knew you would."

"But... I don't want to lose you, Stephan."

"Oh, my love." Stephan pulled her into his arms. "You can never lose me. You are my life mate, I am yours and the day will come when we will be reunited. But *that* doesn't mean your love for Jotham has to end, any more than him loving you means his for Lata must. The life with the ancestors is an amazing place, Jacinda, where love is celebrated."

"Yours and mine."

"Yours and Jotham's."

"Jotham's and Lata's."

"I'm confused, Stephan. I don't know what to do."

"Follow your heart, my love, just as you did with me. You followed your instincts. You made no mistakes and because of it, I was able to fulfill my destiny. Now you must do the same with Jotham. If you do, our world will continue on this bright new path... " Clipping a rose, he handed it to her.

Looking down, Jacinda was shocked to see not a violet rose, not a golden one. Instead, a tiny new bud was just starting to open. Its base, House of Protection violet, while the tips of its petals were House of Healing gold.

One House.

Looking back to question Stephan, she found him gone.

∞ ∞ ∞ ∞ ∞

"She's right, you know."

"Hmm," Jotham asked sleepily, enjoying the gentle fingers running through his hair. "Who is?"

"Jacinda."

"What?!!" Jotham's eyes flew open to find Lata smiling down at him. "Lata?"

"Hello, my love."

"What? Where?" His eyes flew around the room only to discover he wasn't on his shuttle, he was in the garden.

His garden.

Next to Lata's rose bush.

"Jacinda is right, you know. You will meet the ancestors before you should if you keep on as you are."

Jotham frowned at her. "What are you talking about, Lata?"

"You. You've always been destined for greatness, Jotham, but you will achieve none of it if you continue on as you are."

"I don't understand."

"I left you before I should have, my love, because I refused to recognize the signs, didn't follow my instincts. I was young and stubborn and believed nothing bad could ever happen to me. After all, I was the *Queen*." She gave him a sad smile. "I was wrong and now both you and Barek blame yourselves for what was never your fault."

"It was my fault, Lata."

"No, my love, you did everything you could. The fault is mine. All mine, and I don't want you to make the same mistake."

"And what mistake is that?"

"The one where I thought I could handle everything alone. I couldn't, and you can't either. If you continue to try you will fail, just as I did."

"Lata..."

"Our world is on the brink, Jotham."

"The brink of what?" he demanded.

"Of greatness or great destruction. It could go either way and you are the pivot point."

"Me?" Jotham felt himself pale.

"Yes, my love, you. But you have to be there to make it happen."

"I don't understand, Lata. How can I possibly do more than I already am? I'm..."

"Tired. I can see that. So can Jacinda."

"Jacinda..."

"You love her, Jotham." Lata's eyes were soft and full of understanding as she spoke.

"Lata..."

"It's all right, my love." She reached out, running her fingers down his cheek, soothing him as she used to. "It takes nothing away from you and me. If I could have, I would have brought the two of you together sooner. I hated to see you so alone and struggling, but Stephan had his own destiny that he needed to fulfill before the two of you could be together."

"I worried..."

"That I would not approve." Lata leaned over and kissed his lips. "Jotham, she is the only woman I would approve of because she truly *loves* you."

"I know she cares about me, but love..."

"How could she not love you, Jotham? You're a wonderful man."

"I've made mistakes with her, Lata. I've been impatient, demanding, I expect her to do as I say."

"And does she?" Lata's eyes sparkled with mirth, knowing the answer.

"No. She argues with me. Tells me when I'm wrong."

"Good. Someone needs to."

"Lata, stop teasing me, I'm serious." Jotham suddenly realized he was discussing another woman with his life mate.

"And I'm so glad you are, my love." Lata looked at him with understanding eyes. "Jacinda *sees* you, but more importantly, she understands what your duties should entail... and what they shouldn't. She isn't going to let anyone, not even you, intimidate her. She will make a magnificent Queen."

"*You* are my Queen, Lata." Jotham sat up sharply.

"I am," Lata acknowledged, "but that doesn't mean she can't be too. It's always been her ultimate destiny, Jotham. You've seen it for yourself."

Jotham knew she was referring to Jacinda's royal mark, but for him to take a Queen from another House...

"What you're suggesting..."

"Will change our world forever," Lata agreed.

∞ ∞ ∞ ∞ ∞

A steady beeping dragged Jotham from the deep sleep he had fallen into. Blindly reaching out, he hit the button to answer the comm.

"What is it?" he demanded.

"Majesty, we are fifteen minutes out of Kisurri," Chesney's voice informed him.

"Understood." Disconnecting, Jotham relaxed back into the bed and while he pulled Jacinda closer, his mind was on the strange dream he'd had.

It had to have been a dream. Right?

"Jotham?" Jacinda roused sleepily in his arms, rubbing her cheek against his chest.

"Hmm?" Her next words had him stiffening.

"I just had the strangest dream."

"You did?"

"Yeah." She lifted her head to look at him. "Was that Chesney I heard?"

"Yes, he was letting us know we are fifteen minutes from Kisurri."

"Oh, I guess we'd better get up then."

"In a minute." Jotham sat up and leaned back against the wall and pulled her across his lap so she was in his arms, facing him. "Tell me about your dream."

"I..." she hesitated.

"It involved Stephan, didn't it?"

"Yes." Jacinda's eyes widened as she looked at him. "How could you possibly know that?"

Jotham knew he had to be honest with her. "Because I just had one with Lata."

Jacinda felt her eyes start to fill. "Praise the ancestors! That means it wasn't a dream, that it was actually an encounter and..."

"And?"

"Stephan was actually holding me in his arms."

"As Lata was in mine."

Jacinda gave him an uncertain look. "And she was okay with..."

"Us being together?"

At her nod, Jotham gave her that little half smile from the left side of his mouth that always made her heart beat a little faster.

"Yes." Now it was Jotham's turn to look uncertain. "Was Stephan?"

"Yes."

Silence reigned for several minutes, each lost in their own thoughts. Jacinda tried to understand everything Stephan had told her. He said she needed to follow her instincts, her heart, and both were telling her she needed to tell Jotham how she felt. Needed to tell him now.

"I need to tell you something, Jotham."

"You can tell me anything, Jacinda."

"I'm in love with you."

"Jacinda..." Before he could say more, she put gentle fingers over his lips.

"I'm not sure I'm happy about it."

"What?" Jotham pulled away from her fingers, his heart that had leapt at her first words now fell.

"I never wanted to be involved with a King. If I had, I would have stayed in the House of Healing. It's why I always steered clear of you at the Academy." As she spoke, she traced his full lower lip. "I worked so hard to try and not end up here, but it seems the ancestors have other ideas."

"You don't wish to share your life with me?" Jotham felt his heart begin to ache.

"Of course I do!" Jacinda instantly denied. "I love you. You! What I don't love is the thought of watching another man I love working himself to death. I can't do it again. It will destroy me."

"Jacinda, Stephan died..."

"Because I didn't stand up to him, make him keep his promise to slow down, to cut back. He promised he would stop chairing so many committees, that he would delegate more. He did neither and you are even worse."

"Jacinda, I am the *King*. There are things that only I can do."

"Yes, but there are things that you don't need to do, like being involved in the labor talks for the Sokol Corporation. There's no need for it, and in truth, it's detrimental for the workers every time you are."

"What are you talking about?!!" Jotham took great pride in that work. "They are always my top priority."

"Sokol knows that. He also knows how much your people love and respect you and he uses that. He knows if he presents them with a contract that you've approved, they will accept it, no questions asked. Every time they do, his share of the profits increases."

"How can you know this?"

"It was one of the new committees Stephan was chairing before his death. He was investigating Sokol after he was approached by several disgruntled workers."

"Why didn't they go to the Chair of the Labor Committee?"

"Because Pajari chairs that committee and Sokol is his biggest supporter."

Jotham couldn't believe what she was telling him. How could he not have known this? All he was trying to do was help his people.

"And you do." Jacinda saw he hadn't realized he'd spoken out loud. "But by doing so much, you don't have the time to give any of it your full attention. You're no longer that new King, the youngest ever crowned, trying to prove yourself. You are not that newly-widowed King trying to fill those suddenly empty nights to keep your mind off of what you had lost."

"How can you know that?"

"Because I was there, Jotham. I saw it all and then I did the same thing after Stephan died. The nights were always the worst, especially in the beginning. But it's time for it to stop. *You* rule the House of Protection, Jotham. It doesn't rule *you*. Not like this."

Jotham just looked at her, letting her words sink in. Everything she said was right. He had felt he needed to prove himself in those early cycles. He didn't now. He had demanded to take on more and more after Lata's death because he couldn't stand to return to his rooms and know they were empty. Now when he wanted to clear time, time to spend with Jacinda, something always interrupted. But how did he step back now?

"I understand what you are saying, Jacinda, and you are right. But I can't just abandon these duties, to do so would be like abandoning my people."

"I would never suggest that, Jotham, but you can assign those duties to someone else."

"There is no one else."

"Not even Barek?" She saw she had surprised him.

"Barek?"

"Yes. He is your heir, shouldn't he start to learn the responsibilities that will one day be his, from you? Not be thrown into them unprepared as you were?"

"I... I never considered it before. Barek never expressed a desire to be more involved."

"Just like he never expressed an interest in knowing more about his mother?" she quizzed gently. "He is his father's son, Jotham. He watched and learned from you and it's made him a very good, strong, and proud man. It's also made him a very private one."

"Yes." Jotham nodded his agreement.

"When it comes to men like that, sometimes you just have to be very blunt to get them to tell you what they are thinking."

"And if that doesn't work?" He caressed her cheek with a knuckle.

"Then you yell at them, at least I do. Tears work well too, but only when it's absolutely necessary."

"I find it hard to believe you ever had to take it that far with Stephan."

"Oh no, never with Stephan. Yelling always made my point with him. I only ever had to pull out the tears with my father."

Jacinda smiled gently at the memory. "My mother taught me how."

"What could you possibly have had to cry about to get your father to agree to?"

"My Union with Stephan."

A discreet knock stopped Jotham from replying.

"Yes?"

"Majesty, I need to inform you that we are beginning our descent."

"Thank you, Chesney, we'll be out in a moment."

"Yes, Majesty."

"Jacinda," he cupped her cheek, stilling her when she went to move away. "We *will* talk about this again when there is more time. But right now, I have something I need to tell you."

"What?"

"I'm in love with you too."

Chapter Nineteen

Jacinda lay across Jotham's chest, propped up on her elbow as she watched him sleep. She still couldn't believe this amazing man loved her.

Her.

Jacinda Michelakakis.

When they arrived in the dead of the night, they were quickly shown to a private wing and informed that the High Admiral and the Queen were expecting them for first meal at seven.

Now the second sun was just starting to rise and Jacinda knew they would need to rise soon too. She wasn't sure what type of reception she was going to receive from the Queen and High Admiral, but she hoped it wouldn't cause problems for Jotham. She knew he thought they would welcome her with open arms, Jacinda wasn't so sure.

What she *was* sure of was that Jotham loved her, and she loved Jotham. Together they would figure the rest out. No, it wasn't the life she expected, being a King's... companion, but she wouldn't shy away from it either. She of all people knew how precious love was.

"Do you know how much I love waking up with you in my arms?" Jotham's husky words pulled her thoughts back to him. "How much I love you?"

Jacinda smiled gently down at him. "As much as I do you?"

"More," he told her stretching up to capture her lips.

It had been cycles since Jotham had woken up to a beautiful woman staring down at him. The last had been Lata and now because of his 'encounter' with her he could experience and love again with no doubts and no regrets.

Jacinda let him take control of the kiss, wrapping her arms around his neck as he rolled her onto her back. They both sighed heavily when there was a knock on the chamber door.

"Yes?"

"Majesty, I was just letting you know you have thirty minutes."

"Thank you, Chesney."

"One of these times we are going to wake up without Chesney interrupting us," Jacinda teased.

"Yes, we will." Giving her one more, hard kiss he rose then held out his hand. "Come on, my love, I'll let you use the shower first."

∞ ∞ ∞ ∞ ∞

Jacinda walked confidently beside Jotham as they were escorted through the Queen's Wing to the private eating area of the Royal family. She was trying not to be nervous but found she was. Not because of who she was meeting, but because they were Jotham's friends and she wanted to make a good impression.

The chatter of voices could be heard through the closed doors. When the guard knocked on the door, the chatter ceased.

"Enter," came the command and when the guard opened the doors, Jacinda was surprised at what she saw.

A long table was set in the middle of the room and seven pairs of eyes turned to see who had interrupted their meal.

"Jotham," William rose as he greeted his old friend. "Come in, I saved you some food and I want you to know it wasn't easy, not with the way these four rascals eat." He eyed the boys sitting at the table.

With a hand on the small of her back, Jotham guided her to William. "I believe it. I've seen the way these monsters eat. Will, you remember Jacinda Michelakakis, don't you?"

"Yes, of course. Hello, Jacinda, it's been a long time. Won't you sit?" He gestured to the two empty seats, pulling the closest to him out. "Cassandra will be back shortly, Sabah was being fussy so she went to lay her back down."

"It has been a long time, thank you." She took the seat next to him.

"Let me make the introductions. The one at the end down there, shoveling food in his mouth is our oldest, Kayden. Next to him is Brett, Peter and Cyndy's son. Across from them is Jacob and Willie, our second and third sons. Say hello to Madame Michelakakis, boys."

"Hello, Madame Michelakakis." The four quickly obeyed then went back to eating.

"Hello," Jacinda smiled, remembering how much her own boys used to eat.

"This is Peter Chamberlain and his wife, Cyndy."

"Hello." She acknowledged the couple that sat across the table.

"Madame Michelakakis," Peter Chamberlain greeted while his wife gave her a small smile.

"As I said, Cassandra will return shortly." He gestured to the empty chair to his right. "Coffee?" he asked lifting the container in front of him.

"Please," Jacinda smiled her thanks. She hadn't yet had a cup.

"So, Jotham, how was your flight? You got in earlier than I expected."

"It was fine and you can thank Jacinda for that, she packed in record time."

"Really?" William raised an eyebrow at that. "You'll have to teach Cassandra that trick."

"Teach me what trick?"

Jacinda watched as the sound of his wife's voice had William immediately rising to pull out the empty chair for her. "How to pack quickly. Did she go down okay?"

"Yes." She sat. "Hello, Jotham."

Jacinda saw the warmth in the Queen's eyes as she greeted Jotham. They quickly cooled as she glanced at her, waiting.

"Good morning, Cassandra," Jotham replied. "I'd like to introduce you to Jacinda Michelakakis. Jacinda, Queen Cassandra Zafar."

"Majesty," Jacinda bowed her head slightly.

"Madame Michelakakis." Cassandra acknowledged her before looking to her husband. "So are you saying I take too long to pack?"

William frowned slightly at his wife's coolness to Jacinda. "There are times."

"Hmm, I guess I'll have to let you start packing for yourself then."

"Michelakakis? Lieutenant Michelakakis is your daughter?"

Jacinda looked over to find herself under the gaze of Peter Chamberlain's brown eyes. "Yes, Stephie was thrilled to be selected for your advanced training program, although I'm sure she'll be mortified when she finds out I called her by her childhood nickname."

"Daughter? I didn't realize any of the trainees were women." Cyndy frowned at her husband.

"I never thought it important, Pixie."

"But you said this is the most aggressive training program you've ever put together, that you've already had to cut a third of the class.

"Pixie...." Peter gave her a warning look.

"What?" Cyndy demanded.

"It's alright, Captain. I have the greatest faith in my daughter."

"You don't believe she's among the ones already cut?" Peter asked curiously.

"No," Jacinda's answer was swift and decisive. "My daughter has never failed at anything, once she's set her mind to it, and she's set it to graduate from your groundbreaking program. So she will." She saw Peter's lips twitch.

"I see where the Lieutenant gets her confidence from."

"Oh no," Jacinda waved a dismissing hand, "trust me. That all comes from her father."

"He was an Assemblyman for the House of Protection, wasn't he?"

Jacinda looked back to Cassandra, sure the Queen already knew the answer. "Yes, for nearly forty cycles."

"But you're not."

"I'm sorry. I'm not what?"

"From the House of Protection."

"No. I was born into the House of Healing."

"Where your father was also an Assemblyman."

"Along with both my grandfathers and several other ancestors."

"Yet you wed a man from the House of Protection."

"As you did. I've never believed it should make a difference what House your life mate comes from."

"You believe Stephan Michelakakis was your life mate?" Cassandra raised a questioning eyebrow.

"No. I *know* Stephan was my life mate."

"Hmm."

William frowned at his wife, then turned his attention to Jacinda. "Stephan was a good man. We had many spirited conversations."

Jacinda pulled her gaze from Cassandra. "Spirited. Really? You mean you argued loudly, don't you?"

"At times," William smiled and looked to Peter. "If his daughter has half his belief, dedication, and stubbornness she will be an invaluable asset when she completes Peter's program."

Peter nodded slightly, letting William know he understood. He would have to take a special interest in Stephanie Michelakakis' training.

Jacinda took a sip of her coffee and grimaced slightly at its strength, then set it down to add a cube of sugar before she slid the sweetener toward Jotham, knowing he would want it.

"Is there a problem with your coffee?" Cassandra asked coolly, bringing Jacinda's attention back to her.

"No, it's just a little strong. I normally drink a milder blend from an establishment in Pechora."

"Pittaluga's?" William asked longingly causing Cassandra to frown.

"Yes." Jacinda looked back to William.

"I haven't had a cup of his special blend in cycles."

"I brought two pounds of it with me for my sister. I'm sure she won't mind parting with one."

"I didn't think Pittaluga sold his special blend."

"It's a closely guarded secret, but I'm sure he'd be more than willing to send some to you, High Admiral."

"It's Will, Jacinda. We've known each other for far too long to stand on protocol, at least in private."

"Alright. Will."

Jotham shot Will a grateful smile.

"I wasn't aware you two were that well acquainted." Cassandra's tone became even cooler as she looked from her husband to Jacinda.

"I've known Jotham and Will since our Academy days, and while we did have several classes together, I was a cycle ahead of them."

"You're *older* than them?"

"Cassandra!" This shocked exclamation came from Cyndy.

Jacinda wasn't shocked. It seemed the Queen was wanting to get her digs in. Well, two could play at that game.

"Yes, I'm older. As such, I was never part of Jotham and Will's special 'tutoring' program."

Will, who had just taken a sip of his coffee, choked.

"Tutoring?" This question came from a grinning Peter. "Really, Will?"

"I... Well... we were young and..."

"Jotham, I'm surprised at you. I thought you met Lata at the Academy."

The censure in Cassandra's voice was unmistakable and Jacinda wasn't going to stand by and allow it to happen. Especially not when it was because of something she'd said.

"He did," Jacinda spoke first. "And as soon as he met her he never 'tutored' another woman. He is a very loyal man."

"I thought you didn't know him all that well back then," Cassandra challenged.

"I didn't, but my sister, Palma, was Lata's roommate. She visited our home quite often and we were friends."

"I find that... surprising," Cassandra gave her a disbelieving look.

"Why?" Jacinda challenged back. "You don't know me and you never knew Lata. *We* did." She gestured to William and Jotham. "She was one of the sweetest, kindest, most loving woman you'd ever be lucky enough to meet. She also had a wicked sense of humor. She loved Jotham and she loved her son. The universe has been a dimmer place since we lost her."

Silence reigned for a moment at Jacinda's impassioned, heartfelt words. No one could doubt she meant every one of them. Including Cassandra.

"Lata was all those things," William agreed breaking the silence. "She could also be quite the... rule-breaker."

Jotham and William exchanged a look they thought only they understood.

"Are you referring to how you used to distract the other girls on the floor so Jotham could sneak into Lata's room?" Jacinda asked, giving William a too innocent look as she took a bite of her meal.

"I... How did you know about that?" William demanded giving Jotham a shocked look. "Palma always went home whenever we did that!"

"Palma *never* went home, unless it was for a holiday," Jacinda told them emphatically.

"What?" It was Jotham's turn to give her a shocked look. "But Lata always said Palma had gone to see her family."

"She had." She gave him a teasing smile. "Me. She would pack a bag and spend the night in my room. It was the only way the two of you could have any real time together without everyone watching."

"Thank you," Jotham reached over and squeezed her hand.

"It's not like I did anything. I just let my sister sleep on the couch. I'm not sure what you did once I graduated."

"Were you in security too, Jacinda?"

Peter's question pulled Jacinda's gaze away from Jotham's little smirk that said he'd never tell.

"No. I served in communications on the Talon." Jacinda answered him.

"Communications?" Cassandra asked.

"Yes, I was in charge of monitoring all incoming and outgoing communications, not very exciting, but necessary."

"Yes, it is." William agreed, looking at Cassandra. "It can get hectic with the unpredictability of the volume you can get."

"Yes, the only thing reliable was Jotham's nightly call to Lata." Jacinda took another bite, unaware of the shocked looks she was receiving from not only William and Cassandra but also Jotham.

"You always knew when Jotham called Lata?" The stillness of William's tone had Jacinda looking up to find her staring into the eyes of the High Admiral. Straightening, she answered.

"Of course, he called her at eight every night unless he was on duty."

"How could you possibly know that?" Jotham asked, frowning at her.

"Because of your Royal Coding." Jacinda didn't understand why that seemed to upset him.

"You broke the Royal Coding?" Cassandra demanded, her expression tense.

"Of course not!" Jacinda instantly denied. "That code is unbreakable!"

"Then how did you know?" Jotham asked quietly.

"Because of the way the communications system used to be set up." She frowned at Jotham. "Different priority levels ran through different systems. Only you or Admiral Kannon ever had the authority to *send* a communication at that level, and there were only three comms that had that capability. Admiral Kannon's, on the bridge and in his private chambers, and the one in your quarters. I brought it to the attention of Captain Jaq that while no one knew what was being communicated, Jotham was still at risk as they would know his location."

"And what was Jaq's response?" William asked tensely.

"He informed me not to worry my pretty little head about it. That men were in charge and handling it."

"Jaq was always an ass," William spat out, tossing his napkin down on the table in disgust.

"Yes, but he was an especially big ass to women," Jacinda told him quietly.

"Why?" The soft question came from Cyndy.

"He didn't believe women should be allowed to serve in the Fleet," Jacinda told her. "He felt they were a 'distraction' and served no 'real purpose.'"

"Chauvinist pig," Cyndy muttered causing Jacinda to frown in confusion.

"He said that to you?" Jotham demanded angrily.

"To me and every other woman under his command. It's why so many women requested transfers."

"But you didn't. You served both cycles of your tour on the Talon," Jotham reminded her.

"I wasn't going to let that old foab..." she cut herself off, suddenly remembering the children were still at the table, "bully force me out of a position I loved."

"Good for you." Cyndy nodded her approval.

"I'd say your daughter has a lot of you in her." Peter eyed her with a new respect in his gaze.

Jacinda just smiled.

"It was you," Jotham's quiet words had Jacinda losing her smile to look at him.

"What did she do?" Cassandra demanded, her eyes hardening on Jacinda.

Jotham ignored Cassandra and concentrated on Jacinda. "You were the one who brought it to Stephan's 'attention.' It's because of you that the entire communications system was upgraded and the codes changed."

"You were the reason it changed, Jotham. Not me," Jacinda denied.

"Because Stephan brought it to *my* attention. Why didn't he just say it was you?" When Jacinda just looked at him, he pressed. "Jacinda?"

'Because I wasn't from the House of Protection," she finally admitted.

"What the hell does that have to do with it?" Jotham demanded.

"Jotham, think back," Jacinda told him softly. "You know how divided the Assembly was back then. You had just taken the throne and Stephan's and my Union was barely six cycles old. There were those who would have voted against funding that project just because *I* was the one who had voiced the concern."

"I never even considered it could have been you," Jotham spoke quietly. "I always thought it was Will." Jotham looked to his old friend.

"Me?" William gave his friend a shocked look. "Why me?"

"All Stephan would ever say was that it was someone who served in the Coalition and was a friend of mine. Who else was I to think it was?"

"Why didn't you ever say anything, Jacinda?" William asked.

"Because it wasn't important. What was important was that there was no way a Royal could be targeted in the Fleet. That's all that mattered."

"King Jotham?"

"Yes, Kayden?" Jotham looked down the table to find him the focus of confused eyes.

"Who is Lata?"

Every adult at the table sucked in a shocked breath at the innocent question and watched Jotham swallow hard.

"Lata is the Queen of the House of Protection," Jacinda finally answered for Jotham.

"She is the Queen?" Kayden frowned looking to his mother. "Why haven't I ever met her then?"

"She died, Kayden," Jotham spoke quietly looking at the boy. "Cycles before you were born."

"Like Grandpa Jacob did?" he asked quietly.

"Yes."

"Oh." Kayden was silent for a moment. "I'm sorry. You must miss her. I'd miss Mom if she were gone."

"Thank you, Kayden," Jotham replied tightly.

Uncaring about who saw, Jacinda reached over to squeeze Jotham's hand that was fisted on the table, giving him her silent support. Jotham gave her a grateful look and laced his fingers into hers. The action wasn't missed by any of the adults at the table.

"Mom, may we be excused?"

Cassandra looked down the table to find three empty plates, and her youngest shoveling the last of his in as fast as he could. He obviously didn't want to be left behind.

"Yes, but remember you're to be in the classroom at eight."

"Mom?"

Jacinda's gaze went to the smaller, thin boy who sat next to Cyndy.

"Go ahead, Brett, have fun."

"Thanks, Mom." And with that, all four quickly left the room.

Before the door could close, Javiera stepped into the room. "Cassandra, there is a comm for you." Her eyes traveled over the room. "Jacinda?" Her shock at seeing Jacinda sitting there was evident.

"Hello, Javiera."

"Hello. What in the world are you..." she trailed off when she realized whose hand Jacinda was still holding. "King Jotham."

"Good morning, Javiera," Jotham acknowledged not moving his hand.

Cassandra rose wiping her mouth. "I'll take it in my office." Leaning down, she kissed William. "I'll talk to you later."

"Trust me, you will." William gave her a hard look.

Nodding her understanding, she straightened and left the room. With a last look at Jacinda, Javiera followed her.

"High Admiral." A guard wearing House of Knowledge blue entered. "There is a comm coming in from Nuga." Both William and Jotham instantly stood.

"Jacinda," Jotham looked down at her.

"Go. It's why you're here. I'll be fine."

Leaning down, Jotham gave her a quick, hard kiss. "Thank you." Then Jotham and Will left the room.

"I need to get going too." Peter gave his wife a quick kiss and stood. "I'll see you tonight, Pixie. Madame Michelakakis, it's been a pleasure meeting you."

"You too, Captain, and please call me Jacinda."

"Only if you call me Peter."

"Agreed." And with that he was gone. Jacinda looked around the suddenly empty table then smiled at Cyndy. "So, what should we do now?"

Chapter Twenty

"I love this spot." Cyndy sat down on the bench in the Memory Garden.

Jacinda looked around the small walled-in garden taking in the large stone with a name carved into it.

"Jacob Chamberlain," she read.

"Peter and Cassandra's father."

"He died during the Regulian attack on Earth?"

"Yes. Victoria snuck out the back door and followed Cassandra as she helped Lucas after he crash landed and was hurt."

"I had heard that."

"Peter wanted to go, but he had just gotten back from a mission." Cyndy continued to look at the stone. "He injured his shoulder and leg and Cassandra knew he couldn't support Lucas' weight. We didn't know Tori was even gone until we headed for the shelter."

"You must have been terrified." Jacinda couldn't imagine it. If one of her children were out, alone during a Regulian attack, she would have gone crazy."

"I was, but I was three months... moon cycles along with Brett and Peter wouldn't let me go look."

Jacinda watched Cyndy's eyes cloud over as she remembered.

"I remember when the ground began to shake and tremble. It knocked us off our feet, then Peter was up and started sealing the door. I was screaming at him to stop! I was pounding on his back, clawing at him. He was sealing my baby outside."

"I can't even imagine..." Jacinda felt her throat close up and couldn't speak at the thought of what this small woman had gone through.

"What does it say about me, that I never once thought about Cassandra or Jacob?" Pain-filled eyes turned to Jacinda. "All I cared about was Victoria."

Jacinda found she could no longer stand and sat down next to Cyndy, taking her hand. "It says you are a loving mother. Victoria was your priority, as she should have been."

"I think I went crazy for a while. Peter just held me and cried, begging me not to give up."

"He was protecting what he had left. The woman he loved and his child yet to be born."

"None of us would have survived if any of them had made it to the bunker."

Jacinda had to strain to hear the words Cyndy was whispering like a deep dark confession.

"What?"

"The bunker was only stocked with four years of food." Cyndy's eyes were flat as they looked at her. "Without the others there, Peter was able to stretch it to nearly nine."

"Four years...." Jacinda knew she meant cycles.

"Yeah. Four years for four people."

"But there were five people in your family then, Cyndy. You, Peter, Victoria, Cassandra and Jacob."

"Jacob never planned on getting into that bunker." Her eyes turned to the stone. "It took me a while to realize that."

"What do you mean?"

"Jacob was deeply in love with Peter and Cassie's mom. She was killed in a car accident when Cassie was nine and Peter eighteen. It devastated him. He couldn't even look at Cassie because she looked so much like Cassidy. He finally had to send her away... to boarding school."

"Boarding school?"

"I don't know if you have them here. The closest thing I've heard to them is your Academy."

"At nine cycles?" Jacinda couldn't believe it. Carinian children didn't enter the Academy until they were fourteen cycles, and even then Jacinda had thought it too young when her own children went.

"Yes. It really hurt Cassie, made her pull away from people to books. Knowledge, she used to say, never left you."

Both women were silent for a moment, then Cyndy suddenly stood and walked to the stone.

"I'm sorry. I shouldn't have told you about all that. No one wants to hear something like that, especially a stranger."

"Cyndy..." Jacinda slowly walked to the small woman. "Have you talked to *anyone* about this?"

"They all already know about it, so why talk about it?"

"I'm not talking about the actual events. I'm talking about the guilt you feel."

"Guilt?" Cyndy turned confused eyes to her.

"Yes, guilt, about being grateful that the other three *didn't* make it to the bunker," Jacinda said quietly.

"That's not true!" Cyndy nearly shouted at her. "I'm not *grateful*! That would make me..."

"Human," Jacinda finished before Cyndy could. "Your *son* is alive because they *didn't* make it. Your *husband* is alive because they *didn't* make it. *You* are alive because of it. It makes you *human*."

"It makes me a *monster*, a horrible person."

"No, it doesn't."

"Cassie, Tori and Jacob they all died..."

"But they didn't die," Jacinda broke in, "not all of them."

"I didn't know that then."

"But you do now. Cyndy, I can't begin to imagine what you went through. Believing you'd lost nearly your entire family. Being sealed in that bunker and having to deliver a baby, not knowing if it was the only world he'd ever know. As parents, we always want the best for our children and try to give it to them. I'm sure you did what you could."

"I did. It wasn't much, but..."

"And from what I've seen of him, he isn't suffering any lasting effects from that time. He's growing, playing, interacting with his cousins."

"He is, he still needs to build up his strength and catch up on his schooling, but I've never seen him smile so much."

"And Peter, he's back doing what he loves."

"Yes."

"And now you know that Cassandra and Victoria are fine too. Your daughter is beautiful, wed to her life mate, and has a career that she loves."

"Yes."

"And Cassandra the Queen, wed to one of the finest men I've ever met, with a family of her own."

"Yes."

"You also know that Jacob," Jacinda looked at the stone, "never intended on getting into that bunker."

"No, he didn't."

"Then let go of the guilt. As terrible as it all was, it was the only way it could have happened for you all to survive. And while I never had the privilege of meeting Jacob Chamberlain, I do believe he would want you to forgive yourself."

"He would," Cyndy whispered.

"Then *do* it. Only you can. You have so much of your life left to live, Cyndy." Jacinda paused, then asked the question she rarely would. "How old are you anyway? I know Victoria is eighteen, but you don't look a day over thirty."

Cyndy just looked at Jacinda, stunned for a moment, then started to laugh... and laugh... and laugh until tears were streaming down her face and she had to wrap her arms around her stomach because it hurt so much.

"I'm thirty-nine," she finally got out.

"Seriously?" Jacinda's eyes narrowed. "I think I hate you."

"Really?" Cyndy asked wiping away her tears. "Why? I've honestly never seen a woman as beautiful as you. When you and Jotham walked in this morning, you stole my breath. The two of you together... my God, you looked perfect together."

"I... thank you. It's still new and we're trying to find our way."

"Aren't we all?"

The statement was revealing to Jacinda. "Cyndy, I'd like to ask you a question if you don't mind, but I don't want to insult you."

"Ask."

"What did you do back on your planet? Were you just a wife and mother or did you do something else? I don't mean that as an insult because it's basically what I am."

"It didn't sound that way around the table," Cyndy told her moving to sit back down on the bench. "It sounds to me like you were instrumental in making sure the Royals were safe when they were out with the Fleet."

"No one is ever 'safe' when they are out in the Fleet."

"But you did what you could, and that means my nephews are safer because of it, so thank you."

Jacinda blushed at the compliment. "So what about you? Tell me about Cyndy Chamberlain."

"Cyndy Chamberlain..." Cyndy leaned back, putting her arms on the back edge of the bench to support her weight as she closed her eyes, then tipped her head back to absorb the warmth of the Carinian suns. It was something she'd never get enough of. "Well, I started out life as Cyndy Griffin, a small town girl with a big dream."

"What was your dream?"

"To sing. To sing so beautifully that the whole world stopped and listened." She chuckled at the unrealistic dream. "I was so young when I dreamed that."

"How old were you?"

"Five."

"*Five!*" Jacinda couldn't believe it. At five, all she knew she wanted was another cookie.

"Hmmm, all I ever did was sing, from the moment I woke up to the time I went to bed. It drove my parents crazy so they finally hired a teacher, hoping that being forced to sing would make me not want to. They were wrong. It just made me sing more. By the time I was ten I was winning competitions and by twelve I had a record deal."

"Record deal?"

"It was something on Earth that allowed me to make music and get paid for it."

"At twelve?"

"Hmmm, I was considered an amazing new star. I started touring, going out to sing in front of large groups of people and making lots of money... credits. It pretty much destroyed my family."

"I don't understand? You and Peter?"

"Not that family, my parents." Cyndy sighed heavily. "You see back on Earth, a person wasn't considered an 'adult' capable of making their own decisions until they were eighteen."

"It's similar here although there are exceptions."

"There were on Earth too and at sixteen I discovered that my parents, who were in charge of my finances, were spending every penny I made. There should have been millions set aside for me and there wasn't. So I went to court and became what was called an emancipated minor, meaning I was considered an adult and could control my life and finances. My parents never talked to me again, unless they needed money."

"I'm sorry."

"So am I, but it's the way it was. So anyway, I continued to tour. Then I did a concert for the troops, the military like your coalition, and I met Peter."

"How old were you?"

"Just turned twenty. He just stood there, beside the stage and watched me. He didn't sing along or hoot and scream. He just watched me like I was the only person in the room. I was used to people, especially guys, *trying* to make me feel special, but he *did*."

"You loved him."

"From the moment I saw him, but we came from such different worlds. I was always travelling and he had to stay at his base. If I could come visit, he would suddenly have to leave on a mission. It just wasn't going to work."

"But it did."

"Yeah, but not until after a lot of heartache and soul searching. When I got pregnant with Tori, I stopped touring. It was only supposed to be for a couple years, but then the Regulians took her, and she was so traumatized.... She was getting better and I was just starting to consider going back when they returned."

"The Regulians?"

"Yes, and the rest you know."

"You've had an amazing life, Cyndy."

"I guess that's one word for it."

"What word would you use?"

"Insignificant."

"What?!!" Jacinda couldn't hide her shock. "How can you say that? You've got two beautiful children, a husband that obviously adores you, and you survived the Regulians not once, but twice! How can you say it's been insignificant?"

"Because I have nothing to contribute here."

"I..."

"My daughter is full grown and happy, she doesn't need me. My son is growing and learning about things I know nothing about, and I can't help him. My husband... well he's back doing what he's always excelled at, training and protecting. They've all found their place here and then there's me... sitting in a Memory Garden staring at a stone."

"Then find your place."

"How? It's not like I have any skills that are needed here."

"You can still sing, can't you?"

"Well, yeah... not as well as I used to, the dust... but I'm sure no one on Carina would want to hear it."

"Come on," Jacinda stood and held out her hand. After a moment's hesitation, Cyndy took it.

"Where are we going?"

"I happen to know someone that would know if anyone *would* want to 'hear' it."

∞ ∞ ∞ ∞ ∞

Palma stood dumbfounded in the doorway. She'd had no idea who could be at her front door at this time of the day, but it definitely hadn't been her sister and the Queen's sister-in-law, she was the image of her daughter, Victoria.

"Are you going to let us in, Palma, or just stand there?" Jacinda asked.

"I... what... Oh, sorry. Of course. Please, come in." Stepping back, she allowed them in then led them into her living room. "Please. Sit."

"Palma, this is Cyndy Chamberlain. Queen Cassandra's sister-in-law."

"An honor to meet you, Princess Cyndy," Palma curtsied slightly.

"Uh, what? I'm not a princess," Cyndy instantly denied.

"Umm, Cyndy," Jacinda spoke up. "Actually you are. Your husband is the Queen's brother, which means, had they grown up on Carina their mother would have been the Queen, making Peter a Prince and you as his wife, a Princess.

"Well shit," Cyndy spit out, making Jacinda smile.

"Cyndy, this is my sister, Palma Metaxas."

"It's a pleasure to meet you," Cyndy replied. Getting over the shock that she had a title, she let her eyes travel from Palma around the room, stopping on what looked like a piano.

"Would you like something to drink? Coffee maybe?" Palma asked.

Jacinda watched Cyndy closely and immediately noticed how she seemed to still when she saw the Pianola tucked into the corner of the room and hid her smile.

"Why don't I help you make some coffee." Jacinda rose from the couch. "I brought you some of Pittaluga's special blend."

"You did!" Palma asked excitedly.

"Yes, and Cyndy has never had it before. Cyndy, we'll just be a few minutes. Make yourself at home." Jacinda told her even though it was her sister's house, taking Palma's arm she led her away.

∞ ∞ ∞ ∞ ∞

"Jacinda, what in the name of the ancestors is going on?" Palma demanded as soon as they were out of earshot. "You show up here without even calling..."

"Can't I come visit my sister if I want?" Jacinda asked, trying not to smile.

"Of course you can! You know that! Stop trying to change the subject. You show up and you bring with you the Queen's newly arrived sister-in-law. The one it's being whispered about that is on her deathbed. The one no one has been allowed to see. You bring her *here*? With no Royal Guards?"

"Really? She hasn't been allowed to meet *anyone*?" Jacinda frowned at the 'royal guards' part.

"Only trusted Palace staff, like Javiera, and you know how tight-lipped they can be."

"Yes."

"So how did you sneak her out of the Palace? No, the better question is what were you doing at the Palace?"

"What I'm doing there can wait for another time." Jacinda held up a finger silencing her sister. "Seriously, I'll tell you, but what matters right now is Cyndy."

"Why? What's wrong with her?"

"*Nothing* is *wrong* with her, she's just struggling with all the changes she's had to face. Palma," Jacinda looked her sister straight in the eye. "I have *never* met a more amazing woman. What she's survived... the life she had on Earth... I want her to have just as an amazing life here, and I need you to help me with that."

"*Me!*" Palma squeaked. "What can *I* possibly do?"

"Palma," just as Jacinda started to speak, they both heard the first tentative notes coming from the Pianola. The notes of someone exploring the instrument for the first time. Slowly, the notes grew in strength and confidence turning into a melody.

"She's..."

"A musician. An artist. A singer."

"That's what she was on Earth?" Palma couldn't hide her shock.

"Yes, and she doesn't think she can continue to do that here, that there is no place for her here. That's why I brought her to you."

"Is she any good?"

No sooner had Palma asked, a husky voice joined the melody playing on the Pianola, and both women froze. Coffee forgotten, they let the music wrap around them and it dared them to come closer.

∞ ∞ ∞ ∞ ∞

Cyndy couldn't take her eyes off what she knew was a musical instrument, tucked away in the corner of the room. It was obviously well used and loved and it called to her.

Rising, she moved closer and saw that it resembled a piano, even down to the black and white keys. She needed to know if it sounded the same. Sitting down, she ran her fingers over the keys and smiled. It was the same. Amazing.

Without conscious thought, her fingers began to play an old familiar melody and she smiled. When it ended, she played it again, hesitantly adding the words, testing the feel of them, wondering if she could still sing them. What she discovered was that her voice was huskier, deeper, more mature than it had been the last time that she had sung the song and she suddenly realized she'd never truly sung it before. Oh she'd thought she had, thought that she had fully understood the words about not knowing her own strength, but she had been a child then, one who had yet to experience the traumas life could inflict on someone. Now she truly understood and sang with a conviction in her attitude and voice she'd never had before.

When she finished, she felt as if a piece of her very soul had been returned to her. With tears freely flowing down her face, she closed the lid to the Pianola.

"That was the most incredible thing I've ever heard," Palma whispered, tears running down her own cheeks as she stood at the opposite end of the Pianola.

"I'm sorry," Cyndy stood, wiping the tears from her own eyes before clasping her hands behind her back as if she were a naughty child caught doing something she shouldn't. "I shouldn't have played it without asking."

"Ancestors, Cyndy, why would you think that?" Jacinda asked.

"Because... well I mean I could have damaged it or something."

"Cyndy," Palma moved closer to her, "that Pianola has been in my husband's family for hundreds of cycles. It's a treasured family heirloom that my husband plays daily, and in all the cycles we've been wed, I've *never* heard a more beautiful sound come from it."

"I... thank you. I still shouldn't have..."

"Done something you loved? Something that made you feel whole?" Jacinda asked.

"How could you possibly have known that?"

"Because I *heard* it, Cyndy. In your voice. My ancestors, if this is you singing not as well as you used to then, I can't imagine what you sounded like before. It must have been like hearing the universe sing."

∞ ∞ ∞ ∞ ∞

"What do you mean she's not in the Palace?" Jotham demanded surging to his feet. He and William had just finished up a two-hour comm with Lucas. The Guardian had been sent to investigate the explosion on Nuga, as they were the closest ship to the planet. It had been the largest loss of life on the planet since the Regulians had attacked back in 49 and they all wanted answers.

"I'm sorry, Majesty," Deffand spoke. "I was only just informed she had left the Palace. Apparently, the order regarding her security level wasn't immediately relayed to the Palace guard. When she requested a limisin, one was issued."

"Jotham," William spoke up. "She will be alright."

"I might add, High Admiral, that she left with Princess Cyndy."

"What!" Now William surged to his feet. "With no Royal guards?!!"

"Two Palace guards accompanied them."

"Where did they go?" William demanded.

"The guards reported that they went directly to Palma Metaxas' residence."

"Hadar!" William roared.

"Yes, High Admiral!" Hadar came rushing into the office.

"Have my limisin brought around immediately. Tell Paa I want two more filled with Royal Guards."

"Yes, High Admiral!" Hadar hurried away to follow his orders.

"If Cassandra finds out about this, there will be hell to pay," William muttered, looking at Jotham. "What was Jacinda thinking taking Cyndy outside the Palace walls?"

Jotham bristled at the condemnation in his friend's gaze. "First of all, why shouldn't Cyndy be allowed outside the Palace walls, and second, why is Cassandra treating Jacinda this way!"

"Jotham..."

"Don't use that tone on me, Will. Cassandra spoke to Jacinda as if she were the enemy as if she were someone to suspect."

"The same way you treated Cassandra when you first met her?"

"Are you saying this is some kind of payback?"

"NO! I'm just saying the situations are similar. You are someone Cassandra greatly cares about and respects. She knows you've been hurt in the past and doesn't want it to happen again. And Jotham, we both know the lengths she will go to protect those she loves."

"I don't need protection from Jacinda. What I need is for my friends to accept that she is in my life."

"Give her some time, Jotham. Cassandra doesn't know Jacinda the way we do, she doesn't know that she has had struggles of her own. You know, I hate to admit it, but I'm almost afraid of what will happen when those two becomes friends. Can you imagine?"

Jotham looked at his friend thoughtfully. Jacinda had always been a confident and powerful woman in his Assembly. He knew she and Evadne Terwilliger, as wives of the longest-serving Assemblymen, had seen to many of the duties Lata would have performed, had she lived, when especially important events occurred within the House of Protection. What would she do if she had complete authority?

"They will change our world," he found himself whispering, then smiled. "I can't wait."

"King Jotham," Deffand's words drew his attention.

"What is it?"

"I was just informed that Madame Michelakakis and Princess Cyndy have left the Metaxas residence and are returning to the Palace."

"Hadar!" William shouted again.

"High Admiral, your limisin is currently pulling up."

"Cancel it. King Jotham and I will be heading to meet the returning limisin."

"Yes, High Admiral."

Chapter Twenty-One

Jacinda and Cyndy were laughing as they walked through the corridors of the House of Knowledge.

"Oh, that was wonderful, Jacinda. Thank you so much!" Cyndy hugged her new friend.

"I didn't do anything but introduce you to my sister, Cyndy." Jacinda smiled as she returned the hug.

"Whose husband just happens to be the Director of the Arts for the House of Knowledge!"

"Sometimes, the ancestors decide to smile on us." And did they ever today, Jacinda thought.

Arm-in-arm, they turned the last corner putting them just outside the guarded doors of the Queen's Wing. Looking down the corridor, they saw William and Jotham striding toward them, frowns marring both their handsome faces.

"Oh!" The women waited and Jacinda's gaze traveled from William to Jotham wondering what was going on. "Is something wrong?"

"Yes." They said together.

"Peter? Brett?" Cyndy's fingers dug into Jacinda's arm, the fear easily heard in her voice.

"No!" William exclaimed and was instantly at Cyndy's side. "No, Cyndy," he reassured her, his tone a great deal gentler this time. "They are fine. It is you we were worried about."

"Me?" She looked up at him in shock. "Why in the world would you be worried about *me*?"

William couldn't believe the honest surprise he heard in Cyndy's voice. Did she really believe no one worried about her? Her next words, to his dismay, confirmed it.

"You all leave after first meal. You go and live your lives and I don't see you again until last meal."

"Cyndy..." William started, only to be cut off.

"No one ever asks *me* where I've been. What *I've* been doing. So why ask *now*?"

Jacinda was shocked at the way the tiny woman stood up to the High Admiral. It was the first real spark of anger she'd seen in her. Anger to Jacinda's way of thinking, she had every right to.

"Cyndy, you're still recovering," William said trying to calm her.

"So is Peter. So is Brett. Yet you always ask them about *their* day. Do I really matter so little?"

"Of course not!" William instantly denied.

"Maybe it would be best if we took this conversation somewhere more private," Jotham suggested looking to the guards who were doing their best to not listen. Nodding at them, they opened the doors of the Wing. Putting a hand at the small of Jacinda's back, he guided her into the Wing, giving her a hard look.

Jacinda frowned back. What was Jotham so upset about? They'd taken no more than a few steps into the room, the doors closing behind them when they burst open again and Cassandra stormed into the room, anger flowing off her in waves.

"Tell me I am misinformed!" she demanded, her eyes flying around the room, calming only slightly when they found Cyndy.

"Cassandra..." William tried to calm his wife. Cassandra rarely got enraged, but when she did it was never a good thing.

"Don't you 'Cassandra' me, William! Tell me that this woman," her arm swung out to point at Jacinda. "Did *not* take my sister-in-law outside the Palace walls! That she was stupid enough to take only Palace Guards!"

"*Excuse me,*" Jacinda found her own anger growing. "Just who do you think you are calling me *stupid,* your *Royal* Highness!"

"You!" Cassandra walked right up to the taller Jacinda. "How *dare* you take her outside the walls! How dare you even think about it without asking *permission!*"

"*Permission?*" The Queen's words enraged Jacinda further. "I wasn't aware that *Cyndy* needed your *permission* to do *anything!*"

"You have no idea what she's been through!" Cassandra fired back. "How fragile she is!"

"*Fragile?*" That word exploded from Cyndy, as she shoved a shocked Jacinda aside to stand toe to toe with the much taller Queen. "How *dare* you talk about me as if I wasn't even here, Cassandra! As if I should be allowed no say in my own life!"

"Now, Cyndy," Cassandra's tone immediately turned placating, which only enraged Cyndy further.

"You might be the *Queen,* Cassandra, but you know *nothing* about what I've been through and do you know *why?*" Cyndy didn't give her a chance to reply. "Because you never *cared* enough to *ask!* To *listen! Neither* of you did!" Her gaze turned to the High Admiral, who was listening closely. "You listened to the others, but never once asked *me!* Why? Am I somehow less because I can't train your men!" Her gaze returned to Cassandra. "Or because I'm not as 'teachable' as Brett is? Maybe it would have been better for everyone if I had just died!"

"NO! God, Cyndy! NO! How can you even think that?" Anguish filled Cassandra's face and voice.

"Because that's what your actions say! *Jacinda* is the only one who actually sat down and *talked* to me! She listened, asked questions, and treated me like a living, breathing person with thoughts and feelings of my own. Not like someone that needed to be watched, placated, then patted on the head and sent on her way!" Cyndy angrily wiped away the tears that were streaming down her face. She turned to Jacinda, who stood beside her, silently watching the drama unfold.

"Thank you, Jacinda, for listening, for helping, and for being my first real friend here on Carina. I hope you will continue to be."

"Of course I will be, Cyndy." Jacinda reached out, gently squeezing her arm. "Nothing's happened here that can change that."

"Thank you." After giving Jacinda a quick hug, Cyndy rushed from the room.

∞ ∞ ∞ ∞ ∞

Silence echoed through the room after Cyndy's departure, at least until Jacinda rounded on the Queen.

"What in the name of the ancestors is wrong with you?!!" Jacinda found herself nearly trembling with rage. "It's one thing if you want to be condescending and a b'osh to *me*, after all you are a *Queen* and that's what you tend to do!" Jacinda sneered at the title. "But that amazing woman," she pointed to the door Cyndy had just exited through, "is a member of your *family*. Has becoming Queen so warped your mind that you've forgotten that *family* is the most important thing there is in this life?!!"

Jacinda was about to continue when the devastated expression on the Queen's face penetrated her rage. She watched as Cassandra turned to William, who immediately swept her off her feet when she started to crumble to the floor. Giving Jacinda a furious look, he carried Cassandra out of the room, but not before Jacinda heard her whisper.

"What have I done, William?"

∞ ∞ ∞ ∞ ∞

Jotham said nothing as he gripped Jacinda's elbow firmly as he led her from the Queen's Wing to the Royal Wing assigned to them. Deffand and several members of his Royal Guard followed. They would discuss what just happened, but right now he was more concerned about her leaving the Palace without telling him *or* with the proper security.

"Do you want to tell me what you thought you were doing?" he demanded, the moment the doors to their wing closed, pulling her around so she faced him.

Jacinda had remained silent as Jotham led her back to their chambers, still trying to understand the change in Cassandra's demeanor. There was no way she could have faked that, the Queen had been devastated. Jotham's words had her giving him a hard look.

"What are you talking about?"

"You left the Palace without informing anyone and without the proper security!" The fear that had gripped his heart when he'd first discovered her gone returned. He couldn't, wouldn't lose her.

"We had security, Jotham. We had two guards with us."

"*Palace* guards, not *Royal* guards!"

"And your point?" she asked raising her eyebrow at him.

"Do not play dumb with me, Jacinda! You know Royal Guards have a more specialized training in defense and security!"

"Of course I do! My daughter is training to become one, but that doesn't mean that *I* need one to go visit my sister!"

"You are *here*! You are with *me*! *That* means you need them!"

"Jotham..." She put a hand on his cheek hoping it would calm him. "No one *knows* I'm here, let alone with *you*. I was never at risk and neither was Cyndy."

"But you *could* have been!"

"Jotham..."

"I will not lose you, Jacinda! I won't! I won't survive it again!" His mouth crushed hers as he lifted her off her feet.

Jacinda wrapped her arms around Jotham's neck, sinking into the kiss, letting him control it, somehow knowing he needed to. He needed to make sure she was with him, safe, whole, and alive.

Breaking off the kiss, Jotham buried his face in the curve of her neck, his arms tightening around her.

"Ancestors," he whispered against her skin. "Don't ever do that to me again, Jacinda. My heart can't take it." Lifting his head to meet her gaze, he let her see the truth in his eyes. "Promise me that from now on you will take guards with you. *My* guards! Guards that understand how vital you are to me."

"Jotham, I'm here." She kissed his lips. "I'm safe." She kissed him again. "I will do nothing to put myself in danger. I promise."

"Promise you will always take Royal Guards with you," he demanded stubbornly.

A knock on the door stopped Jacinda from responding. Slowly, Jotham returned her to her feet then turned to open the door.

Turning away from Jotham, Jacinda took a deep breath and lifted a shaky hand to make sure her hair was still presentable. It had been a morning filled with a great deal of drama and she needed a moment to catch her breath.

Turning, she found Cassandra walking through the door, William at her side and knew she wasn't going to get it. Straightening her shoulders, she prepared herself for whatever was to come next.

Cassandra watched Jacinda's shoulders stiffen, as if she were bracing herself for an attack, and knew that was her fault. Her attitude at first meal had created this situation, and while Jacinda would probably never believe it, she *did* put her family before everything else, and that included her pride.

"I know I have no right to ask this of you, not after the way I've treated you, but could we sit down and talk? About Cyndy..."

Shock kept Jacinda silent, but Cassandra took it as a refusal.

"Please," Cassandra pleaded.

"Cassandra..." William took a step toward her.

"No, Majesty," Jacinda took a step toward Cassandra, then stopped realizing she'd been misunderstood when Jotham gave her a shocked look and shook her head. "What I meant was yes, please sit." Jacinda gestured to one of the couches. "I will tell you whatever you want to know if it helps Cyndy."

All four of them sat, William and Cassandra on one couch, Jacinda and Jotham across from them on the other, the lines of support clearly drawn.

"Your sister-in-law is an amazing woman, Majesty," Jacinda began.

"I know that. I've always known that, and please call me Cassandra."

"Why now?" Jacinda asked.

"Because, although you couldn't prove it by my actions today, I'm not normally such a b'osh." She gave Jacinda a smile that held no humor. "I normally give a person a chance. I know what it's like to be judged unfairly, without even having said a word. But with you..."

"But I arrived on the arm of someone you consider a close friend, family even, and you protect your family."

"How can you possibly know that?"

"Because Cyndy told me. She told me what your father did... after your mother's death."

"She told you about that?" Jacinda watched Cassandra reach out and grab William's hand, her knuckles turning white.

"Yes, while we were in the Memory Garden. She told me a lot of things."

"Please, will you tell me what she said?" Tears filled Cassandra's eyes. "Cyndy has always been like an older sister to me. She's the one that got me and Dad talking again. She was the only one that could pull me away from my studies. She was the one that encouraged me to go out and do field work," Cassandra reached out to rub William's ring. "I owe her so much... "

"She sees herself as insignificant in our world," Jacinda told her bluntly.

"What?!!" Three sets of eyes looked at her in shock, even William's. While he had realized Cyndy was struggling, he hadn't realized it was with anything like this.

"That was my reaction too, but she feels that everything that made her who she was on Earth is gone here."

"But I don't understand *why*," Cassandra began.

"That's because you are more comfortable with knowledge than with people."

"Cyndy told you that," Cassandra didn't make it a question.

"Yes. She was trying to explain why you treated me the way you did." Jacinda just shrugged. " But Cyndy isn't like you, Cassandra, she's an artist."

"How did you know that?"

"Because I heard her sing."

"Cyndy *sang* for you? *Today*?!!" Cassandra whispered.

"At Palma's, and I have to tell you it was the most amazing thing I've ever heard."

"She was famous back on Earth," Cassandra told them quietly. "She traveled the world and performed for thousands upon thousands of people."

"And she gave it all up when she had Victoria."

"Yes, I know she planned on going back..."

"But Victoria needed her after the Regulians took her."

"Victoria was so traumatized that it took all of us to get her back. But Cyndy was the most important one. She would sing to her when the nightmares came. Sometimes all night long."

"She was her child and her child needed her. Her *family* needed her."

"Yes."

"Now they don't."

"What?"

"Victoria doesn't need her. Bret doesn't need her. Peter doesn't need her. She gave everything she was to take care of her family and now they don't need her. Not here. Not like before. Is it any wonder she's feeling lost?"

"I never considered that... why didn't I ever consider that?" Cassandra's eyes turned to William full of self-condemnation.

"It isn't your fault, Cassandra." William turned her so she was facing him. "None of us realized what she was feeling. We were too worried about getting her here and getting her well."

"There's more that she's feeling," Jacinda told them quietly.

"What else could there possibly be?" William asked.

"Guilt."

"Guilt? What could Cyndy possibly feel guilty about?" William demanded, but Jacinda just silently looked at Cassandra. She could see the thoughts flying through her eyes until understanding suddenly flared in them.

"Oh my God!" Cassandra whispered. "Poor Cyndy."

"Cassandra, what are you talking about?"

"The bunker, Dad's bunker. He personally stocked it, but only for four."

"Four?" Jotham frowned at Cassandra. "That can't be right."

"It is because he meant it for his family, never himself. I always knew that. Four people. Four years." Tears began to run down Cassandra's face as she looked at Jotham. "They were sealed in there for nearly nine. If Victoria and I had been in there..."

"You would have all died." Jacinda finished for her. "It nearly destroyed Cyndy when Peter sealed that door. You were out there. Her baby was out there. But then as time went by..."

"She was grateful because it meant Brett and Peter had a chance to live." This time Cassandra finished the sentence. "It's how I would have felt if Peter and Cyndy had been outside and I was sealed in with William and our children." She looked to her life mate. "It would have eaten at my soul, but it's how I would have felt."

"It's eating at Cyndy's."

"How can I ever fix this?" Cassandra whispered.

"You can't, only Cyndy can, but you can help her," Jacinda told her.

"How?"

"By letting her sing." Jacinda turned to look at Jotham. "You should have heard her today, Jotham. It was as if when she opened her mouth the universe sang." She turned her gaze back to Cassandra. "She needs to sing, Cassandra, it's as much a part of her soul as her family is."

"Then she sings." Cassandra wiped the tears from her cheeks, straightened her shoulders and started to rise. Then she looked at Jacinda and slowly sank back down finding herself at a loss. "I don't know where to start."

"I'd say that's why the ancestors brought me here." Jacinda immediately replied. "Because I know *exactly* where to start."

"I thought *I* brought you here." Jotham wrapped his arm around her, pulling her close as he kissed her cheek. He had never been prouder of her than he was at this moment.

Jacinda just raised an eyebrow at him then looked at Cassandra. "What is it about you Royals? You always think everything is about *you*." Her lips began to smirk. "It's a good thing he's cute or I might have to rethink this whole thing."

"Hey!" Jotham leaned away pretending to be upset while William and Cassandra laughed.

"I don't think I've ever seen anyone put you in your place so nicely, Jotham." Cassandra looked at Jacinda with a new appreciation in her eye. "So tell me where we start."

"Well first, we find a Pianola and get it moved into Cyndy's quarters. You've got to have one *somewhere* in the Palace."

"I... William?" Cassandra looked to William and for the first time, Jacinda truly saw the bond between them, the connection. They truly loved each other and relied on each other.

"There are several, all in the Public Wing, which is why Cyndy's never had access to one. I'll get one moved."

"No. I will." Cassandra interrupted him. "It's not the job of the High Admiral to have furniture moved around the Palace."

When William went to open his mouth to argue, Jacinda interrupted.

"Excuse me, but I'm sure Javiera could see to that for you."

"Yes, that's right, Javiera. What next?" Cassandra demanded.

"Well, the next step I think is up to you." Jacinda looked to Cassandra. "You know Cyndy better than I do, but I think she can be very stubborn."

"That is totally true."

"So I'm not sure if Director Metaxas should come here or if she should go to him."

"Director Metaxas? My Director of the Arts?"

"Yes, Birgin is my brother-in-law, my sister Palma's husband, and after hearing Cyndy sing today, Palma was immediately on the comm to him. He will tell her honestly if there is a place for her music here on Carina."

"Of course there is!" Cassandra's tone had turned all Royal at the possibility that it wasn't.

"Cassandra," William put a soothing hand on Cassandra's arm. "You can't decree people to like Cyndy's music. She needs to know she's hearing the cold, hard truth."

Cassandra sighed heavily but nodded her head. "You're right, but I just want to make it right for her."

"You can't, as much as you want to, my love, you just can't. You can only support her. The way you do all of us." William squeezed her arm.

"Again you're right."

"Is that two or three times now I've heard your wife admit she's wrong?" Jotham teased. "I think we may need to mark that in the record books."

"Shut up, Jotham." Cassandra shot back and Jacinda found herself laughing.

Chapter Twenty-Two

Jacinda woke as the bed slightly dipped. Opening her eyes, she found Jotham's violet ones staring back at her.

"You're back," she said huskily reaching up to caress his cheek. He and William had left when another call had come in from the Guardian and Cassandra left shortly after to attend to her duties.

After making sure everything had been unpacked correctly, Jacinda had laid down on the bed for a short nap. Apparently, it had gone longer then she had planned.

"I am," Jotham told her kissing her lips.

"You need to rest." She could see the fatigue in his eyes. "Come. Rest with me."

"I can think of other things I'd like to do." Even as he spoke, he settled deeper into the bed.

"And we will. After we rest." Jacinda reassured him.

Wrapping up in each other's arms, Jotham laid his head against her chest and let out a tired sigh. "Just for a little while."

"Rest, Jotham." She gently ran her fingers through his thick, black hair as she felt him relax into sleep. As she did, she noticed the first strands of gray starting to make their appearance and smiled slightly. Jotham would look even more distinguished with gray at his temples.

She thought back to his words from before Cassandra and William had arrived, about his concern for her security. She understood his concern, especially after the way Lata died and her accident, but she was nothing like Lata. She never intentionally put herself at risk and she wasn't a member of the Royal family. There was not a reason for her to have Royal guards. Now how was she going to get Jotham to understand that?

∞ ∞ ∞ ∞ ∞

Jacinda tipped her head back, letting the water flow through her hair, rinsing away the cleanser she'd rubbed into it. She carefully slid out of the bed without waking Jotham when she woke again. She knew they needed to leave soon to have last meal with William and Cassandra, but she wanted him to get as much sleep as he could.

Jotham worked so hard. He was so dedicated to his people, always putting them first, that it was time someone put him first. Turning, she let the spray cleanse her face, washing away her sleep and grime from the day. Her breath caught when her breasts were suddenly cupped from behind.

"Jotham!" she gasped as she was pulled back against a hard body.

"You didn't wake me." He nipped her ear lobe in punishment.

"You were tired," she argued back, rubbing against his growing erection.

"I don't care. I don't like waking up without you. It makes me think this is nothing but a dream."

"Jotham..." His words touched her heart making it ache for him.

"I don't want it to be a dream, Jacinda." His mouth started to work its way down her neck his hands taking ownership of her breasts. "I want it to be honest and true and real."

"It is Jotham." She tipped her head to the side giving him better access to her neck. "I wouldn't be with you if it wasn't."

Spinning her around, Jotham's mouth attacked hers as he backed her up until she was against the wall then lifted her off her feet.

Jacinda gasped into his mouth, her hands instinctively gripping his shoulders as her legs wrapped around his waist.

"You are mine, Jacinda!" His hardened shaft nudged her slick entrance and he plunged in.

"Jotham!" Jacinda ripped her mouth away from his, her nails digging into his skin at the intensity of the pleasure filling her.

"Mine, Jacinda!" Pumping into her, the sound of skin slapping against skin filled the steamy chamber, each thrust going deeper than the one before. "Just mine!"

"Yes, Jotham!" Jacinda cried out, throwing her head back. Never had her pleasure built so quickly. "Ancestors, yes!"

Jotham could feel her channel tightening around him, it had his balls tightening and that familiar tingle at the base of his spine grew. He knew he wasn't going to last much longer, but he refused to go without her.

"Come for me, Jacinda!" he demanded driving even deeper into her welcoming body. "Come for me now!"

Jacinda couldn't believe how her body responded to Jotham. How he was able to command it, but he could and she screamed as her orgasm exploded through her.

The moment Jacinda's channel tightened around his shaft, Jotham cried out and with one final thrust erupted.

∞ ∞ ∞ ∞ ∞

Jacinda gave Jotham a small smile as she felt his thumb caress her lower back, where his hand rested as he guided her toward the Queen's Wing for last meal. Deffand, along with several guards, followed a discrete distance behind them. She was still feeling slightly stunned by what had happened in the shower. Never had she experienced an orgasm like she had with Jotham. Never had her entire body reacted like that. Just thinking about it had her taking a trembling breath. She knew if they weren't expected for last meal they would be in bed.

"Are you alright?" Jotham asked feeling the slight tremor that ran through her.

"I'm fine, just... thinking." She saw Jotham's eyes flare with desire as he realized what she was thinking about.

"We won't stay long," he promised pulling her closer so she was tucked under his arm.

Her cheeks flushed, but she nodded her agreement.

Guards opened the doors to the Queen's Wing as they approached. As they proceeded inside, Deffand and the other guards remained outside the Wing. Jotham paused, then turned to Deffand.

"You will see to what we discussed earlier while Jacinda and I are here." He didn't word it as a question.

"Yes, Majesty. Your other guards will remain in the event you need them."

"That will be fine." Turning back, he led Jacinda away.

∞ ∞ ∞ ∞ ∞

Jacinda couldn't help but laugh at the chaos they found when they entered the room where last meal was to be served. William was on his knees, his two oldest boys hanging from his back trying to pull him down while Willie attacked from the front.

"We've got you this time!" Kayden declared as he felt his father start to lean forward.

"You think so?" William challenged and suddenly twisted, wrapping an arm around Willie to pin him, Kayden and Jacob fell to the floor, his fingers going to where he knew they were most vulnerable.

Suddenly the room filled with shrieks and giggles.

"Stop, Dad!" Kayden demanded as he unsuccessfully tried to escape.

"What? You attack, three against one, and expect me to not retaliate?" William asked keeping the three caged underneath him.

"Please, Daddy!" Willie's young voice begged between shrieks.

"Alright, but only because we have company." William's eyes were sparkling with mirth as they looked up at Jotham and Jacinda. "You'll have to thank Jotham and Jacinda for saving you from the tickles you deserve."

Settling back on his knees, William helped each boy up, giving them a hug and kiss. As he rose to his feet, Willie wrapped his arms around his neck, and William lifted him as he stood.

"Hi, King Jotham." Willie greeted, as his father moved across the room. "Thanks for saving us."

"You are most welcome, Willie. You do know that your father is ticklish too." Jotham smirked at William.

"Yeah, Mom showed us, but *we* can never get close enough," Willie pouted.

"I'm sure you will one day," Jotham encouraged.

"Alright, enough about my weaknesses." Leaning down, William put Willie on his feet. "Go wash up for last meal. It will be here soon."

"Yes, Daddy." All three chorused and hurried out of the room.

"Cassandra's putting Sabah down and the Chamberlains should be here soon. Peter and Cyndy had some things to discuss. Would either of you like something to drink? Wine? Ale?"

"A glass of wine would be lovely," Jacinda said and took the long-stemmed glass William handed to her while Jotham took the tumbler of Carinian ale.

"Any new information on Nuga?" Jotham asked taking a sip of his drink.

"It looks like human error and negligence. There's evidence that the manager of the mine wasn't making the repairs and upgrades he was ordered to. Instead, he was pocketing the credits."

"Has he been found?"

"Yes. He will be charged with corruption and the deaths of nearly five-hundred."

"The explosion was that extensive?" Jacinda couldn't hide her shock.

"It occurred during the shift change," William informed her. "The two largest shifts of the day."

"That mine is run by the Sokol Corporation, isn't it?" Jacinda looked at Jotham and saw his jaw clench.

"Yes, it is." William gave her a considering look. "How did you know that?"

"Stephan had been investigating the company at the time of his death," Jacinda told him. "I'm not sure what happened to the investigation after his death."

"Interesting."

"I might still have some of his files if you would like them."

"You do?" Jotham looked at her in shock. "I thought all his files were turned over to the Assembly."

"Stephan liked to work from home a lot so he kept copies there. The secure home comm he worked on is still in his office. No one ever requested it and I never gave it a thought. I have the codes."

"Stephan gave you his codes?" William frowned at her.

"He wrote them down, sealed them and locked them in our home security box. So they would be available if ever needed. I'd forgotten about them until just now."

"When we return, I would very much like to see what Stephan had compiled," Jotham told her reaching out to touch her cheek. "I want to know what he found out and why it was never brought to my attention after his death."

"Then you'll have it."

The sound of the door opening ended the conversation and they all turned to see the Chamberlains enter the room.

Brett walked in front of his parents a bag slung over his shoulder, his eyes searching the room.

"The boys are in their rooms washing up," William told Brett knowing who he was searching for.

Brett looked up at his mom.

"Go ahead, Brett. You haven't washed up yet either." Cyndy smiled down at him.

"Thanks, Mom." Brett was gone in a flash.

"Drink Peter? Cyndy?" William inquired.

"Wine please," Cyndy answered crossing the room. Peter silently followed frowning at Jacinda.

"Is there something you want to say, Captain?" Jacinda asked, not the least intimidated by his hard look.

"Peter!" Cyndy frowned fiercely up at her husband.

"Yes, there is." Peter ignored his wife. "While I don't appreciate you taking my wife out of the Palace without the proper security, I do appreciate what you did for her." Peter looked into the glass William had handed him then looked back to Jacinda before continuing on gruffly. "It's been a long time since I've heard Cyndy sing because she was happy. So thank you."

Jacinda found she could only nod, her throat tightening at the depth of emotion she could see in Peter's eyes. He truly loved his wife.

"Cassandra had a Pianola delivered to our rooms," Cyndy told Jacinda, her face beaming. "Peter had to pull me away from it for last meal."

"I'm surprised your fingers aren't cramping from all the playing you've been doing on it." Peter leaned down, kissing the top of Cyndy's head.

Cyndy smiled up at him flexing the fingers of her free hand. "I am out of practice. It's going to take a while, but I'll get it back."

"I know you will, Pixie."

∞ ∞ ∞ ∞ ∞

Jacinda couldn't hide her smile as she watched young Willie eye her half eaten piece of Fudge Torta. He'd plowed through his own piece as if he'd been afraid one of his brothers might take it from him. Now he raised hopeful violet eyes to her.

This time when they sat down for their meal, Jotham had sat next to William and Jacinda found herself having a lively conversation with the youngest of William's sons, his namesake, and the boy had charmed her.

"Do you really think you have room for more?" Jacinda asked quietly.

"It's Torta," Willie said as if that explained everything and in truth it did.

"You have to ask your mother first."

"Oh. Mommy?" His question said in that small innocent voice only a child could have, had Cassandra looking to her youngest son.

"Yes, Willie?"

"Mommy, Jacinda isn't going to finish the rest of her Torta, so she wants me to eat it. So can I?"

Early in the dinner, when Willie was struggling to pronounce her last name, Jacinda told him and the other boys they could call her Jacinda. Now she smirked slightly at his blatant stretching of the truth.

"Oh she does, does she?" Cassandra asked looking at the fudge already smeared around her youngest son's mouth.

"Yes, Mommy."

Jacinda watched as the most powerful Queen, Carina had ever had, melted under the pleading violet eyes of her child. Jacinda knew what Cassandra was seeing when she looked at the boy. While all William's sons resembled him in some way, his namesake was the mirror image of him. And Jacinda knew Cassandra would never be able to resist him, not when he looked at her that way.

"What about your brothers and Brett?" Cassandra asked.

"They're bigger so they already got a bigger piece," Willie argued back.

"I see. Well, I guess it would be terrible for it to go to waste."

"It would, Mommy. It really would." Willie agreed nodding his head.

"As long as it's okay with Jacinda, then it's fine."

Willie turned his little eyes on Jacinda. "Please?" he pleaded.

Picking up her dessert plate, Jacinda set it on his empty one. "Here you go, little man."

Turning back to Cassandra she smiled. "You are so going to be in trouble when the girls start calling."

"Don't I know it." Cassandra agreed shaking her head. "I can already hear the hearts breaking."

"Just like their father. He and Jotham pretty much had free run of the Academy as far as the girls were concerned."

"Girls!" The disgust in Kayden's voice was easily heard. "Dad, you liked *girls*? In the *Academy*? I thought you said all you did there was train and study."

All eyes turned to William to find him frowning at Kayden.

"All you did was study and train?" Jotham started to chuckle. "Really, Will?"

"I was talking to my son who was six at the time, Jotham," William hissed at him. "What was I supposed to say?"

"I'm sure it was during his last few cycles, Kayden." Jacinda decided to bail him out.

"Oh," Kayden replied as if that made all the difference.

"You know, I have a grandson around your age. He doesn't like girls yet either."

"You have grandchildren?" Cassandra looked at her in shock.

"Two grandsons," Jacinda told her proudly. "From my second son, Ethan. Danton, my oldest, has yet to have a Union and Stephanie, well Stephanie is currently focusing on her career."

"I can't wait to be a grandmother," Cyndy said sighing. "But Victoria is a lot like your Stephanie. She wants to establish her career first, so I'll just have to snuggle up on Sabah until she and Lucas decide to have one of their own I can spoil."

"Every baby needs that," Jacinda said.

"True." Cyndy agreed.

"Especially Sabah," Willie piped in as he ate the Torta, "because she's special."

"Of course she is. She's your sister." Jacinda smiled down at the face that had even more Torta smeared across it.

"Not because of that, but because she has *two* birthmarks," Willie told her.

Jacinda's eyes widened in shock and a heavy silence fell over the room. Willie was the only one who didn't seem to notice.

"Yeah, she's got one on her leg like Mom's and one on her arm like us." Willie proudly pulled his sleeve up to reveal the Arrow birthmark on his arm proclaiming him a royal from the House of Protection.

Jacinda sat stunned. How was this possible? They were the sons of the Queen of the House of Knowledge. They should have no birthmark, yet there it was and just as dark as the one on their father's arm, meaning they were in line for the throne of the House of Protection! If they all had this... and Sabah had both... Ancestors, the purists would go crazy.

"William." His father's stern voice had little Willie looking at him in confusion. "What were you told about the birthmarks?"

"That we shouldn't talk about them with anyone not family," Willie immediately replied.

"That's right."

"But isn't Jacinda family now? Like King Jotham?" He looked from his mother to his father in confusion. "You always said only family got to eat at this table."

Jacinda watched William close his eyes and knew he was searching for patience. She'd had to do it too many times herself when dealing with her own children.

"Did I do something wrong?" Willie set down his forc as his little lower lip began to tremble. "I overheard you tell Uncle Peter how something bad could happen to Sabah if the wrong people found out. Is Jacinda wrong people? Did I hurt Sabah?"

"No, Willie." William was instantly up and at Willie's side, pulling his trembling son into his arms. "No, Willie. You did nothing wrong. You followed every rule we gave you perfectly. Jacinda isn't 'wrong people' and Sabah is fine."

"Can I go check?" Willie questioned. "I want to make sure."

"Go." William put Willie down and the boy immediately scurried out of the room, the last bite of his Torta forgotten.

"Boys, if you're done you can go play," William told them as he returned to his chair.

"Yes, Father." Kayden immediately stood and left the room.

"Yes, Father." Jacob followed Kayden.

"Yes, Uncle William." Brett followed Jacob and they all followed Willie. Silence was left in their wake.

Jacinda looked from Peter to Cyndy to Cassandra to William, then to Jotham before finally returning back to Cassandra.

"Sabah wasn't fussy when we arrived for first meal and you weren't 'putting her down' before last meal because it was her normal time."

"No," Cassandra answered.

"I see." Jacinda nodded her face blank. She couldn't believe how much it hurt. She, better than most, understood why the birthmarks needed to be kept hidden. She even understood William and Cassandra not telling her, but Jotham? Jotham, who claimed he wanted her to be a part of his life? Part of his friends' lives? Yet he kept something like this from her when she'd told him about her birthmark? Their being together was going to be hard enough, but if there wasn't trust they didn't have a chance.

"Jacinda..." Jotham reached out, but she pulled her hand out of reach.

"Just so it's on the record," Jacinda stared directly into Cassandra's eyes, ignoring Jotham. "I would never reveal what I accidentally learned here today. It would serve no purpose but to stir up the purists and they have never been among my favorite people. The ancestors have allowed this to happen for a reason and it's not my place to dispute them."

"Thank you, Jacinda." It was William who spoke.

"Not a problem, High Admiral." Jacinda looked to the man she'd always considered a friend and suddenly realized she had been naive. He was the High Admiral and a King, not her friend because of a casual acquaintance over forty cycles ago. Lifting the napkin from her lap, she wiped her mouth then set it on the table. "Thank you for a lovely meal. If you'll excuse me, I think I'll retire. The trip here seems to have tired me more than I expected."

Jotham immediately pushed his chair back as she rose.

"No." She touched his shoulder momentarily. "Stay. I know you have things to discuss with the High Admiral. Cyndy. Peter." She nodded to each of them, then with a last look at Jotham left the room.

∞ ∞ ∞ ∞ ∞

"That could have gone better." Jotham threw his own napkin down disgusted with himself. Rising, he began to pace.

He had seen the betrayal and hurt that had flashed through Jacinda's eyes before they'd gone blank, blocking him from her thoughts. How had things gone so bad, so quickly? He hadn't considered that Cassandra and William were intentionally keeping Sabah away from Jacinda. It had never occurred to him, but Jacinda had instantly understood.

The boys' birthmarks, while unusual, could be explained by stating that William's bloodline was that strong. But Sabah's..... The birthmark for the House of Protection had never appeared on a female before.

Just like the birthmark for the House of Healing had never appeared on one. Yet Jacinda carried it, over her heart instead of on her hand, but she still carried it. She had trusted him with that secret.

He hadn't trusted her...

Not with any of his secrets.

How could they truly build a relationship without trust?

Trust took time to build and it was the one thing Jotham had little of. Because he'd intentionally made it that way. To fill the empty nights and the emptiness inside him. Both were filled now, with Jacinda, because of Jacinda. If he lost her now, it would be his own fault.

Gripping the cool stone of the balcony railing, Jotham was surprised to find himself outside, overlooking the Queen's Garden bathed in the light of the full moon. Taking a deep breath, he inhaled the dry, lightly-scented air of Kisurri, so different from the moist air of his own garden back in Pechora. A garden filled with the scent of roses.

Roses Lata had planted.

Roses given to her by Jacinda's mother.

The two were as intricately intertwined in his life as the stems of that bush were.

"It will be okay, Jotham. Jacinda will understand."

"Oh, she understands now, Will. She understands perfectly." Jotham tipped his head up to look at the stars. They had once seemed so exciting for him, the thought of getting out there and exploring them. And he had, for a while, but they didn't pull at him now the way they did as a young man. Now all he wanted was to be here with Jacinda.

"I should never have gone on that second tour, Will."

"What?" William looked at his friend in shock, wondering at the change in topic.

"I was only required to serve one cycle, but I wanted everyone to know that I wasn't there just for a token assignment like it was for Dadrian. I wanted everyone to know that I earned every medal I wear on my jacket, that my father hadn't just granted them to me."

"You did, Jotham. No one can ever dispute that."

"But why did I let it matter so much? The only person's opinion that should have mattered to me was Lata's. That decision that need cost me a cycle with Lata. It cost you your Union with Salish.

"We were young, Jotham, trying to find our way."

"Would you make the same decision now as you did then, Will? If you were needed, would you return to the Fleet, leaving your wife and children behind, knowing you may never see them again?"

"No." William didn't even have to think about it. "I've done my time, Jotham. I know who I am and know I've earned my position. I've sacrificed and lost for it. I won't do it again."

"Neither will I." Jotham turned to his friend and straightened. When he spoke, he spoke to him as the King of the House of Protection to the High Admiral. "I am officially informing the High Admiral that I am recalling Prince Barek Tibullus from active duty in the Fleet."

"What?" William couldn't hide his shock.

"I want him back on planet within two weeks."

"He's going to be furious."

"It doesn't matter. Its time he started to learn the duties of the King. He can't do that serving in the Fleet."

"Jotham," William felt his throat tightening. "Are you ill?"

"No." Jotham dropped his 'Royal air' when he saw the honest concern in Will's eyes. "No, Will, I'm perfectly healthy but I'm tired. I'm tired of carrying this burden alone and I've been reminded that I don't have to."

"By Jacinda."

"Yes. I don't want Barek to have to go through what I did, Will. Being thrown into the position when your father suddenly dies. I had so little training on what the King's role truly was and had no one I felt I could truly rely on. If it hadn't been for Stephan Michelakakis, I don't know what I would have done."

"Is that why you supported his and Jacinda's Union?"

"No. I supported their Union because it was the right thing to do. Can you imagine what we would have lost if my father had forced him out?"

"I'm sure King Kado wouldn't have..."

"He sent Stephan a letter, Will," Jotham's eyes were hard as he met his. "It told him to choose between his wife and his position."

"Seriously?" William couldn't hide his shock.

"He sent it right before he died. Jacinda told me about it, so I had Chesney go through my father's old papers and there it was. How could I not have known my mother and father were 'purists'?"

"Jotham..."

"If he'd still been King, he would never have supported your and Cassandra's Union, Will. He never would have given you his protection."

William was silent for a moment then nodded. "No, he wouldn't have."

"Our entire world would have suffered because of that decision."

"That you recognize that is what makes you a great King, Jotham. You're firm but fair, you protect but don't try to control, and you are loyal and true. You have dedicated your entire life to your people and we are better for it."

"I dedicated my life to my people because I have had nothing else to live for. Not after Lata died. I was busy, so I didn't have to deal with what I had lost. How I had lost it and why I had lost it. Barek suffered because I couldn't even handle seeing Lata's image, because I refused to speak of her or allow anyone else to speak of her in my presence. How could I have done that to my own son, Will? To Lata's son?"

"You were young, Jotham, younger than Barek is now. You had a lot to deal with."

"That's the polite, easy answer, but the truth is I became my father. I put my 'duties' over those I loved. I did it to Lata too. If I hadn't been spending so much time trying to prove I deserved my position, I would have realized what it was costing me. I'm not going to make that mistake again."

"With Jacinda."

"Yes. I love her, Will. I want to be with her... really *be* with her... not just show up for meals that are always interrupted."

"Jacinda would understand, Jotham."

"She does, but she's also stated it's not the life she wants." Jotham saw Will's eyes widen in shock and smiled. "Oh she understands it's going to happen, but she doesn't want it to be the norm. Do you know that the meal we just had is the first the two of us have ever had together that wasn't interrupted?"

"We always make sure that unless it is vital, that we're not to be interrupted during meals. Cassandra insists we need to have 'family' time together. If we don't, we lose touch."

"Cassandra is a very smart woman. It's taken me nearly sixty cycles to learn that. I'm not going to lose Jacinda like I did Lata, and I'm finally going to truly connect with my son. We are going to talk about his mother, about his life, and about what he sees as the future and who he might want to share it with."

"And if that person isn't from the House of Protection?" Will couldn't help but ask.

"Then I'll step down, make him the King, and then he can choose whomever he wants."

"Jotham!" Will couldn't hide his shock. Something like that had never been done in the history of Carina!

"Our world is changing, Will. Sons born to the House of Knowledge carry the House of Protection birthmark. It's future Queen could possibly rule both Houses. The Houses are merging, Will. You and Cassandra are the first, but I don't see you being the last."

William was silent for a moment, just looking at his friend and King. "I will have the orders drawn up and transmitted immediately," he told him. "I suspect you'll be receiving a transmission from Barek before first sun."

"I'm sure I will."

Chapter Twenty-Three

As Jacinda approached the outer doors of the Queen's Wing, she found herself pausing. She knew if she left, Jotham's guards would escort her directly back to the Royal Wing. Jotham would follow shortly because he knew she was upset and he would want to explain. It might be childish of her, but she didn't want to talk to him right now. She needed some time and a place where she could be alone for a while. She knew exactly where she needed to go.

Changing directions, she passed through the doors she knew would take her out into the Queen's Garden. She knew she shouldn't be in the Garden without permission, but right now she didn't care. Letting the light of Carina's moon guide her, she followed the path Cyndy had shown her earlier to the Memory Garden.

As soon as she crossed the threshold, it was as if she were being wrapped up in a warm, welcoming hug and she felt tears fill her eyes. Was this what Cyndy experienced when she came here upset? If it was, Jacinda totally understood the draw.

Moving to the bench she sat, letting the feeling of acceptance and love sooth her hurt feelings. Who was it coming from? Stephan? Lata? Jacob? Her eyes traveled to the stone that was bathed in the warm glow of the moon.

"You must have truly been an amazing man, Jacob Chamberlain, to still be able to touch the lives of so many."

She didn't receive a reply, but then she hadn't expected one. What she did get was the soft crunch of footsteps along the path. Leaning back into the shadows, she hoped that whoever it was would just pass by. That didn't happen either and her eyes widened as she was surprised by who entered the garden.

Brett.

Carrying the bag, he'd had before slung over his shoulder.

"Hi, Grandpa." Brett sat cross-legged down in front of the stone and talked to it as if the man was sitting there. "Sorry I'm late, but last meal was a little different tonight. King Jotham was there and he brought this *really* pretty woman with him. I drew her, see?" He reached in to his bag, and pulled out a piece of paper and held it up to the stone. "Aunt Cassie wasn't very happy about it at first meal, she was kinda mean to her, but she seemed better at last meal. At least until Willie told her about Sabah's birthmarks." Brett set the paper aside.

"Anyway, what else happened today? Oh, Mom and Dad were arguing, they never think I can hear them from my room, but I can, especially when Dad yells. Then they suddenly stopped and I heard the strangest sounds. I came out and Mom was sitting there playing this thing she said was a Pianola, crying and smiling. Even Dad was. So I guess it's a good thing."

His voice turned into a whisper. "I still don't understand half of what my tutor is saying, Grandpa. I know he thinks I'm stupid, maybe I am."

Jacinda had been content to sit there in the shadows without letting Brett know she was there. She realized while listening to him that he did this every night, that his talking to the stone was a lot like Cyndy's talking to it. It was something that didn't judge or criticize him, but she couldn't just sit there and let him think he was stupid. "You're not, Brett."

Brett spun around, his eyes wide when Jacinda leaned forward so he could see her in the light of the full moon.

"What are you doing here?" he asked.

"The same thing you are, I think. I wanted some time alone and this is the perfect spot."

"Yeah... well... I'll just go and let you..." He turned and started gathering up his things.

"You're not stupid, Brett." Her words halted his movements.

"You can't know that," he whispered.

"I can, but you tell me why you think you are?"

"Because I don't learn as fast as Kayden and Jacob. They're *way* ahead of me in all our classes."

"That's because they have had cycles to learn what you just are. What else?"

"The teacher... he looks at me and just scowls when I can't answer a question."

"He shouldn't do that. Everyone learns differently, Brett, at their own speed and in their own way."

"Even Mom is disappointed in me." He turned sad eyes to her.

"What are you talking about? You could never disappoint your mother. She loves you."

"But I do. When I ask her to help me like I used to back in the bunker, she just shakes her head at me and walks away. I've even seen tears in her eyes. She's so disappointed in me she cries." He dropped his head in shame.

"Oh, Brett, no." Jacinda dropped to her knees and wrapped her arms around the boy, surprised to find how thin he still was. "That's not why."

"Then why?" The eyes he raised to hers begged for answers.

"You're Mom doesn't help you, Brett, because she *can't*."

"What?" Brett gave her a confused look.

"She doesn't know the answers to the questions either, Brett," Jacinda told him again.

"Mom knows *everything*," he argued back angrily.

"Back on Earth, maybe she did, but you're not on Earth anymore, Brett, and your mom is having to learn things just like you are. She walks away because she doesn't like letting you down. Doesn't want you to think that *she's* stupid."

"Really?"

"Really, and if you ask her, I'm sure she'll tell you the same thing."

"I could never think Mom was stupid."

"As she would never think you were." Jacinda hugged him. "Can I see what you drew?" she asked gesturing to the piece of paper still face down on the ground.

"Drew?"

"The drawing of me. The one you showed your grandpa."

"Oh," Brett's gaze turned to the paper. "It's just a dumb drawing. I shouldn't be doing them. I should be concentrating on my school work or I'll never get into the Academy."

"Is that what your teacher has been telling you?" Jacinda felt her anger at this man beginning to grow. "That you *have* to get into the Academy?"

"Well, yeah. All the Zafar men go there and both Dad and Grandpa Jacob went into the military on Earth. I *have* to go too."

"Oh, Brett." Jacinda's heart broke for the boy. "No one *has* to go to the Academy. It's a choice."

"Dad would be disappointed if I don't," he whispered.

"Did *he* say that to you?" Jacinda demanded.

"Well no, but..."

"But nothing, Brett." Jacinda used her best 'mother's' voice. "Never let someone else *tell* you what your father thinks. If you have a question, ask *him*. You might not always like the answer, but at least you'll know it's the truth."

"Alright."

"So can I see the drawing?" She gestured to the paper he still held in his hand.

"I guess, but it's not very good."

"Well, since the best I can do is stick figures I'm not one to judge."

"Stick figures?" Brett frowned at her.

"Yeah, you know." Jacinda put her finger in the dirt, drew a circle with a straight line from it for the body, with two lines jutting off from the end of the line for the legs and then one on each side of the line about half way up for arms. "See?"

Brett giggled. "That doesn't look like anyone."

"True, but it's the best *I* can do. So can I see?"

"Okay," he said softly then very slowly, he handed her his drawing.

Smiling at him, Jacinda knew she was going to tell him she liked it no matter how it looked but turning it over she found herself speechless. She expected to find a very rudimentary drawing, one better than hers but what she found was extraordinary.

With just a few simple lines, Brett had captured her profile in a way that anyone that knew her would recognize her. Everything was perfectly proportioned and accurate, right down to the fine lines around her eyes and mouth. That was something she wished he hadn't noticed.

"This is absolutely amazing, Brett."

"Really?" He looked up at her with hopeful eyes. "You like it?"

"Oh, yes. Do your mom and dad know you can draw like this?"

Brett just shrugged his shoulders. "I used to do it a lot in the bunker. The dust always seemed to get in, so I'd use whatever was on hand and draw something. Usually something from one of the books we had, but sometimes I'd draw Mom or Dad. They'd last for a while, but then more dust would get in and cover it. I'd just do another one. They seemed to make Mom happy."

"I'm sure they did." Her gaze went to his bag. "Do you have more?"

"You want to see my other drawings?"

"If you are willing to show them to me. It's up to you."

Slowly, Brett reached into his bag and pulled out a thick tablet, running his hand over its cover. "Tori gave me this when she discovered I liked to draw. She told me I didn't have to worry about them disappearing, that I could draw whatever I wanted and I could always have more paper. She also gave me 'pencils'. Did you know they come in different colors?"

Jacinda had to force back the tears that wanted to fill her eyes at this young boy's pure astonishment that a simple pencil could come in *colors*. "I actually did. Have you used them much?"

"Not much. I thought I should save them and only use them when really necessary."

"Brett."

"Yeah."

"On Carina, colored pencils are like paper. You can get more."

"Honest?"

"Honest, so if you want to 'color' something in you can."

"Okay."

Slowly, Brett opened the tablet and began to show her his work. There were landscapes, black and white of course, but most of the tablet was filled with drawings of his life since arriving on Carina. Drawings of Cassandra and William, with their heads close as if they were discussing something. Of his parents holding hands. Of his newly discovered cousins, each doing something she knew they shouldn't be. There were guards and flowers, and what she knew were statues. There was even one of Fudge Torta. It was as if everything he saw he had to put down on paper and he did it beautifully.

Brett said nothing as he closed the tablet and she knew he was waiting for her to tell him she hated what he had poured his heart into.

"Brett, I told you how terrible I was at drawing."

"I understand." His chin dropped to his chest.

Jacinda put a gentle but firm finger under his chin and raised it until he looked her in the eye.

"You don't. What I'm saying is that just because *I* can't draw and create anything as amazing as what you have here, it doesn't mean I can't recognize beauty and talent when I see it. What you've drawn here is beyond amazing and you are only nine. You may not like what I'm about to say, but I'm going to say it."

"What?" Brett asked in a scared little voice.

"You will never go to the Academy."

"But..."

"You, Brett Chamberlain, are meant for the Art Academy at Montreux."

"What? What's that?"

"It's a very important school, your sister Tori graduated from there. They only take the very best in that field of study."

"But I could never do what Tori does."

"You don't have to, all you have to do is what you do."

"What's that?"

"Draw, Brett." She carefully took the tablet from his small hands and opened it to its first page, the landscape that she somehow knew was his first glimpse of the new world he had been brought to. "Let them see the beauty of this world through your eyes. Color our world, Brett, and it will never be the same."

"Do you really think I can?"

"I really do, and if your Grandpa Jacob were here, he'd tell you that too."

∞ ∞ ∞ ∞ ∞

"What do you mean you didn't escort her to our Wing?!!" Jotham demanded of his guards.

"Majesty, she never left the Queen's Wing." One of his guards told him.

"You're telling me she never came out these doors?"

"No, Majesty."

Jotham looked to Cassandra's guards and they nodded that she hadn't passed them. "Stay here!" he ordered. "Notify me immediately if she passes."

"Yes, Majesty." All the guards nodded.

Jotham's mind was racing. Where could she have gone? He knew she was upset, but Jacinda wouldn't try to circumvent Royal Guards. She knew better.

A slight breeze caused a curtain to billow inward and Jotham realized behind it was the door that led to the Queen's Garden. Knowing that's where she would have gone, he followed.

Jotham let his instincts and the Carina moon guide him and found he was outside the Memory Garden. He was about to enter when he heard a voice, a very young voice.

Jotham unashamedly eavesdropped as Brett and Jacinda spoke. He shared her anger at how the teacher was treating Brett, and he would bring it up to Will. His heart also ached for the little boy trying so hard to be like his father. Jotham remembered doing the same thing. Gaining his father's attention and acknowledgement had been a driving force in his young life. It was only after he went to the Academy that he'd begun to find his own path, starting with Lata. But still, that desire had been in him, it had driven him to prove himself in the Academy, in the Coalition, and to the Assembly. He had no doubt his father would frown on his relationship with Jacinda, just as he had with Lata. It made him smile because he knew it meant it was right.

Hearing Jacinda's reaction to the drawings made him want to see them for himself. He'd heard Jacinda give out 'polite' truths before, you couldn't be in politics without knowing how to give them, but all he heard in Jacinda's voice was awe and sincerity. No matter what Jacinda had said about not being able to draw, he knew she had an amazing eye for style and beauty. If she thought Brett belonged in Montreux, then he must. He may be just as big a prodigy as Victoria had been.

Hearing the crunch of gravel along the path, Jotham turned to find Peter walking toward him and he headed down the path so they could speak without being overheard.

"What are you doing here, Jotham?" Peter asked frowning.

"I was searching for Jacinda. It seems she decided to take a walk before returning to our Wing."

"I was looking for Brett. He likes to come out here before bed."

"They found each other in the Memory Garden."

"Really." Peter crossed his arms over his chest. "So why are we standing here talking instead of in the Memory Garden?"

"You know, I never met your father, but from what Tori and Cassandra have told me he was truly an amazing man."

"He was."

"He served in your military too, I understand."

"Yes."

"And that had an influence on you. After all, every little boy wants to do what their father does. To connect with him on that level."

"I suppose so, yes." Peter frowned at Jotham. "Where are you going with this?"

"You were very successful, emulating your father, and those skills are sought after here."

"Yes."

"Yet you never would have qualified for the Academy *here*. You don't meet the minimum height requirement."

"I realize that."

"Brett doesn't."

"What are you talking about?"

"I took a page from your daughter's book and accidentally overheard Jacinda and Brett talking."

"You mean you blatantly eavesdropped." Peter openly acknowledged he knew of his daughter's habit.

"Yes, and Brett thinks he *has* to get into the Academy, not only because you and your father served, but because all his cousins will be going."

"Shit!" Peter swore softly. "I just want my son to be healthy and happy. I could care less if he follows in my footsteps."

"I'm glad to hear that because from what I heard I believe your son is going to be more like Cyndy than you."

"Like Cyndy? You mean a singer?"

"No, but an artist just the same. He has been showing Jacinda the drawings he's done."

"Tori got him that tablet. He takes it with him everywhere. The look of awe on his face, when she told him his drawings wouldn't 'disappear' anymore, is something I'll never forget."

"Jacinda was truly impressed with his work, something hard to do because she has a discriminating eye. She even mentioned Montreux."

"The school Tori graduated from?"

"Yes."

"Brett doesn't want to be a doctor, Jotham."

"Of course not, but Montreux is the premier art school on the planet. If Brett's as good as Jacinda thinks he is, then *that's* where he needs to go."

"We've got years... cycles before we have to worry about that."

"Not if he's a prodigy like his sister is, like his mother is." Jotham started to chuckle. "I don't envy you, Peter. Here you are the most sought after security trainer on the planet, already a legend. Yet your wife and two children are going to overshadow you. Some men might have a problem with that."

"Some might," Peter agreed. "But not me."

∞ ∞ ∞ ∞ ∞

Jacinda silently walked beside Jotham as Deffand and the other guards escorted them to the Royal Wing. She and Brett had left the Memory Garden and found Jotham and Peter talking further up the path. After a few words, Peter had taken Brett's hand and led him away. Jotham had taken her arm and done the same.

Now they entered the Royal Wing and the guards fell away except for Deffand.

"Majesty, your request has been taken care of. It will be here by morning."

"Thank you, Deffand. Go get some rest. We are secure here."

"Majesty?"

"The guards have been doubled patrolling the walls and they have been made aware of Jacinda's status. You haven't taken a break since we've arrived. Go. Rest. Or you're no good to me."

"Yes, Majesty." He gave Jotham a stiff bow. "Madame Michelakakis." He gave Jacinda another one, then turning on his heel, he left.

"My status?" Jacinda asked raising her eyebrow.

"That of being a Royal."

"I'm not a Royal, Jotham," she corrected him.

"You are." He ran a light finger over her birthmark, hidden under the bodice of her dress. "Because of this and because you are with me."

"I've had the birthmark my entire life. It means nothing, and Royal companions are never considered Royal."

"You are more than a 'companion,' Jacinda and you know it. I love you."

"I know." She put a gentle hand on his cheek before stepping away. "But that still doesn't change my status, Jotham."

"It does if I say it does."

"Jotham, there are things that even you can't just decree."

"That may be, but when it comes to your protection I can." Jotham held up his hand. "We can argue about what you will accept at home once we return there. But here, you are with me, and you will be protected as a Royal because you are that important to me."

Jacinda opened her mouth to argue, but Jotham put a finger across her lips, silencing her.

"I owe you an apology," he continued.

"You owe me nothing, Jotham."

"I do," he gave her a sad smile. "I have no excuse for why I didn't tell you about the birthmarks except for the fact that I have kept my own counsel for so long that I forget I no longer have to."

"You are the King, Jotham. Of course, you are going to keep your own counsel.

"Did Stephan?"

"That was different."

"How? Stephan did important work. He affected lives. Are you going to tell me he never asked you your opinion? Your counsel?"

Jacinda remained silent, knowing she'd be lying if she denied it.

"You trusted me with your secret, Jacinda." Again, he touched her hidden birthmark. "Yet I've trusted you with none of mine."

"My birthmark has never been an issue before, Jotham. I was eighteen before it ever even appeared. It was so light that I never even worried about someone noticing it. It's only been in the last few cycles that it has darkened to the point that I make an effort to conceal it."

"It's darkening?" Jotham frowned.

"Yes."

Jotham shook his head, it was something to consider but not right now, right now he had more important things to discuss.

"You have always been honest with me, Jacinda. Sometimes brutally so, but I haven't done the same with you. There are things about me you don't know. Things that I've done that I'm not proud of. Lies I have allowed because they benefited me. I would like to tell you about them. If you would allow me to. They might change the way you feel about me and I couldn't fault you if they did. But I want a real relationship with you. One where we share... everything. The triumphs and the defeats, the beautiful and the horrible. I want it all. With you."

"I can't imagine anything you could tell me that would change my feelings for you, Jotham, but I agree, we can't have a real relationship if we're not honest with one another."

Chapter Twenty-Four

"I need to start by telling you about Rani." Jotham looked at her as she sat facing him on the couch he led her to. "I know it was... surprising to many."

"Shocking is more like it." Jacinda wouldn't lie to him, not if they were going to build a relationship. "No one even suspected you were involved."

"That's because we weren't."

"Excuse me?"

"We weren't *involved*. Not in any way, shape, or form."

"But, I don't understand. She had your *son*, Jotham!"

"I know, and I can't explain how it happened." Jotham surged to his feet, running a frustrated hand through his hair. "I mean I know 'how' it happened, but I don't 'remember' it happening. I was blind drunk."

"What? You don't remember?"

"No." Jotham took a deep breath and forced himself to reveal to the woman he loved, how he created a child with a woman he barely knew.

"Rani and I had met several times in my office to discuss a program she was trying to start for the orphans of Coalition members."

"There was already a program for that," Jacinda informed him. She had sat on the committee herself.

"Yes, but Rani wanted to expand it."

"I see." But she didn't.

"It started storming during one of our meetings and I couldn't, in good conscience, send her out into it. So I invited her to join me for a last meal."

"I'm sure she jumped all over that." Jacinda couldn't stop herself from spitting out the words. While *she* hadn't personally known Rani before she had conceived Dadrian, her sister *Palma* had and Palma hated her. A telling statement for her normally kind-hearted sister. Rani had been in Lata and Palma's class at the Academy. She had tried to get Palma to change room assignments as soon as they'd arrived at the Academy. Stating that the daughter of an Assemblyman shouldn't be forced to room with a commoner. It didn't matter that Rani's family could be considered 'common' as her father only *worked* for an Assemblyman, but somewhere in the distant past she claimed a 'Royal' ancestor.

"She accepted and we moved our meeting to my private rooms."

"You took her into your bed chamber?" Jacinda felt slightly sick at the thought that Rani had once been in the same bed she had.

"No! Of course not. We ate in the outer chamber." Jotham forced himself not to pace. He needed to face this. "I really don't remember much after that. I drank so much wine that the next day Chesney had to remind me that I called him from my private office comm to schedule a meeting for the next day."

"Wait! What?" Jacinda's fingers dug into the fabric of the couch. "You left the room?"

"I must have, but I don't remember it. All I remember is waking up on the couch with a terrible headache."

"So why do you believe you drank too much wine?" Jacinda demanded.

"Because the bottle was empty and I had a hangover."

Jacinda's mind was flying. That wasn't like Jotham, not even in those terrible cycles immediately following Lata's death. He *never* over-drank.

"You had the wine tested. Right?" she challenged.

Her words had Jotham frowning at her. "There was no wine to test. I told you. The bottle was empty. Rani told me what happened later. I drank too much wine and things... got out of hand."

"She claimed you attacked her?"

"No. She said it was consensual. I apologized and we both agreed to never discuss it again."

"At least not until Rani ended up pregnant. At least tell me you checked to make sure Dadrian was yours."

"Of course I did! Dadrian was mine."

"Alright."

"Rani was just as upset about it as I was, Jacinda."

"Oh, I'm sure she was." Jacinda's tone was filled with scorn and disbelief. She remembered how smug Rani had been every time Jacinda had seen her after it had been announced. She lost that look when Jotham refused to make her his Queen.

"Why don't you believe she was?" Jotham frowned.

"Because you never drink so much wine that you black out, Jotham. The only possible way that could ever happen is if the wine was drugged."

"What!!?" Jotham's eyes widened at her in shock.

"Think about it, Jotham," she leaned forward on the couch, her elbows resting on her knees as she spoke. "You left Rani alone with the wine, that you remember. You remember nothing after you returned. You woke up with a terrible headache. If I told you that had happened to Will, what would your first reaction be?"

"That he'd been drugged..." Jotham whispered.

"Yes."

"But why? Why would she do it?"

"Because she believed if she were to conceive your child, you would be forced to make her your Queen. Something she'd been promised by..." Jacinda trailed off.

"Finish," Jotham ordered.

"She was promised by your mother that she was *her* choice for your bride since she had a 'royal' ancestor somewhere."

"Rani told you this?"

"Me?" Jacinda scoffed in disbelief. "No. Palma. When she tried to get her to help break the two of you up."

"My mother supported her." Jotham was shocked.

"Especially after you left for the Coalition. Without you there to witness it, Rani upped her attacks on Lata." Jacinda tipped her head slightly to the side. "You never noticed how Rani wasn't allowed in the Palace when Lata was alive?"

"No. I hardly noticed another woman when Lata was alive."

"Good answer." Jacinda gave him an understanding smile.

Jotham finally gave in and started to pace, his mind racing. If Jacinda was right then, he hadn't betrayed his wife, his Queen. He had been drugged, tricked, but the real victim here was Dadrian.

"That explains so much," Jotham said quietly.

"What do you mean?"

"All Rani could talk about was how we would raise our 'son' together. How he would change the House of Protection. Once I made it clear that I wouldn't be making her my Queen it all changed."

"I can imagine."

"No, you can't." Jotham looked at her with shuttered eyes. "I didn't want him, Jacinda. If she had informed me sooner, I would have insisted she end the pregnancy."

"Jotham..."

"I know it was wrong, that it went against all I believed in, but Lata was the only woman I wanted having my children. It felt like a betrayal at the most basic level to allow him to be born."

"But the law is the law," she said quietly, her heart breaking for him.

"Yes. She was too far past the time that it would be the taking of an innocent life."

"You made the right choice, Jotham."

"Did I? You don't know my other secret, Jacinda. The one where Dadrian betrayed not only me, not only Barek but every citizen on Carina. He caused thousands of deaths and was never held accountable for it."

"What are you talking about, Jotham? Dadrian fell down the stairs in the Royal Wing of the House of Protection.... Didn't he?"

"Yes, but he fell down them because he was running away. Running away because William and Cassandra discovered he had been trying to assassinate Barek."

"What?" Jacinda's normally golden skin turned a deathly pale. "Jotham..."

"Cassandra discovered what he was trying to do when she was investigating who was responsible for the destruction of Earth."

"Audric," she supplied.

"Yes. She was able to link transmissions Dadrian made to Barek, with those that allowed the Regulians to carry out speed attacks on the Fleet."

"The ones that destroyed the Talon? The ones that for a time we all thought killed Barek?"

"Yes."

"That's why Cassandra was so suspicious when I said I knew when you contacted Lata."

"Yes. Cassandra broke the codes. Barek had just arrived back on planet when Dadrian was confronted with what had been discovered."

"And the codes?"

"Cassandra made sure no one would ever break them again."

"Good."

"That's all you have to say? Good?"

"What did you expect?"

"I expected you to ask why I never informed the Assembly of his betrayal. Why I never admitted to my failure not only as a father but as a King. I expected..."

"Jotham! Stop!" Jacinda surged to her feet grabbing his arm when he would have turned away. "You are not responsible for what Dadrian did. He was a grown man."

"I was his father! Maybe if I had given him more attention...

"I can't tell you if that would have made a difference or not," she told him honestly. "What I can tell you is that you are the same man that raised Barek. They were both given the same opportunities, the same chances. How they chose to use what they were given was up to them."

Jotham's shuttered gaze slowly began to open. "You're not disappointed in me for not reporting to the Assembly as I should have? I had planned to, planned to announce it before Cassandra's Challenge, but Will and Cassandra persuaded me it would harm Barek if I did. Then they destroyed all the evidence linking Dadrian to the attacks."

"Oh Jotham, no! I could never be ashamed of you. I'm just sorry you had to go through all that alone, that you have had to carry the burden of it all these cycles. Will and Cassandra were right, you know. If you had revealed what Dadrian had done..."

Jacinda shuddered slightly at the thought. "The Assembly would have lost its faith and trust in you, in Barek, and in the House of Protection. Cassandra might never have been able to take her place as the rightful Queen. Audric would have succeeded in keeping control of the House of Knowledge and Valerian would still be High Admiral. Our world would be a very different place and not one I'm sure I'd want to live in."

Jotham felt his eyes fill with tears and didn't even try to stop them as he lowered his forehead to rest against hers. Her unwavering support moved him. He had worried he would lose her when he revealed not only Dadrian's actions but also his own response to it.

"Ancestors, Jacinda." Wrapping his arms around her, he pulled her close capturing her lips in a soul-searing kiss. "I love you."

"I love you too." Carefully she wiped away the tracks of his tears then gave him a sexy little smile. "Take me to bed, Jotham."

He was quick to obey.

∞ ∞ ∞ ∞ ∞

Jotham woke and lying on his side, curled a strand of Jacinda's long, silken hair around a finger as he stared down at her as she slept. They barely made it to the bed before Jotham had been inside her, and once in the bed, they had loved each other late into the night. Now, with the first sun barely starting to rise, she slept peacefully beside him, her breath coming out in little puffs from between her lips.

He couldn't believe how content he was to just lay and watch her. It felt so natural, so right that he knew he would do whatever it took to keep her with him. The side of his mouth quirked slightly as his comm went off playing Barek's tone.

William had been right, Barek was going to contact him before first sun.

Rolling away from Jacinda, he swung his legs over the edge of the bed and picked up his portable comm.

"Do you know what time it is, Barek?" Jotham demanded in the way of a greeting.

"First sun should be rising by now. You are always up by then. I want to know why I'm being recalled."

"Because I ordered it."

"That I know," Barek said in a disgusted voice. "What I don't know is why."

"Something has occurred that you need to be made aware of, as it will affect not only you but the entire House of Protection."

"What?"

"I want to discuss it with you face to face, Barek. It's important. You need to be on planet."

"Dad... are you ill?"

"No! Why does everyone keep asking me that?" When Barek just gave him an uncomfortable look, Jotham frowned. "Barek?"

"You work all the time, Dad, just look how quickly you answered my comm. My guess is you have a meeting planned for before second sun rises."

"I don't." Jotham reached behind him to rub a hand down the naked leg Jacinda was moving under the covers and made sure Barek couldn't see her through the comm. "And the only reason I answered the comm so quickly was because I knew you would be calling, demanding answers. I *need* you here, Barek."

Barek's eyes widened on the other end of the comm. When had his father ever told him he *needed* him. Oh, he had told him that he loved him before, that he respected him and was proud of him, but never had he told him that he *needed* him.

"I'll be there as soon as it can be arranged."

"Thank you, Barek."

"You don't need to thank me, Dad, all you've ever had to do is ask."

"I realize that, now... and Barek."

"Yes?"

"This move will be permanent."

∞ ∞ ∞ ∞ ∞

Jacinda woke to Jotham moving to answer his comm. Was the man ever going to learn that he didn't have to get up at first sun? Not wanting to distract him or let whoever was on the comm know she was in bed with him, she carefully began to stretch.

Finally waking up enough to really hear Jotham's words, she stilled just as his hand caressed her calf. He was talking to Barek... about him coming home... permanently. Was he really going to start letting Barek take over some of his responsibilities? Had he taken to heart what *she* wanted and taken action?

"Jotham?" she queried, pushing up on her elbows when he disconnected from Barek.

"Good morning." Dropping his comm, Jotham twisted and he captured her lips in a soft but firm kiss as he slid back over her, settling between her legs as he pressed her back into the bed.

"Good morning," she whispered back, her arms and legs wrapping around him as he nuzzled her neck. "Jotham?" she asked as she felt his shaft press against her.

"Umm?"

"Did you really just recall Barek?" Jotham lifted his head to look down at her. "Permanently?"

"You didn't think I would."

"I thought it would take you some time to consider it. I didn't know what you would decide."

"Have you ever known me to be an indecisive man, Jacinda?" He tilted his hips so the head of his shaft pressed against her opening.

"No, it's one of your strengths," she told him in a slightly, breathless voice.

"So you are aware that once I decide something, I remain firm." He thrust forward filling her completely.

"Yes!" Jacinda exclaimed as her entire body arched up.

"And once I set my course I do not deviate." He began to slowly move inside of her, making sure he hit that spot that he knew drove her crazy.

"Yes!"

"If you knew this, then why did you doubt I would take the steps needed to satisfy you?" He thrust harder.

"Because I didn't expect you to move so fast," she cried out.

"You want me to move slower?" He immediately slowed his thrusts to the point his shaft dragged along the sensitive walls of her channel still swollen from their loving the night before.

"Jotham!"

"Or do you prefer fast?" He began to pound into her, knowing he was driving her higher.

"Both! Either! I don't care! Just don't stop!"

"Oh, I'm not going to!" Jotham growled into her mouth. "You are mine, Jacinda, and I'm never going to stop loving you!"

∞ ∞ ∞ ∞ ∞

"Will. Cassandra." Jotham waited until he had their attention before he continued. First meal had been pleasant enough, the children chatting happily, while Cyndy, who had sat down next to Jacinda, talked amicably. Sabah wasn't present. Once the boys left for the morning, Jotham spoke.

"I think you need to reconsider me being second father to Sabah." Everyone looked at Jotham in shock, including Jacinda.

"What!" William who had been about to rise sat back down with a thud. "Jotham, why?"

"Jacinda is a part of my life." He let his gaze travel from his friend to Cassandra. "An important part and she always will be. If the worst were to happen then *both* of us would have a hand in raising Sabah. Given your attitude toward her, I think you should choose someone else."

"Jotham." Jacinda put a hand on his arm. "You don't have to do this. *You* are the perfect second father for Sabah, whether you have to assume the responsibility or not. Cassandra might be the Queen *now*, but she didn't grow up the heir. She will never fully understand the pressure and attention that brings from the moment you are born. Not even Will fully understands. Only you and Barek can truly help guide her through that. Don't let what's happened here affect that little girl's future. Not because of me."

"You know as well as I do, Jacinda, that every decision we make affects the future and my *decision* is that you matter more than ever being a second father, even to one of Will's children."

Silence reigned around the table as Cassandra pushed back from the table and left the room, without a word.

"I'm sorry, Will." Jotham looked to his oldest friend and hoped this wouldn't change that friendship.

Will just raised his hand to silence him, his eyes remaining on the door Cassandra had gone through. It didn't take long for Cassandra to return, carrying a squirming Sabah. She walked over to where Jacinda still sat.

"This is our daughter, Sabah," Cassandra told her and after kissing Sabah's forehead leaned down to set her in Jacinda's arms that immediately cradled the precious bundle.

Sabah immediately stilled when the new arms surrounded her. Her sparkling blue eyes stared up at Jacinda with more intelligence than one so young should have. Then she blew a bubble and Jacinda laughed.

"Well aren't you just adorable." Leaning down, Jacinda rubbed her nose against Sabah's. "I bet you already have your daddy wrapped around this little finger." She lifted it to kiss.

"She does," Cassandra confirmed moving to resume her seat. "All she has to do is peep and William is at her side." Cassandra gave her husband a disgusted look. "If she cries, he's calling the Healer."

"All Daddies are like that with their daughters." Jacinda cooed at Sabah causing her to giggle. "It's good for them, it makes them remember all those naughty thoughts they had about girls growing up. Yes, it does." Jacinda cooed to Sabah. "And they suddenly realize there's going to be some boy out there that will be thinking the same things about *their* daughter and do things like sneak into the showers. It makes them crazy." Jacinda looked up to see both William and Jotham were pale as they looked from her to the innocent bundle in her arms. Looking at Cyndy and Cassandra, they all started to laugh. Peter just snorted.

"Lucas was just lucky my daughter was already in love with him when I met him. Otherwise, he would have found himself on the wrong end of my fists."

"Peter!" Cyndy turned to him in shock. "Lucas is a wonderful man!"

"True, and the only one that I would trust our Tori with, but I still would have made him work to prove it."

"William says he will let Sabah date... when she's thirty."

"Good luck with that," Peter looked to William. "You do remember she is a Chamberlain, don't you?" Peter looked from Cassandra to his wife. "They tend to do whatever they want."

"Sabah is a Zafar." William reminded him proudly.

"True, but she's still a Chamberlain and a Qwes. Honestly, William, with those three names I think you are screwed."

"Shut up, Peter." William chucked his napkin at Peter hitting him square in the face.

Sabah's head turned hearing her father's voice, her little eyes searching for him. The moment she found him, she began to squeal and squirm, her little arms reaching for him.

"See what I mean?" Cassandra said as William immediately rose to go to his daughter.

"Stephan was the same," Jacinda told her, relinquishing Sabah to her father. "Every little peep, unless it involved a dirty diaper."

"William seems to always miss those too."

"As did Peter."

The three women looked at their men.

"Hey, don't look at me." Jotham through his hands up in mock surrender. "I never had a daughter."

"So you're saying you changed Barek's dirty diapers?" Jacinda challenged.

"I... well... I can't remember now."

"That means you never did," Cyndy told him decisively. "If you had, you would remember." Jacinda and Cassandra nodded in agreement.

∞ ∞ ∞ ∞ ∞

"So, Jacinda, Kia will be here later this afternoon, have you given any thought to the dress you want her to make for you?" Cassandra asked.

"Dress?" Jacinda looked to Cassandra in confusion. "For what?"

"For the Royal Ball next month."

"Oh, I won't be going to *that*." Jacinda waved a dismissive hand turning her attention back to William and Sabah.

"Oh yes, you will be," Jotham corrected.

"Jotham, that Ball is for the Kings and Queens of Carina, and their Assemblies."

A Royal Ball only ever occurred every five cycles and was always hosted by a different House. It allowed the House to present itself in the best light. It also allowed all the Houses' Assemblymen to meet and mingle. This time the House of Knowledge was hosting it.

"And you will be at my side." Jotham gave her a hard look.

Jacinda silently gazed at Jotham, she could see the resolve in his eyes. If they did this, there wouldn't be any need for an announcement because word would spread like wildfire. There would be no going back if they did this.

"Are you sure about this, Jotham?" she asked quietly. "I won't be offended if you go without me. We agreed we weren't going to make any 'official' statement."

"We also agreed we would openly spend time together. I want you at my side, Jacinda."

Slowly she nodded. "Okay, I'll have to let my children know beforehand though."

"And I'll be telling Barek when he arrives on planet." Jotham leaned over and kissed her. "It will all work out, Jacinda."

Jacinda prayed to the ancestors that he was right.

Chapter Twenty-Five

Kia was surprised to find Jacinda with the Queen when she arrived at the Palace to discuss the gown Cassandra wished made for the Royal Ball. She was even more surprised when she was informed Jacinda needed a gown too.

"You will be attending the Ball with Danton?" Kia asked frowning. She had never heard of an Assemblyman's *mother* attending the Ball before, not even the late wife of one.

"No," Jacinda spoke up before Cassandra could. "Would you mind if I looked through your sketch book while you work with Cassandra? I wasn't aware until a short time ago that I would be attending the Ball and need a little time to decide what I want."

"Of course. If that is alright with you, Majesty." Kia looked to Cassandra.

"It's fine, Kia. I have a meeting in thirty minutes and you and I have already discussed what I want. Did you bring the fabrics?"

"Yes, Majesty."

Jacinda tuned out Kia and Cassandra's conversation as she tried to decide what type of gown she should wear. With Stephan, she always knew. It had to be elegant and stylish but understated because she was there to support Stephan, not outshine him. Flipping through the pages of Kia's book, nothing seemed appropriate.

"Jacinda. Jacinda!" Cassandra spoke louder finally drawing Jacinda's attention.

"I'm sorry. I was lost in thought."

"I could see that." Cassandra smiled at her. "I was just trying to tell you that I was done. Kia is here for as long as you need her. And Jacinda..."

"Yes?""

"Jotham is a very self-assured man. He knows who he is, and his place in this world. You need to present yourself the same way if you are going to stand by his side." With that, Cassandra left the room.

"Jotham?" Kia looked at Jacinda in shock. "You are going to accompany *King Jotham* to the Royal Ball?" Kia's mind began to swirl.

"Yes," Jacinda told her simply.

"King Jotham. House of Protection King Jotham?" Kia repeated wanting to be sure she understood.

"Yes, Kia."

"Then, my friend, your dress must be *spectacular* for every eye will be on you. *You* will be all they talk about. Just as Cassandra was when she appeared at her first Ball. And you must stand tall, proud, and confident at the King's side."

Jacinda took a deep breath wondering if she was ready for this.

"You are." Kia moved to sit beside her. "Jacinda, I have had the honor of knowing you for many cycles and consider you a friend. You supported Pazel and me when no one else would. You've always had impeccable taste. However, and I hope you don't take this the wrong way, you have never truly shone. You have always made sure you were there in the background supporting."

"It was my role," Jacinda informed her.

"Maybe for an Assemblyman's wife, but that is not who you are standing beside now. Now you are standing beside a King. The most respected one on the planet. You need to show that you *can* stand on your own while still supporting Jotham, just as the High Admiral does with Cassandra. If you trust me, I believe I can design you the perfect dress."

"Kia, I am in your hands."

Kia pulled out her sketchpad and quickly began to draw. The gown would be House of Protection violet with an undergarment of black, enhancing its depth of color. It was a form-fitting sheath with no sleeves, that would cling to her figure before pooling out around her, a short train following behind her as she moved. It was only when they got to the applique, that would accent the bodice, waist and train that they disagreed.

"You said this dress needed to represent who *I* am, that *I* needed to shine."

"Yes," Kia agreed.

"Then the applique needs to be House of Healing gold." She saw the shock in Kia's eyes. "It's where I come from. It's who I am.

"Only Cassandra has ever blended the colors."

"Well now, I am. If you can't do it, Kia, I will find someone who can. Because I refuse to be something I'm not. I am House of Healing. I will represent that in this dress."

Kia gave her a considering look and suddenly realized that their world was about to change again. "Yes, Majesty."

"Kia, I'm not royalty, you don't need to address me like that."

"You may not be yet, but I have a feeling you will be before long."

∞ ∞ ∞ ∞ ∞

"Mother?"

The sound of her daughter's voice had Jacinda turning, a smile breaking out on her face as Stephanie rapidly approached her. After her fitting with Kia, Jacinda had wanted to clear her head. She checked in with Deffand and informed him she was going to take a tour of the Public Wing. It had been cycles since she had been in the House of Knowledge, back when Yakira had been the Trustee, and she wanted to see what changes Cassandra had made.

"Stephanie!" Jacinda greeted happily.

"Mother." Stephanie grabbed her and pulled her to the side of the room. "What are you doing here?"

Jacinda frowned at her daughter. "Well, at the moment I'm touring the Public Wing to see what changes Cassandra has made."

"Cassandra?" Stephanie looked at her mother, shocked at how casually she used the Queen's name, almost as if they were friends. "You mean Queen Cassandra!"

"Is there someone else here named Cassandra?"

"Mother!" Stephanie hissed. "Please tell me you're not here checking up on me!"

Jacinda looked at her daughter, stunned at the accusation. Stephanie was a thirty-four cycle woman, and while Jacinda would always worry about her, she stopped 'checking up' on her when she turned eighteen. "You honestly think I have nothing better to do than come and check up on you? I have a life you know."

"I'd like to think you do, but I ran into Aunt Palma this morning and she told me you were here and that I needed to speak to you."

Jacinda wanted to slap her own forehead, then she wanted to slap her sister's. She hadn't gotten a chance to explain to Palma why she was here. Who she was here with. Now Stephanie thought *she* was why her mother was here.

"My being here has absolutely nothing to do with you, Stephanie. It's totally unrelated."

"Then why are you here? Where are you staying?" Stephanie demanded. "It's not with Aunt Palma."

"No, it's not." Jacinda knew she would have to eventually tell her children about her relationship with Jotham, but she thought she would have a little more time to decide how to break it to them. Apparently, she was wrong. Taking a deep breath, she told her daughter the truth. "I'm staying here at the Palace. In the Royal Wing."

"In the Royal Wing?" Stephanie frowned, her mind racing. "But King Jotham is currently staying in the Royal Wing."

"Yes, he is," Jacinda confirmed.

"But how can both of you be staying there? How can you be? You're not a Royal."

"No, I'm not." Jacinda silently waited, her daughter wasn't stupid. It wouldn't take her long to figure it out.

"But..." Stephanie's eyes widened and Jacinda watched her take a stumbling step back. "No," she whispered. "It's not possible."

"Why isn't it?"

"You can't be *involved*," Stephanie barely breathed the word, "with King Jotham."

"Why can't I be?" Jacinda queried raising an eyebrow at her.

"Because he's the *King*!" This time the words exploded from Stephanie causing heads to turn in their direction.

"Keep your voice down!" Jacinda ordered sharply. "I know he is the King, Stephanie, but Jotham is also a man. A man I happen to care a great deal about."

"But... but... Father."

"Would want me to continue living, to find happiness again if I could. The same way I would want him to if the situation was reversed."

"But this will change everything!" Stephanie ran an angry hand through her hair. "If this ever gets out it will ruin any chance I have to get on a Royal detail."

"*That's* what you're worried about?" Jacinda couldn't hide her shock or disappointment. "How this affects you and *your* future?"

"Mom, what did you expect? I've worked my whole life to get to where I am. I've sacrificed so much..."

"Oh, and I haven't?!!" Jacinda demanded. "I've sacrificed more than you will *ever* know. For you, for your brothers and for your father, but I won't sacrifice Jotham, not for your *career*."

"Madame Michelakakis, is there a problem?" Deffand walked up, his expression blank as he looked from her to Stephanie.

"No, Captain. Thank you. My daughter and I were just having a disagreement, but we're finished. Would you mind escorting me back to the Royal Wing?"

"It would be my pleasure, Madame."

Deffand gave Stephanie a hard look before he extended his arm to Jacinda and led her away.

Jacinda waited until they had exited the Public Wing before she spoke again. "Were you following me, Nicholas?"

"Of course I was," he told her simply.

"I was still within the Palace."

"Yes."

"I informed you where I was going."

"Yes."

"Yet you still felt you needed to follow me?"

Deffand paused for a moment, then led Jacinda to a quiet alcove. "In all the cycles I have served Jotham, I have never seen him this happy and it's because of you. I want to make sure he stays that way, and that means keeping you safe at all times. You're just going to have to get used to it."

"Oh I am, am I?" Jacinda arched an eyebrow at him.

"Yes," Nicholas wasn't intimidated at all, "you are. Jotham has made it quite clear that your safety is his top priority. When we return to Pechora, you are to have your own personal guards. They are being selected as we speak. Jotham is not taking the chance of losing another woman he loves."

Jacinda opened her mouth to argue but snapped it shut as Deffand continued.

"It's what you would expect if it were any other woman."

Jacinda narrowed her eyes at Deffand, not liking that he was right. "I don't like it, but you are right, Nicholas."

"I know." Taking her arm, they began walking again.

"You don't have to be so smug about it," Jacinda huffed at him.

"Smug? Me? Madame Michelakakis, I have no idea what you are referring to."

"Yes, you do. So will you be in charge of my guards?"

"Yes, Madame."

"Alright, but there are going to be some rules they have to follow."

"As long as they don't interfere with your safety that won't be a problem."

∞ ∞ ∞ ∞ ∞

Jacinda proudly stood beside Jotham in the Memory Garden that evening, silently listening as the Guide recited the ancient words over Sabah, held by Jotham, that would forever bind their lives together. Sabah's sapphire blue eyes were wide, but she remained quiet as if she understood the significance of the moment.

"May the ancestors watch over you and guide you on this journey that is your life. May you leave this world better than when you entered it and may you be loved."

With those final words, the ceremony was completed and Sabah began to coo, clapping her little hands together in approval, causing everyone to laugh.

"Thank you, Jotham." William walked over to his friend and for the first time since her birth, his daughter didn't immediately reach out for him.

"It was my honor, Will." Jotham lifted Sabah, kissing her chubby cheek, taking in that amazing scent that only a baby has. He then handed her to her first father, knowing Will needed her in his arms. Turning, he found Jacinda right there, supporting him, an understanding smile on her face as she stepped into his arms. Closing his eyes, he rested his chin on the top of her head, taking in the scent of roses she always seemed to carry and thanked the ancestors for the gifts they had bestowed on him.

"That was amazing, Jotham." Jacinda quietly spoke into his chest, feeling the steady beat of his heart. "I could see the bonds building between you and Sabah." Pulling back slightly, she looked up at him in awe. "The House of Protection and the House of Knowledge are now forever linked."

"They are," Jotham agreed sealing his words with a kiss. "So are you going to tell me what you and Stephanie were arguing about in the Public Wing?"

"Who says we were arguing?" Jacinda arched her eyebrow.

"Deffand." Jotham selected two flutes of wine from the tray of a passing servant then handed one to her.

"Oh really?" She took the glass but didn't sip.

"He was just doing his job, Jacinda." Jotham knew that look and knew he was going to have to do some fast explaining.

"Really? So his job is to inform you of a private conversation between myself and my daughter? I thought it was security."

"It is, you know that, but it's more than that, especially with you."

"Why especially with me?"

"Because Nicholas cares about you. He considers you a friend. He also knows I love you. He's going to tell me when he thinks something or someone has upset you."

Jacinda took a sip of her wine thinking about what Jotham had said. She understood it. She did. She just didn't like it, taking a deep breath she spoke. "If I'm going to accept the security you have Deffand arranging, there are going to be some guidelines, Jotham. My private conversations are *mine*... for me to tell you about... if I feel you need to know."

"You would keep things from me?" Jotham demanded.

"It's not that I'm going to *keep* things from you, but I have the right to decide *when* to tell you something. Like a confrontation with my daughter that has upset me."

It was Jotham's turn to take a deep breath and as he looked over Jacinda's shoulder, he saw William lean down to listen to something Cassandra was telling him while Cyndy was listening to Peter.

Couples. Couples talking and listening to each other.

It had been a very long time since he had been part of one and it seemed his skills were rusty.

"You're right." He looked back to Jacinda. "I'm sorry. I'm a little out of practice at being part of a couple. I'm used to demanding information and being given it."

"You mean you're spoiled." The affronted look on Jotham's face had Jacinda laughing.

"I wouldn't say spoiled, but..."

"Spoiled," she told him. Reaching up, she patted his cheek. "As I said before, it's a good thing you're so cute. Otherwise, I might have to rethink this whole thing."

"Oh really?" Wrapping an arm around her waist, Jotham pulled her body flush against his and captured her lips in a hard kiss until he felt her melt against him.

"Hey you two, cut that out. There are children present here."

William's teasing voice had Jotham reluctantly breaking off the kiss. Seeing Jacinda's dazed look almost made it worth it.

"Rethink *that*," he whispered then kissing the tip of her nose, stepped back and watched her blush.

Jacinda felt her cheeks heat as she looked around to find every eye in the garden was on them, including all the boys. Clearing her throat self-consciously, she took a sip of her wine.

"Come on, let's take a walk." Jotham put his arm around her waist. "We'll see you all tomorrow before we leave." He told everyone in the way of a farewell and led her from the Memory Garden.

"Definitely spoiled," Jacinda teased slipping an arm around his waist, happily walking beside him.

"Perhaps," he said noncommittally.

They walked for several minutes in a comfortable silence, enjoying the last rays of Carina's third sun."

"Will you share with me what Stephanie said that upset you so?"

Jacinda sighed but knew they had to address this. "Apparently, Stephanie ran into Palma yesterday and Palma told her I was in Kisurri."

"I don't understand. Palma doesn't approve of our relationship?"

"I never got the chance to tell her. We were both so amazed by the way Cyndy could sing that we never got around to it."

"So what *did* she tell Stephanie?"

"Only that she needed to talk to me. Stephanie, for some reason, took that to mean that I was here checking up on her."

"Why would she think that?"

"I honestly don't know. I do know she has worked extremely hard to get to where she is. I know that while the attitudes toward women serving have changed since I served, there are still areas where even if a woman excels, she is excluded because of her gender."

"Jacinda, you have to know that there *are* some areas where a man is just better suited, where his strength is needed."

"Not every situation requires extreme strength, Jotham. Sometimes skill and intelligence are more important."

"That's true."

"It's why Stephanie was so excited to get accepted into Peter's class. She saw it as a validation that she could take her career to the next level. Now, because of *our* relationship she's worried she'll never get that chance."

"Why would she think that? I have nothing to do with Coalition assignments."

"Not directly, no, but we both know you have influence."

Jotham said nothing because it was true.

"Stephanie is concerned that because of our association she won't be able to apply for the position she most desires."

"What position is that?" When Jacinda just looked at him, Jotham felt his heart begin to beat harder. What position could Stephanie possibly want? "Jacinda?"

"I'm not sure I should tell you," she told him, her eyes full of indecision.

"Jacinda," Jotham cupped her cheek. "You have to know you can tell me anything. I'm not going to do anything that would interfere in your daughter's dreams."

"What if I want you to?" Jacinda whispered, finally admitting what she was really afraid of, that she would ask Jotham to interfere.

"Jacinda?" This time he cupped both her cheeks, refusing to let her turn away from him. He didn't like seeing her like this. "Tell me. Trust me."

"Stephanie wants to be the first woman ever accepted into a Royal Guard... into *your* Royal Guard." Jacinda's eyes filled with tears.

"Shhh. Don't cry, love." Jotham wrapped his arms around her offering what comfort he could.

"I've always encouraged my children to follow their dreams. Supported them. What does it say about me, as a mother, that I hope she doesn't achieve this one?"

"That you love and worry about your daughter," he immediately told her. "Give her some time, Jacinda."

"I just... " she pulled back, letting the tears run down her cheeks.

"Just what?"

"Was just hoping that they would understand. My children. I knew this was going to affect them, but I thought it would be Danton that would be the most upset by it."

"Because he's an Assemblyman."

"Yes, our relationship directly affects him, but Stephanie..."

"It still may not affect her, Jacinda, because she's right, there's never been a woman in any Royal Guard and there may never be."

"Why? Why not?"

"Because no Queen wants another woman around her King day and night."

"If that's true, then why are there men in a Queen's."

"Because that's the way it's always been." Jotham had the grace to look uncomfortable. "I'll honestly admit I've never considered a woman for my Guard, but in my defense, none have ever applied."

"Are you sure about that? I thought Deffand went through all the applicants."

"He does, but he then sends the most qualified to me for final approval."

"So you wouldn't know if a woman applied."

"I... well, I guess I wouldn't." Jotham used his thumbs to wipe away the tracks of her tears. "It will be okay, Jacinda. We'll find a way to make it all work."

Chapter Twenty-Six

Jacinda sat back in her seat on the shuttle and opened the large folder Brett had shyly handed her after first meal that morning.

Inside had been a large, colored portrait of her and Jotham from the waist up in the Memory Garden, gazing at each other. Brett had captured the moment perfectly. The way Jotham's fingers seemed to be caressing her back. The way Jacinda stared up at Jotham, a barely there smile on her lips, as she leaned closer to him.

Jacinda had dropped down to her knees hugging the boy. "It beautiful, Brett."

"You really like it?" he asked with questioning eyes.

"I do, there's just one problem with it."

"What's that?" he whispered.

"You didn't sign it." Jacinda smiled at him. "Would you? Then I can have it matted and framed because I know just where I want to hang it."

"Really? You're going to hang it up?"

"I am. So will you sign it for me?"

"I didn't know I was supposed to..." He frowned at the drawing. "Where?"

"Well most artists sign it in one of the lower corners, where it can be seen but not distract from the drawing, but it's up to you where you want it."

"Mom?" Brett looked up to Cyndy, silently begging her for help.

"Sign it here, Brett." Cyndy pointed at a spot about an inch up from the lower right hand corner. "That way people can still see it when it's framed."

"Both my names?" he asked.

"Yes, baby," Cyndy told him.

After clearing a spot on the table, Brett carefully took the portrait from Jacinda and set it down. Reaching down, he pulled out his precious colored pencils and after several moments of contemplation chose a color.

They all watched as, biting his lower lip, Brett very carefully printed his name.

Brett Chamberlain.

"Is that okay?" His concerned little eyes turned to Jacinda.

"It's perfect, Brett. Thank you." Leaning down she kissed his cheek and Brett blushed.

"Can I go play with the boys now?" Brett looked to his father.

"Go ahead," Peter told him smiling.

With that, Brett carefully put away his art supplies, grabbed his bag, and took off running.

"Thank you, Jacinda. You made his day." Cyndy squeezed her arm.

"He made mine. I can't wait to get this up. You really have to see about getting him an art teacher."

"Already done," Cyndy told her. "Cassandra contacted Director Birgin and he recommended someone that will be here today."

It had taken several more moments of hugs and goodbyes before Jotham had been able to escort her to the shuttle, and they had departed for Pechora.

∞ ∞ ∞ ∞ ∞

"He is truly talented," Jotham told her leaning over to gaze at the portrait. "Do you really have a place to hang it?"

"Oh yes, it's going right above that small table along the wall between the living room and kitchen." She already knew the mat and frame she wanted.

"On the wall between the living room and kitchen?" Jotham frowned thinking about where she was suggesting and what was already there. "But that's in the main traffic area of the house. You already have an arrangement of visuals there. All of you and Stephan."

"Mm-hmm," she said absently, still looking at the drawing. "I'll find somewhere else for them. I always wanted just one visual there but never found one large enough that seemed right. This will be perfect."

"You would take the other ones down?" Jotham didn't try to hide his shock. "The visuals of Stephan and put one up that included me?"

"Yes." Jacinda frowned at him. "Why are you so shocked?"

"I don't know, I guess I just didn't expect you to be willing to replace Stephan with me."

"I'm not," Jacinda instantly denied, turning to face him. "You can never replace Stephan, Jotham, and I don't say that to be hurtful, but Stephan was my husband for nearly thirty cycles. We had children together. He will always be an important part of my life, of my past, one that I will always proudly display and talk about, but that doesn't mean I can't make room for *you*. *You* are part of my future and I'm just as proud of that."

Jotham felt his throat tightening as she spoke, never in his life had he felt so humbled yet overcome all at the same time. Jacinda was making room for him, not just in her life, but in her home, in her family, and in her memories. She was willing to openly display to everyone just how important he was to her without reducing Stephan's importance. It was something he had never thought possible, but again, she was proving him wrong.

"I don't know what to say," he told her leaning forward to kiss her. "Except that I love you and I will forever thank the ancestors for bringing you into my life."

∞ ∞ ∞ ∞ ∞

Jacinda let out a heavy sigh when she was finally able to close her front door and shut everyone out.

Jotham hadn't wanted her to go home. He had wanted her to go stay at the Palace with him, even though he would be busy until after ten with meetings catching up on all that had occurred while he was gone.

They had argued, but he'd finally agreed she needed to return home as long as she took Deffand with her and let him sweep the house before she entered.

Jacinda had only agreed because he allowed her to notify Myesha before they arrived, so she wouldn't be alarmed.

"I take it, it went well?" Myesha asked in a way of a greeting.

"Yes and no," Jacinda informed her, collapsing on the couch.

"Oh, you are going to have to explain that, Jacinda Michelakakis." Myesha handed her one of the glasses of wine she'd poured when she knew Jacinda was on her way. She knew her longtime friend/employer, and whenever she returned from a trip, the first thing she always wanted was to relax with a glass of wine.

"Oh bless you, Myesha." Jacinda took a small sip before she started. "Well, let's see. After a rather bumpy start, Cassandra and I were finally able to find some common ground."

"The Queen took a disliking to you?" Myesha demanded.

Jacinda smiled at her friend bristling on her behalf. "I won't say it was 'dislike' exactly, it was more her being reserved and cautious. I am a stranger after all, one brought in to the inner sanctum of her family. It didn't help that I took her sister-in-law Cyndy out of the Palace to meet Palma... without Royal Guards."

Myesha choked on the wine she'd just sipped. "*Without* Royal Guards? Jacinda! What were you thinking?!!"

"I wasn't," Jacinda admitted. "I just wanted to get her to Palma."

"Why?"

"Because back on Earth, before she had Victoria, Cyndy had been a professional singer."

"Really?" Myesha gave her an intrigued look. "Was she any good?"

"If her voice now, which she claims is rusty, is anything to go by, then she must have been exceptional."

"Palma thought so too?"

"Oh yes."

"I still can't believe you didn't take *any* Royal Guards. Praise the ancestors, Jacinda, she is a Princess!"

"I know, and, believe me, Cassandra tore into me about it, but in the end it worked out. Cyndy is going to meet with Birgin and he's even going to meet with their son, Brett." Jacinda smiled wishing she could be there to see Birgin's reaction to Brett's drawings. She would have to remember to call him and find out.

"Why would Birgin want to meet with Brett?"

Instead of answering, Jacinda opened the folder she'd set on the coffee table and slid it toward Myesha.

"Oh... my... ancestors...." she whispered in awe, making sure she set her glass far away before leaning in for a closer look. "I thought he was just a boy, a child."

"He just turned nine," Jacinda told her.

"What!" Myesha's eyes flew to Jacinda and saw her nod that it was true. "This is amazing."

"I know. I'm going to contact Kasmira to have it matted and framed."

"But Kasmira *restores* art."

"I know but, Myesha, this is truly a masterpiece. A first of many I believe that we will be seeing from Brett Chamberlain and I want it treated properly from the very beginning."

"It will also help that she's family and won't tell anyone of the subject matter."

"Well, there is that but I don't care who she tells. It's going to get out sooner rather than later... it already is."

"What are you talking about?" Myesha demanded. "I haven't said *anything* to *anyone*!"

"Oh, Myesha! No! I'm not saying it's because of *you*! I never doubted you wouldn't say anything. No, I'm talking about Stephanie."

"Stephanie?"

"Yes. It seems she and Palma ran into each other and Palma told her I was in Kisurri and that she needed to talk to me. She found me in the Public Wing of the Palace and... let's just say she didn't take my being there with Jotham well."

"She'll come around, Jacinda." Myesha reached over to squeeze her hand. "It just surprised her. You know how she idolized her father. She's not going to like anyone else at your side. King or not. Give her some time."

"That's just the problem, there isn't going to be much time." Jacinda took a deep breath then looked at her friend. "I'm going to be attending the Royal Ball... at Jotham's side."

"Jacinda...." Myesha's hand covered her mouth in shock. "The arrival of the Royals at that Ball is broadcast not only across the planet but also throughout the fleet! You arriving on Jotham's arm..."

"I know. I need to talk to Danton and Ethan about it, so they're prepared." With a sigh, she finished her wine and stood. "I guess I should get on that. Myesha..."

"I'll unpack for you. Don't worry."

"Thank you, my friend." Jacinda turned to leave then paused and turned back. "Are you going to be okay with this, Myesha? With all these changes? Jotham has insisted I have security which means they are going to be around the house. Watching and checking on who's coming and going and that includes you."

"I'll be fine with it, Jacinda." Myesha tipped her head to the side, thinking. "You know, the real problem is going to be Madame Nitzschke."

"Oh, praise the ancestors!" Jacinda closed her eyes, her laugh holding no humor. "I'd forgotten about her."

"Yeah, well we'd better warn your security. *They* may be the ones in need of protection if she gets hold of one of them."

∞ ∞ ∞ ∞ ∞

"Young man! Young man!"

Lieutenant Green turned from speaking to another guard and frowned at the woman making her way up the sidewalk. He didn't believe her to be a threat, except to his sense of style because the clash of colors and patterns she was wearing hurt his eyes.

"Young man, I want you gone! This a respectable neighborhood and I won't have you loitering around here." When she turned to make her way up the drive, Kort moved to intercept her.

"Madame, I'm sorry, but I can't allow you any further," he told her firmly.

"*Allow* me!" Madame Nitzschke shrieked. "Allow *me*? This is *my* neighborhood, young man! Do you know who I am?"

Kort wasn't about to admit that he didn't. The last few days had been a whirlwind of assessing and choosing the correct guards as King Jotham had ordered for Madame Michelakakis. They were still compiling information on her family, friends, and neighbors.

"Madame Nitzschke," Jacinda called out having just stepped out her front door when she'd heard her neighbor start in on Lieutenant Green. "How are you today?"

"I'm upset that's what I am! How dare you, Jacinda! This is a respectable neighborhood and you have men lining up outside your house!"

Green looked at the woman in shock. Did she really think they were here to *see* Jacinda? He saw Jacinda wasn't shocked.

"Madame Nitzschke," Jacinda clenched her teeth. "I would like to introduce you to Lieutenant Kort Green. If you notice his uniform, you will see he is a member of King Jotham's Royal Guard."

"You think that makes it okay that he and all these other men," she waved her hand around wildly, "are loitering around out here!"

"We are not *loitering*," Kort stepped between the two women. He had enough of this old biddy. "We are Madame Michelakakis' security."

"Security! What have you done now, Jacinda?" Madame Nitzschke demanded trying to step around Green, who was blocking her. "Move, young man."

"No." Green gave the woman a hard look and several other guards moved in to back up their Lieutenant.

"Lieutenant," Jacinda put a careful hand on his arm. "Let me by. I have known Madame Nitzschke for cycles. She's no threat... except to someone with fashion sense." She said the last part quietly and while she heard the other guards snort, her eyes remained focused on Green. When he finally nodded, she stepped around him.

"Madame Nitzschke, I'm sorry I wasn't able to give you advance notice of the added security around my home. I've always appreciated your concern for your neighbors safety and welfare."

Madame Nitzschke sniffed at her, but she did stand a little taller. "Someone has to do it."

"I know and you've been doing a wonderful job. Lieutenant Green here," she gestured behind her, "and several of his men are now going to be patrolling around my home."

"Why?"

"There's no reason for you to know that. What you need to know is that you don't have to worry about them being here." Jacinda smiled at her. "Now if you'll excuse me, I was just on my way out. Have a wonderful evening, Madame Nitzschke." Turning, Jacinda walked away.

Kort watched as Madame Nitzschke gave him and his men one last go over before she spun on her heel and clicked away. Turning, he found Jacinda moving toward her transport.

"Madame Michelakakis!" He ran to catch up with her. "What are you doing? Where do you think you're going?"

"I have some errands to run, Lieutenant."

"I wasn't informed you were going anywhere."

"Well, I'm informing you now."

"That's not how it works, Madame Michelakakis. You must inform me *first* and *then* I will decide if it advisable."

"Look, Lieutenant." Jacinda rounded on him, causing him to take a quick step back. "I know you have a job to do, but I have a life to live and I am *not* going to let *you* decide if I can. Right now, I'm going to Comorin to have last meal with my second son, Ethan, and his family at his home. Now, you can either get in my transport with me, get into yours and follow behind me, or stay here. I really don't care, but I'm going." Sliding behind the wheel she slammed her door.

Kort found himself racing around the transport getting in the passenger side, as he yelled for the men he wanted to follow and the ones he wanted to stay behind.

"Now, Lieutenant," Jacinda spoke as she backed out of her drive. "We need to set some ground rules."

"Ground rules?"

"Yes. First, my name is Jacinda. I understand there will be times you will need to address me as Madame Michelakakis, but I prefer Jacinda. Second, I will try and I stress the word *try*, to give you advance notice of where I am going and when. I'm new to this level of security so you're going to have to be patient with me."

"Madame Michelakakis..." When she gave him a hard look before returning her gaze back to the road, he quickly corrected himself. "Jacinda, my job is to keep you safe, no matter what."

"I understand that, Kort. May I call you Kort?"

"I... yes, of course," Kort stuttered.

"Good. Now back to the matter at hand. I understand your job, but what you have to understand is that there isn't anyone out there that wants to hurt me."

"You can't be sure of that, especially now that you are with the King. There are bound to be some that are not happy about that."

That had Jacinda quietly thinking. There *were* going to be some that would be upset that she and Jotham were together. To the purists, she would always be from the House of Healing and that meant she should never be with someone from the House of Protection.

"Point taken, Kort."

Chapter Twenty-Seven

"Oh, Jacinda, it's so good to see you. Come in." Kasmira hugged her mother-in-law pulling her into the house.

Kasmira absolutely adored Jacinda, although it hadn't started out that way. Jacinda had intimidated her at first, after all she was the wife of a powerful Assemblyman, she was beautiful, and she was the mother of the man she loved. It hadn't taken her long to realize that while Jacinda *was* all those things, she was also just a woman that loved her children and wanted them to be happy. After that, they became great friends.

"Ethan is running late, you know how that is." She was about to shut the door when she saw the man standing there... a man wearing a Royal Guard uniform. "Ah... Jacinda."

"Hmm?" Jacinda looked behind her. "Oh. Kort, this is my daughter-in-law Kasmira Michelakakis. Kasmira, this is Lieutenant Kort Green of the King's Royal Guard."

"Ma'am," Kort nodded to Kasmira.

"Lieutenant," Kasmira replied. "Please, won't you come in?"

"No thank you. Madame Michelakakis, we will be outside." With a slight bow, he turned and walked down the path.

Kasmira slowly closed the door then turned to give Jacinda a questioning look.

"Yes, I know I need to explain, that's why I'm here. But first, where are my grandsons?"

"They're at a sleepover. I'm sorry. They were already gone when you said were coming. Do I need to go get them?"

"No." Jacinda was disappointed but realized it was probably for the best. "Let them stay. This is going to be difficult enough without upsetting them too."

"Jacinda?" Kasmira put a concerned hand on her arm. "Are you okay?"

"I'm fine." Jacinda squeezed her hand reassuringly. "Honestly, I just have some news I need to tell you and Ethan."

"Okay." But Kasmira didn't sound convinced. "Let's go into the living room and sit down. Ethan shouldn't be much longer."

"Could we go into your workshop instead?"

"My workshop?"

"Yes, I have something I'd like you to frame for me." She lifted her hand to show her the large folder she carried.

"Alright."

∞ ∞ ∞ ∞ ∞

Kasmira stared in astonishment at the drawing before her. She didn't know what to say. What to feel. Intellectually, she could look at it, and know she should be seeing a simple, pencil-colored drawing because that is what it was. But emotionally, it was so much more. Every line was perfectly placed, capturing the motion and emotion of the couple on the paper.

It was a masterpiece.

It was shocking.

It was Jacinda and King Jotham.

Personally, she didn't know how to react to that. How would Ethan?

"The artist is Brett Chamberlain."

"Chamberlain?" Kasmira forced her gaze from the content of the drawing to the signature in the lower corner, no not a signature but a carefully printed name by what seemed to be a childish hand.

"Yes, Queen Cassandra's nephew. He's nine."

"Nine!" Kasmira's eyes flew from the signature to Jacinda then back to the drawing, forgetting about the subject matter, she concentrated on the massive skill she knew it had taken to convey so much with the simple lines.

"Nine. He has had no formal training, but that's going to change. He gave this to me and I would like it treated and framed as the masterpiece it is."

"I can understand why," Kasmira said nodding then looked up. "But Jacinda...."

"Hello! Where is everyone?" Ethan's voice echoed through the house.

"Come on," Jacinda took Kasmira's arm. "Let's go find Ethan and I'll tell you what's going on."

∞ ∞ ∞ ∞ ∞

The meal was a somewhat a stilted affair with Ethan's gaze going from his wife to his mother, frowning.

"Alright what's going on?" he finally demanded. "What's wrong?"

"There's nothing *wrong*," Jacinda pushed her plate away, "and as I've already reassured Kasmira I'm fine, but something *has* occurred that I need to tell you about. First I have a question."

"Alright," Ethan leaned back in his chair.

"What do you know about the Sokol Corporation?"

"The Sokol Corporation?" Ethan tossed down his napkin in disgust. "You mean besides the fact they have Assemblyman Pajari in their pocket and, therefore, win every government contract?!!"

"That," Jacinda agreed, "but what else? Have you heard anything about substandard practices causing accidents?"

"A few." Ethan frowned at her. "Mother, why are you asking?"

"Because of Nuga," Jacinda told him.

"Nuga? You mean the explosion there?" Ethan looked to Kasmira. "I thought it was caused by the Regulians."

"It wasn't, but that isn't public knowledge yet, Ethan."

Ethan watched as his mother gave him that look she had given him so many times in the past, telling him this was important.

"Alright," he nodded that the information would go no further.

"The explosion was caused because the manager of the mine lied about making the required repairs and upgrades."

"What?" Ethan couldn't hide his shock. "Why would he do such a thing?"

"So he could keep the credits."

"But Sokol is in charge of Nuga," Ethan told her.

"I know that."

"How would you know that?"

"Because at the time of his death, your father was chairing a committee that was looking into Sokol's practices."

"Really? Why didn't I ever hear anything about that?"

"I don't know. Just as I don't know what happened to the committee after Stephan's death. I forgot about it until the explosion."

"Mom... you don't think it had something to do with Dad's death. Do you?"

"What? No!" Jacinda instantly denied, never had she even considered that. "Your father died from a massive heart attack, Ethan. It had nothing to do with Sokol!"

"Alright, then why are you taking an interest in this *now*?"

Jacinda took a deep breath knowing her next words would change her son's life forever. "Because I was in Kisurri when it was discovered what caused the explosion."

"I don't understand," Ethan frowned at her.

"I was invited to Kisurri to attend Princess Sabah's Second Father Ceremony."

"*You* were?" Ethan didn't try to hide his shock. "Why? By whom?"

"Jotham," Jacinda told him simply.

"Jotham? As in King Jotham?"

"Yes."

"*King* Jotham invited *you* to attend Princess Sabah's Second Father Ceremony... who is her second father?"

"Jotham is."

"Why do you keep referring to the King by only his first name?"

"Because I went there *with* Jotham, Ethan." Jacinda watched as understanding suddenly filled her son's eyes, along with shock and disbelief.

"No!" Ethan's chair clattered to the floor as he surged to his feet. "No, that's not possible."

"Ethan, calm down." Kasmira rose putting a hand on his arm.

"You knew about this?" he demanded of his wife.

"I only just found out before you got home," she told him softly.

"I... I don't understand this. How could this be? How did it happen?"

"Sit down, Ethan." Jacinda, who had remained seated, looked up at him. "Please. I know this is coming as a complete surprise to you and honestly it surprised me, but I'd like to explain."

"Explain? What's there to explain?"

"Come on, honey, this is your mother. Let's sit down and listen."

Jacinda sent Kasmira a grateful look as Ethan finally sat.

"I've known Jotham for cycles, from back in my Academy days. You know that Lata and your Aunt Palma were roommates."

"Yes, but I never knew you two were involved."

"We weren't," Jacinda instantly denied. "Never. From the moment, Jotham saw Lata she was the only one for him. Just as your father was it for me."

"Then how..."

"Things change, Ethan. Loved ones die, but life goes on." Jacinda took a deep breath. "Several months ago, Jotham contacted me. Why doesn't matter, but because of it we started to... communicate and see each other occasionally. We have a lot in common: history, mutual friends, and interests. Our feelings for each other naturally grew from there."

Ethan silently stared at his mother, calmly sitting there as she spoke. Everything she said made sense, but she was his mother and he'd never considered...."

"It was unexpected, Ethan. Neither of us was looking for a new relationship, but sometimes life gives you a gift and I'm going to accept this gift."

"No matter what your children think?"

Jacinda opened her mouth then shut it, not sure how to answer him.

∞ ∞ ∞ ∞ ∞

"Ethan, I think there's something you should see." Rising, Kasmira held out her hand to the man she loved. "I think it will help you understand."

"What could possibly..." he began.

"Please, trust me it will," Kasmira told him.

After a moment, he took his wife's hand and let her lead him back to her workshop. At first, he couldn't figure out what she wanted him to see. There was a large drawing on her worktable. While thanks to her, he'd come to appreciate art more, he didn't know how it was supposed to help him 'understand' what his mother was telling him.

"Kasmira..." he started.

"*Look* at it, Ethan, at who is in it, at what they are feeling."

It was only then that he realized the drawing was of his mother and King Jotham. He didn't know where they were, but the background didn't matter because it was the expression on his mother's face that had his throat tightening.

For the first time since his father had passed, he saw the sparkle back in her eyes. She was happy and... in love... his mother was in love. Looking at the other image, he took in the expression of a man who he had never considered as anything more than a title. It was an image he recognized for he had seen it all his life, but somehow it seemed different. Less stern. More relaxed maybe. He didn't know the King well enough to be sure. He doubted anyone did. Then his eyes went to where Jotham's hand rested, on his mother's back, and no one could question the gentleness of his touch or the possessiveness. He loved the woman in his arms. Ethan's mother.

Raising his eyes, he saw his mother hesitantly standing in the doorway waiting for his reaction.

"You love him," he whispered. "Jotham. You really love him."

"I do," Jacinda admitted.

"Then we'll make it work."

Smiling through her tears, Jacinda walked over and mother and son embraced.

∞ ∞ ∞ ∞ ∞

"So that's why you have Royal Guards," Kasmira said as they sat back in the living room with a glass of wine.

"Royal Guards?" Ethan frowned at his wife. "I didn't see any Royal Guards."

"Well, you're not supposed to, now are you?" Kasmira shot back making Jacinda smile.

"Yes, Jotham insisted on them, although we're still working out the details."

"Well, I for one am glad he's taking the precaution because you know once this gets out it is going to cause an uproar."

"I know," Jacinda sighed heavily. "Which is why I'm here telling you now. We had planned not so much on keeping our relationship a secret, but private, because in all honestly, it isn't anyone else's business but ours and our families."

"So what changed that?" Ethan asked sitting back to put his arm around his wife.

"Stephanie and the Royal Ball."

"I don't understand… Wait, Stephie is training in Kisurri."

"Yes. When she discovered I was there, she became… upset. She thought I was checking up on her. So I told her the truth." Jacinda looked down at her glass of wine. "She didn't react very well. Actually, I'm surprised she hasn't already contacted you."

"I did have a message from her saying she wanted to talk to me, but it didn't sound urgent so when Kasmira called to say you were coming for last meal, I figured it could wait."

"Well, now you know."

"What were you saying about the Royal Ball?" Kasmira asked.

"Jotham has asked me to attend it with him."

"With him? As in *with* him? As in *arriving* with him?" Kasmira's eyes got wider with each question.

"Yes." Jacinda understood Kasmira's surprise. "Kia is making my gown."

"That means all of Carina will know," Kasmira whispered.

"Yes, which is why I'm telling you now. I still need to tell Danton."

"This is going to affect him the most. You must know that, Mom." Ethan gave her a sympathetic look.

"I do, I just hope..." A knock on the front door had her pausing.

Frowning, Ethan rose and went to answer the door. "Yes."

"Pardons, Mister Michelakakis, might I speak with your mother."

"Kort?" Jacinda walked up behind Ethan. "Ethan, this is Lieutenant Kort Green. He is in charge of my security detail."

"Are you any good?" Ethan demanded causing Kort to raise an eyebrow.

"Yes. I'm very good," Kort replied.

"You'd better be because if anything happens to my mother, I'll kill you."

"Ethan!" Jacinda couldn't believe he just said that.

"I don't believe you'll get the chance, Mister Michelakakis. King Jotham will have my head first."

"Oh really!" Jacinda said in exasperation. "Now that's enough you two. Kort what did you need?"

"There is a stoirme brewing. It would be best if we left before it hit." Just then a loud rumble of tuono could be heard.

Jacinda wanted to argue but then remembered how Lata had died and knew that if Jotham knew she was out in a stoirme he would worry.

"Alright, Kort." She turned and saw the surprise in her son's eyes and just shrugged. "I don't want Jotham to worry. Kasmira?"

"I totally understand." She walked over and gave Jacinda a hug. "We never finished discussing how you want the drawing framed."

"It's going in the living room, Kasmira. I want it to match the frame around Stephan's portrait if the proportions fit. I trust your judgment. You know my tastes."

"I do. Be safe and we'll talk soon."

"We will."

∞ ∞ ∞ ∞ ∞

"Would you mind driving, Kort?" Jacinda asked as they walked to her transport and she saw him glance at her in surprise.

"Of course not, Madame Michelakakis."

Jacinda waited until they were on their way before she spoke. "You're surprised I asked you to drive."

There was a moment before Kort spoke. "Yes, I am. You insisted on driving here."

"True, and normally I wouldn't hesitate to drive home, even with the approaching stoirme. But I also know Jotham is going to find out and worry. If you're driving, I can talk to him when he calls."

"You believe King Jotham will be contacting you?"

"Yes, because I'm sure you informed him where I was."

"Of course I did."

"Of course you did. So when someone informs him there is a stoirme in this area... and someone will... he's going to worry and call." Just then her personal comm rang. Reaching into her bag she pulled it out and raised an eyebrow at Kort.

"Hello, Jotham."

"Jacinda, where are you?"

"I'm in my transport heading home."

"There's a stoirme heading toward Comorin."

"Yes, Kort informed me, that's why we left early. Kort is driving right now."

"Good, he's an excellent driver."

"Yes, well, how was your day?"

"Busy. You would have thought I was gone for a moon cycle. I'm in-between meetings right now. I'm going to be working late."

"I figured that was going to happen."

"Did you now?" Jotham teased.

"Yes, it's what always happened whenever Stephan returned from a trip." She smiled into the comm. "This isn't my first go-round, Jotham. It's fine. I need to talk to Danton tomorrow anyway and that will be easier to do if I'm at home tonight."

"That's not what I was inferring."

"I know, but it would still be best. We're close to an hour out of Pechora and I still need to unpack. By the time that's all done, it will be extremely late. It's best I just stay at home tonight."

"I know you're right, but I don't like it. I've already gotten used to waking up with you in my arms."

"I know, I'm not looking forward to it either. Do you think your schedule will clear up enough that we could have last meal together tomorrow? At a reasonable time?"

"I'll make sure it is. Pack a bag," he ordered.

"Alright."

"Call me when you get home so I know you made it safely."

"I will," she promised knowing it was important to him.

"I love you."

"I love you too."

Chapter Twenty-Eight

"Mother!"

Jacinda was just coming in from having coffee in the garden the next morning when she heard her first son calling out her name.

"I'm back here, Danton," she called out a smile on her face. "Good morning. I was just getting ready to call you."

"I just bet you were! What in the name of the ancestors is going on?" he demanded in the way of a greeting.

"Good morning, Danton," Myesha walked in handing him a cup of coffee. "Here, you look like you could use this."

"Thank you, Myesha," Danton forced himself to respond politely.

"You're welcome. I'm off to see my grandchildren, Jacinda."

" Alright, give them hugs for me."

"I will. And you, young man," Myesha pointed a finger at Danton. "You control that temper of yours. You're not so old that I still can't put you over my knee if I need to."

"Yes, ma'am," he told her, his cheeks darkening.

Jacinda held back her smile as she moved to sit down. She just loved how Myesha, with just a few words, could turn her strong, confident thirty-nine cycle son back into a bashful, five-cycle. She waited until the front door closed before speaking.

"So, Danton, who have you been talking to?"

"Last night I received a comm from Madame Nitzschke, ranting about how the King's Royal Guard had you under house arrest. Then this morning, very *early* this morning, Stephanie contacted me to say you had been at the House of Knowledge, staying in the Royal Wing *with* King Jotham!"

"Well, it's good to know Madame Nitzschke still can't get a story right." Jacinda just shook her head. House arrest? Really? The old bat saw her drive away.

"And Stephanie?"

"Always could."

"Mother." Danton slowly sat down on the couch across from her. "What are you saying?"

"You know exactly what I'm saying, Danton."

"But..." His gaze went to his father's portrait hanging over the fireplace mantle. "That's impossible."

"Why?"

"Why? Well... just because it is!" Now he surged to his feet. "Mother, you can't be *with* Jotham! He is the *King* of the House of Protection!"

"I am well aware of that, Danton. I've known him nearly my entire life. He's also just a man."

"He is using you! Just like he has every other woman!"

"What other women, Danton? Name one."

"Rani!" he spit out.

"Seriously, Danton? That was over thirty cycles ago. Name another."

"I... a..."

"You can't because there hasn't been any other 'woman.'"

"That doesn't matter. This can't go anywhere, Mother, and when it ends.... What's going to happen then?"

"I don't know, Danton. All I know is that I love him. As much as I loved your father, I love Jotham. I know it's going to be difficult, especially for you and Stephanie, but that's why I wanted to talk with you this morning. So you'd be prepared."

"Prepared! How am I supposed to *prepare* for becoming the joke of the Assembly? No one is ever going to take me seriously!

They will all think I was only elected because my mother is *with* the King!"

"*You* know that's not true."

"That doesn't matter!"

"Of course it does! It's the only thing that matters! You can't control what others think, Danton. You know that."

"You have to end this, Mom, before it gets out or I'll have to give up my dream of being an Assemblyman."

"Give up your dream." Jacinda carefully set her cup aside as she rose.

"Yes, you've always known it's been my dream to serve in the Assembly."

Slowly, she walked over and gripped the mantle, her knuckles turning white as she looked up at Stephan. Her heart and mind were in chaos. All her life she'd done her best for those she loved, even when it wasn't what she wanted. She had left her House for Stephan, endured the snubs and comments and stood proudly at his side because she loved him. She even let him continue on in the Assembly longer than he promised because it had been his dream, his first love, and she wanted him happy.

Now, Danton wanted her to give up Jotham so *he* could be a part of that same *damn* Assembly. Because of what others would think of *him*. Could she? Should she?

"No." The word escaped her lips quietly at first then stronger the second time. "No!"

"No, what?"

"No. I've given up enough of *my* dreams for that damn Assembly. Never again!" She spun around to face him. "I won't give up Jotham. Not for you and not for Stephanie. I'm sorry if my *loving* Jotham makes it harder for you to achieve *your* dreams, but I've never known you to back down from a challenge just because a task was difficult. I told you that first day in your office that being an Assemblyman wasn't going to be easy. That many lose their way in that place and start believing that *their* own wants and needs are more important than other people's are. I told you there would be many tests, that life isn't always black and white or easy. It seems you failed this one."

Jacinda watched her son pale at her words.

"I would like you to leave now, Danton."

"Mother...." He rose unsure of what to do. His mother had never spoken like that to him before with such disappointment and hurt in her voice and eyes.

"Leave, Danton, before things are said that can never be taken back."

And unlike the strong, confident man that had arrived just a short time ago, full of self-righteous anger, he left wondering when he had become everything he'd sworn he'd never be.

∞ ∞ ∞ ∞ ∞

Jacinda's legs trembled as she sat down on the couch. She knew her children were going to be shocked and would need time to adjust but she never for a moment thought they would expect her to end the relationship.

When had she stopped knowing her own children? Rising, she looked around the room and felt the walls closing in on her. She needed to get out of here. Needed to be able to breathe.

Striding into her bedroom, she threw what she'd need into a bag, left a note for Myesha, and headed out the front door.

∞ ∞ ∞ ∞ ∞

"Majesty," Chesney leaned over speaking quietly, when Jotham turned his head to listen, the others in the meeting continued to speak. "Madame Michelakakis has just arrived. Green reported she seemed unusually... quiet."

Jotham frowned, wondering what was wrong. "Thank you, Chesney. Gentlemen, let's take a short break. Chesney will see to anything you need." With that Jotham left the room to find out what had happened.

Striding into his Wing, Green walked up to him. "She is in the garden, Majesty."

"Do you know what happened?"

"No, Sire. All I know is that Assemblyman Michelakakis arrived and shortly after he left she informed me she wanted to come here."

"Alright, thank you, Green." Jotham was about to leave then turned back to the Lieutenant. "And thank you for getting Jacinda home safely last night. She told me how heavy the rain became."

"It was my honor, Majesty. She is truly a special woman."

"She is," Jotham agreed then left to find that special woman.

∞ ∞ ∞ ∞ ∞

He found her in the center of the garden, her arms wrapped around her waist, staring at Lata's rose bush. Walking up behind her, he wrapped her up in his arms and pulled her back against him.

After a moment, she relaxed against him with a heartfelt sigh.

"What's wrong?" he asked, dipping his head to nuzzle the shell of her ear.

"I didn't mean to interrupt your day."

"You didn't." He kissed the soft skin behind her ear.

"I know you were planning on back-to-back meetings today so you could clear your schedule for tonight."

"Doesn't matter. *You* are what matters, now tell me."

"I just didn't think my children would react the way they have. I mean I knew they would be surprised, shocked even, but..."

"But? What did Danton say to you?!!" Jotham demanded.

"How do you know it was Danton?" She turned, putting her arms around his waist and looked up at him

"Because you told me you were going to be talking to him today."

"Green told you he arrived at my house this morning." She didn't make it a question.

"Yes," he answered her honestly. "I take it he didn't react well to the thought of his mother being involved with another man."

"You know I don't think that even crossed his mind. All he seemed to care about is that it was *you,* and how it would affect *him,* affect *his* career." The tears of hurt she'd been able to hold at bay began to fill her eyes. "After I demanded he leave, I just couldn't stay there so I came here to you."

Jotham's touch remained gentle as he wiped the tears that ran down his love's cheeks even as his anger for her son grew. He would never have believed Danton would hurt his mother like this if Jacinda hadn't told him herself. Perhaps Danton wasn't the man Jotham thought he was.

"I'm glad you did. You always can, you know. Come to me."

"I know," she gave him a watery smile, "that's why I came, but I didn't mean to disrupt your schedule. I just wanted to walk in your garden and clear my head."

"I'm glad. Did you bring a bag?" His hands ran down her back, molding her body to his. Jacinda smiled up at him, a sexy little smile that had his heart beating faster.

"I did," she told him stretching up to teasingly kiss his lips. "So you'd better get back to work so we can have our evening together."

"We will. Will you be staying here all day?"

"If you don't mind."

"I don't mind at all," except for the fact that he'll be wishing he was with her all day. "Contact Chesney if you need anything. Otherwise, know you have free run of the Palace. Nothing is off limits to you. Do you understand?"

"I... Yes. I do. Thank you."

∞ ∞ ∞ ∞ ∞

Adelaide Pajari had a smug smile on her face as she walked through the doors of the Palace. It had taken her cycles to get to this point. Cycles of suffering and sacrifice to get her family back to where it belonged, a power within the House of Protection.

No woman now had more influence than she, well other than Evadne Terwilliger did, but really how much longer could *that* woman go on? Adelaide had been worried; she could admit that to herself. Jacinda Michelakakis had been an issue in the Assembly but with her husband's death, all the influence that peasant from another House had disappeared and had become hers.

Had Adelaide realized that was all it would take to get rid of Jacinda, she would have found a way to end Stephan Michelakakis cycles earlier than his natural death. Her own husband, Elliott, should have realized it and brought it to her attention, but he was weak. If Stephan hadn't met the ancestors before that b'osh, Cassandra's, challenge she would have done the same to Stephan as Audric had done to Vane, the love of Queen Yakira's life.

Now, her conscience was clear and *she* was one step away from becoming the most powerful woman in the House of Protection. Once Shosha gained Barek's attention and she 'accidentally' conceived, then she, Adelaide Pajari, would *rule* the House of Protection. Just as her bloodline was always meant to.

Right now, her husband was in a meeting with King Jotham and several other Assemblymen. A meeting Jotham had requested because he knew just how important Elliott was. Well, he wasn't, not without her, but Jotham would never know that. Men were so easy to manipulate.

Her smile slipped as she turned and spied Jacinda Michelakakis stepping into the room from the Public Garden. What was she doing here? Striding across the room, Adelaide confronted her.

"You don't belong here, Jacinda Michelakakis!" she demanded. "You're not even from this House! You need to leave."

Jacinda hadn't noticed Adelaide until she'd been in her face, and while her words hadn't surprised *her*, she could tell they had Kort, who had been trailing discretely behind her.

Slipping a hand behind her back, she made a 'stop' gesture that she hoped Kort understood.

"Why, hello, Adelaide. What in the world are *you* doing here?" she asked in the most benign of voices.

"Me? I *belong* here! You, on the other hand, *don't*!"

"And why don't I, Adelaide?"

"Because you are from the House of Healing! It's where you should have *stayed*!"

"Really?" Jacinda raised an eyebrow at her. "King Jotham has made it quite clear that *he* believes the integration of the Houses is a good thing."

"Yes, well he is wrong in his beliefs."

"You are challenging King Jotham?"

"Of course not! I am simply stating a known fact," Adelaide told her as if she should understand.

"Known to whom?"

"Anyone with any breeding, which is something *you've* never had," barked Adelaide.

"Really? Do you really believe a little drop of royal blood received generations ago gives you the right to judge me? You don't even have a birthmark."

"It's more than you have," Adelaide sneered at her. "Now you need to leave before I call security."

Kort, who had remained silent during the exchange, finally spoke up. "Is there a problem here, ladies?"

Adelaide's eyes were cool and dismissive until she took in the uniform Kort was wearing. "Yes, Lieutenant. This... woman... doesn't belong in this House. She might even be a threat. As an Assemblyman's wife and loyal supporter of King Jotham, I demand you remove her."

"You've gone too far this time, Adelaide," Jacinda told her.

"I haven't even started yet, Jacinda."

"Lieutenant," Jacinda turned to Kort, "I believe it is time for me to leave."

"Yes, Madame, I believe it is," Kort agreed.

"That's right, Lieutenant, get her out of here. That's an order!" Adelaide's smile turned vicious as she watched the retreating back of the woman she had always hated. She didn't even see that Kort guided Jacinda toward the more secure wings of the

Palace, instead of out of it. She was too busy wallowing in her supposed triumph.

∞ ∞ ∞ ∞ ∞

"You should have let me handle her," Kort told her as he escorted her to the King's Wing.

"She is an Assemblyman's wife, Kort. Do you know what could have happened to you if you had confronted her? How it would have reflected on this House?"

"You are the King's..."

"Companion," she finished for him. "As such I will never be a recognized figure in this House. Ball or no Ball. Adelaide Pajari wasn't stating anything that others won't be thinking. Now if you'll excuse me, I'd like to be alone."

∞ ∞ ∞ ∞ ∞

"Gentlemen, I believe I am up to speed, so let's call it a day." Jotham looked at the Assemblymen around the table and saw the quickly hidden surprise on their faces as they gathered up their papers and left Jotham's office.

"Majesty, this is your schedule for tomorrow." Chesney handed it to him and waited to see if he wanted to make any changes. After a moment, he saw Jotham nod.

"That will be fine, Chesney. Thank you."

"Your last meal will be arriving in approximately an hour. Would you like it set up in the garden? The temperature there is perfect for it."

Jotham thought about it for a moment. Jacinda loved the garden, but he also wanted some privacy.

"On the patio."

"I will inform Morven, Majesty."

"Thank you. I'll see you tomorrow, Chesney. Goodnight." Rising, Jotham went to find Jacinda.

"Goodnight, Majesty." Chesney smiled at Jotham's back. He was liking the changes Jacinda's presence was making.

∞ ∞ ∞ ∞ ∞

"There you are," Jotham's words had Jacinda looking up from the book she was reading. She was curled up at the end of one of the couches in his living room, her legs tucked up under her, looking beautiful and graceful even though all she was doing was sitting there.

"Here I am," she smiled up at him, closing the book. "Are you done for the day?"

"I am. " He sat down next to her, tucking her bare feet into his lap as she turned to face him.

"How surprised were they?"

"They?"

"Whoever you were meeting with. I mean it's just past six. I'm sure they thought the meeting would run late, very late."

"Yes, I guess they were slightly. They'll just have to get used to it. I have a life beyond them now. Thanks to you." Leaning forward, he gently kissed her lips.

Jacinda let Jotham's words soothe her as they touched and kissed. This *was* where she was meant to be, and she wouldn't let what her children, Adelaide Pajari, or anyone else thought change that. Wasn't that what she had told Danton just that morning? Maybe it was time she truly lived up to her own words.

"I love you, Jotham."

"And I love you." He reached up tucking a strand of hair behind her ear. "What did you do today?"

"Not much, I wandered around the Palace, reacquainting myself with it. I was surprised to see how little it had changed in the last ten cycles."

"Was it supposed to?" Jotham frowned questioningly.

"Well, I expected to see at least *some* changes, especially in the Public Wing."

"Why there?"

"Well, the Public Wing is basically a reflection of the House of Protection itself. It is all that most of the population sees, and that is why it needs to accurately represent our past, but also needs to be a reflection of the present and our future."

"And you don't feel it currently does that?"

"Oh it's got the past down perfectly, but where is the work of the current artists, where are our latest achievements displayed, such as the Guardian? Young people come here to learn about who they are and where they come from. The older ones... many of them come here to remember."

"I don't understand," Jotham frowned at her. "Remember?"

"You've never noticed those that come and just sit in front of certain exhibits? Like the one of the Battle of Fayal?"

"I... No. I guess I haven't."

"Madame Lindgren comes on the anniversary of the Battle every cycle and quietly sits there all day. She lost her father, brother, and husband in that battle."

"How do you know that?"

"I saw her sitting there once and sat down next to her. She told me all about how her father loved her mother. How her brother and husband were best friends and joined the Coalition together, and how all three served on the same ship. Their bodies were never returned to Carina, and she said it comforts her, makes her feel closer to them when she sits there on that day."

"I see. I take it that wouldn't be something you would remove."

"Ancestors no!" She looked at him in shock. "Update maybe. Maybe make it more interactive with recordings from those that survived; telling of their experience and from those, like Madame Lindgren, telling of the cost. Make it *real* for those that see it as just *history*."

"That's an incredible idea."

"It's one Evadne and I discussed when she and I were Co-Chairing the committee in charge of that room. I'm surprised she hasn't implemented it by now. I thought she took over that committee."

"I'm not sure who is chairing it now, but I do know that *you* should be the one in charge of it. Your ideas are groundbreaking."

"Oh, I couldn't!" she immediately denied.

"Of course you could. You have amazing ideas and you've done it before."

"No, Jotham, I don't mean that I couldn't *handle* it, I mean that I *couldn't*. That position is always held by the wife of an Assemblyman, at least since Lata's death."

"You're saying Lata used to be in charge of that?"

"Yes," Jacinda frowned at him. "It's part of the Queen's duties. Of course, she normally selects a committee from the wives to do the actual work. It was always considered the highest honor to be chosen for it."

"And Lata chose you for it."

"Along with some others."

"I see. I'll check into who is chairing it now, and see what they have planned." He leaned over and gave her another kiss. "Now, how would you like to have last meal on the patio?"

"I think that sounds lovely."

∞ ∞ ∞ ∞ ∞

"That was wonderful, Jotham." Jacinda set her forc down and leaned back in her chair.

"I'll let Safford know you enjoyed it," he told her as he refilled her wine glass. "Do you have any preference for first meal?"

Groaning, she rubbed her stomach. "I can't even think about that right now. Whatever you normally have will be fine, as long as it includes coffee."

"Pittaluga's coffee."

"You remember that?" she asked raising an eyebrow at him.

"Of course. It's important to you, although I have to admit I was as in the dark as Will. I didn't know Pittaluga sold the beans. You, Jacinda Michelakakis, are obviously very special to Mister Pittaluga." Jotham leaned back in his own chair as he watched Jacinda blush. "Oh, you have to tell me what that blush means."

"It's nothing," Jacinda waved her hand dismissively and then rose from her chair. "Shall we walk off that wonderful meal?"

"We can," Jotham wrapped an arm around her waist, pulling her close as they started down a path, "but you're still going to tell me."

"It's nothing, really."

"Then tell me."

Jacinda thought back, trying to decide what to tell him. "Pittaluga's hasn't always been where it is now."

Jotham frowned thinking back. "It hasn't?"

"No, forty cycles ago it was on the edge of the Trunt District."

That told Jotham a lot. The Trunt District forty cycles ago hadn't been a very prosperous area, still wasn't, and he realized it was something he hadn't given proper attention to. Once Barek started taking over some of his duties that would change.

"I discovered the original location not long after my Union. I was exploring Pechora, trying to learn my way around, and the smell of that wonderful coffee pulled me in."

"You were in the Trunt District? Alone?" Jotham's hand tightened around her waist protectively.

"I didn't know any better. As I sat there, Mister Pittaluga served me the best coffee I had ever had. Then he warned me that I shouldn't come back, that it wasn't a safe area for me. He even walked me back to my transport so he knew I wouldn't be harmed. When I arrived home, I told Stephan about it, thinking he would find it humorous. He was furious."

"As he should have been," Jotham whole-heartedly agreed, a cold shiver running down his back at what could have happened to her. "Fuck, Jacinda, what were you thinking?"

Jacinda shot him a startled look. Jotham rarely used profanity, it was a sign of how upset he truly was. "I didn't know any better. I was new to Pechora, and as someone from the House of Healing, no one was willing to tell me it was dangerous."

"You were an Assemblyman's wife!" Jotham argued.

"That the Queen had taken an open dislike to. No one was foolish enough to go against Queen Johanna."

"Ancestors, Jacinda, I'm sorry."

"You have nothing to apologize for, Jotham. It was nearly forty cycles ago and had nothing to do with you." Before Jotham could say more, she went on. "And in the end it worked out for the best."

"How can you say that?"

"Because I met Mister Pittaluga and fell in love with his coffee. To keep me from coming there, he would deliver beans to me." Jacinda smiled as she remembered. "Several cycles later his business burned down."

"That happens quite often in the Trunt District."

"Yes, Stephan told me it happened when business owners wouldn't pay protection credits."

"Yes."

"Well, when Stephan learned of the fire he offered to sell Mister Pittaluga a piece of property he owned in central Pechora that had been vacant for cycles."

"Pittaluga's."

"It is now. Because of that, Mister Pittaluga sells me his special blend."

"I'd say that's a good reason."

"Pfft," Jacinda waved a dismissive hand. "That building was just sitting there empty, doing no one any good. Mister Pittaluga did all the work to make it into the special place it is today. We only sold it to him."

"I think Mister Pittaluga would see it differently."

"We only repaid his kindness to me."

"You did more than that. You gave him the chance to succeed."

∞ ∞ ∞ ∞ ∞

Jotham wasn't sure when he had a more enjoyable, relaxing night. After their walk in the garden, they had returned to the patio. Jacinda curled up into his side as they sat on a lounger, sipping wine and watching the third sunset.

Uninterrupted.

When was the last time that had happened?

"It's really beautiful here, Jotham."

"You know, it's been cycles since I've watched third sunset."

Jacinda just snuggled deeper into his side saying nothing. She knew what he wasn't saying. He hadn't seen the sunsets because he would always be in meetings. Stephan had missed many too, just not as many as Jotham had. Her sudden yawn caught her off guard.

"Oh, I'm sorry," she said covering her mouth.

"I think it's time we get you into bed. My bed. For the entire night." The possessiveness and satisfaction in his voice was unmistakable.

"You really like the thought of that, don't you?" she smiled up at him.

"Yes." Standing Jotham swept her up into his arms, striding through the open doors. "I hardly slept last night because I kept reaching for you and you weren't there."

"I'm here now," she reassured him wrapping her arms around his neck.

"Yes, you are, and I'm going to take full advantage of it."

The wicked smile on Jotham's face told her there would be a lack of sleep tonight as well. "Lucky me," she told him, kissing his neck in response.

Chapter Twenty-Nine

Jacinda raised her arms over her head stretching her slightly sore muscles, a satisfied smile breaking across her face. It had been an amazing night in Jotham's bed. A night filled with laughter and loving, gentle touches and whispered words.

Rolling over she reached for him, intending on starting the day on the right note, only to find him gone. Frowning, she sat up and looked at the time. While first sun had fully risen, second had just started to. Jotham was up early, but not as early as he could have been. They were making progress.

Getting out of one of the most comfortable beds she had ever slept in, she reached for her robe and went in search of her man. That put a smile on her face. Her man. She had a man again.

"Jotham, that better be Pittaluga's coffee I smell," she teased entering the living room only to freeze. Oh, ancestors! What had she done?

∞ ∞ ∞ ∞ ∞

Jotham had risen with the first sun. He'd wanted to make sure Safford had gotten his message about Pittaluga's coffee, and that he had told Pittaluga it was for Jacinda. He had, and now there was a steaming pot of coffee and a table full of food waiting for Jacinda. A knock on his private door had him frowning. He had ordered they were not to be disturbed. Walking over, he jerked open the door.

"Barek! What are you doing here?" Jotham quickly glanced at the closed door of his bedroom.

"After you called, I had Lucas drop me off at the Bering space station. There was no reason for me to continue on to the border only to turn around and come back. The High Admiral sent the

Arrow to bring me home. I only just arrived and came straight here. Oh, wonderful! First meal, I'm starving."

Barek started pouring himself a cup of coffee then frowned as he realized the table was set for two.

"I thought you didn't know I was coming?"

"Barek..."

"Jotham, that better be Pittaluga's coffee I smell."

Barek spun around to see Jacinda Michelakakis entering the room from his father's bedroom, wearing a silky robe. It was obvious she had just gotten out of bed. When she saw him, she froze.

"Barek..." she whispered, a dark flush growing on her cheeks as her eyes flew to Jotham.

Jotham was immediately across the room, wrapping his arms around her; knowing she thought she had just created a problem. "It's okay."

"*This* is why you called me home? Why you withdrew me from the Coalition? To tell me you have become involved with Jacinda?" Barek couldn't believe it.

"No!" Jotham instantly denied. "Not entirely," he amended.

"Then why?" Barek demanded.

"I'll just step out so you two can be alone." When she started to step out of Jotham's arms, they tightened around her.

"No. I've talked *alone* nearly all my life. I don't want to be alone anymore. Come. Sit down and have some coffee. It's from Pittaluga's."

Barek silently watched as his father settled Jacinda in a chair, even going as far as pouring her coffee himself, before turning his attention back to Barek.

"I ordered your return because it's time for you to start assuming some of the duties of the future King."

"What?" Barek found he was slowly sitting down in the other empty chair at the table. "You said you weren't ill."

"I'm not," Jotham immediately told him. "But I want to be able to spend more time with Jacinda *and* I don't want you to go through what I did if something *should* suddenly happen to me."

"You want me to start dealing with the Assembly, to actually be *involved* in the ruling of our House?" Barek couldn't keep the disbelief out of his voice or the hope.

"Yes."

"Finally," Barek quietly said.

Jotham frowned as Barek leaned in and looked at him with an expression he didn't understand.

"What do you mean, finally?" Jotham asked.

"I never thought you would ever allow it, that I would never be worthy enough in your eyes."

"What?!!" The word exploded out of Jotham. "Why would you *ever* think that?!! You've always been *more* than worthy, Barek."

"Then why have you never given me more than the most basic of ceremonial duties? Why have you allowed me to stay in the Coalition longer than any other heir ever has?"

"Because I thought you loved being there and because...."

"And because?"

"Because I needed something to fill up my empty days and nights. Something to make me feel my life had some meaning after your mother died."

"It wasn't because you thought I wasn't capable?" Barek found himself asking.

"Ancestors no! Barek, with your knowledge of the law and your experience in the Coalition you will be the most well-rounded King this House has ever had."

"You truly believe that?"

"Yes."

"And you're willing to let me learn, to start fulfilling my destiny."

Jotham's throat tightened at the thought his son believed he was holding him back from being what he could be. "Yes."

"Thank the ancestors," Barek switched his gaze to Jacinda. "And thank you, Jacinda."

∞ ∞ ∞ ∞ ∞

Jacinda silently ate as she listened to Jotham and Barek talk. An extra plate and cup were quickly delivered for Barek. It had been a little uncomfortable at first, sitting there in her robe, knowing that Barek knew she'd spent the night in his father's bed. But Barek seemed to have no problem with the relationship, unlike her children.

Soon the conversation turned to what duties Barek would be assuming and Jacinda was somewhat surprised at how eager Barek was. There was an excitement in his eyes she'd never seen before. Looking at Jotham, she knew he saw it too.

This was how Stephan and Danton would have looked if Stephan were still alive. Stephan would have loved to be able to guide Danton through the intricacies and nuances that were the Assembly. Working together, the two would have been unstoppable, just as Jotham and Barek will be.

"Jacinda?"

Jotham's question pulled her from her thoughts and looking from Jotham to Barek she realized he must have been trying to get her attention for some time.

"I'm sorry. What were you saying?"

"I was just telling Barek about Stephan's investigation into the Sokol Corporation and how I wanted him to look into it."

"Oh, yes. I did ask Ethan what he had heard about Sokol." Jacinda wiped her mouth and set her napkin aside. "His first response was that Keane Sokol had Assemblyman Pajari in his pocket and because of that Sokol is guaranteed all important government contracts."

"That's not right," Barek told her.

"Right or not, it is what's happening. Pajari chairs the contracts committee, so he has the final say. Ethan also said there were rumors of Sokol's substandard practices causing accidents." She looked to Jotham. "I did get into the safe and Stephan's files were still there. I brought them with me. I'll just go get them."

Jotham enjoyed the gentle sway of Jacinda's hips as she walked away and knew if Barek weren't there he would be following her.

"You really need to learn how to be more subtle, Dad," Barek told him shaking his head.

"Really?" Jotham's eyes remained on Jacinda until she was out of sight before turning to his son. "Why?"

"Why? Because if you're not, everyone will know."

"I plan on everyone knowing. That's why Jacinda will be at my side when we enter the Royal Ball."

"Really?" Barek's eyes sharpened on his father. "You know that's going to cause a stir, especially among the purists. It's one thing for you to be *involved* with a woman from another House, but it's an entirely different matter for you to publicly *acknowledge* her."

"Be that as it may, there's nothing they can do about it."

"They can make Jacinda and her children's lives miserable."

"Then they will answer to me." Jotham's eyes became hard as he spoke.

"Only if Jacinda tells you." That had his father giving him a questioning look. "From what I've seen, Jacinda is a very independent woman, Dad. She isn't going to come running to you if someone's rude to her. She'll deal with it herself."

"Here they are," Jacinda announced re-entering the room carrying several folders and stopping Jotham from responding.

∞ ∞ ∞ ∞ ∞

Jacinda quickly found the files she'd brought and thought about changing clothes before returning, but quickly dismissed the idea. Walking back toward the open door, she paused hearing Barek.

"You know that's going to cause a stir, especially among the purists. It's one thing for you to be *involved* with a woman from another House, but it's an entirely different matter for you to publicly *acknowledge* her."

"Be that as it may, there's nothing they can do about it."

"They can make Jacinda and her children's lives miserable."

"Then they will answer to me."

"Only if Jacinda tells you," Barek reminded him. "From what I've seen Jacinda is a very independent woman, Dad. She isn't going to come running to you if someone's rude to her. She'll deal with it herself."

"Here they are," she said pretending she hadn't overheard their conversation. "Stephan had several files and I haven't had time to go through them." She set them down in front of Barek.

"I'll read through them and see what I can find. You said you talked to Ethan about this?"

"Yes, Ethan now runs the Zhao Corporation for his father-in-law."

"They deal with producing mining equipment too, don't they?" Barek queried.

"Among other things, yes."

"Would he be willing to work with me? To answer questions?"

"I'm sure he would, he was quite upset with the deaths on Nuga."

"And Danton? Do you think Stephan ever talked to him about this?"

"I... that I don't know. They talked all the time, but Danton had just turned thirty when Stephan died. I don't know if Stephan would have discussed an ongoing investigation with him."

"I'll speak with him." Barek stood gathering up the files. "Jacinda, I just want to say how truly wonderful I think it is that you have entered our lives." He leaned down placing a kiss on her cheek. "If this old man gives you any problems, let me know and I'll take care of him."

"Old man!" Jotham exclaimed in feigned outrage causing Jacinda to laugh.

∞ ∞ ∞ ∞ ∞

Jotham leaned against the doorframe of the bathroom and simply watched Jacinda and knew he never really appreciated watching a woman get ready for her day before. He had always been too busy getting ready for his own.

Jacinda slipped out of the room when Chesney had called. By the time he finished, she had showered and wrapped herself in a towel and begun rubbing lotion into her dewy, golden skin. She started at her feet, resting first one and then the other on the edge of the large tub he never used, slowly working her way up her legs.

Jotham had never seen anything as erotic as watching her hands glide over her own body. Seeing her fingers massaging the lotion into the golden skin, he groaned silently, torn between the desire to be touching that silky beautiful skin and watching her touch herself.

Where would those hands go next?

He found out as she moved on to her shoulders, working her way down her arms before she reached as far as she could over her back.

"Here, let me help you with that." His words had her head spinning around, her eyes widening as she looked at him; her long, gorgeous hair piled high on her head, exposing the delicate curve of her neck.

"I thought you were on the comm."

"I was. Now I'm with you." He picked up the bottle she set on the counter and squeezed a generous amount into his hand. The scent of roses that he always associated with her filled his senses.

Slowly, he began to spread scented lotion over the soft skin of her shoulders, working his way down until he reached the towel barrier. Slipping a finger underneath, it gave way exposing her slender back. Unhurriedly, he ran his thumbs down her spine the rest of his hands followed, caressing the outside curves of her generous breasts, and then narrowed in over her ribs and her svelte waist, before stretching out again to caress her hips. Hips that twisted slightly under his attentions.

"Do you know what you do to me?" he asked as his hands slowly made a return trip up her back. "I watch you walk in front of me, and I can't take my eyes off you. Off how gracefully you move, the gentle sway of your hips. It makes me so hard."

Jotham couldn't stop from pressing his enlarged shaft against her buttocks proving it. "Even Barek noticed."

"What?" Jacinda asked breathlessly, trying to understand his words.

"He caught me watching this luscious ass as you walked into the bedroom." His hands had worked their way back down to knead said flesh. "And told me I needed to learn to be more subtle or everyone would know."

"What did you say?" she asked pressing back against his hands.

"I told him I *planned* on everyone knowing. I'm not going to hide how I feel about you, Jacinda. About how much you mean to me." His hands, slick with lotion, slid around and up to cup her breasts. "How much I want you."

Jacinda's head fell back onto his shoulder. "Ancestors, Jotham! That feels amazing!"

"It will only get better," he promised squeezing her breasts one last time before his hands arrowed down her soft stomach to the curls between her thighs, pulling her back against him, his cloth-enclosed shaft pressing up between her cheeks.

"I'm going to hold you to that." Reaching behind her, she turned her head as she grabbed the back of Jotham's neck and pulled his mouth down to hers for a searing kiss.

Jotham turned her in his arms, lifting her as he did, setting her on the vanity, causing her to shriek at its coolness.

"Jotham!" she cried out even as her legs wrapped around his waist.

"I will never give you up, Jacinda." Ripping open his pants, he set the tip of his shaft at her wet entrance. "Never lose you." Slowly he pressed into her, his muscles shaking with restrained desire. "You are mine!"

"Yes, Jotham!" Tightening her legs, she pulled him home. "Yours!"

Shouting out, they found heaven together.

∞ ∞ ∞ ∞ ∞

Barek frowned over what he found in Stephan Michelakakis' files. How could this have been going on for so long undetected? Ethan had been right, at the time Stephan had compiled this information. Sokol had been awarded *every* major contract for over ten cycles. It had been nearly another ten since then, was it still true? He needed to find out.

Rising, he went to find the one man that could help him, his father's aide, Chesney.

"Good morning, Mister Chesney," Barek greeted, walking into his father's outer office.

"Prince Barek!" Chesney was instantly on his feet. "I didn't know you were on planet."

"Permanently, Chesney."

"Excuse me?"

"Has my father not told you yet? I have left the Coalition and will now be working along with my father in the ruling of our House."

"Really? No, the King has not yet informed me of that." As he spoke, a smile broke out across Chesney's face. It seemed Jacinda was having a bigger effect on Jotham than he'd thought.

"Well, I'm sure he will be but right now I need your help."

"Of course, Sire. What can I do for you?"

"I need to contact Ethan Michelakakis and don't have his code."

"I can find that for you, Sire."

"Thank you. Could you also compile for me a list of all the mining contracts for the last ten cycles and send them to my comm?"

"The last *ten* cycles, Sire?" Chesney couldn't hide his shock.

"Yes. Also, I'm going to need my own aide since I'm going to be here full time."

"I will compile a list for you, and you can interview them."

"Great, thank you, Chesney. I'll let you get back to preparing for your day."

∞ ∞ ∞ ∞ ∞

"I... Umm..."

Ethan frowned as he heard his secretary stuttering into the comm as he entered his office. Honeycutt was the most unflappable person he knew. What could have her in such a state?

Relief filled her eyes when she saw him. "He's just walking into the office, Sire. If you'll hold for just a moment, I'll transfer you to his comm." Pushing a button, she put a hand over her heart. "Thank the ancestors you're here."

"What is going on?" Ethan demanded.

"Prince Barek is on the comm for you."

"Prince Barek?"

"Yeesss," she hissed at him. "So get into your office and answer your comm!"

If Honeycutt hadn't been with the company for over twenty cycles, and someone he utterly relied on, he would never allow her to talk to him like that.

"Alright. Calm down, Honeycutt."

"Calm down? Have you ever *seen* the man?" She fanned her face with her hand. "He's gorgeous."

Ethan's eyes widened in shock. Honeycutt was old enough to be the Prince's mother. Honeycutt's next words told him Ethan had spoken out loud.

"That doesn't mean I don't have eyes. Now go." She shooed him on.

Entering his office, Ethan sat down at his desk. Taking a deep breath, he composed his face then pressed the button that would connect them.

"Prince Barek, sorry about the delay. What can I do for you?"

"I had first meal with your mother this morning," Barek said getting straight to the point.

Ethan raised an eyebrow slightly in surprise. It was still quite early, barely eight and Barek was obviously in the Palace. How could he have had first meal with his mother? Unless she was at the Palace....

"She told me she had spoken to you about the Sokol Corporation," Barek continued.

"Yes," Ethan's tone was noncommittal.

"I've read through your father's files and have compiled the same information to date. I am not happy at what I am learning."

"The Palace must sign off on all those contracts, Sire," Ethan told him stiffly.

"And we both know my father takes the recommendations of the Committee. It's their job to review and choose who's the best fit for each project."

"Yes, that's how it *should* be."

"What I'd like to know is why haven't *you* ever brought this to the attention of the Palace?"

"And who would I report it to, Sire? Assemblyman Pajari, who heads the committee? To do so is business suicide. He would block us from *any* contract and inform others he was 'displeased' with our company. I have over a thousand people and their families that rely on me for their livelihood. I will not jeopardize them. I play the game, submitting an honest bid so everything appears legal, knowing it will never be accepted, and go on."

Barek was silent for several moments looking at the information before him, then he frowned. "You say you've been submitting bids for contracts?"

"Of course. If you don't, Pajari won't throw you any crumbs, especially to the Zhao Corporation since my Union to Kasmira."

"Your Union? Why would Pajari care about that?" Barek demanded.

"Because to him, I am not truly from the House of Protection, and as such shouldn't be allowed a contract."

"You were born into this House, as your father was."

"But my mother wasn't, and to Pajari's way of thinking, that means neither am I."

"Well he's wrong," Barek told him outraged that an Assemblyman would act in such a way, "and I want you to know I don't feel that way."

"That's good to know."

"Do you have copies of those contracts?" Barek asked changing the subject.

"The ones we submitted?" Ethan asked confused.

"Yes."

"Of course. Why?"

"Because in all the files I've read, I haven't found one recorded bid submitted by the Zhao Corporation."

"What? That's *impossible*! I personally delivered every bid, Pajari demanded it."

"He demanded that of everyone or just you?"

"Just me."

"And your father allowed this?" Barek couldn't believe it.

"I never told him. It's for me to handle."

"You are a great deal like your mother, aren't you?"

"Excuse me?"

"Your mother. She is an amazing woman. Independent. Strong. Living her life on her own terms. It must have been... fascinating... being raised by her."

"It had its moments."

"I can imagine. You do realize she's now facing the biggest challenge of her life, being with my father."

"So you know." Ethan gave him a sharp look.

"Yes, and I heartily approve. The changes I have already seen in my father are truly amazing. I've never seen him this happy or relaxed." When Ethan didn't immediately respond, Barek frowned. "You don't?"

"I'll admit I was shocked when she told us." Ethan sat back in his chair looking Barek in the eye as he did. "I am still not fully on board, even though she says she loves him."

"Why?" Barek demanded.

"Because my mother is going to be the one that bears the weight of this relationship. She's the one that's going to be criticized and judged, and not just by the purists. It's going to upset her, even though she would never say it. I don't want her upset. She's my mother."

"She will be protected, Ethan."

"You know as well as I do that you won't be able to protect her from what people say. She will be the first companion of an unwed King. None of the normal courtesies will be followed."

"I hadn't considered that." Barek frowned not liking the thought of what might be said.

"I can assure you my mother has. Nevertheless, she's not going to let it deter her. When she loves someone, there's no length she won't go to for them."

Chapter Thirty

Jacinda stepped back, crossed her arms over her chest and smiled. It was perfect, just like she knew it would be. Kasmira had done an amazing job framing Brett's drawing making sure it shined. She couldn't wait for Jotham to see it.

"It truly is a masterpiece, Jacinda," Myesha told her standing at her side.

"It is, Brett is going to have an amazing future."

"I believe you," Myesha said. "Oh, Palma called earlier. She wants you to call her back."

"Alright." With one last look at the portrait, Jacinda picked up her personal comm and walked into the garden. It was a beautiful day and she wanted to sit outside and enjoy it. Palma answered on the second ring.

"I've waited as long as I can! You have some explaining to do, Jacinda Crocetti Michelakakis!"

Jacinda found herself laughing at the putout expression on her sister's face. She had forgotten to call her and explain and for Palma to wait a week was a new record.

"Hello, Sis. It's nice to see you too."

"Don't you use that polite tone on me, Jacinda. It never worked with Mom, and it won't work with you."

"Liar."

"Okay, so it did work with Mom," Palma smiled at her. "Now stop trying to change the subject! I want to know what is going on!"

"Are you sitting down, oh favorite sister of mine?"

"I'm your *only* sister," Palma told her, "and yes, I'm sitting."

"This has to stay just between us," Jacinda told her. "At least for a while."

"Jacinda..." Palma's 'I'm irritated with my older sister' tone changed to one full of real concern. "What's going on?"

"I'm involved with King Jotham," she told her plainly.

A stunned silence greeted her statement for several moments. "Define 'involved.'" Palma quietly demanded.

"'Involved' as in being his companion."

"Companion.... Jacinda..." she whispered horrified.

"I love him, Palma."

"I...." Palma really looked at her sister's face and could see it was the truth. Her sister was in love. "I believe you. And Jotham?"

"Loves me too," she immediately replied.

"Is this why you were getting those visuals for Barek?"

"No! I told you why I was doing that. Jotham and I weren't anywhere close to being involved then. I was furious with him for never showing Barek visuals of Lata and I told him so."

"You told off the King?" Palma just looked at her then started to laugh. "Oh, my ancestors, Jacinda... only you..."

"Only me what?" Jacinda demanded.

"Only *you* would have the guts to tell off a King."

Jacinda had the decency to blush. "Yes, well, you know me..."

"I do." Palma stopped laughing and turned serious. "You've always stood up for what you felt was right, for what you believed in and for who you love. I've always admired that about you, Jacinda. I want you to know that, and to know that I'm here for you if you ever need to talk, or just get away, or just... anything. We're family. We stick together."

"Thank you, Palma, and I might have to take you up on that sooner than later."

"What? Why?"

"Because I'm going to be attending the Royal Ball with Jotham."

"You... Jotham... Royal Ball..." Palma's eyes widened with each unfinished sentence.

"Yes. So in a few weeks everyone will know."

"Ancestors, Jacinda. No companion has *ever* attended a Ball. For Jotham to take you... that's big... really big."

"I know," Jacinda smiled at her sister. "Now tell me what Birgin thought of Brett."

Palma knew what her sister was doing. She was changing the subject to something she was more comfortable with and Palma let her. "Oh my ancestors, Jacinda! The talent that runs in that family! Birgin is beside himself with anticipation."

Sitting back, Jacinda smiled as she listened to her sister.

∞ ∞ ∞ ∞ ∞

Barek walked down the corridor of Assembly Hall seeing exactly who he was looking for in the group of Assemblymen that had just exited an office.

"Prince Barek!" Elliott Pajari exclaimed seeing him walking toward them. "I didn't know you were in the Hall today." Of course, he knew he was back on planet, everyone knew but no one knew why he was, so soon after the Guardian had departed.

"Yes, well it was unplanned and I was hoping to speak with..."

"Yes, yes, of course. We'll just go to my office." Pajari cut him off, looking over his shoulder to give the other Assemblymen a self-important look. "I'll have my aide clear my schedule."

"Assemblyman Michelakakis," Barek finished the sentence and saw Pajari's eyes widen before he spun around to glare at Danton.

"You wish to speak with me?" Danton asked coolly causing more than one Assemblyman to give him a startled look.

"If you have the time, of course," Barek replied just as coolly. "I know it's presumptuous of me to just show up."

Danton suddenly realized they were drawing a great deal of attention as he and Barek silently stared each other down. "Of course I have the time, Prince Barek." He swung his arm out. "My office is this way."

Barek knew where Danton's office was. "Gentlemen," he nodded to those left behind, then proceeded in the direction Danton indicated.

Danton let Barek enter his office first, gestured to a chair, then walked behind his desk and sat. "So what can I do for you, Prince Barek?"

Barek silently stared at Danton, taking in the closed look on his face and the tension in his body. The man was obviously on the defensive, and Barek realized it had to do with his mother. Never one to shy away from a challenge, he met it head on.

"So is your problem with me, personally, Assemblyman Michelakakis?" Barek had to give Danton credit, he never so much as blinked at his accusation.

"I have no problem with you, Prince Barek."

"So your attitude is because of the relationship between our parents."

"Why are you here, Prince Barek?" Danton demanded.

"I thought you might be interested in helping me finish what your father started, but now I see you're nowhere near the man your father was or the man your mother believes you are. Good day, Assemblyman Michelakakis, and good luck. Someone as narrow-minded you is going to need it." Barek stood and began to walk out of the room.

∞ ∞ ∞ ∞ ∞

Danton watched Barek rise, his thoughts in turmoil. He had, in fact, been in turmoil since his argument with his mother nearly a week ago. He was still trying to come to terms with what he had discovered. About his mother. Moreover, about himself. All of his life he had tried to live up to the ideals of his parents. In his eyes, they had been the ultimate couple. His father was the handsome, powerful Assemblyman, and his mother was the beautiful, perfect wife. Yet what had made them truly shine was the undeniable love they had for each other. It had been there in every touch, in every gesture, and in every word, they said to one another. It was something he never doubted. Now he did, and in doing so, he doubted himself.

He had disappointed his mother, badly. In addition, in doing so, he had disappointed himself and his father.

'Your mother is an amazing woman, Danton,' his father told him once. *'Meant to do amazing things. She changed my world with her love and made me a better man. I've often wondered what would have happened if instead of loving me, she had loved a King, as her mother had hoped. Imagine what everyone's world would be like if that had happened.'*

Maybe it was time they all found out.

"Wait!" Danton surged to his feet.

Barek slowly turned.

"I am not narrow-minded, but I will admit I am having a problem with my mother and your father being involved."

"Why?"

"Why? Because she's my *mother*! Which in my family means she loves my *father*! And *only* my father."

"She still does, but she also loves *my* father and he is a better man for it."

Barek's words had Danton stilling, they so closely echoed his father's that it was as if Stephan were speaking to him. Maybe it was time for Danton to listen.

"She tends to have that effect on a man," Danton agreed heavily. "Could we start this conversation over? Please? My mother is already upset with me, if she finds out I was rude to you, I may never get back in her good graces."

"Knowing your mother, I doubt it will take much. She is a very forgiving woman." Barek returned to his seat.

"She is," Danton agreed, sitting. "But she also believes you don't have to be rude to make your point."

"You don't have to be, but sometimes rudeness just feels good."

"Agreed." Danton smiled at Barek. "But I'll deny it if you tell my mother I said that."

Barek couldn't help but laugh that this thirty-nine cycle man was still worried about disappointing his mother then realized he was the same way with his father.

∞ ∞ ∞ ∞ ∞

"So do you want in?" Barek asked after he explained why he was there and gave Danton some time to read the files he'd brought.

"Fuck yes. I do! I can't believe I didn't know about this, or that Ethan never said a word! I'm going to beat the crap out of my little brother the next time I see him!"

"He felt he needed to handle it himself," Barek told him quietly.

"Fuck that! We're family and family helps one another. Family sticks together, even when times are tough."

"Does that include your mother? Because times *are* going to get tough, especially with her attending the Ball at my father's side."

"What? What are you talking about?" Danton demanded.

"The Royal Ball." Barek frowned. "Jacinda didn't tell you?"

"We didn't get past her relationship with your father," Danton finally admitted.

"I see. Well, she will be attending the Royal Ball at the House of Knowledge, at my father's side."

"He's willing to go public with their relationship?"

"My understanding is that they haven't been trying to keep it a secret, just private."

"Little is 'private' in the life of a Royal," Danton told him.

"You might be surprised," Barek told him thinking about Dadrian. "But they are both trying to make this about *them* and what *they* want. I'm now permanently on planet and am going to assume some of my father's duties so he and Jacinda can have more time together."

"You are..." Danton realized what that was going to mean, not just for his mother, but for the Assembly.

"Yes, there is a great deal I still don't know when it comes to the Assembly, but I'm going to learn. And things like this," he gestured to the files sitting on Danton's desk, "are not going to be allowed to happen."

∞ ∞ ∞ ∞ ∞

"What is going on, Elliott?" Adelaide stormed into her husband's office, not caring that his aide was trying to stop her. She had her own sources within the Hall and had been informed how Prince Barek had chosen to speak with Danton Michelakakis instead of her husband.

"Adelaide, what are you doing here?" Elliott quickly disconnected his call before turning to face his wife.

"What am *I* doing here? What is Prince Barek doing here talking to *Danton Michelakakis* instead of you?!!"

"I don't know. Danton seemed as surprised as I was."

"Something is going on," she told him sitting down in a huff.

"Adelaide, you always think something is going on," Elliott told her dismissively.

"Because something always is!" she fired back. "You can't tell me you don't find it strange that Barek is on planet when he should be on the Guardian with our daughter! Or that now he's requesting to talk to a new Assemblyman, and not just *any* Assemblyman but Danton Michelakakis! I can't believe we have to deal with another one of *them*! It was bad enough that he was elected, but then to take his *mother* to the Assemblyman's Ball! Unheard of! Then for Barek and Jotham to feel *obligated* to dance with her!"

"Is that how you saw it?"

"Of course! Why else would they! Did I tell you I saw Jacinda in the Public Wing last week?"

"No, no you didn't." Elliott leaned back in his chair.

"Well I did, and I had a member of the King's Royal Guard escort her out of the Wing." Adelaide had a self-satisfied smile on her lips as she remembered the man leading Jacinda off under her orders. For too many cycles, everyone had treated Jacinda as if she belonged in the House of Protection. As if she were important just because she had a Union with a standing member of the Assembly.

"And he did it?" Elliott gave her a shocked look.

"Of course, he knew who *I* was. Now back to Prince Barek. What have you heard?"

"All I've heard is that King Jotham requested Barek return and that the High Admiral sent the Arrow to retrieve him."

"I wonder what was so important." Adelaide's mind was racing.

"I've got some feelers out. Hopefully, we'll know soon."

"Hmph, that's not good enough. Not with the Royal Ball coming up. I need to know if Barek is going to be attending, so you can get Shosha back on planet and there."

"First, there is no way you can get Shosha back, not after the strings I had to pull to get her on the Guardian. Secondly, she never would be allowed to attend. You know it's only for Assemblymen and their wives."

"She would be allowed if she went with Barek."

"With Barek...." Elliott shoved his chair back. "Adelaide, have you finally lost your mind?"

"Don't talk to me like that, Elliott!" Adelaide's face began to turn red. "Never talk to *me* like *that*! You would be *nothing* if it weren't for me. Do you hear me? NOTHING!!! *I'm* the one that made sure you were elected! *I'm* the one that made sure you got on the most influential committees! And *I'm* the one who made sure the Pajari name is one to be feared and envied!"

"And I did nothing?" Elliott's hands rested on his desk as he rose and leaned forward. "*I'm* the one that chairs those committees, Adelaide, not you! *I'm* the one with the power and the prestige. *You* are nothing more than my *wife*!"

"Nothing more?!!" she shrieked. "Nothing more?!! Why you little foabhor! You would be nowhere without me! You would have nothing! Be nothing!"

"I would be *happy*!" he fired back. "Now get out of my office, Adelaide. Go buy something. Go make someone else miserable. I have work to do!"

Adelaide gave her husband a furious look then spun on her heel and stormed out of the room. Elliott's aide pushed away from his desk, as she stormed through the outer office, trying to get as far from the enraged woman as he could. Adelaide Pajari was known to lash out at anyone available when she was like this. The woman was totally unstable.

∞ ∞ ∞ ∞ ∞

"Deffand, I'm going to be leaving the Palace," Jotham told him.

"Yes, Majesty. May I inquire when and to where?"

"As soon as Safford has the picnic lunch packed, and I'm going to Jacinda's."

"Yes, Majesty. I will inform Green that we will be arriving. I assume you will be eating in Jacinda's garden."

"Yes."

"I'll make sure security is informed."

"Thank you, Deffand." Jotham disconnected the call and looked up to see Barek was just entering his office.

"Can't stay away from her, can you?" Barek grinned at his father. So much had changed in the last few weeks. His father was more relaxed, he smiled more, real smiles, and he laughed. Oh, he took his duties just as seriously as ever, but they were just that... duties, not his life as they had once been and that was all thanks to Jacinda.

"I haven't seen her since yesterday," Jotham said by way of explanation. "She had some meeting in Pechora that ran late and stayed at her house."

Barek just shook his head at his father's putout look. It was something he never expected to see. "So you're going to surprise her."

"Yes. I contacted Myesha, so she knows. What did you need?"

"I've finished compiling and analyzing all the information on the Sokol Corporation's contracts." Barek's face turned serious as he sat down.

"And?"

"And he should never have been awarded a single one of those contracts. His bids were overinflated and the materials listed were often substandard or completely wrong."

"And yet Pajari awarded him the bid."

"Yes. It's a complete cluster-fuck, Dad. Nuga is just the tip of it. There are at least a dozen other sites that have the potential to be just as bad if not worse."

"I want a complete investigation, Barek! Fuck!" Jotham surged to his feet to pace. "There are thousands of lives at risk here!"

"I know and I've already started the investigation. Not only into Sokol but also Pajari."

"Quietly?"

"Of course. I've also contacted Ethan Michelakakis to see if his company would be willing to assist us in cleaning up this mess."

"And?"

"He's more than willing, as long as it's understood he has complete authority over who is hired, who is fired, and who the inspectors are."

"Why?"

"He doesn't trust Sokol's people or some of our inspectors. He wants results and recommendations that he can trust, and I can't blame him. Not after the way he and his company were treated."

"Agreed." Barek had informed Jotham how Pajari had made Ethan personally hand-deliver his company's bids. Something no other company had to do. It infuriated him, especially with it being one of Jacinda's children. "Anything else?"

"I have Danton questioning the other Assemblymen."

"You think that's wise?" Jotham raised an eyebrow. "Someone is bound to tell Pajari about it."

"They might, but Danton is a new Assemblyman, hence his questions about how different committees are run, how specific decisions are made, and by whom, should seem normal."

"True. Good call, Barek."

Barek smiled at his father's praise.

Jotham answered his buzzing comm. "Yes?"

"Majesty, Safford reports that your lunch is ready and on its way to your limisin."

"Thank you, Chesney." Jotham immediately rose. "Is there anything else, Barek?"

"No. Will you be back tonight?"

"Unfortunately yes. I have several meetings later this afternoon. Join us for last meal?"

"I would like that."

∞ ∞ ∞ ∞ ∞

"I'll get it, Myesha," Jacinda called out over her shoulder as she walked down the hall to answer the front door. Opening it, a smile broke out across her face. "Jotham!"

Leaning down, Jotham kissed those smiling lips. He stepped into the house carrying a large basket. "I brought lunch."

"You did?" Her eyes went to the basket.

"Yes, I thought we could have it in your garden."

"That would be lovely."

"The table is all set for you," Myesha announced walking toward them drying her hands on her apron. "Would you like me to take that out for you, Majesty?"

"Thank you, Myesha. And Myesha?"

"Yes, Majesty?" she asked taking the basket from him.

"Please call me Jotham?"

A blush traveled across Myesha's cheeks. "I... yes, M... Jotham." She stuttered before hurrying off.

Jacinda watched her long-time friend and housekeeper hurry off and shook her head, her eyes teasing as she looked back to Jotham. "You are a bad man, Jotham Tibullus, flirting with another woman, and right in front of me, in my own home even."

Jotham wrapped his now free arms around her, pulling her flush against him. "You know *you* are the only woman I'm interested in *flirting* with." Saying that, he gave her a deep, hard kiss.

"Hmmm," she hummed when Jotham finally let her back up for air. "I love the way you 'flirt,' Jotham." She looked up at him with desire-filled eyes.

"And I love you." He kissed the tip of her nose. "Should we go see what Safford made for us?"

"Yes." Turning in Jotham's arms, they walked arm-in-arm toward the garden when Jotham suddenly stopped. "Jotham?"

"It's up." He paused before Brett's drawing on the wall.

"Yes." Jacinda smiled softly as she looked at it. "Kasmira did a wonderful job framing it, don't you think?"

"She did." But what caught his attention more was how the drawing of the two of them just seemed to belong there, as if they were always meant to be. "Thank you, Jacinda."

"For what?" she asked, looking up at him.

"For making me a part of your life. For openly including me in it."

"I wouldn't have it any other way." Reaching up she touched his cheek. "Ready to eat?"

"Yes."

∞ ∞ ∞ ∞ ∞

Jotham sat back in his chair in his private office and stared at Lata's portrait. The one he had taken from the wall next to his outside the King's Wing, not long after she met the ancestors. He hadn't been able to stare at it publicly, hadn't been able to just walk by it and know she was gone. It had gutted him.

He had it hung here, covered for many cycles until he had been able to look at it again. Now he wondered if it wasn't time it returned to the place of honor Lata deserved. Rising, he walked over to the portrait. Reaching up, he gently caressed Lata's cheek.

"It's time, my love." Carefully he lifted it off the wall.

"Chesney."

"Yes, Majesty?" Chesney looked up from the screen he was studying, stunned to see Jotham walking toward him carrying a piece of framed artwork from his office.

"Will you contact Barek for me and have him meet me in the corridor outside the King's Wing."

"I... yes, Majesty... right away, Majesty." Chesney blindly pressed his comm as Jotham exited the office.

∞ ∞ ∞ ∞ ∞

"Father? Chesney said you wanted me to meet you here?" Barek frowned as he exited the King's Wing, seeing his father just standing there looking at the wall. The guards posted at the doors looked distinctly uncomfortable. Looking past them, he saw Deffand hurrying toward them. Obviously, he was informed the King was outside the Wing.

"I thought you would like to help me with this," Jotham said quietly.

"With what?" Barek looked from his father to what rested against his legs, its back facing him. It looked like a portrait. His eyes flew from it to the blank space on the wall, his heart beginning to pound. Could that be what he thought it was? Was his father doing what he thought he was?

"With putting your mother's portrait back where it should always have been."

Barek swallowed hard before speaking. "I would be honored to."

Deffand and the other guards watched in awe as for the first time in their lives, they saw the portrait of Queen Lata hanging next to King Jotham. She stood proudly in the portrait, wearing her royal robes and crown, holding her scepter in one hand while her other rested on her stomach. The look in her eyes, while steady, held just the slightest hint of mischief. She was beautiful.

"There," Jotham said stepping back, a smile that was a mix of sadness and pride on his face. "You're back where you belong. I'm sorry it took me so long, my love." The slight breeze that brushed across his cheek had his eyes filling and he knew his life mate forgave him.

"She was truly beautiful," Barek said quietly.

"She was, inside and out, and she loved you so much.... She would be very proud of the man you've become, Barek." Jotham turned and faced his son.

"I hope so."

"Never doubt it. Be true to yourself and both of us will always be proud of you." Jotham looked at the portrait again and this time truly smiled before turning to Barek. "Come on, this moment deserves a glass of ale."

"I can agree to that."

∞ ∞ ∞ ∞ ∞

Jotham handed a glass of ale to Barek, together they turned and looked at the now empty spot on the wall of his private office.

"To your mother," Jotham raised his glass.

"To Mom," Barek agreed raising his own glass before taking a sip of the well-aged ale.

"I need to tell you something, Barek. Something I know you're not going to like." When Barek said nothing, he continued. "Did you ever wonder why Jacinda and I suddenly started seeing each other, after all these cycles?"

"I did wonder but assumed it had something to do with Stephan." Barek raised his glass to take a sip.

"Not in the way you think. I asked Jacinda to meet with me because of you... and Amina Michelakakis."

"What?" He lowered his glass. "What are you talking about?"

"At Victoria and Lucas' Union, I noticed the interest you took in Amina. It concerned me as I knew relatively little about her. When I realized she was related to Stephan Michelakakis, I contacted Jacinda and asked for her help."

"You had Jacinda spy on Amina?" Barek felt his face start to flush in anger.

"Spy is a strong word. I asked Jacinda for her assistance, to make sure Amina would be suitable."

"Suitable!" Barek spat out through clenched teeth.

"Yes. You are the heir to the throne, Barek. You can't just choose *anyone* to be your Queen."

"You have no right! It has nothing to do with you! It is *my* choice!"

"I have *every* right." Jotham grabbed Barek's arm to stop him from turning away. "I am the King and your father! It's my duty..."

"Duty! I'm a duty!" Barek raged at him. "I can't believe Jacinda went along with this!"

"She didn't," Jotham told him quietly. "I believe she was even more enraged than you are right now." He slowly released Barek's arm. "She sat in this very room and tore into me like no one ever has. Not even Lata." He glanced back to the empty spot on the wall.

"She said no?" Barek asked giving his father a shocked look.

"Vehemently. She told me that it was *your* choice and that I had no right to interfere. She went as far as to say your mother would have been ashamed of me. She was right, Lata would have been."

"She would have?"

"Oh yes, your mother would have been irate and I should have realized it. It seems I have more of *my* parents in me than I want."

"I don't understand."

"Only after Jacinda and I... resolved our differences did I discover certain things about my parents."

"Such as?"

"They were purists, Barek." Jotham looked at his son with regretful eyes.

"What? No... that can't be."

"It's true. I never knew, never even suspected it. Not until Jacinda told me about the letter."

"Letter. What letter?" Barek demanded.

"It seems my father was going to make Stephan choose between his wife and his career."

"What?" Barek gave him a disbelieving look.

"I had the same reaction. Disbelief. So I had Chesney search King Kado's papers and he found the proof. A handwritten letter demanding Stephan choose."

Barek found he had to sit down and moved to a chair. "I can't believe it. How could..."

"They weren't much kinder to your mother, Barek." Jotham quietly told him.

"What?"

"I didn't know that either or didn't want to, I'm no longer sure. Palma told Jacinda how they offered Lata no assistance, no training even though I'd made it clear to them she was my choice."

"They hoped you'd change your mind while you were in the Fleet."

"Yes."

"They never really knew you, did they?" When Jotham just looked at him, Barek chuckled. "Once you reach a decision, you never change it."

"Rarely," Jotham corrected. "Rarely change it, because even a King can be wrong. He just needs someone brave enough to tell him when he is."

"Like Jacinda," Barek said.

"Exactly like Jacinda," Jotham agreed.

"And Amina?" Barek's eyes went blank as he asked.

"I will not intefere... as a King... but as your father, I make no promises. You are my son. I love you and I only want the best for you."

"What you think is best for me and what I do, could be radically different. Just as your parents were about you."

"True." Serious eyes met Barek's. "All I want is for you to find true happiness and love, Barek, as I had with your mother, as I have rediscovered with Jacinda. The crown you will one day wear won't be nearly as heavy if you have love in your life."

Chapter Thirty-One

"Pajari, what the *fuck* is going on?!!"

"What are you talking about, Keane?" Elliott asked looking at the flushed, furious face of his biggest financial supporter through his comm.

"The investigation going on of my company!"

"Keane, I warned you it was going to happen after the explosion on Nuga."

"You said they would be investigating *Nuga*! Not that they were going to be investigating *all* of my contract sites. You especially didn't tell me the investigation was going to be conducted by the Zhao Corporation. By Ethan Michelakakis! Personally!"

"What?" Elliott couldn't keep the shock off his face. "That's *impossible*! I have final say on what is investigated."

"That's what *I* thought! It's what I pay you for! But Ethan Michelakakis showed up at my Central site with an order signed by Prince Barek!"

"Signed by Barek? But Barek doesn't have any real power, not as the heir. Jotham's never given him any."

"Well, it seems he does now! You had better *fix* this, Pajari, or I'll find someone else to give my support to!" With that threat, Keane disconnected.

Elliott sat back in his chair, his mind racing. What the fuck was going on? Barek was signing orders? That can't be right. Barek will be returning to the fleet shortly... wouldn't he? Pushing a button on his comm, he connected with his aide.

"Yes, sir?"

"Get me the Palace!" he ordered. "Now!"

"Yes, sir!"

∞ ∞ ∞ ∞ ∞

"King Jotham's office," Chesney answered the comm.

"This is Assemblyman Pajari, put me through to King Jotham."

"I'm sorry, Assemblyman, but King Jotham is not available at this time." Chesney barely kept the satisfaction off his face that he could tell the presumptuous man that. "Could I relay a message to him?"

"Yes, inform the King that I need to speak with him about the Sokol Corporation," Pajari ordered.

"If you are referring to the current investigation, then you need to speak with Prince Barek, as he is in charge of it."

"Prince Barek is?" Pajari's eyes widened.

"Yes. Would you like me to transfer you to his aide?"

"Barek has an aide?!!"

"Of course. So would you like to be transferred?"

"Yes."

"One moment then," Chesney told him and hitting a button transferred the call.

∞ ∞ ∞ ∞ ∞

"Prince Barek's office."

"This is Assemblyman Pajari," Elliott told the face of a man he'd never seen before, hoping to intimidate him. "I need to speak with Prince Barek immediately."

"Let me see if he is available, sir." He put Pajari on hold before the man could say another word.

Barek smiled at his new aide. He had handled Pajari perfectly. Barek had been expecting this call. It had actually taken a little longer than he thought, but he was sure that was because Sokol had been chewing Pajari's ass.

"Keep him on hold for a few more minutes then transfer his call in to me."

"Yes, Sire."

∞ ∞ ∞ ∞ ∞

"Assemblyman Pajari, what can I do for you?"

"Prince Barek, I'm sorry to bother you, but I was informed by your father's aide that I needed to speak to you regarding the Sokol Corporation. I'm sure he is wrong."

"Chesney is never wrong. Why are you inquiring about Sokol, Assemblyman?"

"I... Well, I received a call from Keane Sokol, owner, and President of the Sokol Corporation. And he was quite... upset... when Ethan Michelakakis showed up at one of his mining sites with an authorization, signed by you, to investigate the facility."

"I'm sure he is upset, and he'll be even more upset when he realizes *all* the facilities that he received a government contract for are being investigated."

"What?!! But... but I chair the committee that decides who is to be investigated."

"So I've been informed." Barek gave Pajari a steady stare and saw the other man begin to sweat.

"Then how..."

"How what, Assemblyman?"

"Then how is this happening when *I* didn't approve it?"

"It's happening because my father gave *me* complete authority to investigate what happened on Nuga and make sure it never happens again. Anywhere."

"Of course, of course. What happened on Nuga was a terrible tragedy and it must be investigated, but there are certain procedures that need to be followed, Prince Barek, so that the People's confidence can be restored."

"I totally agree, Assemblyman Pajari."

"Sire, that can't be done if you are starting something you aren't going to be here to finish."

"What makes you think I won't be here to finish it?" Barek demanded coolly.

"Because these things often become long, drawn out, and complicated things to investigate. I know I've been involved in many of them and with you returning to the Guardian..."

"I won't be returning to the Guardian, Assemblyman. I have officially resigned my commission and will now serve permanently at my father's side."

"I... I was not made aware of that, Sire."

"Should you have been?" Barek let Pajari hear his sarcasm. "It was a private, personal matter between myself and my father. As such I will now have plenty of time to investigate what happened on Nuga."

"Yes, of course. I agree and I can have a group of trusted inspectors on Nuga in just a few days. I will demand immediate answers from them so Nuga is repaired and running properly. There is no need for the investigation to go further than that."

"I disagree, Assemblyman. I have studied all the contracts granted to the Sokol Corporation, and they always list the same suppliers, the same personnel, and many times identical test results..." Barek let that hang there for a moment. "Because of this, I believe the corruption and mismanagement that led to the explosion on Nuga goes much further than just Nuga. Therefore, every site that Sokol manages that has received a contract from the House of Protection will be inspected by those that *I* trust."

"But, Sire, Ethan Michelakakis... He is a competitor of the Sokol Corporation. He will state there are problems where none exist."

"What makes you believe that?"

"Because, as I've said, he was never able to secure a major contract with us."

"Why is that? I've looked over his bids, in many cases they came in more favorably than Sokol's."

"One must look at more than just the bottom line when one considers awarding a contract, Sire. There is reputation and, of course, how they performed with past contracts."

"The reputation of the Zhao Corporation is without reproach, Assemblyman Pajari."

"When Harbin Zhao ran the company, yes, but the last ten cycles that's been lost with his son-in-law running it. Ethan Michelakakis."

"You question Ethan Michelakakis' ethics? With a father like Stephan? An Assemblyman you served with?"

"Yes, well, Stephan was a good man, but he wasn't perfect and made some large errors in judgment, as far as I'm concerned. His son is just the product of that."

"A product of what? Assemblyman Pajari?" Barek's tone had become deathly cold, but Pajari didn't seem to notice.

"A product of a mixed bloodline. When that occurs, it's no wonder the child has no concept of what it is to truly belong to a House and, therefore, has no loyalty."

"Just so I'm sure I understand, Assemblyman Pajari. You believe that Ethan Michelakakis is *not* a member of this House, even though he was born here and his father *was* from this House."

"But his mother *isn't*."

"Jacinda Michelakakis might have been born in the House of Healing, but she wed a man from the House of Protection, she has lived *here* for nearly forty cycles."

"That still doesn't make her a member of *this* prestigious House!"

"And that is your basis for believing Ethan would lie?"

"Of course, and in doing so he would sully the good name of a true and loyal member of this House."

"I see."

"Good, so I will inform Keane he may have Ethan removed by any means he sees fit."

"No." Although the word was quietly spoken, it froze Pajari as if he had been stunned.

"No?" Pajari questioned.

"No. You see Assemblyman Pajari, *I* trust Ethan Michelakakis, emphatically. He is *my* choice for this position and he will report directly to *me*. You can inform Keane Sokol that if I hear of him interfering with Ethan and the investigation he is conducting in *my* name, in any way, that he will be brought up on charges of gross negligence in the death of nearly five hundred people."

"I..." Pajari's eyes bulged at Barek.

"Have a good day, Pajari."

∞ ∞ ∞ ∞ ∞

"No! Absolutely not!" Jotham words were hard and said as the King.

"Jotham..." Jacinda's words were gentle as if she were dealing with an upset child.

"I don't want you to go without me."

"It's only a few days early, Jotham, so Kia can make the final alterations to my gown." She put a hand on his arm. "It's important to me, that this dress reflect well not only on me but on *you*."

"I could care less what it 'reflects,' Jacinda. I know," he held up his hand as she opened her mouth. "I know that's the wrong thing to say, but it's true. I have never seen you at an event that you didn't look amazing, Jacinda. You could be wearing a rag and you'd still outshine every other woman in the room."

"Jotham...." Jacinda's eyes softened.

"What I care about is that you are going to be away from me. Half a world away, and it doesn't matter that you'll be staying in the Royal Wing at the House of Knowledge. I'll still worry because I'm not with you. Kia can make the alterations once *we* arrive."

"Kia is going to be up to her eyeballs making alterations for Cassandra and others. She's already doing me a favor by making the dress on such short notice. It's the least I can do to work around her schedule."

"Jacinda..."

"Plus it'll give me a chance to hopefully talk to Stephanie."

Jotham heard the worry in her voice. "She's still not answering your comms?" He knew how upset Jacinda was about that even though she tried to hide it.

"No. So I thought I would try face-to-face this time."

Jotham took a deep breath. He knew she needed to do this and he needed to let her. It didn't mean he needed to like it. "Alright, but you will take my personal shuttle, a full guard, and you will *use* them." The look in his eyes told Jacinda not to argue. "All the time, Jacinda."

"Alright," she agreed.

"And you'll call me. Every day. Every night."

"I will."

"And..."

"Jotham." She put gentle fingers over his lips, stilling his words. "It will be fine. I will be safe. I won't take any chances."

"Swear it," he ordered.

"I swear."

∞ ∞ ∞ ∞ ∞

Green walked into Deffand's office and sat down. He knew Jacinda planned to stay at the Palace that night *after* she convinced Jotham to let her go to Kisurri early, without Jotham. He couldn't help but smile because he knew she *would* convince the King. He had already told his men to pack and be prepared to leave.

"What's put that smile on your face, Green?" Deffand demanded looking up from the report, he was reading.

"Jacinda. She wants to leave for Kisurri early." His smile grew. "Without Jotham."

"Oh, that's not going to go over well." Deffand set his report aside.

"No, but she'll convince him."

"True. I'd better let my men know we'll be leaving early too."

"You think Jotham will change his schedule and go with her?"

"No, he has some meetings he can't miss. But I do think with her gone, he's going to rearrange his schedule and be working late so he can get there earlier." Deffand was about to pick up the report when a look crossed Green's face Deffand didn't like. "What's wrong?"

"Something happened several weeks back. I keep expecting Jotham to ask me about it, but he hasn't. I don't think Jacinda told him."

"Told him what?" Deffand asked.

"Not long after Jacinda was assigned protection, she was walking in the Public Wing when Assemblyman Pajari's wife confronted her."

"Confronted her? What do you mean 'confronted' her?" Deffand demanded.

"Madame Pajari was ranting on about how Jacinda shouldn't be there, shouldn't be allowed there, and that she needed to be escorted out of the Palace."

"She *what*?!!"

"Jacinda just stood there and took it. She wouldn't let me interfere except to escort her out. Madame Pajari didn't even notice I was escorting her deeper *into* the Palace instead of *out* of it."

"That woman is a menace," Deffand muttered.

"I agree. But what shocked me the most is that Jacinda told me it was what she had expected, that when it was realized she was the King's 'companion' there were going to be even more things said to and about her, and that was just the way it was."

"Jotham is never going to allow that."

"He will if he doesn't know about it."

"So why haven't you told him?"

"And have Jacinda upset with *me*? No way. I report to *you*. You have the responsibility of informing the King, and then Jacinda can be upset with you."

"Thanks a lot, Kort. Here I give you a dream position and you go and throw me under the transport."

"Dream position. Yeah, right. Jacinda is a security nightmare. She's on the go more than Jotham, and more often than not, it's at the spur of the moment."

"And you love the challenge."

"I do." Kort agreed. "Don't worry, Nick, she won't stay mad at you for too long."

∞ ∞ ∞ ∞ ∞

"Hello, Stephanie." Jacinda watched her daughter stiffen and knew she would have turned and walked away if it weren't for Peter Chamberlain walking beside her. Peter had informed her they would be walking this way and Jacinda had taken advantage of it.

"Mother," Stephanie acknowledged coolly. "What are you doing here?"

"I thought we should talk." Jacinda turned her attention to Peter. "Hello, Peter."

"Hello, Jacinda," Peter said smiling at her. "Will I see you at last meal tonight?"

"I'm afraid not. Tonight I'm having dinner at my sister's."

"Brett will be disappointed. He has some more drawings he wants to show you."

"I would love to see them," Jacinda told him honestly. "Maybe if it's not too late when I get back I could call him?"

"That would be fine." Peter turned his attention to Stephanie. "Lieutenant, I'll see you in the training room in fifteen."

"Yes, Captain," Stephanie immediately responded.

Jacinda waited until they were alone before speaking. "You never answered any of my calls."

"I didn't want to talk to you."

"I gathered that, but ignoring a problem doesn't make it go away, Stephie."

"Is talking about it?" Stephanie demanded.

"Not in the way you want, but it might help you come to terms with it."

"And if I don't want to come to 'terms with it,' as you say?"

"Then we are going to have a problem."

"I can't believe you're doing this, Mother!" Stephanie hissed. "What about Dad!"

"What about him?"

"If he were alive...."

"If your father were *alive,* none of this would have happened. I loved your father, Stephanie, still love him, will always love him. But now I also love Jotham and I would no more give him up than I would have your father."

"But..." Stephanie frowned, looking confused.

"But what?"

"How... you always said Dad was your life mate."

"And he was, is, but that doesn't mean I can't love someone else. It's not the same as the love I have for your father, Stephanie. It's different, but that doesn't make it wrong. I'm not the same woman I was when I wed your father and became a wife. It changed me, just as it changed me when I became a mother, just as it changed me when I became a widow. I'm sorry if that upsets you. I know, of all my children, you were the closest to your father because you were his little girl. You idolized him so much more than Danton did or Ethan ever did, and I know you see this as a betrayal to him, but I don't. I see it as a tribute. Your father's love was so true that I know he wouldn't want me to remain alone, not if I found myself in love again."

"You can't be sure of that," Stephanie denied, but she didn't sound so sure.

"I can because it's what I'd want for him if the situation were reversed."

"I... I have to go, Mother. I can't be late for training."

"I understand. But please, Stephanie, think about what I've said because in a few days everyone is going to know."

"What do you mean?" Stephanie demanded. "Is Jotham going to make an official announcement?!!"

"In a way. I'm here because I'm going to be attending the Royal Ball with him."

"What?!!" Stephie took a stumbling step back.

∞ ∞ ∞ ∞ ∞

"Keep your arms *up*, Michelakakis!" Peter's warning came a moment too late and Stephanie found herself on the mat, again, with Woodrow grinning cruelly down at her. She hated Wortham Woodrow. He made no secret that he believed women had no place in security, and as Stephanie was the only remaining woman in this program, she was his favorite target.

"Everyone take a break! Michelakakis! My office!" Peter ordered, spinning on his heel.

Woodrow snickered as he went to get a drink of water.

"What's going on in your head, Lieutenant?" Peter demanded slamming the door shut before moving to his desk.

"Nothing, Sir," she responded standing stiffly at attention.

"I can see that. Otherwise, Woodrow would never be able to take you down with such a telegraphed move."

"Yes, Sir."

Peter leaned back in his chair giving her a considering look. "You, Lieutenant, are the most naturally talented recruit I have ever trained."

"What?" Stephanie gave him a shocked look.

"You're smart, quick to learn and adapt, and realize that brute strength is rarely the answer."

"I... Thank you, Captain."

"Which is why your performance today is so annoying. Now I want to know what is causing it."

"Sir, I'm sorry, it's a family matter. But I swear to you, I will not let it affect my training again."

"You're upset about your mother's relationship with King Jotham." Peter didn't think it was possible, but Stephanie became even stiffer, her eyes piercing his much like her mother's had.

"Sir, while I have nothing but respect for you, *that* is none of your business."

"Normally I would agree with that statement except in this case it affects one of my trainees. So unless you want removed from this program, you will answer."

Stephanie was silent for several moments weighing what mattered to her most and realized that if she failed this program now it would be her own fault.

"Yes. I'm having a problem with my mother's... relationship with King Jotham."

"Why?"

"WHY?!!" Stephanie looked at him as if he were crazy. "She's my *mother* and he's..."

"Just a man."

"That's not true! He's a King, a leader of people, he, and my father..."

"He and your father?"

"They were friends. I used to sneak into my dad's office and listen to him and Jotham talk. I never really listened to what they were saying, but the way they said it. You could tell, even when they were arguing, that they respected each other."

"And you think Jotham has somehow now violated that friendship, that respect, by loving your mother."

"He doesn't love her," Stephanie instantly denied.

"He does," Peter told her quietly.

"He can't."

"Why not?"

"Because if he did, he would be making her his Queen and not his companion." She finally said what was truly bothering her. Her mother was never meant to be a 'companion.'

"Perhaps he will."

"No. He's always said that Lata would be his only Queen."

"To who?"

"My father. Dad wanted him to meet someone once. Can you believe that? My dad trying to set the King up with a woman? Jotham said it then that there would only ever be one woman for him, one Queen, and she was gone."

"People change, Stephanie, time changes us and life changes us. I don't know if Jotham will make Jacinda his Queen, but I do know he loves her. All you have to do is see them together to know it." When Stephanie didn't answer, he asked her a question. "Let me ask you this, if the situation were reversed. If you fell in love with a man, a good man, a man who loved you and wanted to share his life with you. If that happened and your mother felt, you needed to give him up because it might interfere in *her* life. Would you?"

"Of course not! She's my mother! All she's ever wanted is my happiness."

"But you don't want that for her. Should she have died with your father?

Stephanie paled at the accusation. "No!"

"Then let her live, Stephanie. Let her love and be a part of it, be her daughter."

"It's not that easy."

"It is if you let it be. Family is a precious thing, Stephanie. I know that better than anyone. You don't want to lose yours because of *your* selfishness."

"I... I'll think about what you've said, Captain."

"Do that. Now get back out there and don't let Woodrow take you down again."

"Yes, Sir." Spinning on her heel, she left the room.

∞ ∞ ∞ ∞ ∞

"King Jotham?"

Jotham looked up from the comm in his office to find Deffand standing there looking slightly ill at ease.

"Deffand, I'm in for the night," he told him.

"Yes, Majesty, I know. I was hoping I might be able to have a word with you."

"Of course," Jotham eased back in his chair. "What can I do for you?"

"I... something was brought to my attention that I feel you should know about."

"Alright." He didn't think he had ever seen Deffand this uncomfortable before.

"It concerns Jacinda."

Jotham was immediately on his feet. "Has something happened to her? Is she hurt?" She had only left the night before, deciding it would be easier if she slept on the flight to

Kisurri so she could wake refreshed and start her day. He hated watching her get on his shuttle without him, hated knowing he would be sleeping alone for the next few nights.

"No! No, Majesty! I never meant to imply that!"

"Then what?!!" Jotham demanded, his heart still pounding in fear.

"There have been some comments made about Jacinda, *to* Jacinda, that I don't believe you have been made aware of."

"Comments?" Jotham slowly sat down. "What kind of comments? Made by who?"

"Madame Adelaide Pajari."

Jotham groaned. He knew this wasn't going to be good. "What happened?"

"Apparently, Madame Pajari confronted Jacinda in the Public Wing about her not belonging there and demanded she be escorted out of the Palace."

"She what?"

Jotham's voice had gone colder and more lethal than Deffand had ever heard it. "Green was following Jacinda, per your orders and witnessed the entire thing. When he stepped forward to interfere, Madame Pajari took it that he had come to *her* aid, as she is an Assemblyman's wife. Before Green could correct her, Jacinda asked him to escort her out of the room."

"And he did it?"

"Green's immediate concern was to get Jacinda away from a possible threat. I went back and reviewed the recordings. Madame Pajari was acting erratically."

"And why am I just finding out about this now?"

"Green believed Jacinda would tell you about it and that you would then send out a clear and detailed directive in regard to how these situations were to be handled with your..."

"With my?" Jotham asked.

"Companion, Majesty," Deffand replied quietly.

"Companion!" Jotham shot back out of his chair. "Green called Jacinda my *companion?!!*"

"No, Majesty," Deffand immediately denied. "Jacinda called herself that and informed him that he would have to get used to it, because once it became known the two of you were involved, there would be more comments made."

"Fuck!" Jotham ran an angry hand through his hair and began to pace behind his desk, his eyes flying to the empty space where Lata's portrait had been. Why hadn't he considered this? Yes, there were Royals, both men, and women, that had what was politely called 'companions' because many of those Unions were politically motivated like Yakira's, instead of love matches. And while companions were often seen at small private gatherings when the spouse isn't present, they were never acknowledged in public. But Jotham had no spouse, so he hadn't considered it an issue.

"She never said a word," Jotham whispered.

"I gathered that, as did Green, as the weeks passed."

"So why didn't Green tell me?" When Deffand again looked uncomfortable, Jotham frowned. "Deffand?"

"Green knew Jacinda would be upset when you were informed, and he didn't want her upset at *him*."

Jotham's lips twitched at the thought that one of his Royal Guards would be afraid of upsetting Jacinda. "So he wants her upset at you instead."

"So it would seem," Deffand agreed.

"Thank you for bring this to my attention. I will take care of it."

"I... yes, Majesty."

"You have something else you wish to say, Deffand?"

"I... I just want to say that I have the greatest of respect for Jacinda. She is a truly kind woman, and..."

"And?"

"And if someone makes an inappropriate comment about her or to her, in front of *me*, I don't care who they are I will shut them up painfully." Deffand's eyes glittered at the thought.

Now Jotham did smile. "I will give you a medal for it too. Thank you, Nicholas, and I promise you *no one* will be making inappropriate comments about Jacinda."

Chapter Thirty-Two

"Jacinda, thank you so much for coming early." Kia walked up, her hands flying as she spoke.

"It wasn't a problem, Kia, not when you didn't complain about making my gown."

"As if. Clothing you is a joy. How is it that after all these cycles your measurements have hardly changed?"

Jacinda laughed, "Oh, Kia, you are so good for my ego."

"You are good for my business. It's only going to take one look at you wearing this gown at the Ball and every woman on the planet is going to be pounding on my door. Come. Let's make sure everything is perfect."

"Oh, Kia," Jacinda whispered moments later as she looked at the image reflected back at her in the mirror. "This is amazing."

Kia stood behind her, a satisfied look on her face, as she ran a critical eye over the gown. She really had outdone herself this time. The gown had changed, grown since its original drawing a month ago. It was the same, form-fitting sheath, with no sleeves, that clung to her figure. The applique had taken on a life of its own. Once Kia had started applying the beads, she realized she needed to go bold or go home. Instead of the beading just along the hem, she filled the lower quarter with waterfalls full of beads that pooled around Jacinda's feet, arranged in such a way that House of Protection violet shone through as the royal crown. After that, the upper half of the dress demanded more and Kia had answered. She continued the crown theme across the bodice, knowing Jacinda could carry it off. Then on a whim, she'd inverted the design so it accentuated the curve of her hips. It truly was one of Kia's best works.

"Walk," she ordered watching the movement of the gown carefully. "You need higher heels. Zee!" Kia clapped her hands together and the assistant came running. "Four inch heels."

With just a nod, Zee hurried away to get the shoes.

"Kia, four inch? Are you sure?"

"The dress will hang better and you won't have to worry about stepping on the hem, not even when you're dancing." She looked up at Jacinda and knew her concern. "Jotham will still be taller than you by several inches, Jacinda."

"You're sure?"

"Yes. The two of you together... I will be glued to my comm watching how stunning the two of you will look together."

Jacinda blushed, "Thank you, Kia."

"No thanks needed. Now," she said as Zee entered the room, "lift your foot." As Jacinda did Kia changed her shoes. "Now try it again."

Jacinda did and found Kia was right, as usual, the dress did flow better and was just off the floor enough so she wouldn't worry about stepping on it. "You were right."

"Of course I was," Kia told her absently her eyes still on the dress. "Turn. Good. Stop." Kia came up closer, inspecting the beading that flowed along the back of her hip. "The beading is a little loose back here. I will have it fixed and will personally deliver it to the Palace tomorrow."

"Alright." Jacinda turned giving herself one last look in the mirror unable to believe how beautiful the gown was. "Thank you, Kia, I truly love it."

"You are most welcome, Jacinda."

∞ ∞ ∞ ∞ ∞

Jotham sat in his living room and stared at the velvet box that he had placed on the table before him. He had personally gone into the Royal vault to retrieve this particular item, not wanting anyone else to know about it. He wasn't sure what he was feeling as he looked at the box. He never planned on using it again. Had believed Barek would be the next one to, but here he was.

Reaching out, he opened the front latches that held the box closed. Then swinging the sides out, opened it to reveal the betrothal circlet for the House of Protection. It was the sign that she willingly accepted the responsibility and duties that came with her Union to the heir. Or in this case, to the King.

It was a simple piece really, especially in comparison to the crown each Queen designed for herself. This was the only thing they *all* wore, made of gold mined many millennium ago and studded with large, square-cut violet gems that the House of Protection drew its color from. It glowed as it sat in its velvet home, but he knew it would glow even more when Jacinda wore it.

He thought about it before Deffand had informed him what happened with Adelaide Pajari. However, he and Jacinda had wanted to take this slow, even though he had insisted that she attend the Ball with him. *He* hadn't considered what accepting that would cost her, *she* had and yet she had *still* agreed. The moment he had moved Lata's portrait back to where it belonged, he'd known he was going to ask Jacinda to be his *next* Queen. Never to replace Lata, but to be his Queen on her own terms. Well, at least her own terms once she accepted him because they were not appearing at the Royal Ball until she was wearing this circlet.

He knew there would be those that would protest the Union because Jacinda wasn't born into the House of Protection, but the precedent had already been established with Cassandra's Union. It was only the *heir* to the throne, who must wed within his or her own House. He wanted Jacinda, and he was going to have her as his wife and as his Queen.

Closing the box, he went and placed it in his luggage. He wanted to be with Jacinda. He missed her and for once he was going to put his needs first. Walking over to his comm, he contacted Chesney.

"Notify everyone that we are leaving for Kisurri as soon as my shuttle is readied."

"Yes, Majesty. I will make the necessary calls."

∞ ∞ ∞ ∞ ∞

Jotham was shocked when less than two hours later every member of his travel staff along with his security were on board the shuttle, not one of them looking frazzled.

"Deffand!"

"Yes, Majesty?" Deffand was immediately at his side.

"You had no problem getting all the security force here?"

"No, Majesty." At Jotham's disbelieving look, Deffand's face cracked into a smile. "We have all been packed and ready to leave since Jacinda departed, Majesty. I actually won the pool."

"The pool?" Jotham quizzed.

"We all bet on how long it would take after Jacinda left, before you would be following her." Deffand gave him an unapologetic, smug look.

"Have I become that predictable?"

"Only in that you hate being separated from her. I hope to one day be that predictable." Deffand's expression became neutral again. "Was there anything else, Majesty?"

JACINDA'S CHALLENGE

"No, Nicholas, and thank you for everything. I'll make sure Jacinda doesn't stay 'upset' for too long."

"Greatly appreciated, Majesty."

∞ ∞ ∞ ∞ ∞

"Is my drawing *really* hanging on the wall in your house? Like one of those?" Brett pointed to the masterpieces hanging on the walls as they ate first meal.

"It *really* is," Jacinda told Brett. "My daughter-in-law framed it beautifully. You will have to come visit so you can see it."

"Can we, Mom? Can we go to Jacinda's house?" Brett turned excited eyes to his mother.

"We'll have to see. But you realize if we go you will miss your lessons with Mister Johns."

"Oh yeah, I like those," Brett frowned obviously conflicted.

"Maybe when there is a break, you and your parents could come visit," Jacinda suggested.

"Mom?"

"We'll see, Brett. Right now you need to get going or you'll be late for class."

"Okay." Gathering up his things, Brett ran from the room. "Oh, sorry, King Jotham! I'm late," he said as his bag bumped into Jotham just entering the room.

"No harm done, Brett. Have a good day." But he was talking to empty space.

Jacinda spun around in her chair at Jotham's voice. "Jotham! You weren't supposed to be here until tonight!" She was immediately up and in his arms.

"Well, I came early." Leaning down he captured her lips in a hard kiss. "I missed you."

Jacinda felt her eyes go misty. "I missed you too. Have you eaten yet? I think there's some left."

"Right, after those four little monsters got done? Good luck with that." Will smiled at Jotham. "I'll contact Hutu and tell him to send up another plate. The usual, Jotham?"

"Actually, I'm good. I had first meal on the shuttle." He gave Will a hard look. "Do you have some time?"

"Sure. Here or my office?"

"Here is fine, I think Jacinda would like to hear this. Cassandra too."

"I need to get to my trainees. Will, you'll fill me in later?" Peter asked rising from the table.

"Yes."

"I have a meeting with Director Metaxas unless you need me here." Cyndy rose too.

"I see no reason for you to be here," Jotham spoke.

"Come on, Pixie, I'll walk you to your limisin."

"I can get there myself you know," Cyndy teased.

"Yeah, but then I don't get to watch your cute ass as you walk."

"Peter Chamberlain! What am I going to do with you?" Peter's response was lost as they walked away.

"It's good to see them so happy," Will said quietly. "We owe a lot of that to you, Jacinda."

"You would have figured it out yourself. I just sped up the process."

"It would be nice to think that, but I'm not so sure." He looked to Jotham. "Let's at least have some coffee. I need it. It seems Sabah is getting her first tooth and she only wanted me to hold her."

"And you savored every minute of it," Cassandra challenged sweeping into the room.

"I did, but I still need coffee. Pittaluga's coffee."

"You have totally ruined him, Jacinda. When I met him, William would drink sludge. Now... it's Pittaluga coffee or nothing."

"I'm so sorry," Jacinda responded without a hint of remorse in her voice.

"Yeah, I can tell." Picking up the coffee tray before William could pour a cup, Cassandra carried it to the sitting area that overlooked the garden.

"I could have done that, Cassandra," William protested.

"Before or after you drank half the pot?" she asked.

William had the decency to blush.

"That's what I thought. Jacinda?" Cassandra looked to her.

"I'd love some. Thank you, Cassandra."

"Jotham?"

"Please."

"Cassandra...."

"Guests first, William." Slowly, very slowly Cassandra poured William a cup of the so desired brew, then handed it to him laughing. "You are so bad, William Zafar."

"I'll show you bad," he told her before taking a long sip of the coffee. "Later, when we're alone."

Cassandra just blushed in response.

After several moments of everyone enjoying their coffee, William finally spoke. "Well, I have some news concerning those transmissions between Pajari and Stannic."

"Transmissions?" Jacinda raised a questioning brow at Jotham.

"Yes, you know that Rogue Stannic, an Assemblyman for the House of Knowledge was arrested."

"Yes, but mostly it has been pretty hush-hush," Jacinda admitted.

"He wanted me dead," Cassandra informed her bluntly. "Me and all my children."

"I..." Jacinda looked at Cassandra in shock before her eyes pinned William. "Why is he still alive?"

Jotham started to chuckle. "I didn't know you were such a blood-thirsty thing, my love."

"I'm not. Not normally, but Stannic has always been a fucking little foabhor. I just never thought he'd take it to such extremes."

Silence greeted Jacinda's heartfelt statement.

"What?" she asked looking at the three shocked faces.

"Where did you ever learn a phrase like that?" Jotham finally asked.

"Oh please," Jacinda waved a dismissive hand. "I did go to the same Academy you did *and* I served in the Coalition. It's not like I haven't heard it or said it before."

"Yeah, but you are usually so... polite and... tactful," William said.

Cassandra snorted causing Jacinda to look at her and the silent look they exchanged said. *'Men!'*

"So back to this transmission?" she queried.

"After going through his comm it was discovered he was communicating regularly with someone in the House of Protection."

Jacinda didn't even hesitate, "Pajari."

Everyone in the room looked at her in shock once again.

"What *now*?" Jacinda demanded.

"How could you possibly have known that?!!" William demanded.

"Because they are both purists. They believe anyone who isn't from a 'pure' bloodline is beneath them."

"That is absolutely ridiculous!" William scoffed. "There is no such thing as a 'pure' bloodline, not even their own."

"I wouldn't try telling them that." Jacinda gave him a long look. "So I assume the communications were related to Barek and whom he would choose as his Queen."

William looked at Jotham. "Why did we even bother? We wasted the last moon cycle when all we had to do was ask Jacinda."

"Moon cycle?" Jacinda looked at William in shock. "You mean you've been working on this since we left?"

"Yes," This time Cassandra spoke. "The transmissions were complicated to track."

"I'm sure they were. Pajari might be a foabhor, but he's a smart foabhor. So at least now you have the proof."

"Yes," William agreed.

"Why were you so sure the transmissions were related to Barek?" Jotham asked, giving her a questioning look.

"Because Adelaide Pajari is just as sure her daughter is meant to be a Queen, as mine was."

"Your mother thought you were destined to be a Queen?" Jotham asked stilling.

"Oh yes. She and Queen Rea were just sure Yusuf and I would be perfect for each other. It's one of the reasons I was so adamant about going to the Academy, to get away from them and *him*."

"Yusuf has to be at least six cycles younger than you," Jotham said.

"Nine. Can you imagine? They were trying to set me up with a *five*-cycle. And a snot-nosed, spoiled one at that." Jacinda shuddered at the memory.

"He's not now," Jotham informed her quietly, his face blank causing Jacinda to give him a strange look.

"True, but I wasn't interested then and I'm not interested now. The only man I'm interested in is *you*." Leaning over she gave him a kiss.

"Good." When Jacinda would have pulled away, Jotham gripped the back of her neck, keeping her close as he nibbled on her lips, coffee mingling with her unique flavor. Finally, after William cleared his throat for the second time, Jotham released her. Pleased to see her face was flushed with desire.

"Alright you two, you can do that later, back to the matter at hand," Cassandra teased.

"If we must," Jotham said grudgingly. "So Adelaide thinks Barek should be interested in Shosha." It was Jotham's turn to shudder. "My son has better taste than that."

"He certainly does," Jacinda agreed, knowing he was talking about Amina.

"Elliott Pajari did contact Barek though," Jotham told them. "It seems Sokol jumped all over him when Ethan showed up to inspect his Central site."

"Ethan?" Jacinda gave Jotham a sharp look, the soft look in her eyes gone. "*My* Ethan?"

"Umm... well yes," Jotham told her carefully.

"Oh-oh, Jotham's in trouble." Cassandra's off-key singsong voice had Jacinda and Jotham both glaring at her while William cringed as she tried to carry a tune.

"Cassandra, now may not be the right time...."

"You will explain to me *exactly* what one of *my* sons is doing anywhere near Keane Sokol! He's worse than Pajari because he just plays at being a purist. All he cares about is his credits."

"Actually," Jotham figured he better tell Jacinda everything. "Danton is involved too."

The silence filling the room was deafening after Jotham dropped that bomb.

"Excuse me?" The ice that dripped from Jacinda's words chilled everyone in the room.

"Jacinda, Danton has the right to help finish what his father started. So does Ethan. They both want to be a part of this. A part of making sure that *their* House is safe for *all* who live and work there."

Jacinda rose and walked onto the balcony, gripping the railing as she looked out over the garden. She understood what Jotham was saying. She even understood that her sons would want to be a part of this, especially Ethan. He didn't think she knew about what he and the Zhao family had to endure because Kasmira had married him. It was one of the reasons she hadn't complained when Stephan had told her he was going to chair yet another committee. She understood, but that didn't mean she had to like it.

"Jacinda?" Jotham walked out so he was standing directly behind her. Leaning down, he placed his hands over hers, surrounding her with his warmth and protection.

Leaning back, she soaked it all in. "I'm fine. Not happy, but fine." Slowly she turned in his arms, saw the concern his eyes held and cupped his cheek. "I really am, Jotham. I understand why the boys want to be involved, just as I understood why Stephan was. Sokol and people like him need to be stopped. He's like Audric, who killed Yakira's life mate, Vane, so *he* could wed her. He didn't care who suffered or what he had to do, as long as he got what *he* wanted."

"Barek and your sons will stop him."

"Tell Barek to be careful, Jotham. To never meet with Keane without his guard."

"You think Sokol is crazy enough to attack the heir to the throne?" Jotham couldn't hide his shock.

"Valerian was crazy enough to try and kill Cassandra, wasn't he?"

William put an arm around his wife's shoulders, pulling her close as he remembered that terrible moment when Valerian had fired on Cassandra, as they followed the other couple out onto the balcony.

"You're right," Cassandra said causing Jotham and Jacinda to look at her. "You never know what someone who is power hungry will do. Barek is here, isn't he?" Her gaze shot to Jotham.

"Yes."

"Good. We'll make sure his security is increased." Cassandra had gone into full Queen-mode. "Ethan is still in Pechora?"

"Investigating Sokol's Central site," Jotham told her.

"You'll need to up his security. I assume Danton is on the shuttle with the other Assemblymen?" Jotham nodded in agreement. "Is he staying at your Emissary?"

"No," Jacinda answered. "He is staying with my sister, Palma."

"I'll make sure security in that area is increased. If anyone asks it's because Birgin is working with my sister-in-law and nephew."

"Thank you, Cassandra," Jacinda smiled.

"No thanks are necessary, Jacinda. You are not only a friend but part of my family now. That makes your family, mine too, and I protect what's mine."

∞ ∞ ∞ ∞ ∞

Adelaide squirmed in her seat. She hated these 'Assemblymen' flights. Hated being surrounded by so many that were 'beneath' her, but Elliott had refused to charter them a private shuttle, or ask Keane to use his, stating they needed to be seen as 'one' assembly when they arrived.

She found that comical, for they weren't 'one'. There were those that mattered and those that didn't. She was one of those that mattered. Danton Michelakakis was one of those that didn't.

Casually she turned to look behind her and smiled to find Danton seated in the back row, where he belonged. He appeared to be reading something on his comm. Something she was sure was unimportant. As if he felt her gaze, his eyes suddenly lifted and he met her stare straight on.

For a moment, Adelaide felt uneasy. It was if Danton was able to see her thoughts and knew all her secrets. Giving herself a mental shake, she gave him the slightest of smiles before facing forward again.

"Elliott," she demanded quietly. When he didn't immediately respond, she gave him a sharp look and found him looking out the shuttle window apparently lost in thought. "Elliott!" she hissed louder this time.

"Hmm?" he finally responded absently before his eyes focused on his wife. "What did you want, Adelaide?"

∞ ∞ ∞ ∞ ∞

Elliott had been lost in the pleasant thoughts of his companion, Bebe. Yes, he knew she wasn't the brightest of women, but she wasn't demanding and truly cared for him. She was already in Kisurri, staying at an amazing hotel they has discovered on one of their many visits.

Adelaide hated the heat of Kisurri and rarely accompanied him here. The only reason she was accompanying him now was because it was the Royal Ball and she would never miss such an important event.

Tonight, saying he had things to discuss with other Assemblymen, Elliott would meet up with Bebe and they would have a wonderful meal together, followed by amazing sex. Oh yes, he couldn't wait to get to Kisurri.

Adelaide's irritating voice had interrupted his pleasant thoughts.

"What did you want, Adelaide?" he asked crossly.

Adelaide's eyes narrowed at Elliott's tone, but she knew she couldn't make a scene. Not here when Assemblymen and their wives surrounded them. But once she got him alone, she would make him pay for talking to her like that.

"Did you ever find out why Barek was meeting with Danton," she hissed quietly.

Elliott rubbed his chin, gathering his thoughts as he decided what to tell and not to tell Adelaide. He'd learned a great deal from Barek, but none of it concerned Danton. He hadn't told her about the problems with Sokol because he knew how she would react and he hadn't wanted to deal with it. Not until he decided the best way to handle the situation.

He had knowingly lied to Sokol, which was never a good thing, telling him that he was handling the situation. He'd told him that while Sokol had to allow the inspectors in, he would make sure the reports never saw the light of day. Of course, that wasn't going to happen, but he had bought himself some time. Things were starting to fall apart. Once they discovered the full extent of his corruption, the House would strip him of his power and position and the Pajari name would forever be associated with corruption.

He had been under no misconception that this would one day happen especially after the close call he'd had when

Stephan Michelakakis had been investigating him. Elliott's malfeasance would already have been discovered if Stephan had not died. That's when he'd started to prepare. He had started a secret fund, one Adelaide knew nothing about, and that would start his next life. One that included Bebe and only Bebe. Yesterday he put his plans in motion to 'disappear'.

Adelaide could fend for herself, as for their daughter... he felt a slight twinge about Shosha, but it quickly faded. Shosha had always been Adelaide's more than his. She did what her mother told her. He hoped she would survive the fallout, but as for Adelaide... He couldn't care less. The woman had become more and more unstable as the cycles passed and he couldn't wait to have her out of his life permanently.

So what was he to tell Adelaide? It had to be something that would distract her from the real problem.

"No, but I did learn that Barek has resigned his commission in the Coalition and will now be on planet permanently."

"What?!!" Adelaide's exclamation had heads turning to look at her.

"Do you want everyone to know, Adelaide?" Elliott asked already knowing the answer. "Or would you prefer to be the only one?"

Adelaide immediately calmed down, then looked around to discover they had become the center of attention. "I'm so sorry," she said giving her best imitation of a sincere smile. "Elliott just gave me some surprising news. It's fine."

She waited until the low rumble of conversations resumed before turning back to Elliott. "That's impossible! Who told you that?"

"Prince Barek himself informed me of his decision. He felt, because of my position, I should know." The lie crossed his lips easily as he'd been doing it for cycles.

"But Shosha is on the Guardian!" Adelaide pointed out the obvious.

"Because that's where *you* wanted her."

"Well *you* have to do something to get her home!" she ordered. "Shosha needs to be on planet if she's going to attract Barek's attention and be the next Queen."

"There is very little chance of Barek ever choosing Shosha, Adelaide."

"That's not true! Shosha is young, beautiful, has influential parents, and is from a pure bloodline. No other woman even comes close to having all that."

"Perhaps that isn't what Barek is looking for," Elliott taunted, knowing it would infuriate his wife. "Perhaps he is more like is father, whose Union was for love."

"Love is for idiots!" Adelaide spat out dismissively. "What matters is that the Pajari and Tibullus names are forever linked. Get Shosha back on planet, Elliott. I don't care what you have to do and *I'll* make sure the rest happens."

Chapter Thirty-Three

"Danton! It's so good to see you. I swear it's been *cycles*!" Palma wrapped her arms around her nephew. "I swear you've grown a foot since I last saw you."

"You say that every time you see me, Aunt Palma," Danton teased leaning down to kiss her cheek. "I would be at least thirty feet tall if it were true every time."

"Oh, you." Palma pinched his cheek then pulled him into the house. "Leave your bags in the hall, Birgin is in the living room."

Danton smiled and dropped his bags. He always loved coming to his Aunt Palma's house. She was always so open and happy. Not that the home he grew up in wasn't, but it was different here. Here he wasn't the first son of an Assemblyman, he was just Danton, at least he used to be.

"Danton, good to see you." Birgin rose from where he was sitting to cross and shake his hand. "Would you like a glass of ale?"

"I would love one. It was a long flight."

"I can imagine." Birgin turned to get the drink. "Traveling on a shuttle all day with a bunch of stuffy Assemblymen and their wives." Birgin gave an exaggerated shudder.

"Hey!" Danton protested taking the drink Birgin held out. "I'm one of those 'stuffy' Assemblymen now, and really it wasn't that bad. Since I'm a newly-elected and unwed Assemblyman, I was seated in the back row. Which made it possible for me to get some work done."

"You'll never get me to believe it." Birgin handed Palma a glass of wine and they all sat down.

"So, Danton. Are you going to tell me why you wanted to stay here rather than at the House of Protection Emissary with the other Assemblymen?" Palma asked sipping her wine.

"Can't I just want to come spend time with my aunt and uncle?"

"You can, but I know you too well, Danton Michelakakis. For some reason, you don't want to stay at the Emissary." Palma gave him a hard look. "Is it because your mother is staying in the Royal Wing?"

"You know about that?"

"Of course, Jacinda had supper here last night."

"She did?"

"Yes, and I want to know what's going on between the two of you."

"Palma..." Birgin put a cautioning hand on his wife's arm.

"Don't you 'Palma' me, Birgin Metaxas." She gave her husband a hard look. "You noticed it too, and I want some answers." Palma's gaze shot back to Danton. "So tell me, Danton. Why does your mother seem so sad whenever your name is mentioned?"

"She does?" Danton found he had to swallow hard to clear the lump that suddenly formed in his throat.

"Yes, and while she said all the right words about how proud she is and how hard you are working, her heart wasn't in it. That is not like my sister. She has *always* raved about her children. Oh, she's never thought you were perfect, but she always supported whatever path you took. So what's happened to change that?"

Danton set his drink aside. "We had a... disagreement."

"A disagreement?" Palma asked disbelieving.

"An argument... a big argument." He reached up and rubbed the tense muscles on the back of his neck.

"What could you possibly have..." Palma trailed off as she suddenly realized what the problem was. "Jotham."

"Yes. I didn't... react very well when she told me, Aunt Palma." He turned devastated eyes to her. "Not well at all. She asked me to leave the house. We haven't spoken since."

"Oh, Danton...." Palma rose to go sit next to him, taking his hand. "You know she still loves you."

"I'm not so sure about that."

"Well, I am. You're her child. She's your mother. She's always going to love you but, Danton... you have to realize she's more than that. She's a woman too. An amazing woman, who's had an amazing life. She's lived her life on her own terms. I know you kids may not see it that way, but it's true. She knew exactly what she would be facing when she agreed to be Stephan's wife. We all did, that's why we all tried to dissuade her, me included." Palma nodded at Danton's look of disbelief.

"She stood her ground, Danton, telling us all that Stephan was more than worth it. That love, true love, was a gift and one she wouldn't turn away from just because it was going to be difficult. She feels the same way about Jotham. The ancestors have gifted her a second love. Do you truly understand what a rare thing that is?"

"I was so selfish, Aunt Palma, thinking only how it would affect *me* and *my* life when I should have been happy for her. What do I do?"

"Are you really sorry, Danton? Are you really going to be able to accept that Jotham is now an important part of your mother's life?"

Danton took a deep breath. "Yes, to all of it because you're right. My mother is an amazing woman and she deserves to be loved."

"Then tell her that, Danton, and I guarantee she'll forgive you because she loves you too."

∞ ∞ ∞ ∞ ∞

Jotham leaned down and kissed away the moisture from the curve of Jacinda's neck before looking up to meet those amazing eyes of hers in the mirror.

"There's nothing to be nervous about, my love."

"So says the King," she told him smiling softly.

"So says the man that loves you. Now, I better get out of here and leave you alone or neither of us is going to get dressed." With one final kiss on her shoulder, Jotham reluctantly turned and left the room.

Jacinda stared at herself in the mirror and could see the nervousness in her eyes. This would never do. Taking a deep breath, she straightened her shoulders and thought about what was important. It wasn't the people that would be at the Royal Ball tonight. It was Jotham and her family. Her heart ached a little that her family wasn't going to be standing beside her tonight. She still hadn't heard from Danton and didn't look forward to seeing him across the room tonight. She wasn't sure what Stephanie had decided. Ethan and Kasmira were the only two from her family that she knew supported her decision, but they were not here tonight.

Knowing there was nothing to be done about it, she reached for her brush and began to prepare for what was sure to be an eventful evening.

∞ ∞ ∞ ∞ ∞

Danton walked into the Public Wing of the House of Knowledge knowing he was extremely early. He had planned to call his mother last night but then realized that this needed to be face-to-face. He had hurt his mother, something he never thought in a million cycles he would do. He reacted without thinking and had reacted selfishly. That couldn't be corrected over the comm.

Looking toward the guarded doors that he knew lead to the Royal Wing, where his mother was staying with Jotham, he took a deep breath and advanced on them.

"I am Assemblyman Danton Michelakakis, from the House of Protection, and I would like to be taken to my mother."

Both guards silently looked at him for several moments before one looked down at the tablet he was holding. " You are not on our list," he informed Danton.

"Yes, I know that. I would still like to see my mother, Jacinda Michelakakis. She's staying in the Royal Wing."

"I'm sorry, Assemblyman Michelakakis. Without proper clearance, we cannot let you pass."

"Is there a problem here?"

The words came from behind Danton. He turned to find a man, at least five inches shorter than himself, standing behind him. He was wearing a House of Knowledge uniform.

"No, Captain," the guard quickly informed the other man.

"Yes, there is," Danton countered. "I am Assemblyman Danton Michelakakis, and I would like to see my mother, Jacinda Michelakakis."

"She knows you are coming?" the shorter man questioned.

"She knows I am here, she doesn't know I wish speak to her."

"Madame Michelakakis is currently preparing for the Royal Ball. As an Assemblyman, you will also be at the Ball. You can speak to her then."

As the Captain turned to leave, Danton put a restraining hand on his arm. "Now see here, Captain. Just who do you think you are?"

"I am Captain Peter Chamberlain and you will remove your hand or I will remove it for you."

Danton immediately realized that even though the other man was smaller than he was, he was much more lethal. He had heard about Peter Chamberlain and about his amazing skills. It's why Stephanie was so excited to come here. Danton quickly removed his hand.

"Captain Chamberlain, I apologize, but it is of the utmost importance that I speak with my mother before the Ball. Please."

Peter silently stared at him for several moments and whatever he saw on Danton's face must have convinced him. "I will take you to Prince Barek. He can decide if you should be allowed to see Jacinda." Peter turned to the guard, "Notify Prince Barek we are on our way."

"Right away, Captain."

∞ ∞ ∞ ∞ ∞

"Danton, what are you doing here?" Barek demanded pulling open the outer door of the Royal Wing.

"I need to speak to my mother, Barek, *before* the Ball."

"You haven't done that yet?" Barek couldn't believe it.

"No," Danton admitted, "and I need to. She needs to know that I love her and support her in all her decisions. Just as she always has mine."

Barek was silent for several moments, trying to decide if he believed Danton. Nevertheless, in the end he knew it wasn't up to him. It was up to Jacinda.

"Follow me. They're in their private living quarters. Dad asked that they not be interrupted until it was time to leave, but I think Jacinda is going to want to see you."

"Thank you, Barek," Danton's reply was heartfelt.

"Don't thank me yet," Barek gave him a hard look. "If you upset her, you're going to have *two* angry Tibullus men to deal with."

"I'll wait here to escort him back," Peter told Barek.

"I'll have Deffand do it. I know you have a lot going on already. Thank you, Peter, for bringing him here," Barek told him.

"Don't thank me yet. If he upsets Jacinda, he'll also have to deal with two very unhappy Chamberlain men." After giving Danton one last hard look, Peter spun on his heel and returned to his duties.

∞ ∞ ∞ ∞ ∞

Jotham looked down at the box in his hands, surprised to discover how nervous he was. It wasn't like he hadn't done this before but for some reason this was different. This was Jacinda, and he wanted to do it right. He needed to make up for his thoughtlessness at not realizing what everyone would think of her, say to her, and how they would act toward her. No one would ever harm her, not while he was alive. Now all he had to do was get her to say yes.

To being his Queen.

Would she really be willing to do that and assume the responsibilities that came with it? He knew he was asking a lot of her. Asking her to change not only her life but also the lives of her children. Because this would affect them too.

A knock on the door to their private living area had Jotham frowning. He had told Deffand that he didn't want to be disturbed. Striding impatiently toward the door he yanked it open and found Danton and Barek on the other side. Neither of them looked happy.

"What?!!" Jotham demanded.

"I would like to speak to my mother," Danton informed him.

Jotham gave Danton a hard look. He didn't want Jacinda upset before the Ball. He knew it still weighed heavily on her mind, Danton's reaction to their relationship and his refusal to take her comms. She was his to protect now and protect her he would. Even if it was from her own family.

"You had your chance to talk to her before now."

"I know but what I need to say needs to be said in person."

"Danton, what are you doing here?"

Jacinda's words had all three men turning toward her, stunned by the vision entering the room.

∞ ∞ ∞ ∞ ∞

Jacinda was just doing the final check of her gown in the full-length mirror when she heard voices in the outer room and one of those voices sounded like Danton. Spinning away from her image, she went to find out what was going on. Opening the door to the living room, she found not only Danton there but also Barek.

"Danton, what are you doing here?" she demanded walking into the room unaware of the effect of her entrance. She looked from Danton to Barek to Jotham in confusion when no one answered her. Jotham was the first to recover.

"You look absolutely stunning," he told her, slowly approaching and taking in every inch of the magnificent gown she was wearing. It was the perfect combination of House of Protection violet and House of Healing gold, worn as only Jacinda could.

"You're sure it's alright?" Jacinda let him see her doubt.

JACINDA'S CHALLENGE

"It's perfect, just as you are. It makes me want to show you off and not let you out of this room all at the same time." Leaning down, Jotham gave her a deep kiss.

"Ahem," Barek coughed discreetly into his hand to remind them that they were not alone.

Reluctantly, Jotham broke off the kiss. He turned to face Danton but remained at Jacinda's side, showing Danton that they were one.

"Danton, what are you doing here?" Jacinda asked her face still flushed from Jotham's kiss.

"I needed to speak with you, before the Ball." Danton let his own eyes run over his mother. "Ancestors, Mother, I've never seen you look more beautiful. Being in love agrees with you."

"It does," she told him softly.

"Perhaps we should give you two a private moment..." Barek began only to be cut off by Danton.

"No. I need to say this to my mother and for you both to hear it too." Danton took a deep breath then focused his gaze on his mother. "I am *so* sorry I reacted the way I did, Mom. I have no excuse for it and you have every right to be angry with me... to be disappointed in me. I think that hurts the worst, knowing that I disappointed you. You have always supported me, no matter what and the one time you need me... You of all people have the right to be happy, and even an idiot like me can see that King Jotham makes you happy."

Danton's gazed turned to Jotham. "Thank you for making my mother happy again. For loving her. I know my father would approve." His gaze returned back to his mother. "The rest will work out because we're a family, a family with two more members now. Moreover, before long, Stephanie will come around. She's just the most stubborn of the three of us."

"Oh really?" Jacinda quizzed arching her eyebrow, even as her eyes filled at her son's acceptance. "I believe Stephie would say *you* are the stubborn one." Moving forward she hugged her son.

"She'd be wrong," Danton wrapped his arms around his mother and let her loving embrace heal all hurts, just as it had done all his life. "I love you, Mom."

"I love you too, Danton. Thank you for coming here. I know it was hard for you."

"No, it...Don't cry, Mom!" Danton exclaimed. "Are you trying to get me killed?"

"What?" Jacinda pulled back to frown at him. "Danton, no one's going to kill you!"

"Okay maybe not kill," Danton corrected. "But I'll be hurting in the morning if I upset you."

"What are you talking about?" Jacinda turned questioning eyes to Barek only to find him innocently looking up at the ceiling. So she turned her eyes to Jotham. "Jotham?"

"Let's just say, that the men of the House of Protection protect their women," he told her.

"But he's my son!" Jacinda gave him a sharp look.

"It doesn't matter. You're mine, Jacinda," Jotham's eyes hardened. "And *no one* is allowed to hurt or upset you."

"Oh please," she rolled her eyes at him. "You might be the King, but not even *you* can stop that."

"I can do everything in my power to try, which is why...." Turning away from her, he went to the table where he'd placed the box. Opening it, he took out the circlet then slowly walked back to her. "I had planned on doing this when we were alone, but I think now is perfect."

"Jotham? What are you..." Jacinda's words froze when Jotham suddenly went down on one knee before her.

Jotham looked up at her then slowly raised his hands revealing the betrothal circlet.

"Jacinda Crocetti-Michelakakis, I love you. You will be the last woman I will ever love. Would you do me the greatest honor of my life by becoming my wife? My Queen? I know we still have a great deal to overcome and that it won't be easy for us or our families, but I don't want to spend one more day the ancestors have blessed me with, without you by my side. To do so would be pointless."

"I..." Jacinda couldn't get her throat to work. She hadn't expected this, had never expected this. Lata was always to be Jotham's only Queen. She'd made her peace with that. "I... I don't know what to say..."

"*Say yes!*" Danton and Barek exclaimed in unison and when Jacinda looked at them, she found them both grinning like fools as they had in that visual taken so long ago. Looking back at Jotham, still on one knee waiting, she nodded.

"Yes. Yes! I'd love to be your wife, Jotham."

Slowly Jotham rose, his eyes still locked with hers. "And my Queen?"

"If that's what you truly want, then yes," she agreed nodding.

Without another word, Jotham placed the circlet on her head that would announce to all of Carina that *she* was the future Queen. The moment his hands were free, he swept her up in his arms, crushing her against his chest as he captured her lips for a deep, heartfelt kiss.

∞ ∞ ∞ ∞ ∞

"You know, one of us should break them up or they'll never make it to the Ball," Barek leaned over slightly to tell Danton, trying to keep a straight face.

"I defer to you, oh mighty Prince," Danton replied grinning widely. "You, after all, are the heir. It's not like *you* can be sentenced to death for 'upsetting' the King and future Queen." Danton's eyes were full of humor as he looked at Barek. "I, on the other hand, am just a lowly Assemblyman, here only to serve. Oh, and then there's the fact that technically, I'm now your older brother, so suck it up and get in there."

Barek's eyes widened in shock then narrowed, not because of Danton's words but because of the true affection behind them. This is what having a brother was supposed to be like. But he wasn't going down without a fight. "Really, so you think age trumps rank?"

"In family it does." Danton gave him a hard nudge forward with his shoulder. "So get to it."

"Hmph, I can see we're going to have to set some ground rules here," Barek muttered.

"Good luck with that. Ethan and Stephanie have been trying for cycles."

"You know your sister can kick your ass, right?" Barek asked even as he moved forward.

"She can try." Danton just crossed his arms and grinned.

∞ ∞ ∞ ∞ ∞

Barek and Danton were quietly talking as they walked through the Royal Wing.

"Are you sure you don't want to enter the Ball with us?" Barek asked. "You are family now."

"Thank you, but I think it would be better if I stay with the other Assemblymen. It will give me the chance to find and tell Stephanie and also to watch Pajari's reaction. He's been up to something ever since you talked to him."

"Really? What have you found?" Barek demanded.

"Lots of credit movement. He thinks he's being secretive, but I have a friend from my Coalition days that's a whiz at finding things like that."

"Excuse me, Prince Barek." Both men turned not realizing Deffand had walked up behind them.

"Yes, Deffand?" Barek asked.

"Why would Assemblyman Michelakakis enter the Ball with you?"

Barek grinned at Deffand knowing he could tell him. "Because my father just proposed to Jacinda and she accepted. The House of Protection is getting a new Queen." Deffand didn't grin back.

"What?!! Why wasn't I informed? Fuck!" Deffand was immediately on his comm. "Green! I need you and your entire guard armed and outside the Royal Wing in *five*!" His eyes shot back to Barek. "Has anyone informed Chamberlain yet?"

"I don't think so since it only just occurred," Danton informed him when Barek only frowned at Deffand.

"What has you so concerned, Deffand?" Barek asked.

"It had been decided that only the King's Guard would accompany you to the Ball as Captain Chamberlain's trainees would be assisting the House of Knowledge security. But I refuse to trust my future Queen's security to anyone other than our own people. I also need to make sure Assemblyman Michelakakis has protection along with Stephanie."

"I'll be fine, and Stephanie *is* a guard," Danton told him.

"You are no longer *just* an Assemblyman, Sir. You are now directly related to the Royal family. If the purists react badly to this, they could attack you. It's my job to make sure that doesn't happen. Get used to it."

"Barek," Danton turned to him looking for assistance.

"He's right, Danton. While the majority of our people are going to react favorably to this, there are those that will not. No one is going to get close to Jacinda but you.... You know as well as I do it would devastate your mother if you were harmed."

Danton sighed heavily, "Alright, but I don't want them near me until you are about to enter the Ball. It will make everyone suspicious."

"I make no promises," Deffand told him. "Now if you'll excuse me, I need to inform Peter of this change and Green. Prince Barek, you will be remaining in the Royal Wing until we leave?" Although Deffand phrased it as a question, neither man doubted it was an order.

"Yes," Barek told him.

"Good, then Assemblyman Michelakakis, if you would follow me I'll make sure the proper security escorts you back to the Public Wing.

∞ ∞ ∞ ∞ ∞

Adelaide's eyes widened as she watched Danton Michelakakis walk out of the heavily guarded door that she knew led into the inner wings of the House of Knowledge. A place neither she nor Elliott had ever been allowed to enter. Following behind him were several House of Protection Royal Guards.

"Elliott!" she hissed. "Do you see what I see?"

"Hmm?" Elliott's eyes traveled around the room quickly spotting what had his wife so upset, his own eyes widening. "Yes, I do."

"What do you think it means?" Adelaide demanded.

"I have no idea. Why don't you go ask Danton?" Elliott told her shortly, thinking it looked like he would have to move up his plans to 'disappear' with Bebe.

"I was serious, Elliott." Adelaide gave him a sharp look.

"So was I. If you want to know so badly, go ask him." For the first time in his life, Elliott Pajari wasn't going to defer to his wife. She would be on her own soon, just not soon enough for him.

"What has gotten into you, Elliott Pajari?!! You know I can't just go up and *ask*."

"Why not?" he taunted. "Danton just might tell you."

"These things have to be done subtly. Have you learned nothing in all the cycles we've been wed?"

"Oh, I've learned a great deal, Adelaide. A great deal. You just might be surprised."

"Doubtful," she snorted inelegantly. "You've never 'surprised' me in your life, Elliott."

"Things change, Adelaide. Now, do you want to go into the Ball or just stand here and argue?"

Adelaide gave him a sharp look. She wasn't sure what was going on with him, but he had a point. People were starting to give them strange looks. "Let's go," she ordered then held out her arm so he could escort her into the Ball.

∞ ∞ ∞ ∞ ∞

Jacinda stood in front of the mirror, adjusting the circlet so it nestled securely within her hair but was still prominently seen. She still couldn't believe it was on *her* head.

"You look beautiful. You always do." Jotham's image joined hers in the mirror, his eyes full of love. "I'm sorry."

"For what?" she asked turning around to face him.

"For not realizing people would consider you my companion. That *you* considered yourself my companion. That was never my intent."

"That didn't matter, Jotham. *You* were what mattered."

"No. *You* are what matters. You should have told me what Adelaide said to you."

"How did you find out...." Jacinda's eyes narrowed. "Green."

"No, but *how* I found out doesn't matter. What matters is that *you* didn't tell me. How would you have reacted if that had happened to me, or Barek, or one of your children and no one informed *you*?"

"Infuriated," she admitted with a sigh. "It was just..."

"No. Jacinda, there is no 'just.' We are going to have enough challenges ahead of us; we don't need to add more by keeping things that matter from one another."

"You're right. I'm sorry. I should have told you." She wrapped her arms around his waist and looked up at him. "Next time I will."

"There won't be a 'next' time. If anyone says something to you, Jacinda, and I mean *anyone*, you have the right to respond *any way* you want. You always did, my Queen or not."

"I know, and normally I wouldn't have allowed Adelaide to have the last word, but it had been a horrible day and I just wanted to get away. Letting her think she was in charge was the easiest way."

"Ready to show her who's *really* in charge?" Jotham watched a smile bloom on her face making her even more radiant.

"Oh, yes. I can't wait to see the look on her face."

"Then let's go show the people of Carina the most beautiful woman on the planet and the one that holds my heart."

∞ ∞ ∞ ∞ ∞

Stephanie just stared at Peter to stunned to speak. She had been worried when he pulled her aside, thinking he was removing her from the security detail, but she never for a moment thought it could be for something like this.

"Could you please repeat that?" she asked quietly.

"Your mother has agreed to be Jotham's wife. Because of this, I need to pull you from the security detail."

"No! This is where I need to be," she argued back.

"Lieutenant..."

"No sir, I mean it. I know *this* is where I need to be. It's a feeling that's been growing all day. Please, I understand what you are saying, but don't pull me off the security detail. Hardly anyone even knows I'm here. They'll be focused on Mom and Danton. Please."

Peter gave her a considering look. His own instincts had saved him on more than one occasion. He needed to trust Stephanie's.

"Alright, but if I see anyone overly interested in you, I'm pulling you. No questions asked. Agreed?"

"Agreed." Spinning on her heel, Stephanie returned to her post along the wall behind the members from the House of Protection and while her eyes were sharp and clear her mind was in turmoil.

∞ ∞ ∞ ∞ ∞

Danton stood talking to Assemblyman Terwilliger and his wife, Evadne, as the first of the Royals began to arrive. There was never any set pattern to who arrived when at these things. Except for the fact that the House hosting the Ball always arrived first so they could formally greet the other Royals.

"So, Danton. How are you finding your first Royal Ball, so far?" Evadne asked him as she took a sip from her glass of wine.

"I can honestly say it's been a life-changing experience," Danton replied blandly.

"It can be, can't it?" Evadne agreed. "I just love this event. I just wish it happened more than once every five cycles."

"I'm not sure our world could handle that." Danton's enigmatic reply had Evander giving him a sharp look.

"Of course, we could," Evadne missed her husband's sharp look. "Your mother loved this event too. Oh, how I wish she were here. We always had the most amazing time together at these things, and her gowns.... they were always amazing. Queen Cassandra is the only one ever to come close to outdoing your mother. Just imagine what it would be like to have them both here together. It might make someone," her eyes went to Adelaide, "finally realize she has no fashion sense."

Danton subtly looked to where Evadne's gaze had gone and nearly choked on his drink when he saw what Adelaide Pajari was wearing. While it was in House of Protection violet that was the only good thing that could be said about it. The gown that he assumed was supposed to enhance her bony, bird-like frame instead hung from it like weeds blown into a fence. The hair she'd pulled back from her sharp features only enhanced her bird-like appearance.

After the cycles he'd watched his mother dress for these events and knew how much pride she took in being at his father's side, in *supporting* him, Adelaide standing beside Elliott was an affront to his senses.

"I see what you mean," Danton finally replied to Evadne.

Evadne was stopped from replying by the changing of the music announcing the arrival of the host Queen and King. All heads turned to watch the arrival of Cassandra and William, and they didn't disappoint. The High Admiral was wearing his Coalition uniform, and although he was the King of the House of Knowledge, his pants were still the deep violet with a black strip down the leg, representing the House of Protection. His jacket, the snowy white formal one all Coalition members wore, announced his rank on its collar while all the medals he'd earned filled his chest.

At his side, her hand resting lightly on his arm walked Cassandra. Her gown was in a deep sapphire blue that made her eyes stand out, but stitched across its bodice were violet crystals showing her support of her husband and *his* House. On her head was the smaller royal crown she had chosen for the event because of its weight and the short royal robe that she wore just over her shoulders so it cascaded down her back to just reach the floor.

They paused for just a moment inside the entrance, allowing everyone to see them and the polite applause to die down. Then they moved through the crowd, nodding occasionally to those they knew until they reached the official 'royal' area where they would welcome the others.

One by one the other Houses arrived. First the House of Faith, then the House of Growth, followed by the House of Healing. All moving to Cassandra and William to be officially welcomed to the House of Knowledge. A low buzz began to fill the room as everyone waited for the arrival of the last house, the House of Protection. Some were wondering why it was the last to arrive when normally it was among the first. Jotham liked to leave early, as he had no Queen, but perhaps it was because Barek would be accompanying him this cycle. His first Royal Ball.

Danton could feel his own tension growing as the moment was fast approaching that would change not only *his* life but also that of their world. Earlier he'd seen Stephanie standing her post behind him and the look they exchanged told him she knew what would be happening that night. Now he took a slight step back wanting to see the Pajaris' reaction to what was about to happen.

"Danton, is something wrong?" Evander asked noticing the move.

"No, I just wanted a better view."

"Then you need to move closer not further away. Here, you can have my spot, I've been seeing this for cycles."

"No, Evander, thank you but I'm fine right here."

"You're sure?"

"Yes."

Just then the music changed, announcing that the House of Protection had arrived and Evander turned around.

∞ ∞ ∞ ∞ ∞

Barek waited in the common living area of the Royal Wing, wearing his Coalition dress uniform of purple pants and white jacket. He knew he should probably be wearing his more 'royal' attire, but tonight wasn't about *him* and he wanted to be able to help protect Jacinda if he needed to. He couldn't move as well in the royal trappings of a robe and crown. So instead, he'd chosen this.

"My, don't you look handsome, Barek." Jacinda's words had him looking up to find her and his father entering the room.

"Thank you."

"If I were thirty cycles younger, you'd be giving your father a run for his credits." Reaching out, she instinctively straightened one of the medals on his chest that was crooked, as she would have for one of her own children. "There, now you look perfect."

Barek found himself blushing at Jacinda's words and a warmth filled his heart that she would take the time and cared enough to correct something he'd missed. It was something he realized his own mother would have done had she been there. "Thank you." He gave his father a teasing look. "And anytime you want to lose the old man...."

"Stop flirting with my woman!" Jotham demanded, but he was smiling as he said it. "Give me a run for my credits," he huffed, pulling her away from Barek so her back was flush against his chest. "This boy doesn't know nearly enough to handle a woman like you."

Jacinda looked over her shoulder and smiled at him. "You know you're the only man I want, Jotham Tibullus, but that doesn't mean I can't enjoy *looking* at a handsome man. Especially one that's the spitting image of you."

Jotham found he couldn't argue with that and as his eyes ran over his first son he felt a surge of pride that had never been there with Dadrian. He'd finally made his peace with that, and with what had happened, thanks to Jacinda. Now it was time to get on with the rest of his life.

"You know, Barek," Jacinda touched the circlet in her hair. "We never asked if *you* were okay with this."

"Of course I'm okay with it!" Barek gave her a somewhat shocked look. "You've made my father a very happy man and given my mother back to not only me but to our people. I know she would approve of this so I'm extremely okay with it."

"Given your mother back?" Jacinda looked from Barek to Jotham in confusion.

"I placed Lata's portrait back alongside mine in the King's Wing."

"You did?" Jacinda felt her eyes soften, knowing what it had taken for him to do that. "Oh, Jotham...."

"It's where she's always belonged," he told her firmly. "Not hidden away and forgotten by most, and soon your portrait will hang on the other side of mine."

"But..." The King's portrait was always closest to the door.

"It is what I want, for everyone to see the women I love, on either side of me."

"I... Alright... if that's what you want."

"It is."

A knock on the door had them all turning before it opened and Deffand entered, followed by Green. The hall behind them was filled with the men from both guards.

"Majesties," Deffand bowed to all three. "It's time."

"Why is Kort here?" she asked looking to Jotham. "He and his men were supposed to have the night off."

"That was before we were informed of your change in status, Majesty," Deffand spoke first.

"But..."

"It's necessary, Jacinda," Jotham informed her. "Let them do their job. It makes them feel needed."

Jotham's words caused every man to stiffen.

"They are needed!" Jacinda immediately defended the guards. "They perform a very important and dangerous duty!"

Barek hid his smile. He knew exactly what his father was doing. Not only was he causing Jacinda to accept the guards presence, but by her defending them, he was cementing their loyalty to her.

"Then what are we arguing about?" Jotham asked gently and watched Jacinda open her mouth to only close it again, her expressive eyebrow shooting up.

"Sneaky, my love, very sneaky. I see I'm going to have my hands full with you."

"That you are," he agreed. "Shall we go?"

Taking a deep breath, she nodded, "Yes."

∞ ∞ ∞ ∞ ∞

Deffand and the King's guard took the lead while Green and the Queen's followed behind, surrounding the Royals with their protection. Jacinda and Jotham walked in front while Barek walked to her left and just slightly behind.

Jotham could feel the tension growing in Jacinda with every step they took, her grip on his arm tightening.

"Relax, my love. It will be fine."

Jotham's words drew Barek's gaze and he too could see her tension. He didn't like it, and raised his gaze to his father but found Jotham had stopped and turned Jacinda toward him causing everyone to stop.

"We don't have to do this right now if you want more time to become comfortable with everything before we announce our engagement," Jotham told her. "I just felt this would be the easiest way. I'm sorry. I should have consulted you first. Barek can represent the House of Protection. Jotham's hands went to the latch on his robe, ready to remove it to give to Barek.

"No," Jacinda covered his hand with hers stopping him, her eyes full of love but firm. "You have nothing to be sorry for and now is the perfect time. I'm the one who's sorry. I shouldn't be this nervous; I have you at my side." Stretching up slightly, she gently kissed his lips. "Let's do this." Turning, she nodded to Deffand and they started to walk again.

As they exited the more secure wing, Jacinda could hear the music change announcing the arrival of a Royal, and knew her life was about to change forever. Smiling, she knew she was ready for it too.

Chapter Thirty-Four

The guards parted and moved to the side and slightly behind as they reached the entrance to the Ball. Their move allowed the Royals to be seen, but they could still react quickly if the need arose.

The applause that immediately began as the guards parted started to dwindle as people realized that someone was standing *between* Jotham and Barek. A low murmur began to ripple through all of the Houses, and even the Royals, as people began to not only recognize *who* stood between them but that she wore the betrothal circlet.

Doing something never before done at the entrance of a King, Jotham turned Jacinda toward him and kissed her, so there would be no doubt that she was to be *his* Queen.

Jacinda put a startled hand on his chest but returned the kiss whole-heartedly. Her nerves had passed and she was now ready to take her place next to the man she loved.

When the kiss ended, Jotham held out his arm and Jacinda confidently placed her hand on it allowing him to lead her through the crowd and toward her new life.

∞ ∞ ∞ ∞ ∞

"Oh, my...." Evadne Terwilliger's faintly spoken words seemed to echo the feelings of the entire contingency from the House of Protection especially those that recognized Jacinda. Never, had the House of Protection shone so brightly or appeared so regal and it was all due to Jacinda.

The embellishments on the gown she wore resembled the well-worn gold of the House of Healing, but when combined with the House of Protection violet, it seemed to represent something more, the healing of a House.

Evander spun around to give Danton an assessing look, one that Danton silently returned. "You have some explaining to do, young man."

"I don't think there's anything that needs to be explained. Do you?"

Evander turned back to look at Jacinda walking up to the other Royals, the bridal circlet seeming to glow on her head and smiled. "No, I guess there's not."

"No!" Adelaide gasped not caring who heard her. "No! That is not possible!"

"And why is that?" Danton asked, watching as Adelaide Pajari's face became nearly as violet as her obnoxious gown as her gaze followed his mother's progress toward the other Royals.

"Because she's not even *from* the House of Protection," Adelaide spat out her eyes still on Jacinda.

"I believe *the King* is well aware of that," Evander told her.

"Then he should know that this breaks the Law!" Adelaide rounded on the elder Assemblyman and Danton quickly stepped between them.

"There is nothing in the law that states *the King* must wed within his House." Danton's eyes were hard as he looked down at the woman who he now realized was poisonous to his House. "Only that the *heir* must. That was established with Queen Cassandra's Union to the High Admiral."

"*That* doesn't matter! In addition, someone like *you* will not lecture *me*! *This* is the House of Protection and that *woman*," her arm arrowed out to point at Jacinda, "doesn't belong in it.

Danton's eyes narrowed, "I'm sure the King would *love* to hear your opinion of his future *Queen*, Madame Pajari, and before you say anything else let me remind you that she is also *my mother* and I will not tolerate you speaking ill of her in my presence."

"How dare you!" Adelaide puffed out her chest indignantly. "I'm..."

"The *wife* of an Assemblyman." Danton's eyes were hard as they met hers. "While I *am* an Assemblyman. Perhaps you need to be reminded of *your* place in this House."

"How *dare* you! Elliott!" Adelaide turned to her husband for support.

"Shut. Up. Adelaide." Elliott told her in short, sharp sentences causing everyone there to look at him in shock, including Adelaide. "Assemblyman Michelakakis, I apologize for my wife. She has been unwell for some time and I believe it would be for the best if we were to excuse ourselves."

"I think that would be best," Danton agreed and watched as Elliott dragged his struggling wife away, the other members of their Assembly parting to allow them a rapid exit.

∞ ∞ ∞ ∞ ∞

Cassandra didn't try to hide her smile as Jacinda and Jotham approached, even though she was as surprised as everyone else. She had never doubted Jotham's feelings for Jacinda, but she thought it would take him a little while longer to propose. It seemed Jotham was a lot like William, once he found the woman he wanted, he didn't waste any time making her his.

"I, Queen Cassandra and my King, High Admiral William Zafar, would like to formally welcome the House of Protection to the House of Knowledge. Welcome, King Jotham, future Queen Jacinda and Prince Barek." Cassandra recited the formal greeting that was standard at the Royal Ball. Cassandra found the rhetoric tedious, and it was only because William's hand lightly squeezed her waist, that she stopped her eyes from rolling as she spoke.

"Thank you, Queen Cassandra. *King* William." Jotham's lips twitched as he used the title he knew irritated his life-long friend. The slight narrowing of William's eyes was William's only response, but it told Jotham he would get even as he recited the required reply. "On behalf of the House of Protection, it is an honor to be here."

"Thank you, Queen Cassandra. High Admiral Zafar," Jacinda used the title Cassandra had used, knowing it was what Will preferred. When she automatically went to bow her head, Cassandra's quietly hissed 'No' stopped her and Jacinda's eyes flew to hers.

"You are a Queen now, Jacinda," Cassandra whispered for her ears only. "You bow to no one."

"She's right," Jotham leaned over to whisper in her ear. "I'm sorry, I should have said something."

"Queen Cassandra. High Admiral Zafar. I also wish to thank you." Barek spoke, drawing everyone's attention as his father quietly spoke to Jacinda. "It is truly an honor to be here."

"Prince Barek," Cassandra stepped outside of protocol and gave him an honest, open smile. "The pleasure is all ours."

"Thank you, Queen Cassandra, and might I just ask, how is it you grow more beautiful every time I see you?" His words had the High Admiral grunting at him in displeasure as Cassandra laughed.

"You, Prince Barek, are truly incorrigible. Just like a few other House of Protection men I know." Cassandra's eyes traveled from Barek to her husband.

"I do not believe it is just the men from the House of Protection, Queen Cassandra," King Yusuf stepped up now that the formal greetings had been finished. "The men from the House of Healing can be just as incorrigible, given the chance. Prince Barek, wonderful to see you again."

"King Yusuf," Barek acknowledged the greeting.

"Jotham," Yusuf turned his attention to him.

"Yusuf," Jotham returned the greeting already knowing whom Yusuf really wanted to speak.

"And Jacinda...." Yusuf let his eyes travel over her, lingering a little longer than was polite. "It's been a long time."

"It has Yusuf," Jacinda acknowledged. "Over fifteen cycles, if I'm not mistaken. When the Royal Ball was held at the House of Healing."

"Yes, you attended it with your husband. An Assemblyman from the House of Protection?"

"Yes. Stephan. He's been with the ancestors for ten cycles now."

"He has?" Yusuf frowned. "I'm sorry. I wasn't aware of that fact."

"Why would you be? As you said, Stephan was from the House of Protection."

"Yes, but you are from the House of Healing, the daughter of one of *our* Assemblyman. I should have been made aware of such a thing. After all, our families have been close for generations." Yusuf moved a step closer invading Jacinda's personal space. "Had I known, I would have assisted you in your time of need."

Jacinda felt Jotham stiffen at her side and knew he understood exactly how Yusuf meant to 'assist' her. "While I *appreciate* the sentiment, Yusuf," Jacinda gave him a hard look. She wasn't going to let anyone, King or not, talk to her like that. "It is unnecessary and *unwanted*. While honored to say I was born in the House of Healing, my true destiny has always been tied to the House of Protection. It's where I belong. Standing beside the man I love." Jacinda's gaze traveled to the woman who was coming up to stand behind Yusuf. "Hello, Pima, you are looking as wonderful as ever."

"Jacinda." Pima put a hand on her husband's arm not acknowledging the compliment. "This is a surprise."

"It's good to see you too," Jacinda answered as if Pima had given the appropriate response. "How are your children?"

Manners finally kicked in forcing Pima to reply. "They are well. And yours?"

"Fine. Just fine."

Cassandra signaled for the music before turning to William, "I believe that we should start the Ball. Shall we, my love?"

Lifting her hand, William kissed the ring he placed there at their Union. "It would be an honor, my love." With that, he led her to the floor.

"Jacinda?" Jotham held out his arm.

"That would be truly lovely." She took his arm and let him lead her away.

Soon every Royal followed and the Ball officially began.

∞ ∞ ∞ ∞ ∞

"What do you think you are doing, Elliott?!!" Adelaide demanded ripping her arm from his as he pulled her from the room.

"I am stopping you from making a complete idiot of yourself. King Jotham knows *exactly* what he's doing and he is within the law! Do you want to be arrested for threatening the King and his future Queen?"

Elliott's mind was flying. He needed to get out of here and disappear. Tonight! Everything was now making perfect sense.

The in-depth investigation into the Sokol Corporation had to be because Jacinda told Jotham about Stephan's investigation. An investigation he'd stopped after Stephan's death. If that was true, then they were much closer to discovering his deceit then he ever imagined.

"No one would *dare* arrest *me*," railed Adelaide.

"You truly believe that, don't you?" Elliott looked at her in disbelief. "That the *King* is going to defer to *you*? You have lost your mind, Adelaide. *No one* will support you against King Jotham including me."

"I always knew you were *weak*, Elliott."

"Better weak than crazy, Adelaide. Now I am leaving. Are you coming?"

"No! Someone has to keep this atrocity from happening." With that, Adelaide stormed back into the Ball.

Elliott watched Adelaide leave in disbelief. He moved toward one of the guards to inform them that she could be a possible threat then paused. If he warned them, they would prevent him from leaving and he needed to leave, get Bebe, and get off this planet.

Spinning on his heel he pulled his comm out of his pocket and left the House of Knowledge.

∞ ∞ ∞ ∞ ∞

Jotham pulled Jacinda close, not caring what was considered a 'proper' distance. He needed her in his arms, needed to feel her body pressed against him. Yusuf's words had infuriated him. For that little foabhor, King or not, to insinuate something like that to Jacinda... What would he have said if she had attended as his companion instead of his future Queen?

"It's alright, Jotham." Jacinda let her fingers lightly graze the skin along the back of his neck trying to ease the tension she felt there.

"It's not." His eyes bore into hers as his hand tightened on her hip. "He had no right!"

"He's been brought up to believe he does." She continued to let her fingers caress his neck as they moved around the room flawlessly together. "It's one of the things I immediately noticed about you at the Academy. You never expected special treatment, never demanded it. You were the first heir I ever met that didn't act entitled. After meeting your parents all those cycles later, I have to say it surprises me."

Jotham found his humor return and he relaxed at Jacinda's words. "I owe that to Will and *his* parents more than my own," he told her. "I spent a lot of time with them growing up, especially in the summers up at their cabin. Will's mother was a no-nonsense woman and she treated me no differently than she treated her own son. Sometimes I wished she would, especially if she caught me trying to sneak a treat when I'd already been told no."

"She put you in your place, did she?" Jacinda smiled up at him.

"Yes, she did. I truly grieved when she met the ancestors."

"I wish I could've met her."

"She would've liked you," Jotham told her. "You would've liked her. She would've reacted just as you did when I requested you help me with Amina. Actually, you let me off easy compared to what Candee Zafar would've done to me."

"Really? I'll have to remember that," Jacinda teased. When the music began to fade away, she realized that they had been dancing and talking the entire time in front of every Assemblyman on the planet. Not to mention everyone watching the broadcast. Slowly she and Jotham separated and then turned to approach the Assemblymen of the House of Protection.

∞ ∞ ∞ ∞ ∞

Danton, along with every other person in the room, watched as his mother danced with Jotham as though she'd been born to be with him and maybe she had.

No longer was she just his mother.

No longer was she his father's wife.

Now she was a Queen and she shone like one.

Now everyone saw her for who she really was, including himself, and he was in awe to be able to call her Mother. Turning slightly to his right, he caught Stephanie's gaze and saw she was thinking the same thing and he knew Ethan sitting at home watching was too.

As the music ended, his attention turned back to the floor and he watched Jotham lead his mother toward the remaining representatives from the House of Protection.

"I believe an explanation is in order." Evander Terwilliger's words brought Danton's attention back to the front.

"Since when am I required to explain myself to you, Assemblyman Terwilliger?" Jotham demanded somewhat shocked that Evander, of all people, was the one confronting them.

"Pardons, Majesty," Evander quickly responded. "But with all due respect, I wasn't addressing you." He turned his attention to Jacinda. "*You*, young lady, have some explaining to do. I have known you for nearly forty cycles... couldn't you have given me a little heads up?"

Jacinda threw her head back and laughed. Evander was the only one here that could get away with calling her a 'young lady' in that parental-tone everyone remembered from their own childhood.

"Oh, Evander... you've always been able to make me laugh." Jacinda leaned over to kiss his cheek. "Thank you."

"Anytime you need to, I am always available, my Queen."

And with that, a man Jacinda had always respected gave her a deep, formal bow. Immediately, every other man from the House of Protection followed suit while the women all gave her a deep curtsy. Jacinda felt her eyes fill at their acceptance.

"You may all rise," Jotham told them gruffly, their immediate acceptance of Jacinda touching him as well. "And thank you. It means a great deal to the both of us. Now this is a Ball, so it is time we all enjoy ourselves." After that, everyone started to talk and mingle.

"Jacinda!" Evadne immediately grabbed on to Jacinda's hand and pulled her to the side. "Look at you! You're glowing!"

"I am so happy, Evadne."

"It shows. Oh!" Evadne immediately dropped Jacinda's hands as Royals guards moved closer. "I am so sorry! I should never have touched you!"

"Evadne," Jacinda immediately picked Evadne's hands back up and gave the guards a hard glare that had them retreating. "From nearly the moment I arrived in Pechora, you have guided me, supported me, have been my mentor, and a true friend. I hope that will continue because now, more than ever, I will need that friendship."

"It would be a true honor to assist you, Majesty." And again Evadne curtsied to her.

"Mother." Danton walked up to her and kissed her cheek. "May I have the honor of a dance? With your permission, of course, King Jotham." Danton looked to Jotham.

"Really? You feel you have to *ask* if you can dance with your *mother*?" Jacinda raised an eyebrow at her son.

"Tonight? Yes," Danton replied undaunted by his mother's eyebrow. "Tonight is a night of firsts and I want to start out on the right foot. I think we all do."

"You will always be on the right foot with me, Danton, as long as you don't step on my toes as you once did."

Danton tipped his head back and laughed. "I will try not to. Shall we?" he asked holding out his arm to her.

"I would love to."

Jotham watched as Danton led his mother to the floor. He didn't even think they noticed how others parted for them.

"My King," Jotham turned as Evander spoke to him. "I realize my opinion does not matter, but I would like to say I have never been prouder to be an Assemblyman from your House than I am today. With Jacinda Michelakakis as our Queen..." Evander found his throat tightening up.

"She is truly a remarkable woman, isn't she?"

"She is, Majesty. The ancestors have truly blessed our House."

"I believe they have, Evander. I truly believe they have."

∞ ∞ ∞ ∞ ∞

As the night proceeded, Jotham watched as every man was vying to dance with Jacinda. After Danton it had been Barek, then Evander, and then William. When Yusuf stepped forward though, Jotham had had enough. There was no way he was letting that man touch his Jacinda.

"Pardons, Yusuf, but I find my patience has run out with others dancing with *my* Queen. I'm sure you understand." And with that Jotham whisked Jacinda onto the floor for one of the last dances of the night."

"Thank you for saving me. I wasn't sure how to politely tell him to fuck off."

Jotham found himself laughing. "Maybe I should have waited a few minutes longer for I would have liked to see Yusuf's expression when you told him where to go."

"But that wouldn't have helped much with inter-house relations."

"I don't care. The little foabhor needs put in his place." Jotham suddenly realized how late it was. "Are you ready to retire for the night?"

"More than," she told him.

"Then let me tell Barek we are leaving and retire. I feel the need to make love to my Queen."

∞ ∞ ∞ ∞ ∞

"I haven't seen the Pajaris, have you?" Barek asked Danton quietly as they stood togetherin the back of the room watching thier parents dance.

"They left shortly after you arrived at the Ball," Danton replied just as quietly. "Adelaide was becoming quite vocal in her disapproval of the future Queen."

"Really?"

"Yes."

"And they didn't return?" Barek asked.

"No," responded Danton.

"Madame Pajari did." The quiet statement coming from behind them had both men turning to find Stephanie standing in the shadows.

"What?" Barek asked.

"Madame Pajari returned," Stephanie told him, "but she has yet to offer her congratulations to the Royal couple. Instead, she is remaining along the outer edges. Watching."

"She could be a threat Stephanie," Danton told her.

"To the King?" Stephanie questioned.

"To Mom," Danton told her and saw her eyes widen.

∞ ∞ ∞ ∞ ∞

Jacinda smiled as Jotham led her back to Danton and Barek, people parting as they passed. This night had been magical. All her worries had been for nothing.

"NO! I will not allow this!" Suddenly, Adelaide Pajari appeared out of nowhere shoving her way through the crowd, pulling out the restraints that once held her hair, as she lunged at Jacinda.

"No!" Jotham yelled stepping in front of Jacinda, willing to take the strike if it saved his Jacinda when they were both thrown to the floor.

∞ ∞ ∞ ∞ ∞

Jacinda suddenly found herself flat on her back on the hard, cold floor, her breath driven from her as Jotham landed on top of her. She heard the shouts and screams that filled the room, but her only concern was for Jotham, who wasn't moving on top of her.

"Jotham!" She grabbed his shoulders shaking him. "Jotham!"

"I'm fine," he groaned rolling to the side so he was on his knees facing her. "Are you?" His eyes frantically ran over her searching for any sign of injury.

"I'm fine. I just had the wind knocked out of me for a minute." Her eyes in turn ran over him. "Are you sure you're okay?"

"I am. A guard pushed me out of the way." Rising, he helped her to her feet. He couldn't believe how close he'd come to losing her, right here in a room filled with guards. Wrapping his arms around her, he pulled her close and felt the tremors that ran through her as she wrapped hers around his waist.

"Jacinda?" Leaning back slightly, he looked down at her taking in the paleness of her skin.

"I'm fine, just hold me." Jacinda soaked up the comfort Jotham's arms offered and thanked the ancestors he was safe. "I can't believe Adelaide would do something like that."

Jotham looked through the guards that had encircled them and saw that Adelaide was currently being restrained by Green and his men.

"Get her out of here, Lieutenant. I'll deal with her later."

"Mom!"

"Danton, I'm fine." The fear in Danton's call had Jacinda's eyes searching for her son through the guards, but she couldn't find him.

"Mom, you need to get over here! NOW!"

Jacinda suddenly realized the fear in her son's voice wasn't for her and Jacinda's heart stopped. She was immediately out of Jotham's arms and pushing her way through the guards encircling them. "Move!" she ordered and when they finally did, Jacinda froze.

Lying there surrounded by Nicholas, Peter, and Danton, who were on their knees, lay Stephanie. The two metal spears from

Adelaide's hair protruded from her back and her jacket was soaked with blood as she struggled to breath.

"Stephanie!" Jacinda's heart-wrenching cry tore through the clamor-filled room and had everyone quieting.

Jacinda was immediately on her knees next to her daughter, uncaring about the blood or protocol. "Stephie, baby, it's Mom. Talk to me, baby." Tears streamed down Jacinda's face, as her hands fluttered over her daughter not sure where to touch. Finally, she gripped the pale hand that rose toward her.

"Mom?" Stephanie's eyes fluttered open for a moment searching for her.

"I'm here, baby. I'm here." Jacinda lowered her head to the floor making it easier for Stephanie to see her.

"You're okay?" Stephanie whispered.

"I'm fine."

"King Jotham?"

"I'm fine too, Stephanie." Jotham was on his knees next to Jacinda. "Thanks to you, we both are."

A weak smile appeared for a moment on Stephanie's lips before it faded. "I told you, Mom," she whispered weakly. "I told you I needed to be here."

"You did, baby." Jacinda refused to let her voice wobble even as tears streamed down her face. She needed to be strong for her daughter. "And you were right. Now I'm going to tell *you* and you are going believe what *I* tell *you*. You are going to be just fine. The doctor is on his way and he's going to take care of you. Do you hear me, Stephanie?!! You are going to survive this!"

"It's alright, Mom." She squeezed her mother's hand weakly. "Don't cry. I'm not afraid of dying."

"Stephanie Anne Michelakakis, you will not talk that way! Do you hear me? You are *not* going to die! I forbid it!"

JACINDA'S CHALLENGE

"Spoken like a true Queen..." and with those words, Stephanie's entire body seemed to go lax.

"Stephanie!" Jacinda screamed.

∞ ∞ ∞ ∞ ∞

Jotham watched helplessly as Jacinda paced the room, her beautiful gown was now bloodied and torn, but she'd refused to leave her child. Stephanie had been in surgery for hours now. Dr. Bliant had rushed her in the moment he'd seen her and they'd heard nothing since.

Everyone had been in to check on them. Evander and Evadne. Peter and Cyndy. Cassandra and William. But they'd had nothing to tell them. Danton had been on his comm nonstop talking to his brother and aunt, keeping them updated on what had happened while Barek was in constant communication with Green, who was interrogating Adelaide. Rising, Jotham stepped into Jacinda's path and wrapped his arms around her, stilling her.

"Jacinda, you need to sit for a while. You will do Stephanie no good if you collapse from exhaustion."

"I..."

"Mom, Jotham's right," Danton added his voice to Jotham's as he disconnected his comm, exhaustion and worry written all over his face. "Sit, if only for a few minutes. Please, for me."

Finally, she nodded and let Jotham lead her over to the chair next to Danton. The minute she sat she took Danton's hand.

"She's going to be okay, Mom. You know how stubborn Stephie is."

"I do," she squeezed his hand. "She used to work so hard to keep up with you and Ethan."

"We gave her such a hard time."

"You did, but she wouldn't have had it any other way. She loved every minute of it, just as she loves you."

The ringing of Barek's comm had a jarring effect on everyone in the room. Looking down, Barek frowned as he read the message.

"I assume that involves the Pajaris and what happened," Jacinda said to Barek.

"You might as well tell her," Danton told Barek when he saw him hesitate. "If you don't, she'll just wear you down until you do. Trust me she can be..." he gave his mother a slight smile. "Tenacious when she believes she has the right to know something."

Barek looked to his father who nodded.

"Elliott Pajari has disappeared. It seems he left the Ball shortly after your arrival, leaving his wife behind. He may not even know that it was Adelaide that attacked you as the broadcast was immediately cut off at the first sign of trouble."

"I want him found, Barek," Jotham told his son.

"Cassandra is already on it. She's furious that this happened within her House and has ordered all borders closed until he's found."

"This wasn't Cassandra's fault," Jacinda spoke as she rose and started pacing again. "I've known Adelaide for more cycles than I care to remember. She's always been slightly unstable what with her 'purist' ideas. She even spent some time in Atrato cycles ago. But even with all that, I never thought she was crazy enough to take it this far. To attack Jotham at the Royal Ball, in front of thousands of witnesses."

"She was trying to attack *you*, Mom," Danton reminded her gently.

"I know, but Jotham stepping in front of me should have stopped her. She'd never attempt to kill the King. She wants Shosha to wed Barek too badly."

"What?!!" Barek sputtered.

"It's something we discovered when investigating the transmissions between Pajari and Stannic. They had nothing to do with Stannic's attempt on Cassandra. Instead, they dealt with them wanting their daughter to be the next Queen," Jotham stated.

"I don't even *know* their daughter," replied Barek.

"I'm sure that didn't matter to Adelaide," Jacinda told him.

Just then the doors on the other side of the room opened and Bliant stepped in, still wearing his operating suit, stained with blood, his expression bleak. Jacinda reached out blindly and grabbed Jotham's arm.

"Madame Michelakakis," Bliant began. "I'm sorry I didn't have time to properly introduce myself to you earlier."

Jacinda waved her hand dismissively. "I don't care about manners, Dr. Bliant. Just my daughter."

"Yes, of course, I understand perfectly. Your daughter is a very strong and stubborn woman, Madame Michelakakis. The damage done to her back and lung would have killed most people. Your daughter refused to let it."

"So she's going to be alright?" Jacinda demanded, her fingers digging into Jotham's arm.

"I see no reason why she shouldn't, barring any unforeseen complications, but there is something you need to be aware of."

"What?" Jacinda demanded.

"I couldn't save the damaged lung."

"What?" Jacinda paled and Jotham wrapped an arm around her waist steadying her.

"Her attacker appears to have twisted the spears as she stabbed your daughter. They shredded the lung. It was pure luck that she only struck one. If she'd struck both, nothing would have saved your daughter."

"Oh, my ancestors." Jacinda raised a trembling hand to her mouth at the thought of how close she'd come to losing Stephie.

"Because of this," Bliant continued, "she will be unable to maintain the rigorous training level that she does now."

"You're saying she will no longer be able to be a guard?"

"No, she won't," Bliant told her bluntly.

"But otherwise," Jotham finally spoke up, "she'll be able to live a full life?"

"Yes, I see no reason why she couldn't."

"Thank you, Dr. Bliant." Jotham nodded to Bliant.

"I'll let you know when you can see her." His eyes traveled back to Jacinda taking in the circlet she still wore for the first time. "She is still quite heavily sedated, Majesty. It might be better for her if she doesn't see the blood on your gown. I believe it will worry her and I would like to keep her as calm as possible. Her body has been gravely injured and it is going to take it, and her, some time to adjust to having only one lung."

∞ ∞ ∞ ∞ ∞

"I need to let Ethan know." Jacinda ran a shaky hand through her hair, surprised to find she still wore the circlet. "And Palma and..."

"Mom," Danton took her hand stilling it, not liking how she had begun to tremble. "I'll do it. You go change and rest a little before Stephie wakes. She's going to want to see you. Both of you." He looked to Jotham. "To make sure you are okay."

"But..."

JACINDA'S CHALLENGE

"He's right, Jacinda." Jotham squeezed her waist.

"Alright." She gave Danton a weak smile. "Make sure you tell them that she is going to make a full recovery."

"I will." Danton looked at Jotham over her head silently thanking him for his support.

"Come on, Jacinda. Let's get you changed." Jotham led her from the room.

As they left the room, both Guard immediately surrounded them. It was then that Jacinda notice the blood on Deffand's uniform and remembered how he'd immediately been at Stephanie's side.

"Thank you, Nicholas." Reaching out she squeezed his arm.

"Is she..." Deffand found he had to clear his throat.

"She's going to be fine," Jacinda reassured him.

"Thank the ancestors," Deffand whispered.

"And fast acting, well trained guards." She let her gaze encompass everyone there. "Thank you. All of you."

"Captain, we are going to the Royal Wing to change then will be returning. I want guards posted outside Stephanie's room."

"That has already been seen to, Majesty. Captain Chamberlain has personally chosen the men so that we could remain at your side."

Jotham looked to Jacinda and with her nod of approval looked back to Deffand. "That will be fine. I also want security around Danton and Barek increased. Until we know where Elliott Pajari is I'm taking no chances."

"Yes, Majesty." He immediately looked to several men who nodded and remained behind.

With every step they took, Jotham could feel the tremor in Jacinda growing. As soon as they closed the doors to the Royal Wing and were alone, Jacinda collapsed into his arms, letting go of all her fear and grief.

"I've got you, Jacinda," he whispered into her hair as he swept her up into his arms and carried her directly into the bathroom. "I've got you. I love you. Everything's going to be all right. Everyone is going to be fine."

"I know," she whispered clutching at his neck as he allowed her feet to touch the floor. "I know. I just can't seem to stop shaking."

"It's understandable." He carefully set aside her circlet before his hands went to her side, finding the device that held her gown together. "You've been so strong through it all, my love, for everyone. Now you need to take some time for yourself."

"I could have lost her, Jotham. I could have lost my daughter." She laid her head on his shoulder as he undressed her. "I could have lost *you*." The tears streamed down her face as she looked at him.

"But you didn't." He wiped the tears from her cheeks. "I'm fine and Stephanie is going to be. We'll make sure of it. Now come on, my love, let's get you cleaned up." Jotham led her into the shower stall.

"Join me?" Her eyes implored as she stepped in. "I need you."

Jotham immediately began to strip, uncaring where anything landed. "I'm here, Jacinda." Slipping into the shower, he wrapped his arms around her now slick flesh pulling her close. Gently he ran a finger along the birthmark between her breasts. "It's filled with color," he whispered.

"It has?" With her hands loosely gripping his waist, she leaned back. Looking down she saw the golden symbols that before were seen only on the King's hand were now filled with color. "It wasn't like that before the Ball, Jotham?" She looked up at him with troubled eyes.

"It will be fine, my love."

"But..."

"It's the way of the ancestors, Jacinda. When it is a ruler's time, their birthmark fills in with color."

"I know that, but this... no female has ever carried the House of Healing symbol."

"Your ancestors have."

"True, but it's never filled with color."

"Are you sure about that?" Jotham carefully kissed each mark before straightening to sink his fingers in her hair. "You are where the ancestors want you, Jacinda, in my arms. The rest we will work out... together."

"I love you, Jotham."

"And I love you." He slipped a hand behind her neck extending the kiss. "We'll get through this, Jacinda, and whatever else life has to throw at us because we're together." Reaching up he caressed her cheek. "And once Stephanie is well enough, I'm going to make you my wife and my Queen."

"Your wife..." Jacinda gave him a truly brilliant, loving smile. "That's all I want. Well that, and for you to turn around so I can wash your back."

"Is that all you will wash?" Jotham asked feeling his shaft start to lengthen as her hands grazed his hips.

"Well, I guess that will depend on you... my King."

∞ ∞ ∞ ∞ ∞

Michelle has always loved to read and writing is just a natural extension of this for her. Growing up, she always loved to extend the stories of books she'd read just to see where the characters went. Happily married for over twenty five years she is the proud mother of two grown children and with the house empty has found time to write again. You can reach her at m.k.eidem@live.com or her website at http://www.mkeidem.com she'd love to hear your comments.

∞ ∞ ∞ ∞ ∞

Printed in Poland
by Amazon Fulfillment
Poland Sp. z o.o., Wrocław